D0746136

THE LORD
IS MY SONG

CHRONICLES OF THE KING

BOOK 2

THE LORD IS MY SONG

A NOVEL

Lynn N. Austin

Beacon Hill Press of Kansas City
Kansas City, Missouri

Copyright 1996
by Beacon Hill Press of Kansas City

ISBN 083-411-6022

Printed in the
United States of America

Cover Design: Ted Ferguson

Cover Illustration: Dave Howard

10 9 8 7 6 5 4 3 2 1

The Lord is my strength
and my song;
he has become my salvation.

EXODUS 15:2

Dedicated to my children,
Joshua, Benjamin, and Maya—
my favorite "trilogy"

ABOUT THE AUTHOR

Giving "flesh and blood" to biblical characters—that is the intent of author Lynn N. Austin in writing her Chronicles of the King series. *The Lord Is My Song* is the second in the collection.

"I want to show that Old Testament characters were real people, with the same needs, fears, and struggles people have today," she explains. "I want the readers to see that they can identify with them."

Underlying Lynn's novels are common threads that run throughout history, both in public and private life. "The people of the Old Testament were pretty much the same as us," she comments. "Mankind's heart hasn't really changed. There are a lot of parallels between their times and our times—such as between child sacrifice in their day and abortion in our day, to point out only one example."

Lynn is a full-time freelance writer and speaker. She and her husband, Ken—a Christian musician—live near Chicago in Orland Park, Illinois, with their three children. In 1993 she was honored as "New Writer of the Year" at Moody Bible Institute's Write-to-Publish Conference. She is an editor of *Profile*, the journal of the Chicago Women's Conference, and has contributed to numerous periodicals, including *Discipleship Journal, Christian Educators' Journal, Teachers in Focus, Moody, Women Alive, Parents of Teenagers, The Christian Reader, Live, The Lookout, Teen Power,* and *Standard*.

A NOTE TO THE READER

Shortly after King Solomon's death in 931 B.C., the Promised Land split into two separate kingdoms. Israel, the larger nation to the north, set up its capital in Samaria and was no longer governed by a descendant of King David. In the southern nation of Judah, David's royal line continued to rule from Jerusalem.

The narrative of this book centers around events in the life of Hezekiah, who ruled from 716 to 687 B.C.

Interested readers are encouraged to research the full accounts of these events in the Bible as they enjoy this second book in the Chronicles of the King series.

Scripture references for *The Lord Is My Song*
        2 Kings 17:1-23
        2 Kings 18:1-12
        2 Chron. 29—31
        2 Chron. 32:27-30

See also:

        Deut. 17:14-20
        2 Sam. 5:6-8
        The prophecies of Isaiah and of Micah

Prologue

The drenching rains had finally ended, but silvery puddles dotted the streets of Jerusalem as King Hezekiah walked with General Jonadab down the hill from the palace. They followed the route the procession had taken when Hezekiah had been led as a child through the streets to the Valley of Hinnom. Heavy fog blanketed the view ahead of him like a shroud covering the sin and shame of this valley of death. He could barely see the jagged cliffs through the mist as he strode through the valley gate and turned down the narrow divide.

Once again Hezekiah stood face-to-face with his enemy, Molech. The monster seemed smaller than Hezekiah remembered, his roar now silenced as he gazed down from his throne. Rain dripped like teardrops from Molech's face. His soot-smudged belly stood empty and dark, his gaping mouth mute. Heavy ropes shackled him, circling his neck, his chest, his arms, his feet. It seemed unbelievable to Hezekiah that anyone would worship such an impotent creature, offering their children in return for help from this helpless god.

Two teams of oxen waited placidly as the workers harnessed them to the statue. Hezekiah gave the signal, and the foreman's whip cracked. The animals strained forward, the ropes stretched taut. Molech teetered slightly, then crashed to the ground on his side in a heap of soggy ashes and soot. The oxen dragged the deposed god a few more feet, then halted. Molech's arms stretched toward Hezekiah as if silently pleading for help.

"Well, that's the end of him, Your Majesty," Jonadab said.

"If only it were that simple." Hezekiah stared at the toppled idol, remembering his brothers Eliab and Amariah, who had been sacrificed. He felt no victory over his fallen enemy. "There are still plenty of people who'd rather cling to ignorance and superstition than seek the truth. And they're the ones who'll keep Molech alive."

"You think they'll still sacrifice their children now that the statue's gone?"

"I'm certain they will—only now it'll be in secret. You'll need to warn the guards at the valley gate to watch this place after dark, Jonadab. It's been used for child sacrifice for centuries, even before they made this cursed thing."

"And if we catch someone sacrificing here?"

"Bring them to me at once."

Jonadab gestured to the fallen idol. "What do you want us to do with it, Your Majesty?"

"Melt it down and forge weapons from it. Swords, spears, arrowheads, shields. Fill the armory with them. Someday I'll have an army again." The wind lifted a funnel of soot from the empty pit, and specks of ash rose in the air like tiny spirits ascending heavenward.

"Our nation's guilt is very great," Hezekiah said softly. "I don't know how God can ever forgive us for all the innocent blood we've shed in this place." For a moment no one spoke. The workmen and oxen waited in reverent silence.

"Seems like we should say a prayer or something, doesn't it?" Jonadab said.

The workmen looked to Hezekiah expectantly. He drew a breath and recited the only words of the Torah that he knew: "Hear, O Israel. Yahweh is our God—Yahweh alone. Love Yahweh your God with all your heart and with all your soul and with all your strength."

Then he turned and began the long climb back up the hill to the palace.

Part

1

Hezekiah was twenty-five years old when he became king, and he reigned in Jerusalem twenty-nine years. His mother's name was Abijah daughter of Zechariah. He did what was right in the eyes of the Lord, just as his father David had done. In the first month of the first year of his reign, he opened the doors of the temple of the Lord and repaired them.

—2 Chron. 29:1-3

1

(In the northern kingdom of Israel)

Jerusha lay awake in the loft of her square stone house listening to the sounds of morning. She was too excited to sleep. Pink light from the dawning sun filtered through the cracks of the shutters, along with the melody of songbirds in the olive trees. In the stall below her room she heard the heavy tread of the oxen on the stone floor and Abba's voice speaking softly to them as he led them outside. He would feed and water the animals, then hitch them to the cart for the three-mile trip to Dabbasheth.

She stood up, eager to begin this special day, and rolled up her blanket and sleeping mat. She tied back her thick brown hair with a leather thong, then studied her murky reflection in the tiny square of bronze she used for a mirror. Her straight nose and oval-shaped face were deeply tanned from working beside her mother in the barley fields, and she had her father's almond-shaped eyes, as green as the rolling hills after the spring rains. Abba said she was pretty. Could it be true? She returned the metal scrap to its place on the shelf, wishing for a proper mirror.

At 17, Jerusha was as lissome and slender as a young willow tree, her limbs long and graceful. And like the willow, her nature was joyfully resilient, willing to bend with changing circumstances. This morning, instead of her usual work clothes, Jerusha put on the one good dress she reserved for special occasions. Today she would travel to the village with her family for cousin Serah's wedding. The festivities would last for days; she would feast and dance and visit with relatives. Best of all, maybe Abram would be there.

Jerusha had known Abram for years, had grown up with him, seeing him at weddings and festivals and family gatherings. He had always been a quiet boy, the opposite of Jerusha with her carefree outgoing nature. She had hardly noticed him when they were children.

But now that Abram was a man, Jerusha found herself dreaming of becoming his wife, bearing his children, making a home with him on his father's land.

As Jerusha bustled around the tiny loft, humming a wedding tune, her younger sister, Maacah, awoke and rubbed her eyes sleepily. She was small for an 11-year-old and thin as a reed, with thick, dark braids and a round face peppered with freckles. She followed Jerusha everywhere but was much too young to share her older sister's dreams of a husband and babies.

"Why are you getting up so early?" Maacah grumbled.

"Did you forget? We're going to Dabbasheth for Serah's wedding." Jerusha unlatched the shutters and opened them.

Maacah groaned. "We don't have to leave this early." She turned toward the wall, pulling the covers over her head.

"Abba says we have to finish all our chores before we can go. So come on, sleepyhead." Jerusha pulled the covers all the way off her protesting sister and folded them, stuffing them into the wall niche beside her own. Then she climbed down the ladder from the loft to the large main room of the house.

Her mother, Hodesh, knelt in the center of the room by the hearth, grinding wheat with a hand mill for their breakfast. "Oh good—you're up," she said. "I need water." She handed Jerusha the empty jug, then returned to her work, pouring the finished flour into the kneading trough.

Outside, the new day was fresh and clear, the golden sun warm but not yet high enough in the sky to be hot. Jerusha lifted the jar to her shoulder and sang a wedding tune as she skipped down the hill to the well. By the time she returned with the water, balancing the pot daringly on her head, Maacah was up, helping their mother rekindle the fire.

When Abba came in from his chores, he bent to kiss his wife and daughters tenderly. "Ah, Jerusha, my happy little bird. What makes you sing so sweetly this morning?"

She smiled as she cut goat cheese into thick slices for their trip. "You know, Abba—we're going to the wedding today. I'll get to see Serah and Tirza and—"

"And maybe Abram, that handsome son of Eli?"

"I wasn't thinking of him at all," Jerusha replied too quickly. She handed her father a lump of cheese that had crumbled off. "But do you really think he'll be there, Abba?" Jerimoth laughed heartily.

"What's so funny, Abba?" little Maacah asked.

Jerimoth smiled and tugged Maacah's braid affectionately. "Nothing, my little one. It's just that your sister has grown into a woman already. How I wish I could keep my daughters here with me forever!" He sighed and drew Jerusha into his brawny arms. "How lonely we'll be without our little bird to sing for us! But Abram's land is not so very far. Maybe she'll fly back to visit us once in a while, eh?"

Jerusha looked up into Abba's tanned face, loving every line and wrinkle in his weathered skin. "Abba, you talk as if I'm already married. What if Eli's son doesn't want me?"

"Not want you? Ha! If he had his way, you two would be married today instead of Serah and her groom! I'm the one who's making him wait. How I hate to see my little bird leave the nest."

Jerusha's heart pumped faster. "Did he really say he wanted to marry me?" She couldn't hide her excitement and hoped her father wouldn't laugh at her again.

"We shall see about a betrothal," Jerimoth sighed. "After the wedding I'll talk to Abram's father. We shall see."

Jerusha hugged her father tightly. "I love you, Abba!" Jerimoth returned her hug in tender silence.

As they journeyed over the terraced green hills to Dabbasheth, Jerusha could hardly contain her excitement. The slow, steady plodding of the oxen nearly drove her crazy as the animals labored to pull the heavy cart loaded with wine from Jerimoth's vineyard and the food Hodesh had prepared for the wedding feast.

At last they arrived at the tiny, unwalled village and unloaded their cart at Uncle Saul's house, which was tucked behind the shop where he fashioned and sold his pottery. Jerusha helped her aunts and cousins dress Serah in her brightly embroidered wedding gown and place garlands of flowers in her hair and around her chair. Jerusha gazed at her cousin with envy. The next wedding would be her own—hers and Abram's.

The groom's procession paraded through Dabbasheth to the music of flutes and cymbals and tambourines as they came to claim the bride. All the villagers streamed from their homes to join the happy couple, following them joyfully through the streets. Jerusha walked behind the new bride and groom, eagerly surveying the faces in the crowd, hoping for a glimpse of Abram.

Then above the music and gaiety of the procession, Jerusha thought she heard a rumble of distant thunder. She glanced up, but the sun blazed hotly in a cloudless sky. The rumbling grew louder, closer. Gradually the merriment died away as everyone paused to listen.

Suddenly, with the force of a bursting dam, hundreds of Assyrian horsemen poured into the unwalled village square. Swords flashed in the sunlight, and fierce shrieks filled the air while the horses' pounding hooves trampled anyone who stumbled and fell beneath them. Screams of terror replaced the sound of singing and laughter as the villagers tried to flee in all directions. Jerusha stood rooted in place, too stunned to move, frozen in shock by the horror and bloodshed all around her.

"Run, Jerusha!" Uncle Saul screamed. "Run! Now!" In a daze, Jerusha watched him shove her cousin Tirza and Serah, the bride, down an alleyway toward their house. The groom lay on the ground, motionless, in a spreading pool of blood. Jerusha tried to run after them, but her legs moved like heavy stones beneath her.

Suddenly three Assyrian soldiers thundered up the alley toward her cousins. The girls tried to turn back, but two of the soldiers leaned over in their saddles and swooped Jerusha's cousins off their feet, throwing them across their horses. The girls screamed in terror as the soldiers rode away.

Uncle Saul fell to his knees before the third soldier and raised his hands to him, pleading with him. "Don't take my girls! Please, I'll pay any price! Bring them back—I beg you—" The Assyrian drew his sword and in one powerful slash chopped one of Uncle Saul's hands off. Jerusha would have fainted, but suddenly Abba pushed her to the ground.

"Get down, Jerusha! Crawl under the cart! Hurry!" He urged her toward his cart, parked several yards away. She saw her mother and Maacah cowering beneath it, but as in a nightmare she moved as if under water, her body refusing to obey her commands.

All around her, screams and shouts and thundering hooves roared in her ears as she crawled toward the cart. It seemed a hundred miles away. Nearby, a woman cried out as an Assyrian soldier snatched her baby from her grasp and hurled it beneath his horse's hooves to be trampled. Jerusha wept hysterically as she crawled the last few feet toward the safety of the cart. Her mother reached for her hand. She was almost there.

"Get away from her!" Abba cried as rough hands suddenly grabbed Jerusha. She turned, flailing her fists at the Assyrian soldier who gripped her, while Abba attacked him from behind.

"Run, Jerusha, run!" Abba yelled as the soldier released her to fend off her father. She made a desperate scramble for the safety of the cart, half crawling, half rolling, when out of nowhere another pair of strong arms scooped her up effortlessly and threw her across the front of a horse.

"No! Oh, God, no!" she screamed. "Abba, help me! Save me!" She struggled to free herself, but the soldier held her down, pressing his hand into her back. As the horse wheeled around, she saw her father running toward them. Then she heard the soft swish of metal as her captor unsheathed his sword. She remembered the blood and horror of Uncle Saul's severed hand and shouted, "Abba, no! Stay back!"

The Assyrian leaned sideways in his saddle and slashed out toward her father with his sword. Jerusha saw a crimson gash appear across Abba's forehead, and he sank to his knees, his face covered with blood. He disappeared from her sight as the horse pounded up the road, away from the village.

Jerusha screamed as the horse sped faster and faster, away from the clamor and din of Dabbasheth, away from her family and safety. They galloped for several minutes, then the horse slowed and the soldier slapped Jerusha, shouting angrily at her in his strange language. When she didn't stop screaming, he slapped her again and again until she stuffed her fist in her mouth to stifle her cries. She felt numb with fear. He was going to kill her.

"I don't want to die—please, I don't want to die," she whimpered. A few minutes later they stopped near a grove of sycamore trees beside a farmer's field. Several other horses were already tethered there, and Jerusha heard muffled screams and coarse laughter coming from among the bushes. Her heart pounded with a new terror as she realized what was about to happen.

"No—no—please don't," she sobbed. The soldier dismounted and pulled her off the horse, throwing her over his shoulder like a sack of grain. As he carried her into the woods, she saw her cousin Serah struggling desperately, fighting with all her strength against the soldier who pinned her down. When Serah wouldn't stop struggling, the soldier beat her unmercifully, again and again until she no longer moved. Jerusha knew it would be useless to fight. The blows he had already given her throbbed painfully. She wanted to live through this nightmare, and find her way home. She decided not to struggle.

Jerusha knew it was the right decision, but she couldn't make herself stop crying. Her screams blended with the others until the woods echoed with the sound. Even the wind seemed to shriek with fear. Finally, her captor halted and threw her to the ground. The smell of his unwashed body made her gag. She turned her face in revulsion, and he slapped her again, yelling at her angrily.

"Oh, God—I don't want to die," she sobbed. "Not now, not like this. Please, God, please—I don't want to die!"

(In the southern kingdom of Judah)

Zechariah leaned on King Hezekiah's arm as they slowly walked down the hill from the palace. The sound of grinding hand mills and the smoke of early-morning fires filled the air around them, stirring memories for Hezekiah of another morning walk with his grandfather years before. It seemed a lifetime ago. Yet in the week they had been reunited, the bonds of love between them had been rewoven as if no time had passed at all. As they walked through the water gate and down the steep ramp that led out of the city, their robes billowed in the brisk spring wind, and the gray dawn sky threatened rain. Hezekiah shivered.

"Are you sure you don't want to go back inside?" he asked. "Maybe it isn't such a good idea to recite our prayers out here."

"I'm sure. Don't forget—once the Temple is purified, we'll be praying outside every morning in all sorts of weather. Even the rare snowstorm."

"I guess that's true dedication," Hezekiah said, laughing.

Zechariah seemed unchanged to Hezekiah. He had the same flowing white hair and beard, the same noble, dignified features he had loved so much, the same gentle green eyes full of wisdom and humor. But now Hezekiah stood almost a head taller than his grandfather. He smiled, remembering how he had once imagined that Yahweh looked like Zechariah. They reached a terraced olive grove near the Gihon Spring and sat to rest on a low wall surrounding the garden. The trees offered welcome shelter from the cold gusts of wind.

"How's this?" Hezekiah asked.

"Perfect." Zechariah sighed contentedly and gazed in wonder as if seeing trees for the first time in his life. Hezekiah shuddered at this reminder of Zechariah's long imprisonment. "You know, Son, there's a reason I wanted to come out here to pray. When we're surrounded all day by our own creations, it's easy to believe we're more important than we really are." He plucked a slender, silvery-green leaf from an olive tree and twirled it between his fingers. "We need to take a closer look at Yahweh's creations. Can we fashion anything as fragile and perfect as this leaf—or as solid and enduring as those mountains?"

"'As the mountains surround Jerusalem, so Yahweh surrounds His people, both now and forevermore,'" Hezekiah quoted.

"Ah—you still remember. I'm glad. Yahweh has faithfully surrounded our nation all these years, even though our sin and idolatry have hidden Him from sight."

From Hezekiah's palace windows he could usually see the familiar green-and-brown-speckled hills that surrounded Jerusalem. But this morning the clouds had hidden them from view. He bent to pick up one of the dozens of stones that lay scattered on the ground and absently tossed it from one hand to the other.

"I love this sad little nation, rocks and all. I wish it could be like the land of milk and honey our ancestors knew."

"God will answer your prayers in time if you're faithful to Him." Zechariah's trust in God seemed unlimited, Hezekiah's own tiny seed of faith insufficient, especially for the overwhelming task he faced.

"Someday I'm going to win back all the land that's rightfully mine, the land my father lost to the Philistines and Ammonites. We need the farmland of the Shephelah and cities like Beth Shemesh that guard the mountain passes into Jerusalem. Without those passes we have no access to the trade routes." He tossed the stone he was holding toward the Gihon Spring as Zechariah listened patiently, offering neither comment nor criticism. "And we need the fortified cities in the Negev and Arabah. And Elath, our seaport on the Red Sea. These territories once belonged to my ancestors, and they're rightfully mine."

"You remind me of King Uzziah, Son. He brought about an age of prosperity because he dreamed big dreams—and because he loved God. With God you can do anything—anything at all."

Zechariah was silent for a moment before continuing. "But Uzziah's success resulted in pride, not gratitude. When foreign kings honored him for his accomplishments, Uzziah took the credit for himself instead of giving the glory to God."

He rested his hand on Hezekiah's shoulder. "I have dreams for you, Son. But I've lived through the failures of all the others, and I pray that you'll remain strong when you're tested. Pride destroyed Uzziah. His son Jotham was destroyed by bitterness, and your own father by fear. If they had placed their trust in Yahweh, how different things might have been for you!"

Hezekiah felt a restless urgency to begin, to make the changes his country needed as quickly as possible. "You'll help me, won't you, Grandpa? I need to replace Uriah, and I'd like you to fill his position as—"

"No. I won't serve as palace administrator."

"What? Why not?"

"I'm a Levite and a teacher of the Torah. I'll help you with your religious reforms, but not as an administrator."

"But I need you. How can I convince you to change your mind?"

"You can't. I'll never hold a government position again."

"But—I mean, I just assumed you'd return to the position you held under King Uzziah. You know more about running the kingdom than the rest of us put together."

"That's flattering, but an exaggeration, I'm sure."

"Well, what about serving in the Temple, then?"

"I'm much too old for that. Levites retire at age 50. I'm almost 70."

"Grandpa, please—there aren't enough Levites to do all the work, and there are even fewer priests. Maybe some of the younger ones will return to service, but they'll need to be trained and—"

"And so you want to call a wrinkled old Levite like me back into service for a while?"

"Yes. Would you?"

Zechariah sighed and gazed up at the Temple walls, high above them. "I remember the last time I wore my Levitical robes. It was on the day I stopped your father from offering his sacrifice on the Assyrian altar, the day I became a prisoner. When I dressed in my robes that day, do you remember what I told you?"

"No—I'm sorry."

"You begged me to come back when I was finished at the Temple to teach you more about Yahweh. I told you that I might be a little late, but I would be back. Well, I'm much later than I ever dreamt I'd be, but I'll keep my promise to you, Son. I'll teach you Yahweh's laws and assist in the Temple until some younger men can replace me."

"Where should we start? The Temple looks like it's in pretty bad condition."

"It is, but we can start by assigning the priests and Levites to their divisions according to the order King David established. We'll have to anoint a new high priest, and the people will have to tithe the required Temple portion to support us."

"I'll issue the orders. And I'll contribute what I can from the royal treasuries too. But what about the Temple structures? Won't they require restoration?"

"Yes, and I think I know the man to help us. My dear friend Hilkiah has a son who's been trained as an engineer. Hilkiah is a righteous man, faithful to Yahweh, and I'm certain he has trained his son Eliakim in God's laws too."

"Good. I'll send for him to oversee the reconstruction." Hezekiah stroked his beard thoughtfully. "I think the hardest part of my job is knowing who I can trust. Uriah probably wasn't the only one who'd like to take control of my kingdom."

"Whenever power changes hands suddenly, it's a very dangerous time for everyone. You'll need to stand strong until your sovereignty is established."

"My father's government was very corrupt—from the highest official to the lowest clerk."

"Yes. That's why the prophet Micah condemned the leaders of Judah so strongly."

"I've ordered all my father's former advisers to assemble in the throne room later today. I'm going to announce my decision to reorganize the kingdom according to the Law of Moses."

Zechariah's eyes narrowed. "You'd better prepare yourself for a bitter power struggle, Son. Some people are eager to return to the laws of God, but most of the men who've been in control under Ahaz will violently oppose you."

"I know. But how do I prepare for something like that?"

Zechariah lifted his prayer shawl from around his shoulders and covered his head with it. "You pray. And allow the Lord to be your strength. Remember—the Lord doesn't *give* you strength, Hezekiah. He *is* your strength." He gestured to the city walls on the cliffs above them. "When your enemies surround you, you can't rely on man-made fortifications or military power. Trust God." Hezekiah nodded, but he knew he was a long way from understanding and faith.

"Perhaps we should recite King David's prayer," Zechariah said, "written when he was hounded by enemies who wanted to destroy him: 'Deliver me from my enemies, O God; protect me from those who rise up against me. Deliver me from evildoers and save me from bloodthirsty men. See how they lie in wait for me! . . . Arise to help me; look on my plight! . . . But I will sing of your strength, in the morning I will sing of your love; for you are my fortress, my refuge in times of trouble. O my Strength, I sing praise to you; you, O God, are my fortress, my loving God.'"

———◆———

Hephzibah's handmaiden bustled into her bedroom and threw back the filmy curtains that surrounded her bed. "You're not up yet? Come on—your breakfast is ready."

Hephzibah didn't move from where she lay against the pillows. "Bring it to me, Merab. I want to eat it here, alone."

"No, my lady. You can't hide in your rooms forever. You are the king's wife, the others are only his concubines."

"But I don't want to be with them. And they don't want to be with me."

"It doesn't matter what they want. You are superior to them, and they must do as you say."

"They don't even respect me, Merab. They know Hezekiah hasn't sent for me since my wedding week. They mock me."

"Don't make excuses, my lady. Come." She pulled Hephzibah to her feet. "Face them. Claim your rights. And don't allow them to make you a captive in your own palace."

Merab helped her dress, then guided her down the passageway to the dining room. Hezekiah's concubines were already seated around the low table and had begun to eat without her. Hephzibah shivered with dread as she joined them, waiting for their usual taunts to begin, but this morning they ignored her completely. Hephzibah ate quickly and had nearly finished when the chamberlain of the harem hurried in. He stood with his hands on his hips, appraising the women as if trying to select one. His pudgy, white body reminded Hephzibah of bread dough rising in a kneading trough. When the concubines noticed him, their chattering stopped. "I need one of you to come with me," he said. "King Ahaz always liked a concubine to warm up his chambers on a cold, damp day like today, and I'm sure the new king will too, now that his time of mourning is over."

One of the concubines waved her hand and giggled. "Take me—I'll gladly go."

Merab nudged Hephzibah. "My lady, you're his wife. Tell the eunuch you'll go."

"I—I can't." Although she longed to be with Hezekiah, Hephzibah was terrified that he would reject her.

The feisty Merab spoke up. "King Hezekiah's wife will come with you, Lord Chamberlain."

The eunuch stared at Hephzibah with cold, mocking eyes. "You?" He snorted, then turned back to the others, deliberating for a moment before pointing his stubby finger at the girl who had offered to go. "All right—you. But hurry up. The king could return to the palace any time now." He hustled the concubine from the room with Merab close behind, scolding him loudly.

"Oh dear, poor little Hephzibah," one of the concubines said.

"Now why do you suppose she wasn't picked?" another one asked, and they all laughed.

Hephzibah's pain seemed beyond what she could bear. She struggled to her feet and ran from the room, unwilling to let her enemies see her bitter tears. But more painful than their jeers was the knowledge that her husband would soon hold the concubine in his arms instead of her.

She ran until she reached the safety of the hallway, then leaned her forehead against the cold stone wall and sobbed. How much longer would she have to endure this empty, lonely life? She might never be held or loved again.

"Is something wrong?"

Hephzibah whirled around. Prince Gedaliah stood a few feet away from her. He was not supposed to be here. He was forbidden to enter the king's harem. "You're my brother Hezekiah's wife, aren't you?" he asked. He leaned casually against the wall beside her as if he were a regular visitor.

Hephzibah could barely answer. "Yes, my lord. I'm his wife." She saw only a slight resemblance between Hezekiah and his younger brother. Gedaliah was much shorter, with their father's stocky build. His manner seemed spoiled and arrogant. Only the brothers' curly dark hair and wide brown eyes were similar.

"Well, you don't seem very happy, my little sister. Don't you like being married to the new king of Judah?" He moved closer to Hephzibah, and his boldness unnerved her. Her heart raced.

"I—I have to go."

"Wait." Gedaliah grabbed her wrist, and the warmth of his hand seemed to burn her flesh. He wasn't holding her tightly, but she felt powerless to move, as if caught in his spell. "Please don't go, Hephzibah. I just want to talk." His smile reminded her vaguely of Hezekiah's.

"We can't talk. You're not even supposed to be here."

Gedaliah shrugged indifferently and rested his other hand against the wall beside her. She could not escape. "You can't leave until you tell me what's wrong."

"Nothing—I—"

"Then why were you crying? Did my brother do something to hurt you?"

"No—it was the others."

"Tell me." Very gently, Gedaliah brushed the tears from her cheeks. His tender gesture magnified her loneliness until the pain was unbearable.

"The others—they mock me because the king always chooses them—instead—"

"What? Instead of you?" Gedaliah's dark eyes flashed, and he tightened his grip on her wrist.

"Yes, my lord." Fresh tears rolled down her cheeks.

"But why? That makes no sense."

"I don't know why. If he would tell me how I've displeased him, I could try to change or—"

"Don't even talk like that. You can't possibly be to blame. My brother has been making a lot of stupid decisions lately—believe me. But please don't think it's your fault, sweet Hephzibah. I'm sure it isn't."

He brushed away her fresh tears, but more fell in their place. "Listen—I know what it's like for you," he said gently. "I feel pretty useless and unwanted too." For a moment his arrogance vanished, and Hephzibah glimpsed his pain. "My father appointed his younger brother as second in command when he became king. By rights, Hezekiah should do the same. I should be the one to take Uriah's place as palace administrator." Gedaliah's eyes filled with resentment. "But Hezekiah's ignoring me just like he's ignoring you, and he's choosing others instead. So you see? I understand, Hephzibah. I understand how much it hurts." He stood just inches from her.

"You do, my lord?" She thought about Hezekiah holding the concubine in his arms, and another tear rolled down her cheek.

"Yeah, sitting around all day—waiting—hoping. Maybe he'll summon you. Maybe today, maybe tomorrow. But he never does." The prince truly did understand how she felt, and along with her own sorrow Hephzibah was moved with pity for his plight too.

He loosened his grip on her wrist and gently took her hand. "You're so beautiful, Hephzibah," he murmured. "So incredibly beautiful. My brother must be blind. I would never treat you this way. Never."

Hephzibah's loneliness, her longing to be held and loved, grew so great that before she realized what was happening, Gedaliah's arms encircled her, and she was sobbing against his shoulder. "It's all right, Hephzibah," he murmured. "I understand. I understand." She was only dimly aware that it wasn't Hezekiah holding her, but his brother.

"Hey! What's going on? What are you doing in here?" The eunuch's angry voice jolted Hephzibah back to the present, and she quickly freed herself from Gedaliah's embrace. When she realized that she had allowed another man to hold her, she nearly collapsed in fear. They would both be stoned to death.

But Gedaliah's arrogance returned, and he spun around to challenge the eunuch. "I demand to know who's in charge of the king's harem!"

The eunuch seemed momentarily shaken. "I am."

"Then tell me what you've done to make my brother's wife so upset. I happened to be passing by and I found her here, sobbing her heart out. Now I want to know why!"

The eunuch stared, dumbfounded, as if suddenly unsure if he should challenge Gedaliah or answer to him. "I don't know. If she's upset you'll have to ask her why."

They both looked at Hephzibah. She was so frightened she could barely speak. "I—I'm all right. Really I—" And not knowing what else to do, she turned and fled to her room. Even with her door closed she could hear the eunuch shouting and Gedaliah boldly defending her. Horrified by what she had done, she clapped her hands over her ears to escape the sound of Gedaliah's voice until at last the shouting stopped. For a moment all Hephzibah heard was her heart pounding. She waited, terrified, to see what would happen to her. Why had she done such a foolish thing? How had Gedaliah managed to cast his spell around her? She wanted to crawl away and hide.

Suddenly the eunuch burst into her room, his round face quivering with rage. "Do you have any idea what you've just done? I won't have you making a fool of the king!" His hands balled into fists, and Hephzibah cringed, certain he would beat her.

"We were only talking," she whimpered.

"The devil you were!"

"He's—he's my brother-in-law and—"

"Now you listen to me, and listen well! You belong to the king of Judah. No other man is allowed to touch you, ever! Anyone who does is committing an act of treason, a direct challenge to the king's sovereignty. That little weasel would like nothing better than to seize his brother's throne, and he would use you to do it too!" Hephzibah felt faint. Then the eunuch grabbed her by the shoulders and shook her hard. "If you ever do anything that stupid again, I'll have you executed!" Hephzibah knew he meant it. He gave her another rough shake, then stormed from the room.

Hephzibah stood rooted in place for a long time, trembling uncontrollably. Her shoulders ached from the eunuch's grip. At last she staggered over to the tall windows that looked down on the palace courtyard and fumbled with the wooden shutters until they opened. Cold, damp air streamed inside, but numb with pain and sorrow, Hephzibah didn't notice. She hugged herself, rubbing her bruised arms, and suddenly remembered the feeling of Gedaliah's strong arms around her, the masculine scent of his broad chest, the brush of his beard against her hair. She might never be held in a man's arms again. Despair welled up inside her until she wanted to die.

After a long while, she became aware of a flutter of movement in the courtyard, and when her eyes focused she nearly cried out. Hezekiah stood below her window, talking to an older man with a white beard. His voice was low, and she couldn't hear his words, but she watched him longingly as he talked, gesturing with his large, strong hands. Then he embraced the older man and disappeared alone into his chambers. He would find his concubine waiting. Hephzibah was barely 19, but she would be Hezekiah's prisoner for the rest of her life. He didn't want her, but no one else could have her either. She would have to live here alone until the day she died, and she could do nothing about it.

Outside Hephzibah's window, King Ahaz's clock tower loomed in the courtyard. Most of her days would be spent watching the sun's shadow inch slowly up the smooth stone stairs, then back down again. But today it was overcast. There would be no shadow. And Hephzibah would remain frozen in time like this—forever.

◆

Hezekiah returned from his morning prayers with Zechariah feeling more troubled than comforted. Threats of political intrigue and conspiracy filled his thoughts, and his mood matched the gray, dreary day outside. When he entered his chambers, he was surprised to find a concubine waiting for him.

"You look so cold, my lord," she murmured as she glided into his arms. "Sit over here by the fire, and let me warm you."

Hezekiah was still unaccustomed to such lavish attention, but he rather liked it. She was one of his favorite concubines, a lively, attractive girl with raven hair, and she offered him an interesting diversion from his disquieting thoughts. He allowed her to lead him closer to the hearth, enjoying the musky fragrance that trailed in her wake. "This is a nice surprise. I don't remember sending for you."

She cupped her small, soft hands around one of his, rubbing it gently to take off the chill. "The chamberlain thought you might like someone to help warm up your chambers. King Ahaz always did."

At the mention of Ahaz, any stirring of desire Hezekiah may have felt suddenly vanished. He vividly recalled the many concubines who hovered around his father, and the memory disgusted him. The pursuit of pleasure had occupied most of Ahaz's time while his nation had languished in poverty and disarray. Hezekiah pulled away.

"What's wrong?" she asked in alarm.

"Tell the chamberlain that I'm not like King Ahaz. You're dismissed until I send for you." He knew from her expression that he had hurt her feelings. She bowed low and left his chambers without a word.

As the door closed behind her, his problems and anxieties suddenly returned, and for a moment Hezekiah regretted his hasty decision. But he had work to do, a conference with his advisers to prepare for. He rang for his servants.

Isaiah entered the throne room where Hezekiah sat alone and bowed respectfully. "I am honored to meet you, Your Majesty."

"We've met before, Rabbi—a long time ago, in the Valley of Hinnom."

"Yes, of course. I remember."

With the windows shuttered against the rain, the throne room was gloomy, but by the pale light of the lampstands Hezekiah saw that the prophet had aged in the years since he had last seen him. His light brown hair had turned gray at the temples, and flecks of silver sparkled in his reddish beard. But his startling blue eyes, now creased with fine wrinkles at the corners, were still clear and penetrating. Isaiah wasn't tall and had only a slim build, but his presence seemed to fill the room.

"Your Majesty, I've heard you've decided to embrace the laws and covenant of Yahweh. For that, you've earned my respect. But you've also made many enemies, and you'll need to be a man of conviction and courage in the days ahead. My prayers are with you."

"Thank you. Rabbi, I would like to ask you to return to your rightful place among the nobility. You're one of the few men I can trust, and I would greatly covet your advice."

Hezekiah didn't get the immediate response he had expected. Instead, Isaiah stared thoughtfully at him, studying him, for what seemed like several minutes. The prophet's strange silence puzzled him. Any ordinary man would have quickly leaped at the opportunity for power and position. But he was beginning to see that Isaiah was no ordinary man.

"No one has been appointed to replace Uriah as palace administrator yet," Hezekiah continued. "My grandfather suggested that I ask you."

Again the prophet seemed lost in thought. But finally Isaiah shook his head, giving Hezekiah his answer even before he spoke.

"I'm sorry, Your Majesty, but I can't accept your offer. I'm honored—more than I deserve to be—but I can't accept it."

Isaiah's refusal frustrated Hezekiah. For the second time today, one of the most qualified and trustworthy men in the nation had refused a position of power second only to his own. He couldn't understand it.

"May I ask your reasons, Rabbi?"

"My reasons? They are rather difficult to explain. Earlier in my life I yearned for a position like the one you've offered me. You might say it was my life's ambition. Even now I admit it tempts me. But I've accepted another commission, and I must work to finish that job first."

"I'm afraid I don't understand. There's no other job in the nation that's more important than palace administrator, except mine."

Isaiah smiled a brief, warm smile that faded in a flash. "It's a long story."

"I'd like to hear it. I'm curious to know what could tempt a man of your obvious intelligence away from such power."

"Very well. My story begins when I was a young man, grandson of King Joash, rapidly rising in the court of my cousin King Uzziah. He was one of Judah's greatest kings. I idolized him, and I worked hard to please him and to gain a position of power in his magnificent government."

Isaiah talked rapidly, using quick, decisive gestures to emphasize his words. "When God's judgment fell on Uzziah, I was stunned. I considered it unfair and much too harsh for a man of Uzziah's greatness and accomplishments. I directed my anger and bitterness toward God because He had cursed Uzziah, making him an outcast, a leper. When the king finally died, he left a void in my life that his son Jotham could never fill. Uzziah was a great man, an outstanding king, and his shameful death shook my life to its foundations.

"The same year that he died, I experienced an even greater shaking. As I worshiped at the Temple, the mountain of God suddenly began to heave and quake beneath me, and I was hurled to the ground."

Isaiah's manner changed suddenly. His voice became reverent, as if reciting words that were very sacred to him. "I saw the Lord. The Holy One of Israel. And all the earthly power and glory of King Uzziah blew away like—like ashes in God's presence. All my life I'd worshiped a mortal king. Now I saw the Eternal One, the King of Kings.

"He was seated on a lofty throne, high and exalted, and the train of his robe filled the entire Temple. Hovering about Him were mighty seraphs, each with six wings. With two of their wings they covered their faces, with two others they covered their feet, and with two they flew. In a mighty, echoing chorus they sang, *'Holy, holy, holy is the Lord Almighty! The whole earth is filled with His glory!'"* Isaiah pronounced each word with deep reverence and wonder until the room seemed to resonate with the majesty of Yahweh's holiness. "At the sound of their voices, the doorposts and the thresholds of the Temple shook to their foundations, and the entire sanctuary filled with smoke."

"I saw the Lord," he repeated in awe. "And suddenly I saw myself for the first time. I saw my sin and unrighteousness, and I cried out, 'Woe is me! I am ruined! For I am a man of unclean lips, and I live among a people of unclean lips, and my eyes have seen the King, the Lord Almighty!'" Isaiah closed his eyes as if once again he saw himself in the light of God's holiness.

Hezekiah waited, transfixed, until the prophet finally opened his eyes and continued. "God's judgment on King Uzziah wasn't harsh," he said. "If anything, it was merciful. For Uzziah had dared to approach the holy God in His dwelling place. No mortal man, not even a king, is worthy to stand before the Lord Almighty. And now I, too, was condemned to die as I stood before God. Then one of the seraphs flew to me with a live coal, which he had taken from the altar with tongs. With this coal he touched my mouth and said, 'See—this coal has touched your lips; your guilt is taken away, and your sins are all forgiven.'"

Isaiah paused again, as if overwhelmed by the memory. "Did I deserve such forgiveness? Did I deserve God's mercy and pardon for my sins? Certainly not. Above all else, God is holy and just. But for those who repent, He is also merciful. Then I heard the Lord say, *'Whom shall I send?'* and *'Who will go for us?'* And I said, 'Here am I. Send me!'

"You see, He gave me back my life, just as He gave back yours, King Hezekiah, in the Valley of Hinnom. And so I said, 'Send me.' Then Yahweh said, 'Go and tell my people this: Though you hear my words repeatedly, you won't understand them. Though you watch and watch as I perform My miracles, still you won't know what they mean. Dull their understanding, close their ears, and shut their eyes. I don't want them to see or to hear or to understand, or to turn to me to heal them.'"

Hezekiah already knew some of the abuse Isaiah had suffered in his work for God, including physical threats and exile by King Ahaz. Yet Isaiah was willing to continue his thankless job, even if it meant turning down political power. Men like Isaiah were exceedingly rare.

"When will your work for Yahweh be finished?" Hezekiah asked.

Isaiah gave another fleeting smile and shook his head. "I asked, 'For how long, Lord?' and He answered, 'Not until their cities are destroyed—without a person left—and the whole country is an utter wasteland. And they are all taken away as slaves to other countries far away. And all the land of Israel lies deserted.'"

The prophet's words alarmed Hezekiah. He wanted to know if this part of the vision would be fulfilled within his lifetime, during his reign, but he was afraid to ask. Perhaps it would be better not to know.

"Yet a 10th—a remnant—will survive," Isaiah added, as if reading his thoughts. "And though the nation is invaded again and again, and destroyed, yet Israel will be like a tree cut down, whose stump still lives to grow again."

"Rabbi, I understand why you can't serve in an official capacity. But may I still come to you for advice?"

Isaiah smiled and spread his hands helplessly. "My own advice would be of little use to you, I'm afraid. But I promise to reveal the Word of the Lord to you, just as I did to the kings before you. Whether or not you heed that Word will be your decision, as it was theirs."

Hezekiah sat alone for a long time after Isaiah left, trying to decide whom to appoint as palace administrator. Isaiah's refusal had greatly disappointed him. The prophet was an amazing man, and, like Zechariah, he possessed a deep relationship with God. Hezekiah found it curious that neither of these devout men wanted a share in administering the government. The job of palace administrator was an important one. Hezekiah needed someone intelligent and uncorrupted, someone who would support his reforms and whom he could trust as a friend, someone who was faithful to Yahweh. He knew someone who fit every requirement but the last one: Shebna, his tutor. He would make an excellent choice except for the fact that he refused to believe in the existence of God. Hezekiah continued to ponder a mental list of all the officials and nobles in his government, weighing each of their qualifications carefully, but he always returned to the same conclusion. None of them was as qualified or trustworthy as Shebna.

Frustrated, he finally decided to send for Shebna, to seek his advice in making this difficult decision. All his life Hezekiah had relied on Shebna as a springboard for his ideas, to help him examine all aspects of a problem and make a choice. Now he felt a sense of relief as soon as Shebna arrived. How he admired Shebna's keen, sharp intellect! The dark, lanky Egyptian had been his closest friend for as long as he could remember, and Hezekiah knew he could come straight to the point.

"Shebna, I've asked the two most qualified men I know—Zechariah and Isaiah—to serve as palace administrator. They've both refused."

"Both of them? That is astounding!"

"Their reasons were even more astounding." He rose from his throne and began to pace restlessly, his hands clasped behind his back. "So where do I go from here? Who's left? My brother Gedaliah?"

"I do not think that would be wise."

"But my father set a precedent—"

"Gêdaliah lacks the experience for such an important job."

"Let's be honest, Shebna. I'm inexperienced, too, thanks to my father."

"But you have always worked diligently, my lord. That will quickly compensate for your inexperience. Prince Gedaliah does not work except for personal gain. I doubt that he would care about the good of the nation."

"That's what bothers me the most about my brother. He seems to have inherited our father's love of pleasure." Shebna said nothing, but his grim expression confirmed his agreement. "So, who's left? The truth is, I want to appoint you, but—" Hezekiah sighed in frustration and stopped pacing.

Outside the shuttered window the slashing rain beat against the wood. When he turned back, Shebna nodded. "I understand. I am not Judean. I am Egyptian."

"Shebna, I need someone who's not connected to Ahaz's administration, someone who can't be bribed. I know I can trust you, but I don't know about the others. They say one thing and believe another, but—"

"But you know what I believe and do not believe," Shebna finished for him.

"I'll admit, your lack of faith is a big problem for me. I need your sharp mind, your advice, your loyalty. You're not an idol worshiper, but—"

"Your Majesty, more than anything else I want to continue to serve you in your new government. But I can never say I believe in Yahweh. I would be lying if I did."

"And I'm determined to build my kingdom on Yahweh's laws. I don't know how we can reconcile that."

The Egyptian pondered for a moment as thunder rumbled in the distance. "Your Majesty, consider this: I have read your code of laws, your Torah, and found them to be good laws. I would have no problem becoming a Jew externally. I will even submit to your rite of circumcision. But you must understand that my religion is only external. I have no faith in any god."

"There are probably many external Jews in my court who are trying to fool me into thinking they're believers," Hezekiah said. "You could have done the same thing just to obtain power. At least you're honest." He thought for a moment about what Shebna had suggested. "You would really agree to follow all the laws, Shebna—including circumcision?"

"Yes. But you had better think it through carefully, Your Majesty. You are certain to meet with opposition to my appointment. My religious views are not a secret, nor would I lie about them if anyone asked. But I would not wish to cause a controversy for you so early in your reign."

Hezekiah knew he needed Shebna. There was no one else. And the thought that his appointment would spark a controversy didn't deter him. In that moment he decided.

"I'm the king. I don't need to justify my decisions to anyone. I want you to serve as my palace administrator."

The eerie silence that suddenly filled the little grove of trees terrified Jerusha more than the sound of screaming had. She lay on the ground in a daze of shock and pain, listening. The agonized cries had stopped. The other girls were dead. And now Jerusha's captor would kill her too. She looked up and saw him standing over her, slowly removing a short dagger from his belt.

"No—please." Her terrified voice was barely audible. "Please don't kill me."

She stared into his dark face and saw him clearly for the first time. He was lean and muscular, catlike, with wavy black hair and a short, squared-off beard. His deep-set eyes glinted cruelly beneath thick, straight brows. "Please don't—," she begged.

His black eyes narrowed as if considering her plea. Then he grabbed her hand and jerked her roughly to her feet. Numb with fear and pain, Jerusha could barely stand, but he shoved her down the path ahead of him, pressing the point of his knife to the base of her spine to keep her moving.

As she stumbled through the trees, Jerusha discovered the fate of the other captives. Their mutilated bodies lay scattered all over the grove. When she saw her cousin Serah's body, recognizable only by the embroidered wedding dress, Jerusha fell to her knees and vomited. The Assyrian began to laugh, and the sound of his laughter, eerily out of place amid the horror all around her, was unlike any true laughter she had ever heard—sadistic, cruel, malignant. Suddenly he grabbed her hair and thrust her head back, pressing the blade of his knife to her throat. Fear pulsed through Jerusha's body. She was going to die.

But a moment later he released her again and stared into her face. Then he grunted, and his thick brows arched questioningly. Jerusha understood. He was offering her a choice; submit to him or die. She had only a moment to decide.

Terrified, she bowed before him, clinging to his feet. "Please, I'll do anything. I don't want to die." He spat on her, then pulled her to her feet by her hair and shoved her down the path. They found the other soldiers waiting for them beside the horses, and immediately Jerusha's captor began barking orders. The men moved quickly to obey him. She saw that he was older than the rest, probably in his mid-30s, and clearly in charge. They bound Jerusha's hands and tossed her like baggage across the back of a horse, then rode off with her.

For almost a week the soldiers made their way north in a wave of violence. Again and again they descended on unsuspecting villages and farms, looting and killing and destroying until Jerusha grew sick from the terror and bloodshed. How many thousands of people had they murdered and mutilated? How many vineyards and olive groves had they devastated? She soon lost count. She wondered if the Assyrians had destroyed her father's little farm outside Dabbasheth and prayed that they hadn't. Abba loved his land more than life itself. Beloved Abba. Jerusha wept when she thought of him and his desperate efforts to save her. She tried to remember his smile, his voice, but could remember only the Assyrian's slashing sword and Abba's face, covered with blood.

Please, God—please let him be all right. She remembered Mama and little Maacah huddling, cowering, beneath the cart. Had the soldiers discovered them? Had they taken Maacah captive too? *Please, God . . .* Jerusha vowed to live, to find out what had happened to her family. Her love for them gave her the will to survive the endless days of terror and cruelty. Somehow, someday, she had to find a way to escape and return home. It was all she thought about in the days that followed.

At last they reached their destination, many miles to the north. The Assyrian camp lay sprawled like a vast black wasteland around a besieged city. Thick smoke and the scent of death hovered everywhere until even the air carried the metallic taste of blood. The world seemed dark and oppressive to Jerusha, and she saw more soldiers and chariots and horses than she imagined existed. Her chances of escaping from such a dreadful place seemed hopeless. Her captor, whose name was Iddina, terrified Jerusha. There was no mistaking the sadistic cruelty in his dark eyes. The sight of him, the smell of him gagged her. But when she remembered the mutilated bodies left behind in the little grove of trees, she knew her only hope of survival was unquestioning submission.

It was early evening when they arrived in the camp, and Iddina led her to the officers' section, where the larger, three-roomed tents offered more luxuries than the enlisted men's quarters. Iddina stopped beneath one of the few remaining trees, and Jerusha saw three more Assyrians, dressed in officers' tunics like his, seated on mats beneath the tree, eating their evening meal. Nearby, a woman bent over a hearth, surrounded by clay cooking pots, water jars, and storage vessels. Her cowering, skittish movements reminded Jerusha of a beaten dog.

The other officers seemed pleased to see Iddina and greeted him with hearty shouts. Then Iddina pushed Jerusha in front of them, proudly displaying her like a hunter with his trophy. The men quickly lost interest in their food and gaped at Jerusha with undisguised lust. She edged toward Iddina for protection. Without warning, he slapped Jerusha across the face and shoved her back toward the other men. They began to laugh at her with the same cruel, sadistic laughter she had heard from Iddina. Then one of the men shouted at the woman who knelt by the hearth, and she jumped up and hurried over to them.

Jerusha was shocked to see by her clothing and features that she was also from Israel. Behind the deadness in her eyes and the lifeless pallor of her skin Jerusha could see that the woman had once been beautiful, but now her every movement and gesture reeked of fear. She was looking at Jerusha but seemed to be gazing through her.

"I am Marah," she said in a toneless voice. "They want me to translate for you. Iddina says that the Assyrians always share their spoils of war. He says he will not be selfish and keep you for himself. You belong to all of them now."

Jerusha saw the lust in the other men's eyes and drew back again. "No!"

As swiftly as a pouncing cat, Iddina grabbed her from behind and poised his dagger above her heart. "Iddina says you must choose. Do you still wish to live?"

Jerusha felt paralyzing fear.

"Choose," Marah translated. Jerusha began to sob. There was no choice. Both alternatives horrified her. But her tears only produced more laughter.

"Die, little fool!" Marah said harshly. "Die while you still have the chance to die quickly!" Through her tears Jerusha stared at the waiting men, and they seemed more like animals to her than human beings. The knife remained poised above her pounding heart.

"O God, please help me," Jerusha sobbed. "I don't want to die."

Hezekiah studied the faces of the men bowing in obeisance before him, pledging their support, and wondered how he could separate the honest ones from the impostors. They assembled in an audience before his throne, waiting expectantly for him to begin.

Outside the palace windows, cold, slashing rain pelted the city, turning the creamy beige stones of Jerusalem's buildings a rich golden color. The spring rains, as precious to his nation's economy as gold, had been plentiful this year. Hezekiah hoped they marked the beginning of God's blessings.

The windows of the throne room, shuttered tightly against the rain and wind, admitted little light. Hezekiah had ordered all the torches and bronze lampstands to be lit, but the throne room remained gloomy, the atmosphere tense.

"For too long this nation has stumbled in darkness without God's light to lead us," Hezekiah began, "but this is about to change. As I rebuild this government from the ground up, I intend to rule according to the laws of Moses, and that means changing the way you did things in the past. From now on you will consult the Levites and the teachers of the Law in every judgment and decision you make and in every action you take. We must remain faithful to the laws of the Torah. Positions of authority in my government will be reserved for men who live by those laws and who haven't compromised with idolatry."

A gust of wind whistled outside, and the driving rain beat against the wooden shutters as Hezekiah paused. When no one questioned the fact that Shebna—an unbeliever—sat at his right hand, Hezekiah knew he faced an audience of seasoned politicians skilled at hiding their thoughts and emotions. The throne room was damp and cold, but a trickle of sweat ran down Hezekiah's neck.

"In order to eliminate the bribery and corruption of my father's reign I will personally oversee the administration of all levels of government at first. I'll also hold open court to hear petitions; that will end the injustice toward the poor that's currently taking place at the lower court levels. I'm also instituting a uniform system of weights and measures, and I expect it to be enforced.

"In a few weeks I plan to reopen the doors of the Temple. The regular daily sacrifices will be offered once again, but first the Temple will need repairs as well as cleansing from everything not commanded by Yahweh. The priests and Levites have already begun the consecration. As for the repairs, I've recovered a small sum of gold that Uriah stole from the tribute to Assyria. I consider this treasure Yahweh's, since it originally came from His Temple, and I'm using it to finance the repairs. Would Eliakim, son of Hilkiah, please stand?"

Hezekiah detected a murmur of surprise or perhaps discontent as Eliakim, a newcomer lacking royal credentials, was singled out. "Eliakim, you've been recommended to me as a capable engineer as well as a faithful follower of Yahweh. I'm putting you in charge of the structural repairs to the Temple. You'll also serve on my advisory council."

Eliakim's speechless expression covered a wide range of emotions—astonishment, awe, incredulity, joy. But he quickly recovered and bowed humbly, if somewhat shakily. "I—I am honored, Your Majesty. It will be a great privilege."

"When the Temple is ready," Hezekiah continued, "we'll offer a sacrifice for the sin of our nation and renew our covenant with God. I'll contribute animals from the royal flocks, and I'll expect all the elders and city officials to participate, along with everyone in Judah who wants to ask forgiveness for his sins."

He gazed at the faces assembled before him, trying to discern their thoughts. He believed there was discontent, mistrust, perhaps even conspiracy among them, but he saw no outward signs of it. He needed to shock them into speaking their minds, coax them out of hiding, and see where the battle lines were drawn.

"Finally, I'll open up this last topic for discussion. The Law of Moses requires the people to give a tenth portion to the priests and Levites so they can devote themselves to the Temple and its sacrifices. But the people are already heavily taxed to pay the Assyrian tribute demands. So it seems that the Law of God and the demands of Assyria are in direct conflict.

"If our nation is to have any future, I must consider what I will do about Assyria. The tribute we're forced to send every year is crippling. I'd like to be free from Assyrian control, but I first must consider what would happen if I stopped sending the tribute payments." Hezekiah chose an explosive topic, hoping to elicit a response and discover where the divisions lay. He had expected disagreement, but the sharpness of the conflict startled him.

"You would be committing suicide!" one of Ahaz's advisers shouted. He was an experienced statesman who had served under Kings Jotham and Ahaz. "The Assyrians would begin marching toward Jerusalem with their numberless hordes as soon as they heard of our rebellion."

"That's right," Hezekiah's father-in-law added. "You would be needlessly endangering the entire nation."

"But our nation is called to be a servant of Yahweh, not a servant of Assyria," Zechariah said. He was almost smiling as he deliberately drew out the opposition. A third adviser turned on him sharply.

"Listen—all the nations around us pay tribute as well. Do you think they're all fools? There's a very good reason why our taxes go to Assyria and not the Temple."

"He's right, Your Majesty," General Jonadab added. "I can prepare a detailed report on the Assyrians if you'd like me to. I think you will find it horrifying to read. They are a brutal, merciless, bloodthirsty people."

"And we can't afford to pay more taxes to the Temple," Ahaz's former treasurer added. "The Assyrian demands alone are staggering."

The prophet Micah scrambled to his feet. He wore his left arm in a sling, and his many bruises had discolored to a deep, purplish black. With his tanned, muscular body and simple clothing, he looked out of place among the wealthy nobles, but his passion for his subject was unmistakable.

"It was our nation's sin that caused our bondage to Assyria in the first place. But we can throw off their yoke once we make Yahweh the head of our nation."

"Just a minute!" Shebna sprang from his seat and confronted Micah angrily. "If you want to launch a religious revival and make everyone throw away their idols to worship Yahweh, that is immaterial to me. But it would be disastrous to allow your religious zeal to spill over into your political decisions."

Hezekiah was alarmed that Shebna vehemently opposed Yahweh's prophets. Had his appointment been a serious mistake? Micah stood up to Shebna fearlessly.

"Once we renew our covenant with God and purify the land of idolatry, we can't serve any other master but Yahweh. To give Yahweh's portion to Assyria would be a grave sin."

"If we stop sending the tribute to Assyria, we will be wiped off the map," Shebna said. "We cannot confuse religious idealism with political reality."

"You're wrong." Micah's voice was quiet but firm. "There's no difference between the two. King Hezekiah isn't the true ruler of Judah—Yahweh is. Our forefathers demanded a king like the other nations, but God is our true king. Therefore, there's no difference between our religion and our politics. They're one and the same."

Hezekiah watched the assembled men carefully and noted that most of them disagreed sharply with Micah. The rift between the religious and secular factions was deep. But as he listened to both sides of the argument, Hezekiah was not sure whom he agreed with. Shebna had taught him to make practical, informed decisions based on reason; Zechariah urged him to trust in God's power alone. These two sides of Hezekiah seemed as irreconcilable as the two fighting parties.

Beyond the shuttered window Hezekiah saw a flicker of lightning and heard the answering grumble of thunder a moment later. For his nation's sake, he would try to appease both political factions, and both sides of himself, for as long as he possibly could. With his economy in chaos, his nobility sharply divided, and his nation in a state of turmoil, the next few months of his reign would be challenging enough.

———◈———

Prince Gedaliah left the meeting in a rage. Hezekiah had finally appointed a palace administrator—Shebna. Their father had named his younger brother to the position, and Gedaliah had hoped the tradition would continue. But Hezekiah had not appointed him to *any* position, not even the job of overseeing repairs at the Temple. Some commoner named Eliakim had been given that job.

The prince was furious. He wanted power. And now he wanted revenge against Hezekiah for not granting him any. As he had watched his father's advisers bitterly opposing the new religious faction, he began to see how he might achieve both goals. Why settle for Shebna's position as second in command if he could be king instead? Hezekiah's new policies had angered many powerful, important men among the nobility. Gedaliah would be their obvious choice once they decided they'd had enough of Hezekiah's religion. But first he needed to let them know quietly that he agreed with them. He had made a mental note of all the advisers who spoke against canceling the Assyrian tribute. And when he saw that Shebna was among them, he knew exactly how he could win his support. He waited for him outside the throne room, and as the lanky Egyptian walked through the palace courtyard, he tried to draw him aside.

"I want you to know I was on your side in there, Shebna."

"I do not know what side you are referring to." Shebna walked on, but Gedaliah fell in step beside him.

"Come on—we've known each other a long time, Shebna."

"Yes, since you were a child."

"Right. And ever since Hezekiah and I were children, you've made it plain that you don't go along with all this religious stuff."

"King Hezekiah is well aware of what I believe. What is your point?"

"Well, our king just announced in the meeting that all the key government positions will go to those who follow God's laws. Doesn't it strike you as strange that the very top position went to you—an unbeliever?"

"Not at all. I have assured the king of my willingness to live by the laws of the Torah even though I do not profess belief in Yahweh or any god." Shebna was definitely on his guard.

Gedaliah decided to take a friendlier approach. "That's what I've been trying to tell you. I'm on your side. So are a lot of others I can name. I don't know what my brother is trying to prove with these religious reforms, but frankly I think he's going a little overboard."

He laughed to mask the ambition that drove him. "Now, if I were the king I wouldn't do things his way. I'd let the priests handle religion, and you and I would handle the government. In other words, Shebna, your thinking is more in line with mine than my brother's. You know what I'm saying?" He had dropped the bait. Now he waited to see the response.

Shebna stopped walking, but he controlled his emotions well. "Yes, I know exactly what you are saying. And I think you have greatly underestimated my loyalty to your brother." He turned to leave.

"I'm not finished, Shebna."

"I am. I have nothing more to say to you."

"Well, I have something to say to you, and I think you'd better listen: Hezekiah doesn't know everything there is to know about you."

Shebna faced him again, and his dark eyes bored into Gedaliah's. "I have nothing to hide."

"Oh yeah? Well, I wonder if Hezekiah ever heard the true story of how our mother died—or why."

Shebna turned his back so suddenly that Gedaliah didn't have a chance to see if his expression betrayed guilt or fear. "Not out here," he said as he strode away. Gedaliah hurried to catch up with him.

"Now, what do you really want?" Shebna said after he had closed the door to his chambers. Gedaliah looked around at the rooms that had belonged to Uriah. They should be his.

"What do I want?" Gedaliah repeated. "Let's see—we were talking about my mother, weren't we? Now, I was very young when she died, so I hardly remember her at all. But Hezekiah is a little older than I am. I think he remembers her quite well. And I think you do too, Shebna. Am I right?" Shebna didn't answer, but he looked uneasy. "In fact, if Hezekiah were to learn the true story of her death and your involvement in it—not to mention the part you played in our grandfather's long imprisonment—I think he might have good cause to hold you responsible. What do you think?"

"All I did was tell King Ahaz that your grandfather was teaching Hezekiah. I was new to the palace; I had no way of knowing how the king would react." Gedaliah saw Shebna's fear and savored the power he held over him.

"Oh, I believe you, Shebna. But the question is—will Hezekiah?"

"I did nothing wrong."

"No, more precisely, you did nothing—not when my father beat my mother right in front of you, and not even when he ordered her to be killed. You did nothing."

"Ahaz was the king, for heaven's sake! How could I stop him?"

"It was your fault he found out in the first place, wasn't it?"

"Yes. But how could I have possibly known what Ahaz would do?"

"Kings are mysterious creatures, Shebna. They have a way of doing whatever they please with people who double-cross them. So I guess it's hard to know how Hezekiah will react, too, isn't it?—if he were to find out, that is."

Shebna looked unnaturally pale. "What exactly do you want from me? A job in the government?"

"Yes, for starters. I need your help, Shebna, and you're going to need mine. You can't fight these religious fanatics by yourself. They jumped all over you in the meeting today. And my grandfather and Isaiah both have a lot more influence over Hezekiah than you do."

"No. They have both refused a government position."

"Don't kid yourself. Maybe they don't hold an official title, but their influence over Hezekiah is enormous—especially my grandfather's. I don't know why my brother has allied himself with a bunch of religious nuts, but unless we work together to counterbalance them, it's going to lead to disaster. Like all their crazy talk about rebelling against Assyria. They're dangerous."

"What do you suggest?" Shebna said irritably.

"If like-minded men such as us formed a party to oppose these fanatics, perhaps my brother would be forced to listen to reason. We have to work together. You need me in your government, Shebna. And in return, I'll make sure Hezekiah never learns about your past sins—how you betrayed our mother, then stood by and watched our father beat her half to death before he ordered her execution!" Gedaliah's voice grew steadily louder until he was shouting.

"You have made your point," Shebna said. "And I will see that you get your government position. But understand two things." He thrust his fingers in Gedaliah's face. "First, you will discharge all your duties with integrity. I will not tolerate any corruption. And second, although you and I may challenge some of the advice King Hezekiah receives from the religious extremists, we will never challenge his sovereignty. Understand?"

"I understand. And I guess I'll have to live with your ultimatums—for now. But if these radicals gain any more power, you can bet they'll demand your removal from office because of your unbelief."

"We shall see."

"Yes. We shall see."

❖

Eliakim hurried down the hill to his house after the meeting, his robes flapping, his curly black hair blowing in the wind. He was eager to share the news with his father and didn't care that sprinting through the streets in the rain was undignified. As he passed through the outer gate, he barely had time to kiss his fingers and touch the mezuzah that hung on the doorpost before Hilkiah rushed out of the house to meet him.

"Well? What happened, Son? Why did the king send for you?"

"Abba, you'll never believe it!" he said breathlessly. "I can hardly believe it myself!"

Eliakim leaned against the doorframe, puffing to catch his breath. Hilkiah grabbed Eliakim's arms and shook him.

"So tell me, already! What did the king want with my son?"

"He wants me to work for him!"

"Work for him?"

"Yes!"

Hilkiah clutched his heart with both hands. "Excuse me. I must sit down." He stumbled into the house and sank down onto a bench near the door. Eliakim followed, grinning broadly.

"Now please," Hilkiah said. "Start at the beginning, Eliakim."

Eliakim drew a deep breath. "Remember the night we helped Micah—the night he prophesied to the king? Well, King Hezekiah listened to him, Abba. Really listened and—"

"Yes, yes, I know this part. I took them to see Zechariah at the Temple, remember?"

"While I sat in prison with my throat slit open; remember?" He fingered the gauze bandage on his neck.

Hilkiah waved in annoyance. "I know, I know. Forget your throat."

"It's pretty hard to forget an experience like that, Abba!"

"So, the king invited you to his palace to discuss your throat, Eliakim? Talk sense to me!"

"Abba, King Hezekiah is completely different from what his father was. He's going to purge all the idolatry from the land and govern the nation according to God's Law."

"Praise God!"

"Your friend Zechariah and the other Levites will be advising him. He's going to start by purifying the Temple according to the Law and reopening it for the daily sacrifices. Then, when it's ready, the whole nation will hold a sacrifice and reaffirm our covenant with God."

Hilkiah cried out for joy and leaped up to embrace Eliakim. "God of Abraham! What a glorious day! It's too much. It's too much to even believe."

"Sit down, Abba, and save the dancing for a feast day. I'm just coming to the best part."

"What could be better than reopening Yahweh's Temple? And the sacrifices? After all these years, all our prayers? God of Abraham! What could be better?"

"The king hired me to oversee the repairs at the Temple."

Hilkiah stood blinking, his eyes wide. "Oh, Eliakim. God's holy Temple? You?"

"Yes Abba, me. I'm in charge of repairs. And I'm on the new council of advisers that the king is forming too. He said he wants only those men who've remained true to Yahweh and who never took part in idolatry. Apparently your old friend Zechariah recommended me, and of course Micah—"

"And you didn't want to help Micah. You told me to mind my own business!"

"Let's not go into that again. I've already admitted that I was wrong and you were right."

"'Kings take pleasure in honest lips,' Eliakim. 'They value a man who speaks the truth.' Oh, Son, I'm so proud of you." He grabbed Eliakim again and kissed both his cheeks.

"Abba, you'd better sit down. I want to tell you something else."

"There's more?"

"When the king asked me to serve on his council, I recalled an incident that happened a long time ago. Remember when I came of age and you sent me to Isaiah's house late at night with a message from Zechariah?"

"Yes, I remember."

"Well, something happened that night. I think you would say Isaiah prophesied over me." Hilkiah sat in stunned silence, waiting. "I don't recall the exact words, but he said that one day I would be God's servant. God would summon me to be a father to the house of David. He said I'd have absolute authority, second only to the king's—like the palace administrator, I guess."

"And you never told me all this?"

"Well, it seemed pretty far-fetched at the time, Abba. I was only a kid. In fact, it still seems unlikely. King Hezekiah appointed his former tutor, Shebna, to the position of palace administrator."

"Who is this Shebna? A foreigner?"

"He's Egyptian. That's the only appointment the king made today that didn't make any sense. Shebna's not a Jew, and from what I've heard, he doesn't believe in any god at all. Personally, I don't trust the man. There's something about him—"

"If King Hezekiah follows the Torah, and if you're right about Isaiah's prophecy, then maybe you'll replace Shebna someday. Remember, 'Many are the plans in a man's heart, but it is the Lord's purpose that prevails.'"

Eliakim sighed. "For now, I'm just content to work on Solomon's Temple. It's amazing!"

Hilkiah gave another cry of joy and clapped his hands. "Call all the servants. We're going to have a feast. We'll sacrifice a thank offering and praise God for the great honor He's given this household. We'll invite Uncle Moshe and—"

"Oh no, please, not Uncle Moshe."

Hilkiah stopped midsentence and frowned. "Why not Uncle Moshe?"

"Because he'll bring Aunt Hannah, and she'll have a long list of all the lovely brides she's picked out for me."

"So? Is that so terrible? Aren't you ever going to get married and give me some grandchildren?"

"Not to one of Aunt Hannah's brides, I'm not."

"So maybe some of them are a little chubby. So what? What's wrong with chubby?"

"What's wrong with beautiful, Abba? Beautiful would be much nicer."

"Listen. You wait and see. The matchmakers will be beating our door down now that you're on the king's royal council. Every rich papa in Jerusalem will want you for his daughter."

"You really think so?"

"I know so. You're not such a bad catch, you know—good looking—intelligent—" He tousled Eliakim's hair. "Maybe a bit too skinny, though, and too pale. Yes, you could use a good wife, eh?"

"Just let me choose her, Abba, not Aunt Hannah."

"But we have to invite her to our feast. It wouldn't be right to leave her out."

"Invite whomever you want," Eliakim said, laughing. "Listen, I'll see you later. I just came home to tell you the good news."

"Where are you going now?"

"To work. Repairing the Temple. Remember?"

"Now? You're starting now, in the rain?"

"Sure. That way I can see if the roof leaks."

"Oh, praise God, Eliakim! That I should live to see this day!" Hilkiah clapped his hands joyfully. "Your dear mother, may she rest in peace, would be fainting for joy."

Zechariah's face displayed concern, dismay, disappointment. "I understand your reasons, Son, but I think it's a serious mistake to appoint Shebna to such an important position."

"But there's no one else I trust as much as Shebna. I honestly think I can make it work."

"I don't see how."

The tiny room that was the king's former classroom felt hot and stuffy. Hezekiah crossed to the windows and unlatched the shutters, flooding the room with damp, icy air. The rain had finally stopped, and the setting sun edged the remaining clouds with gold. But Hezekiah was too upset to notice the sunset.

"Shebna's duties will be mostly administrative. I'm relying on you to make sure every decision is in accordance with the Law."

"Will you be going to Shebna for advice?"

"Well, yes. Sometimes."

"How can Shebna make wise decisions without the Lord's guidance?"

"Because he's a brilliant man."

"They're the most dangerous kind. Man's wisdom is foolishness in God's eyes."

Hezekiah sighed in frustration and rubbed his tired eyes. "Well, I had no choice. If there was anyone else who was qualified, I never would have chosen Shebna. I didn't want anyone who was connected with Ahaz because—"

"But Shebna *is* connected with Ahaz. Your father hired him."

"That's different. Shebna wasn't part of my father's government. I want to completely separate my reign from his—"

"You're wise to make that distinction."

"But that doesn't leave very many men to choose from. And the truth is—a lot of them are no more religious or godly than Shebna;

they're just better liars. At least I know where Shebna stands. He won't pretend that his advice is godly wisdom."

Zechariah stared at him gravely for a moment, his face drawn and tired. He opened his mouth to speak, then sighed and shook his head. "Let's not argue about it anymore. We have work to do." He sank down heavily at the table and unrolled one of the scrolls he had brought with him. Hezekiah closed the shutters again and sat down beside him, very aware that he hadn't convinced Zechariah or won his approval of Shebna's appointment. "This portion of the Torah was written for you," Zechariah said. "It's Yahweh's instructions to the kings of Israel. Of course, the king must follow all the laws of the Torah, but these words apply specifically to you, not the people."

"I had no idea any rules or guidelines existed," Hezekiah said, remembering his outburst with Shebna on the day of his coronation. He read the small Hebrew lettering aloud: "When you enter the land the Lord your God is giving you and have taken possession of it and settled in it, and you say, 'Let us set a king over us like all the nations around us,' be sure to appoint over you the king the Lord your God chooses—"

"God chose the house of David," Zechariah said, interrupting. "He promised that David's throne would endure forever. And God chose you. That's why He saved you from Molech. Never forget that." He gestured for Hezekiah to continue.

"'He must be from among your own brothers. Do not place a foreigner over you, one who is not a brother Israelite.'" He looked up from the text at Zechariah. "Or worse still, an Egyptian?" he asked ruefully. Zechariah didn't reply. "Look—Shebna's the least of my problems. The emperor of Assyria is the real king of Judah. He skims the wealth of our land for his own treasuries."

"Yes, I agree. The Torah clearly says, 'Do not place a foreigner over you,' yet that is exactly what Ahaz did when he first sent the tribute to Assyria. But then, Ahaz made no pretense of following the Torah."

Hezekiah stroked his beard thoughtfully. "I purposely raised this question of serving Assyria in the meeting today because I wanted to see where everyone stood. But I'm beginning to see that it's only a matter of time before it turns into a major issue. I don't want to remain a vassal nation, but I don't see how we can free ourselves from Assyria."

"If you renew Judah's covenant with God, then God's part of that covenant requires Him to deliver us from all our enemies."

"Then you favor rebellion?" Hezekiah said.

"I favor obedience to the Word of God, which says, 'Do not place a foreigner over you.'"

"I think I'm a long way from your level of faith. Assyria is the most powerful empire on earth. Maybe if we joined a military alliance with some of our neighboring nations someday—"

"No," Zechariah said firmly. "There are no alliances in God's plan, especially not with Egypt. Read the next part."

"'The king, moreover, must not acquire great numbers of horses for himself or make the people return to Egypt to get more of them, for the Lord has told you, "You are not to go back that way again."'"

"You see," Zechariah said, "alliances with other nations lead to bondage. Joseph started out as Pharaoh's trusted adviser in Egypt, but our fathers ended up as slaves. And Ahaz's alliance with Assyria led to our present slavery."

"Yes, but aren't alliances with other nations necessary? Times have changed since this law was written."

"No. Yahweh's Word will still be valid 1,000 years from now. You don't need to trust in the fickleness of other nations, Son. Put your trust in God."

Hezekiah knew that his faith wasn't very strong. Yahweh had saved him from Molech, but would that knowledge be enough if the powerful Assyrian armies marched against his tiny nation? "I'll be honest," he said. "This is too new for me. I've been taught to rely on the facts and on my own judgment and—"

"Then rely on your judgment and forget all this." Zechariah scooped up the scroll with a sweep of his hand. "But don't try to do both. It won't work. Either your faith in God is absolute, or it's worthless. There's no way to compromise."

Their eyes met and held. Then a slight smile flickered across Hezekiah's face. "I have a lot to learn, don't I? Come on—teach me." He unrolled the scroll again and found his place. "'He must not take many wives, or his heart will be led astray.'" Hezekiah looked up in surprise. "But kings always have harems full of wives."

"Kings don't always follow the laws of the Torah."

"What do wives have to do with anything?"

"King Solomon had 700 wives and 300 concubines, and they led him to compromise his faith in God."

"Wait a minute," Hezekiah said. "Kings are supposed to have large harems so they can produce an heir to the throne."

"God promised that there would always be an heir of David reigning on his throne. Does God need the help of 100 women to fulfill that promise?"

Hezekiah smiled. "No, I guess He needs only one."

"Marriage is a sacred covenant, much like Israel's covenant with God. Our affections must stay pure toward one wife, just as Israel's affections toward God must remain pure, not lusting after other gods. Do you have many concubines?"

"Yes, and I'm not sure I want to get rid of—"

"How many wives?"

"Only one—Hephzibah."

"Good. Do you love her?"

Hezekiah leaned back in his seat. "No. I hardly know her. My father arranged the marriage as a political payback. I've always thought of her as a present from Ahaz, so I guess I never showed much interest in her. I plan to choose my own wife now."

"Does Hephzibah love Yahweh, or does she practice idolatry?"

"I really don't know what she believes. Why?"

"If you decide to be faithful to one wife, as the Torah commands, Hephzibah would be the mother of your heir."

"I really don't know much about her at all." Hezekiah thought back to the day they were married. She had seemed so young, and he remembered how she had trembled when he held her in his arms. But she had a lot of spunk too. He smiled, remembering her daring scheme to get a glimpse of him. Suddenly he felt sorry for her and regretted ignoring her for so long.

"I guess it isn't her fault that she's a gift from Ahaz."

"My beloved wife was the joy of my heart and my most cherished treasure. Hold your wife close to you, Son. Confide in her. Listen to her. Sometimes women see things more clearly than we do. If you win her loyalty and her love, you'll be the happiest man alive. God gives us wives for more than physical pleasure."

Zechariah picked up a clay tablet and a writing tool. "Ancient tradition says that Yahweh dwells amid married couples. You see, here's the word for man—and the word for woman. All the letters are the same except for two. And if you put those two letters together, they form the name of God. If you share a love for each other and for God, His presence dwells in your midst."

Hezekiah was still not sure he wanted to dismiss all his concubines, even if what Zechariah said was true. He turned back to Zechariah's scroll and read: "'Neither shall the king multiply to himself silver and gold—' This won't be hard to obey. The royal treasuries are empty. I only hope this nation will prosper again someday."

"It will, Son. I promise you."

"'And when he sits on his royal throne, the king shall write a copy of this law and he shall keep it with him and read in it all the days of his life, that he may learn to reverently fear the Lord; so that he and his sons may continue long in his kingdom.'"

"Yahweh knows that a king's three biggest temptations are power, pride, and pleasure," Zechariah said. "When we read the history of your forefathers, you'll see how often one of these contributed to their downfall. Yahweh requires you to write the words of His Law yourself so you can study them. The king must have no doubt about what God demands of him."

"Will you come every day and teach it to me as I copy it?"

"Yes, I'll get you started. And there is a promise in this passage of scripture: 'That you and your sons may continue long in your kingdom.'"

"Both my father and his father died relatively young."

"That's no coincidence, Son. It was Yahweh's blessing that Ahaz died before he completely destroyed Judah."

"Sometimes I wonder if it isn't too late already. Rabbi Isaiah doesn't seem to think that the men of Judah will repent and turn back to God. And it all depends on the people, doesn't it? I mean, I can do only so much as king, and if the people don't respond, if they continue in their idolatry—" He stopped, remembering Isaiah's vision of ruined cities and a desolate land.

"God has set before them life and death. We can only pray that they choose life." The old man sighed deeply.

The tiny room had grown dark in the last few minutes as the sun dropped below the western ridge. Zechariah stood. "It's time for prayers." He lifted his prayer shawl, covering his head with it, and Hezekiah did the same.

But before Zechariah closed his eyes to recite, he gave Hezekiah a somber, penetrating look. "When it comes to obeying the Law, you can't pick and choose. If you decide to obey His Word, you must obey all of it." Then Zechariah began to recite, and Hezekiah knew they were back where they started: his grandfather still disagreed with his decision to appoint Shebna.

"Blessed is the man who does not walk in the counsel of the wicked or stand in the way of sinners or sit in the seat of mockers. But his delight is in the law of the Lord, and on his law he meditates day and night."

That evening, drawn by curiosity, Hezekiah decided to visit his wife. He knew nothing about Hephzibah, and the realization that he had ignored her since the week of their wedding had disconcerted him. He wondered how she would react to his sudden appearance after so much time. But when he saw Hephzibah again, it was he who was astounded.

She was a strikingly beautiful woman. She was dressed in white linen and adorned like a queen with golden earrings and bracelets. The fragrant smell of fine perfumes and bath oils filled the room. Hephzibah's long, dark hair hung loose down her back in thick curls. It looked radiant, luxurious, and he had an overwhelming urge to bury his hands in its softness. Hephzibah gazed at him in astonishment when she saw him standing in her doorway. He saw surprise in her eyes and many unspoken questions, but she quickly recovered and bowed low.

"Welcome, Your Majesty. Come in. Shall my servants bring you some refreshments?" Her voice shook, and she kept her head lowered as if awed by his presence.

"No, that's not necessary. You may dismiss them." Before Hephzibah could say a word, the servants disappeared. "You look lovely," he told her. "Your dress, your perfume . . ." He couldn't take his eyes off her. Was this incredible stranger really his wife?

"Thank you," she murmured. "It's all for you."

"But how did you know that I was coming?"

"I didn't."

"You mean you go through this every night? Just in case—?"

"Yes, my lord."

For a moment Hezekiah glimpsed the absurdity of her situation, the hours of preparation and waiting just to cater to his whims. He suddenly felt clumsy and awkward with her, as if for the first time. The discovery that such a beautiful woman had been waiting in vain for him every night stunned him.

She was small and delicate, the top of her head barely reached his chin, and her skin was a golden, tawny color that matched the highlights in her hair. Her deep brown eyes were flecked with gold and fringed with thick, dark lashes that brushed against her cheeks as she stood before him with her head lowered. She seemed so young to him, with a childlike vulnerability that made him want to shelter and protect her. She was his wife, yet the only thing he knew about her was her name. He took her hand and led her to a cushioned couch, then sat facing her. Her hand felt icy, and he cupped it between his own.

"How old are you, Hephzibah?" he asked, trying to shake the disturbing awkwardness he felt.

"Nineteen, Your Majesty." He reached out to hold her other hand. It was icy as well.

"Is it too cold in here? You're shaking. Shall I have the servants light a fire?"

"No, Your Majesty—thank you—I'm fine."

He should have warned her he was coming. She seemed nervous, and he wondered if that was what made it so difficult for him to relax with her. She raised her head to look at him, but when their eyes met he was startled to read in them the depth of her love, a love he knew he didn't return. And he also realized that she was not shaking from cold, but from fear.

"Hephzibah, why are you afraid? Is it because I'm the king?"

"Yes—a little." Her voice was barely a whisper.

"And why else? You can tell me." Her eyes filled with tears, and Hezekiah guessed that he was probably to blame. But he couldn't imagine what he had done to make her cry. Nor did he know how to make her stop. "Have I made you unhappy somehow?"

"I'm the one who hasn't pleased you!"

"What makes you say that?"

"Because you never come to see me like all the others."

"Is that what you think?" Hezekiah was horrified to learn that she had interpreted his lack of interest as her own fault. "It's not that way at all, Hephzibah."

She looked down at her hands, still in his, and her tears continued to fall. "I've failed to give you an heir."

Hezekiah sighed in frustration and let her hands drop. He felt angry with himself and guilty for allowing his hatred for Ahaz to hurt this beautiful woman. He wanted to make things right with her, but he didn't know where to begin. He stroked his beard, trying to think, and remembered Zechariah's words: *Yahweh dwells amid married couples.*

He placed his hands on Hephzibah's shoulders. "Listen—I know we haven't gotten our marriage off to a very good start, but it hasn't been your fault. You've never done anything to displease me. Maybe we should start over again. Do you think we could give each other another chance?"

"Oh, yes! I want that with all my heart!" She gazed up at him with a mixture of hope and joy, and once again her deep love for him shone clearly in her eyes. He pulled her into his arms and felt her tears, warm and wet on his chest as she clung to him with surprising strength.

"I want our marriage to be happy," he said. "I want to know all about you. After all, you'll be the mother of my heir."

She lifted her head and stared at him. "But suppose one of your concubines has a son first?"

Again, he thought of Zechariah's words: *When it comes to obeying the Law, you can't pick and choose.* The Torah instructed him to be faithful to one wife, and if he had to decide between Hephzibah and one of his concubines, there was no contest. None of the others could match her elegance and grace—or her astonishing beauty.

He took a deep breath. "It won't happen. From now on I'll have only one wife, as the Torah commands."

"What?" She stared at him in disbelief.

"It's true. You'll be my only wife."

Hephzibah gave a cry of joy and threw herself into his arms, weeping and clinging to him as if she would never let go. He had surprised himself as well. He certainly hadn't made this decision ahead of time. And as he held Hephzibah close and stroked her soft, fragrant hair, he was equally surprised to discover that he no longer cared about the rest of his harem. How could he have forgotten how beautiful Hephzibah was?

"I know that in time we'll have a son," he said, "maybe by this time next year. But there's really no hurry. I plan to live a long time, so I won't be needing an heir right away."

She looked up at him, smiling through her tears, and Hezekiah was overcome again by her loveliness. "I will give you an heir—I promise! I will bring regular offerings to Asherah, who gave my mother seven sons and—"

"Oh, no." Hephzibah worshiped idols. He released her from his arms and saw the look of terror on her face as she realized she had lost him. In spite of the revulsion he felt toward her idolatry, Hezekiah couldn't bear to hurt her again. He studied her delicate face for a moment, the perfect slope of her nose, the slight almond slant of her eyes, the flush of her smooth, tawny skin.

"Do you believe in Yahweh, Hephzibah?"

"Yes—He was worshiped in my father's house."

"Other gods too?"

"Yes."

"Which ones?"

"The lord Baal, the goddess Asherah—"

"And Molech?" He felt his stomach turn.

"No, my lord. Not Molech."

Hezekiah sighed. Once again he thought of her as Ahaz's gift, and her idolatry didn't surprise him. He knew he was free to divorce her because of it and to choose his own wife, but he was amazed to realize that he didn't want to. Maybe it was because he recognized her deep love for him. Or maybe because she was so very beautiful. Hezekiah didn't fully understand why, but he knew he wanted to give her another chance. He felt irresistibly drawn to her, like the proverbial moth to the flame.

"There is only one God," he said gently. "Yahweh. He is the only God we will ever worship in this nation and in this household as long as I am king. The others are only wood and stone. If you want to remain married to me, you must give up Baal and Asherah and worship only Yahweh." He wondered if he was asking for too much too soon.

"I will do anything for you," she said, and again he saw the love in her eyes. He believed her.

Hezekiah found himself wondering what would happen if he opened his heart to her. He hadn't really loved any of his concubines. *Confide in her. Listen to her. Win her loyalty and her love, and you'll be the happiest man alive.* But how would they begin building a life together? He didn't even know her.

As he gazed around the room, Hezekiah spotted a small lyre. "Do you play, Hephzibah?"

"Yes." Her smile was both shy and radiant.

"Would you play something for me? I love music, but I don't play anything myself. My grandfather is a Levite singer, and, of course, my ancestor David was a musician, but unfortunately I didn't inherit any of their talent."

"Shall I sing too?"

"Yes, I'd like that." She picked up the lyre, strumming and tuning it softly, and he could tell by the way her delicate fingers caressed the strings that she was an accomplished player. But when she began to sing, her voice was the most beautiful sound Hezekiah had ever heard. Sweet and clear, it flowed so effortlessly that she made singing seem easy. He sat entranced, feeling the tension and strain of his day melt away. He wished it would go on forever.

When she finished he sat in silence for several moments, enjoying her beauty, basking in it. Her song had cast a spell over him that he was powerless to break. "Please—sing another one."

She smiled and strummed a few bars of a haunting melody. "This one was written by another ancestor of yours," she said. "'Let him kiss me with the kisses of his mouth—for your love is more delightful than wine . . . Take me away with you—let us hurry! Let the king bring me into his chambers. . . . Arise my love, my fair one, and come away with me.'"

When she finished, he gently took the lyre from her hands and gathered her into his arms.

7

As another long day of hearing petitions drew to a close, King Hezekiah leaned back on his throne. "Are we finished for today, Joah?" he asked the court scribe.

"Almost, Your Majesty. A delegation of priests and Levites from the Temple requests an audience with you."

"Good. Send them in." He turned to Shebna, seated by his right hand. "I've asked them to report their progress in purifying the Temple. Let's hope it's good news for a change."

"Most likely it is another internal power struggle for us to solve. We seem to have plenty of those."

"Now we know why King Solomon prayed for wisdom."

Zechariah, Azariah, and Shimei the Levite entered the throne room, and Hezekiah knew by their beaming faces that they brought good news. Azariah seemed especially old and frail, and as he bowed low before the king he had difficulty rising to his feet again. But he spoke with the vigor and enthusiasm of a much-younger man, willing to tackle an overwhelming job.

"Your Majesty, we have finished cleansing the Temple. We've cleaned the altar of burnt offerings and all its tools and the Table of Shewbread and its equipment. What's more, we've recovered and sanctified all the utensils thrown away by King Ahaz when he closed the Temple. They're beside the altar of the Lord."

Hezekiah couldn't hide his surprise. "You mean everything's finished already? The Temple is purified?"

"Yes, Your Majesty."

"I can't believe it. I thought it would take months to restore. How did you accomplish everything so quickly? It's only been—how long? A little more than two weeks?"

"Sixteen days, Your Majesty," Shimei said. "But some of us have waited a lifetime for this opportunity."

"It's not fancy," Zechariah added, "and there's still a lot of repair work to be done, but it's purified according to the Law. Why don't you come and see?"

Hezekiah couldn't resist the invitation. He hadn't been to the Temple since the night Uriah died. "Lead the way," he said, and, leaving Shebna behind, he followed the three men.

The afternoon was dismal, and a light rain fell as Hezekiah climbed the steps of the royal walkway to the Temple mount. "We can hardly believe it ourselves," Azariah continued breathlessly as they ascended, "but we all worked together as one man. The priests cleaned up the inner room of the Temple and removed everything that was unclean, carrying it into the courtyard. Then the Levites took it down and dumped it in the Kidron Valley. We reached the outer court in about a week and finished everything else this afternoon."

As they arrived at the entrance to the Temple, Hezekiah stopped to admire the spacious open courtyard and the magnificent view from the highest point in the city. Rows of rolling gray clouds hung heavily over the valleys, and Jerusalem looked sodden, rain-soaked, deserted. He walked through the court of women and into the inner courtyard, then stopped just inside the gates. The Assyrian altar was gone, and the huge brazen altar of Yahweh was back in its original place. It loomed above them, 30 feet square and 15 feet high. He watched as one of the priests ascended the ramp to fuel the fire, which hissed and steamed in the falling rain.

"How did you ever move this altar back? It's so huge I imagined it would require hundreds of workers."

"Your new engineer figured out a way for a handful of men to move it as if it weighed nothing," Azariah said. On Hezekiah's left, a team of craftsmen worked to construct a new base of 12 oxen for the brazen laver, like the original oxen from Solomon's time. The huge laver rested crookedly on its improvised base, and raindrops made spreading circles on the glassy surface of the water. Hezekiah walked over for a closer look, running his fingers across one of the oxen's shining wet flanks.

"It's magnificent," he said. "I never saw this laver the way it's supposed to be. Were the original oxen sent to Assyria?"

"Yes," Zechariah said. "Such treasures to give away to a heathen king."

"Our treasures, our wealth, our sovereignty." Hezekiah felt a surge of anger, but for now he was powerless to change the situation his father had created. Perhaps the rededication of the Temple would bring the return of Yahweh's blessings.

"Have all the priests and Levites consecrated themselves?" he asked his grandfather.

"There are more Levites than priests, but we've all performed the ritual of consecration as Yahweh commanded. We're ready."

He looked around again at everything they had accomplished and remembered his disappointment the first time Zechariah had brought him here. It had seemed like an empty ritual, with none of the splendor and majesty that God deserved.

"How long has it been since the daily sacrifices have been offered?" he asked.

"According to the Law of Moses? I don't know—many years," Zechariah said. "Yet Yahweh commanded that a sacrifice be made morning and evening for the sins of the people."

"Then the account of our sin must be very great by now. When can we begin the sacrifices again?"

"Tomorrow morning," Azariah said, smiling.

"Are the musicians ready too?"

"Yes, Your Majesty," Shimei said. "We have organized everything according to the pattern prescribed by King David, just as you commanded. All the Levites from the tribes of Asaph, Heman, and Jeduthun are ready. We have singers, harps, lyres, and cymbals. And we've been rehearsing."

Hezekiah rested his hand on Azariah's shoulder. "I still can't believe everything is ready so soon. You've all worked hard. Thank you."

As he was about to leave, he saw Eliakim hurrying across the courtyard to bow before him. His clothes were soaked, and rain plastered his hair to his head and dripped from his beard.

"I'm amazed at how much has been accomplished, Eliakim. How are the structural repairs coming?"

"Excellently, Your Majesty. I have a very dedicated crew. There's still a lot of repair work to be done, but the foundations are solid. Solomon's original structures were well built, each stone chiseled so precisely that mortar wasn't even necessary, and—" Eliakim paused to sneeze. "Excuse me, Your Majesty."

"We've tried to get him to go indoors for a while, out of the rain, but he won't listen," Shimei said.

Eliakim dismissed their concern with a wave of his hand. "Even the great earthquake from King Uzziah's time didn't seem to damage the main structure. Most of the work will involve repairing the crumbling plasterwork, replacing rotting beams, and restoring what was damaged when the gold was stripped off by King Ahaz." He finished with another sneeze.

"That's very good news, Eliakim. I appreciate your dedication. And I'm ordering you to go home and change into dry clothes."

As Hezekiah walked back through the courtyard toward the palace, a glint of metal suddenly caught his eye. He turned aside for a closer look. In a corner of the courtyard stood a huge metallic snake draped around a brass pole. He called Shimei over. "What's this?"

"It's the bronze serpent that Moses raised up in the wilderness. According to the story, poisonous serpents afflicted the Israelites because of their sin, but when they looked to this bronze serpent, God healed them."

"I noticed it before, but I assumed it was more of my father's idolatry. Is it part of Solomon's original Temple?"

"Well, no. Not exactly."

"Get rid of it, then. It doesn't belong here."

Shimei gazed at him in shock. "But many people pray to it, and some even claim healing—"

"Then the people are misusing it. They've made it into an idol. It's unclean, and I want it out of here."

"But Your Majesty, the people consider it sacred—"

"I don't care. I'll smash it to pieces myself if you don't want to, but it doesn't belong in this Temple. It isn't sacred. It's a hunk of brass. Our worship must remain pure."

"Yes, Your Majesty."

"Tell the priests that I want the sin offering tomorrow to be seven times the usual sacrifice for sin. Offer it for the entire congregation and for the sanctuary, because it was so defiled, and for all of Judah—no, make that for all of Israel and Judah. Even though we're two nations, we're still one people."

"Everything will be done just as you command, Your Majesty."

"Good. Until tomorrow, then."

—◆—

The overcast sky was turning light in the east when Hezekiah descended the broad palace steps to greet the nobles and city elders waiting for him in the courtyard. The crowd streaming up to the Temple seemed large, larger than he had dared hope. Wave after wave of gray storm clouds rolled down from the distant mountaintops into the valleys below, threatening rain. The spring rains had been plentiful this year, and Hezekiah wondered again if God had already begun to bless his nation.

From a distance he heard the bellowing of the sacrificial animals and smelled their scent. Blood had to be shed, atonement made. Suddenly he felt very conscious of his sins, as if they were visibly written on him for all to see. He knew his guilt was very great, and he wondered if he would feel any different afterward.

Azariah stood beside the altar of burnt offering, dressed in the miter and ephod of the high priest. The air above the altar wavered from the heat, and Hezekiah could feel its warmth as he approached. One of the bullocks strained against the rope as it instinctively shied away from the fire, and he identified with the animal in its attempts to escape, remembering his own desperate struggle against the soldiers who had carried him to Molech. Hezekiah placed his hand on the bullock's head, feeling the rough stubble of its fur, and he remembered Uriah's hand on his own head, marking him as the firstborn. The bullock would take his place, would die for his sins. He thought of his brother Amariah, who had died in his place. The high priest did his job swiftly and skillfully, and the bull went limp, its blood filling the ceremonial bowl.

Then there was a flurry of activity around him as the priests slaughtered the bullocks that the chief elders had presented. Carcasses piled up around the altar as basin after basin of blood was poured out at its base. Knives glinted and flashed, the priests' arms turned bloody, their garments stained, but they worked tirelessly, slaughtering the seven rams, then the seven lambs. The Levites helped with the sacrifices, removing the fat for the priests, who carried it up the sloping ramp to the altar. When everything was ready, the high priest began to chant the liturgy, and the men who still remembered the words joined in: "Blessed is he whose transgressions are forgiven, whose sins are covered—" Then everyone fell prostrate in worship as the priests and Levites sang: "I acknowledged my sin to you and did not cover up my iniquity. I said, 'I will confess my transgressions to the Lord.'"

As the congregation rose to their feet, the high priest laid their offering on the altar and stepped back. Then the joyful cry rang out as a pillar of fire ascended into the air. "And you forgave the guilt of my sin. *Selah*. Therefore let everyone who is godly pray to you while you may be found; . . . you are my hiding place; you will protect me from trouble and surround me with songs of deliverance."

The words seemed like a promise to Hezekiah, and he wondered if he would ever have enough faith to trust God for deliverance from Assyria. He looked at his grandfather and knew that he had waited and prayed many years for this day.

With the sin offering completed, Hezekiah gave the command for the burnt offering to begin, and the Levite musicians assembled on the steps of the sanctuary with their instruments. The sound of voices and trumpets in the echoing courtyard, along with the stirring melody, touched a chord in Hezekiah as ancient as his ancestry and brought back tender memories of Zechariah singing to him, comforting him. As the music rose in the morning air, the sacrifices seemed transformed. The splattered blood and slaughtered animals faded into the background as the priests accomplished their tasks in rhythm to the music. It was no longer a scene of carnage, but an act of worship.

"Shout for joy to the Lord, all the earth. Worship the Lord with gladness; come before him with joyful songs—" The aroma of roasting meat filled the air, and Hezekiah found it was a sweet smell, one he would smell every morning and evening as the wind carried it down the hill to the palace.

Hezekiah faced the people. "Now that you have rededicated yourselves to Yahweh, you may bring your peace offerings and thank offerings." The overwhelming response amazed Hezekiah as hundreds of men brought their offerings forward. Zechariah and the other Levites had to take over for the exhausted priests as animals were brought to them in a steady stream. As the morning wore on, a misty rain began to fall, washing gently over the worshipers, and it seemed to Hezekiah that it cleansed the entire city. The Levites continued to praise and sing in spite of the rain until the last offering was finally placed on the fire.

Hezekiah bowed his head as the high priest delivered the benediction: "The Lord bless you and keep you; the Lord make his face shine upon you and be gracious to you; the Lord turn his face toward you and give you peace."

"Amen," Hezekiah murmured. He felt a sense of relief knowing that peace had been restored between him and God. He had a new beginning after so many wasted years; now he could begin to lead his nation on God's path.

Jerusha lifted the tent flap and dragged the heavy water jug over to the hearth, lacking the strength to carry it. Her limbs ached, and she battled waves of nausea. She would receive no compassion or relief even if she was sick, so she struggled with her work in silence, willing her seething stomach to be still. She swatted uselessly at the black flies that swarmed around the food; they hovered everywhere, clinging to dishes and cooking pots. To Jerusha everything about her new home seemed oppressive and evil, as if all the color had drained out of the world, leaving only darkness—the dull black tents stretching endlessly in every direction; the Assyrians' black, curly hair and pitiless eyes; the ever-circling vultures, darkening the sky, blotting out the sun.

Birds no longer sang during the day, drowned out by the cries of human pain and torture and the distant sounds of battle. At night the hyenas and jackals boldly roamed about in the darkness, fighting and feasting on the bodies of the fallen. She couldn't escape the smell of rotting flesh, but to the Assyrians the scent of death was a sweet-smelling perfume. Death was their sport, their way of life, their god.

Jerusha lost track of time as the days and weeks merged together endlessly. Had she been captured a month, six months? She no longer knew, nor could she recall joy or laughter or love. When she tried to remember her home or her family, she found that the memories had faded, merging with the death all around her until she could remember her family only as she had seen them last: Abba covered with blood, Mama and Maacah cowering in fear, the grape arbors and olive groves of her homeland looted and burned. Her life had become an unceasing grind of slavery, preparing meals during the day, being used and abused by Iddina and his fellow officers at night.

"You'd better hurry up." Marah's angry voice brought Jerusha back to the present.

"I can't work any faster. I feel awful."

Marah offered no sympathy but continued to grind grain in silence. From the beginning, Jerusha had shared the three-room tent and all the cooking duties with Marah, but if Jerusha had hoped for any love or friendship, she was soon disappointed. Long ago Marah had retreated to a secret world inside her own mind to escape from the Assyrians and her living death sentence. She had nothing to give Jerusha beyond the basic instructions of their daily work.

Jerusha had guessed Marah to be in her late 30s and was startled to learn she was 20. Marah seemed like an aging, bitter woman, her beauty used up, her youth and innocence long dead. Through the scattered, fragmented sentences Marah offered from time to time, Jerusha learned that she had been captured more than a year earlier during an Assyrian raid like the one on Dabbasheth. Her husband and tiny son had been brutally slaughtered. Now Marah often retreated to a world inside herself, staring sightlessly, her body curled into a huddled ball, rocking endlessly. Once withdrawn, she was deaf, blind, unreachable.

"What's wrong with you today?" Marah asked suddenly. "Why are you so slow?"

"It's my stomach. I feel like I'm going to be sick."

The smell of burning dung reached Jerusha's nostrils, and she could no longer control her nausea. She dropped the dough she was kneading and fled behind the tent.

When she stumbled back to her work again, Marah stood with her hands on her hips, watching. "You're pregnant, aren't you." It wasn't a question, but an accusation.

"No—I can't be—"

"Why not?"

"Because—" Jerusha started to say that only women who are married and loved and have homes and husbands get pregnant, but the words died on her lips. For a painful, bitter moment she thought of her engagement to Abram and the rosy-cheeked babies she had imagined they would have together. It had been her dream, all that she had asked for in life. Then the vision died with the realization of where she was and what she had become.

"You *are* pregnant," Marah said, and Jerusha knew it was true. She covered her face and wept. "I'll take care of it for you," Marah said after a moment.

"What do you mean?" Jerusha couldn't imagine why the cold, unfeeling Marah would offer to care for her child.

"I'll take care of things—so it'll never be born."

"Oh, no!"

"It's better to kill it now before—"

"I could never do that!"

Marah gave her a disgusted look. "Suit yourself. But don't say I didn't warn you." She returned to her work.

Could Jerusha's life become any more unbearable than this? It was already a hideous nightmare she could never awaken from; now she had to face the fact that she was carrying a child. Their baby was growing inside her, and she would have to give birth to it in this dark, evil place. She covered her face again and wept at the hopelessness of it all, her body shaking with her sobs. Why had God abandoned her to this living hell?

"Stop your sniveling and get back to work," Marah said. "If their breakfast is late, we'll both get a beating."

Jerusha knelt and picked up the lump of dough to resume her work. She had no other choice.

———◆———

"Oh, Miriam, it's so good to be home again!" Hephzibah threw her arms around her sister and hugged her warmly. "You're so grown up, Miriam. Turn around and let me look at you." Hephzibah's sister was taller than she was, but she had the same thick, curly hair and deep brown eyes. It was easy to tell that they were sisters. "You've become a woman overnight," Hephzibah said.

"Well I *am* 16 now."

"Come on—let's go sit out in the courtyard under the fig tree and talk like we used to. Remember?"

"It seems like such a long time ago that you were married. And now your husband is the king! I still can't believe it. My own sister is married to the king! What's it like?"

They sat on the ground beneath the tree, and Hephzibah sighed contentedly. She loved this tiny, familiar patch of trees and flowers that brought back so many warm childhood memories. "I'll tell you the truth, Miriam—at first it was very, very lonely. I had no friends, and I missed all of you so much."

"What about your husband? Doesn't being married make up for leaving your family?"

"Well, at first I never saw him. That was the worst part. He was more interested in the rest of his harem, and I was very miserable. I didn't know what I'd done to displease him."

Miriam put her arm around Hephzibah. "We had no idea you were so unhappy. Why didn't you tell us?"

"The loneliness was unbearable. But I couldn't come home, because I didn't want Abba to know that I had failed as a wife."

"And I've been envying you for marrying royalty."

"There wasn't much to envy at first. But ever since he became king everything's changed. Now we spend every evening together."

"So tell me your secret! How did you win him away from his concubines? I hope to have a husband of my own someday."

"I'd like to think it was something I did, but the truth is—I didn't do anything. He says it's against Yahweh's law for the king to have a lot of wives."

"What? Against the law?"

"Yes, I'm to be his only wife from now on. No concubines. And our son will be the next king." She smiled with pride.

"But the kings of Judah always have huge harems. What about King David and King Solomon? Their harems are legendary!"

"I don't understand it—I just know how wonderful it is to finally have my husband all to myself."

"It doesn't make sense. I've never heard of that law before."

"That's not the only new law. I have to learn all sorts of other rules and rituals, too, like special baths and offerings and forbidden foods. Sometimes I get a little jealous of all the attention my husband gives Yahweh. But he says that if I obey all these laws, Yahweh will bless us with a son—many sons."

"Now, that's really crazy. I've never heard of Yahweh granting sons. Everyone knows you pray to Asherah if you want children."

"Shh! Please, Miriam! I'm not allowed to even mention the name of another god. King Hezekiah worships only Yahweh, and I have to do the same."

"He's taking a big chance, then, if he wants to have sons. You'll be barren if he offends the fertility goddess."

"Shh—I know, I know." Hephzibah found it easy to believe in one god when she was with Hezekiah at the palace, but now that she was home, reminded of the old ways, the old loyalties, she felt guilty for heartlessly abandoning Asherah.

"Is it true that the king tore down the big altar of Assur that used to be in the Temple? And even Moses' sacred serpent?"

"Yes, it's all true."

"Well, Abba hasn't been very happy about all the changes your husband is making. Every time he comes home from the palace he shouts about the terrible things that are going to happen to our nation because King Hezekiah has offended all the gods."

"I know—it scares me too. But my husband doesn't believe in any god but Yahweh."

"Do you still believe in them?"

Hephzibah had asked herself the same question many times. She had assured Hezekiah that she would abandon all other gods, but sometimes she felt a lingering fear for deserting them. Was Yahweh really the only god? "I must believe whatever the king tells me to," she said.

"What about your vow, Hephzibah? You pledged a daughter to the goddess's service—remember?"

"That was before—I mean, how was I to know my husband would forbid me to worship Asherah?"

"What are you going to do?"

"Well, maybe once we have a son, King Hezekiah will be a little more open-minded about who I worship. But for now, I want so much to please him. I'll do whatever he asks."

"You really love him, don't you?"

Sweet, warm contentment flowed through Hephzibah, erasing all other concerns. "I love him more than anything else in the world."

"I hope I can learn to love whoever Papa chooses for me."

"You will. Just wait and see. Has Papa been making any inquiries for you yet?"

"I don't think so. He's waiting to see who'll be appointed to the important positions in the new court. Are there any eligible men on the council?"

Hephzibah reached up absently to pluck a leaf off the fig tree. "Shebna, the new palace administrator, isn't married, but he's too old for you. Then there's a new chief engineer named Eliakim who's becoming pretty important. He's a bachelor and—"

"Is he handsome?"

"Yes, in a scholarly sort of way—high forehead, dark, rumpled hair and beard, slim build—"

"I want a husband as handsome as yours."

Hephzibah tossed the leaf at Miriam playfully. "That's impossible. There's no one in the kingdom who's that handsome."

"Do you remember when we snuck out to try to see what Prince Hezekiah looked like?"

"How could I forget?" Hephzibah laughed. "If Abba had found out, he would have had us stoned!"

"Tell the truth," Miriam said. "You were afraid he'd be a fat, ugly toad like his father."

"Well, can you blame me? But when I saw him that day, he was so handsome, with such huge, dark eyes—he took my breath away. I wanted to be his wife more than anything in the world. I was so afraid King Ahaz would change his mind, and I'd never know what it felt like to be held in Hezekiah's arms."

"But now you do." Miriam sighed.

"Yes. The goddess has answered all my prayers."

"And is it as wonderful as you dreamed?"

"Even more wonderful. Someday you'll find out, little sister. I know that my husband doesn't love me yet—not as much as I love him. But I'll make him mine, no matter what it takes."

"Even if it means forsaking Asherah and following a bunch of crazy rules and rituals?"

"Yes, whatever it takes. And as soon as I give him an heir, I know he'll be truly mine—forever."

Hezekiah slowly traced his index finger down the yellowed parchment, then paused. "Is this where we stopped yesterday?"

"Yes, that's it. We were reading about Moses and the plagues of Egypt."

Hezekiah smiled at his grandfather. "I remember the first time you told me the Passover story, when I was a child."

"Yes, you especially liked the plague of frogs, remember?"

"That's because I could imagine the panic in the harem if the ladies woke up with frogs in their beds." They both laughed. Hezekiah had chosen the tiny, cramped classroom where he had spent so much time with Shebna to begin his study of the Torah with his grandfather. Every day they worked together, Hezekiah patiently copying the Law, while Zechariah interpreted it for him. The work bonded them even closer together than before.

"I also remember how you begged me to take you to the Passover feast," Zechariah said, "but of course there was no feast. In fact, there hasn't been one for a long, long time." Hezekiah stroked his beard.

"Now that the Temple has been purified and the daily sacrifices are being offered again, couldn't we reinstate the feast days too?"

"We certainly could. The Torah says—let's see—where is it?" He scanned the scroll, unrolling it. "Here it is. It's talking about the first Passover feast, and it says, 'This day shall be to you for a memorial. You shall keep it as a feast to Yahweh throughout your generations—'"

"Then Yahweh commands us to celebrate it?"

"Yes, and I think reliving such a monumental landmark in our nation's history might help to unify our people."

"When is Passover traditionally celebrated?"

Zechariah's excitement faded. "It's too late. The time has just passed. It was supposed to be held on the 14th day of this month, but we were still purifying the Temple then."

"We'll have to wait an entire year?" Hezekiah's disappointment felt close to anger.

"I'm afraid so."

"Celebrating this feast could have accelerated all our reforms, even more than the covenant sacrifice."

"Yes, I think you're right, Son. The people are ready for a fresh start. With Passover as a reminder of God's deliverance, maybe they would have abandoned their idolatry for good."

Hezekiah rose from his seat and stood in front of the window that looked down on Jerusalem. Sounds from the city drifted up to him—children squealing in play, iron cart wheels rumbling over stone streets, animals braying, shouted greetings and curses. He wished he could remind all these people what God had done for them in the past. "If only we didn't have to wait an entire year!"

Zechariah suddenly sat up straight. "Wait a minute. It seems to me I recall—" He picked up the Torah scroll and began searching through it. "Let me try to find it." As Hezekiah watched his grandfather pore over the tiny, hand-printed letters, he noticed for the first time how tired Zechariah looked. His face was pale with fatigue, his eyelids drooped heavily, and his movements seemed slow and painful. The hard work he had performed in purifying the Temple, then helping with the covenant sacrifice, had taken its toll. The task of slaughtering more than 3,000 animals had tired the younger men, and Zechariah was nearly 70. But he had never complained, nor had his enthusiasm waned.

"Here!" A smile of victory spread across his weary face. "Here's the answer! Some of the Israelites missed the first Passover feast because they were ceremonially unclean. They asked Moses what they should do and—well, here. You read it."

Hezekiah read aloud: "Then Yahweh said to Moses, 'Tell the Israelites: if any of you or your descendants are unclean because of a dead body or are gone on a journey, they may still celebrate it on the fourteenth day of the second month at twilight.'"

He looked up. "Do you think this applies to our situation?"

"Yes, I'm certain of it. Like us, these men weren't consecrated according to the Law at the time of the feast, but Yahweh gave them a second chance during the second month."

"Then let's do it! We'll proclaim the 14th day of the second month as the Lord's Passover this year. Do you think we can make all the necessary preparations by then?"

"With a little hard work, I think we could."

"I'll send couriers with the announcement. And I'll notify the northern tribes of Israel too."

"The timing will be perfect! The religious calendar for the northern tribes is one month behind ours. If we celebrate a month later here, it will coincide exactly with Passover in Israel."

"Then it's settled." Hezekiah crossed to the open window again and looked down on the bustling city. "Jerusalem is the place God chose as the center of worship for all His people. The local shrines and high places must be abandoned for good. Passover will be the beginning. I'm going to reawaken in my people a knowledge of our history—and of our God."

———◆———

King Hezekiah's courier rode steadily during the daylight hours, traveling out of the mountains into the rolling foothills of the Shephelah. So far, the response to the announcement that Passover would be celebrated had been mixed. Men in some towns and villages greeted the news with joy, others with indifference.

He reached the bustling city of Lachish just as the day began to cool off, knowing he would find the new city governor, Prince Gedaliah, seated at the gates along with the elders of Lachish, judging regional disputes and local squabbles. He slowed his horse to avoid creating a dust cloud around them. They were arguing loudly with a short, dark-haired peasant, and several moments passed before they even noticed the courier. When he finally dismounted and the emblem of David on his horse's banners became clearly visible, the discussion halted.

"For you, my lord, from King Hezekiah." The courier removed a document from the folds of his cloak and passed it to Gedaliah.

"Now what?" Gedaliah frowned, then began reading aloud in a voice that seemed to mock the king's words. "'From King Hezekiah to all the men of Judah' and so on. 'Return to the Lord, the God of Abraham, Isaac and Israel, that He may return to you who are left, who have escaped from the hand of the kings of Assyria. Do not be like your fathers and brothers, who were unfaithful to the Lord, the God of their fathers, so that he made them an object of horror, as you see.' . . . and so on. Let's get to the point. Ah, here it is: 'Come—let us celebrate the Feast of Passover together on the 14th day of the second month in Jerusalem. For on this day Yahweh brought our people out of Egypt' and so on. That's about it."

"The king is celebrating Passover? In Jerusalem?" a dark-haired peasant asked in astonishment.

"That's what it says." Gedaliah handed the parchment back to the courier, who rolled it up and tucked it inside his cloak. He was eager to move on to the next village. If he could reach Arad and Beersheba within the next few days, he could then head toward home once again. He walked to his horse and prepared to mount.

Suddenly, the peasant raised his arms to heaven and shouted, "Yahweh, be praised!" His left arm didn't go quite as high as his right, but twisted crookedly at an odd angle. "In the last days the mountain of the Lord's temple will be established as chief among all the mountains; it will be raised above the hills, and all peoples will stream to it. Many nations will come and say, 'Come, let us go up to the mountain of the Lord, to the house of the God of Jacob. He will teach us his ways, so that we may walk in his paths.' . . . They will beat their swords into plowshares and their spears into pruning hooks. Nation will not take up sword against nation, nor will they train for war anymore. . . . All the nations may walk in the name of their gods; we will walk in the name of the Lord our God for ever and ever."

The courier stood rooted in awe as the man spoke. He had heard rumors that the prophets of Yahweh were active in Judah once again, but this was the first time he had heard one speak. The elders of Lachish, however, seemed unimpressed. Governor Gedaliah turned on the prophet angrily.

"Now you listen to me, Micah. We have our own high places and priests here in Lachish, and there's no reason why we should have to travel up to the Temple in Jerusalem."

"It's what Yahweh commanded," Micah said. "He ordained a place for the whole nation to celebrate the feasts and—"

"I don't believe that," Gedaliah said. "The king is just using this as an excuse to take away our local power and autonomy so that he can—"

"No! The king seeks the word of God in everything he does. He knows there is only one true God, and so should you. But instead, you have a temple to the sun god in the middle of your city!"

"We've made peace with the gods of the land. Why should we change our ways and trek up to Jerusalem just to celebrate some ancient ritual? The citizens of Lachish are free to worship whatever gods they choose."

The tension between Gedaliah and the prophet multiplied with every word they spoke. The king's courier mounted his horse. "Listen to me, Prince Gedaliah," Micah said. "If you refuse to destroy your pagan temple and return to Yahweh, His judgment will fall on this city! Quick! Use your swiftest chariots and flee, O people of Lachish, for you were the first of the cities of Judah to follow Israel in her sin of idol worship. Then all the cities of the south began to follow your example . . . Weep, weep for your little ones. For they are snatched away, and you will never see them again. They have gone as slaves to distant lands. Shave your heads in sorrow—"

Gedaliah gave the prophet a shove that stopped him midsentence. "Get out of my city and go back to your farm in Moresheth. Our city is at peace, and you're talking like a fool about exile. Get out! Go home! We don't want you in Lachish."

The courier spurred his horse and rode off to the south, leaving the elders of Lachish to choke in the dust behind him.

◆

Jerusha's father knelt in the rocky soil of his vineyard and gently wove a new green vine through the framework of the trellis. His huge hands, as gnarled as the ancient stumps, handled the fragile shoots tenderly. A few months ago it had seemed to Jerimoth that these damaged stumps could never live again, but the new green stems and leaves that sprang from the blackened trunks flourished in spite of their brush with death. And now the vines spoke silently to Jerimoth, telling him that he must also go on living, planting and harvesting again, in spite of the destruction around him. All his life he had witnessed spring's rebirth after the cold defeat of winter, and he clung to the hope of new life.

He slowly rose to his feet and looked at the row he had just tended. His broad shoulders had a defeated sag, and his green eyes had lost their laughter. He groped over his shoulder for the flowing end of the keffiyeh he wore in a loose turban around his head, then wiped the sweat from his face and neck. His tanned face was as deeply furrowed as his fields, scarred by years of plowing and planting, waiting and worrying.

He carefully studied the rutted road where it disappeared over the horizon, constantly alert, watching for the ominous dust cloud, listening for the rumble of hooves and chariot wheels that would signal the start of another Assyrian raid. But the road lay quiet and still, disturbed only by a gentle breeze that stirred up a funnel of dust and by the fluttering blackbirds as they scratched in the dirt for insects.

On the highest rise of land stood Jerimoth's square stone house, shaded from the brilliant sun by two date palm trees that had stood there for as long as he could remember. He had been born in that house, beneath those trees, as his father had been before him. His wife,

Hodesh, descended the stairs from the flat rooftop carrying a dried bundle of flax to the covered patio where she and their daughter worked. Little Maacah wrestled with the heavy loom, determined to master this new skill she had been forced to learn. Her arms and legs were as thin as the shuttle that she labored to pass back and forth between the threads of the loom. She should be playing with straw dolls, combing the flax for their make-believe hair, yet now she had been forced to grow up and to take over Jerusha's chores.

Thinking of Jerusha brought a stab of pain to Jerimoth's heart, reopening a wound that had never healed. He fingered the jagged scar on his forehead and shuddered at the memory of her terrified, heart-rending screams, knowing he would never be able to accept her loss or erase the agony from his heart. They had found the bodies of Saul's daughters Serah and Tirza. He had helped his brother dig their graves in the soft brown earth, and as painful as this task had been, it had helped Saul accept their deaths and finally understand that he would never see his girls again. But Jerusha? Not knowing her fate—and imagining the worst—tormented Jerimoth. He would never know if her beautiful, vibrant life had ended violently or if she still lived somewhere, suffering unspeakable horrors.

Jerimoth shuddered and silently pleaded, *Please don't make her suffer—please don't hurt my Jerusha—my happy little bird*. He wiped his face again with the end of his keffiyeh and was about to return to his labors when he spotted a small puff of dust on the southern horizon, moving up the road from the village of Dabbasheth.

"Hodesh! Maacah!" he shouted. "Get into the house!" Hodesh dropped her bundle of flax and grabbed Maacah by the hand, pulling the startled child behind her as she raced across the patio and into the house.

Beneath the floor Jerimoth had prepared an empty cistern, hewn from the solid bedrock, in which to hide his wife and daughter during the next Assyrian raid. They were all he had left now, and he was determined to protect them from this violent enemy that was ruthlessly consuming everything he had ever loved.

He sprinted up to the house, lifted the heavy stone lid, and helped them climb in. Then he fitted the lid into place where it blended with the other flagstones on the floor of his house. Only when the woven rug was laid over the hiding place did Jerimoth dare to go to the door and peer down the road again. He saw now that the dust cloud was too small to be a division of Assyrian soldiers, and he felt foolish when he realized that they usually swept down from the north. But he decided to keep his family hidden just the same. He busied himself in the sticky shade of his winepress as the dust cloud sped closer.

The horse's hooves pounded on the hard-packed dirt road in rhythm with his heart, and he shot a quick glance in that direction. The lone rider was a soldier, definitely not Assyrian, but not from Jerimoth's nation of Israel either. The stranger slowed as he approached the row of cedars that guarded the borders of Jerimoth's land, then dismounted near his well. As Jerimoth walked cautiously toward him, the stranger greeted him in Hebrew. "Shalom! May I refresh my horse at your well?"

His face wore a mask of perspiration and dust, finely etched with lines of fatigue, and his lathered horse panted in the searing heat. Suddenly Jerimoth recognized the emblem of the King of Judah emblazoned on the horse's banner.

"You are from Judah?" he asked in surprise.

"Yes, I've come from Jerusalem with a message from King Hezekiah. I just delivered it to the elders of Dabbasheth, and I'm on my way to the next town."

Perhaps the armies of Judah were coming to help Jerimoth's suffering nation fight the Assyrians. He probed for more information. "You've come all the way to Israel? With a message?"

"Yes, and I'll be returning to Jerusalem through the tribal lands of Manasseh and Issachar. King Hezekiah's message will be spread from Beersheba to Dan."

Jerimoth lowered the rope into the well and hoisted a bucketful to the top. He emptied it into an ancient stone watering trough, licked smooth by generations of animals, and allowed the lathered horse to quench its thirst before passing a drinking gourd to the stranger. The soldier drank greedily, splashing the cool water over his dusty face while Jerimoth silently watched. When his thirst was relieved, the stranger looked around and gestured toward Jerimoth's charred land.

"Assyrians did this?"

Jerimoth nodded.

"That's a shame. We've heard that they sometimes raid farms along the border."

"We've suffered terribly at their hands. Sometimes I think Yahweh must have forgotten us to make us suffer so."

The soldier grew attentive. "You believe in Yahweh?" Jerimoth hesitated. It wasn't wise to admit to a stranger which god you worshiped, but the words had already slipped out.

"Yes—I believe in Him."

"Then you'll be interested in King Hezekiah's message." He pulled a scroll from the folds of his tunic and handed it to Jerimoth. Jerimoth read while the soldier finished his water:

"People of Israel, return to the Lord, the God of Abraham, Isaac and Israel, that he may return to you who are left, who have escaped from the hand of the kings of Assyria. Do not be like your fathers and brothers, who were unfaithful to the Lord, the God of their fathers, so that he made them an object of horror, as you see. . . . Come to the sanctuary, which he has consecrated forever. Serve the Lord your God, so that his fierce anger will turn away from you. If you return to the Lord, then your brothers and your children will be shown compassion by their captors and will come back to this land . . ."

There was more, but tears blurred Jerimoth's vision, and he couldn't read further. The scroll trembled in his hand. During all the years that he had farmed his land, raising his crops and his children, he had never acknowledged Yahweh with offerings of thanksgiving. Yahweh had been forgotten until Jerimoth's life had begun to crumble. Now, in anger and despair, he cried out to the silent heavens, wondering why Yahweh had forsaken him. He held the answer in his hands—and also hope.

"Do you think you'll go, then?" the soldier asked.

Jerimoth looked up, lost in thought. "What did you say?"

"Will you be going to Jerusalem for Passover?"

Jerimoth wiped his eyes and finished reading the scroll. "For the Lord your God is gracious and compassionate. He will not turn his face from you if you return to him. Come—let us celebrate the Feast of Passover together on the 14th day of the second month in Jerusalem."

Jerimoth gazed at the soldier. "I've never celebrated the Feast of Passover."

"Me either. It hasn't been celebrated in Judah since before King Ahaz's reign. But our new king has been making a lot of changes, and now he's declared that all the feast days will be celebrated again, beginning with Passover. Not too many people in your country seem interested, though. The elders of Dabbasheth wouldn't even give me water for my horse."

Jerimoth quickly reread the amazing words, memorizing them: "'If you return to the Lord, then your brothers and your children will be shown compassion by their captors and will come back to this land—' Yes," Jerimoth said, "I'm going to Jerusalem for Passover."

"Good. And thanks for the water." The courier mounted his horse and rode up the dusty road to the north. Jerimoth watched until he finally disappeared over the horizon. Then he hurried up to the house and kicked the rug aside to open the cistern. Hodesh heaved a sigh of relief as she climbed out. She fussed over Maacah, brushing bits of plaster from her clothes and hair, and several minutes passed before she noticed the tears streaming down Jerimoth's leathery face.

"What's wrong?" She scanned the vineyard and olive grove, then turned back to Jerimoth. "What happened? Who was it?"

"We're going to Jerusalem for Passover," he said. Hodesh put her hand to his cheek, tenderly brushing the tears from his beard.

"What are you talking about, Jerimoth?"

"If we return to Yahweh, He will bring our Jerusha home to us again."

10

It was becoming a habit that Hezekiah thoroughly enjoyed, to visit Hephzibah every evening and share the events of his day with her. She lavished him with attention as he tried to unwind from the pressures of his reign. She seemed to know exactly what to say to cheer him, to encourage him, to comfort him. Hephzibah's beauty and quick wit far surpassed any of his concubines' shallow charms, and he shared a companionship and an intimacy with her that he had never experienced before. He was beginning to understand what Zechariah meant when he said a wife was given by God for more than physical pleasure. And Hephzibah was beautiful. Just watching her or listening to her sing was a pleasure he looked forward to more each day. No matter how busy his day, Hephzibah had become his addiction.

And so, only a few days before the first Passover celebration, he made his way to her chambers with anticipation and the now-familiar longing to hold her in his arms.

"You look so tired, my lord," she said as she led him to the cushioned couch.

"I am. But there's so much to do—so many preparations." He sank down among the pillows, but his overworked mind couldn't stop planning and calculating.

"You need to relax. You look much too serious tonight." He was struck once again by how tiny and delicate she was, like a beautiful, fragile dish. He wished he could forget everything else and stay here with Hephzibah, but there was too much to do before the feast.

"I can't relax yet. Not until everything's ready. In a few days this city will be bursting with pilgrims—at least I hope it will."

How far would his reforms spread? How responsive would the people be to all his changes? He rose from the couch and walked restlessly around the room, talking and gesturing rapidly.

"One minute I'm wondering where we'll put everyone, and the next minute I'm doubting if anyone will bother to show up. If their idolatry is too deeply rooted—"

"They'll come," she soothed as she followed him around the room. "Why wouldn't they come?"

"Well, it's been so long since Passover was celebrated. Do you have any idea what it means to the people?"

Hephzibah stood on tiptoe, planted her hands on his shoulders, then gently pushed him down onto the couch again. "No. What does it mean? Will you explain it to me, my lord?" Her hands remained on his shoulders, and as she gently kneaded his tense muscles he could feel the strain start to ease.

"Umm. That feels good. Don't stop." She seemed to know what he needed even before he asked. He smiled in spite of himself. "Where was I?"

"You were going to tell me what Passover means."

"Umm. Passover. It's a celebration of freedom, Hephzibah—the anniversary of our nation's deliverance from slavery. God heard our cries of suffering and freed us from serving the Egyptians so we could serve Him. The men of Judah work hard all year in order to live, but when Passover comes, they can lay aside their work for eight days and rest and feast and thank God."

"And how will they feast for eight days if our nation is so poor?" The charming way she cocked her head to one side when she asked a question amused him.

"Good question, my dear lady," he laughed. "That's why I've been so busy. I'm opening the royal storehouses and ordering animals to be prepared from my own flocks and herds. Everyone who comes, rich or poor, will have eight days to relax and to feast and to celebrate Yahweh's goodness."

"Since you're providing the food, it seems to me they should celebrate their king's goodness instead."

"No, I'm not the Messiah. I may be able to feed the people for a week, but the rest of the year we're still slaves to the Assyrians. They demand more and more tribute every year and—"

"Hush!" Hephzibah stopped massaging and put her fingers over his lips. "You have all day to worry about such things. Now it's time to forget about them."

He pulled her onto the couch beside him. "You're right. Help me forget." He kissed her neck, and her warm skin was soft and fragrant. She laughed softly. "What's so funny?" Hezekiah asked.

"Your beard tickles." She tugged on it playfully, and Hezekiah smiled.

"Ah, Hephzibah—you're so good for me. Your laughter—your love. They're just what I need." He held her close and realized for the first time how very precious she had become to him in the past months.

"This is the best part of my day," she murmured, "being with you. But our time together is always too short."

"And I'm afraid it'll be even shorter tonight. I can stay only a few minutes."

"Oh, no."

"I'm sorry. But there's too much work to do."

"Can't your servants and officials do some of it? Do you have to do everything yourself?"

"I'm still not sure who I can trust and who's waiting for a chance to stab me in the back. Remember Uriah?" He poked her back gently with his forefinger. "I'm making a lot of changes in a very short time and probably a lot of enemies too. People resist change. Besides, my father's government was so corrupt that the only way I can be sure things are done right is to do them myself."

"You're scowling again, my lord." She gently smoothed his knitted brow with her cool, soft fingers. "You're not supposed to talk about all your problems—remember?"

"And you're supposed to help me forget my problems—remember?"

"Then I guess I'd better do my job." She took his face in her hands and kissed him with a passion that left him breathless.

Jerimoth sighed and tugged on his beard as he surveyed his vineyard one last time. His family stood beside the cart, waiting. "I guess everything will be all right until we get back."

"It'll be fine," Hodesh said. "Come on." Jerimoth walked around the loaded cart again, examining the wheels, the paired yoke of oxen, the harness fittings. He made certain the new spring lamb he had chosen from his flock was tied securely to the load; then he turned to the young man he had hired to watch over his land while he was gone.

"You'll remember all I told you?" he asked. "You'll remember to watch for my daughter Jerusha? She's coming home."

"I'll watch for her, sir."

Jerimoth sighed again, and with a final, worried glance at his farm, he set off with his wife and daughter to begin the pilgrimage to Jerusalem for Passover. A seed of hope had been planted in his heart, and Jerimoth had nurtured it, clinging to King Hezekiah's promise that the Assyrians would release Jerusha if he returned to Yahweh. They traveled south toward Dabbasheth, skirting the village and its painful memories, then passed through the towns of Cabul and Rimmon. Soon the road turned east, and they journeyed beneath a blazing sun, over the rolling hills to Migdal on the sparkling Sea of Galilee.

There Jerimoth found a caravan of pilgrims headed to Jerusalem, and they joined them for the remainder of the trip, following the lush plains along the banks of the Jordan River. They reached the oasis of Jericho on the fourth day, feeling tired and irritable, their throats parched from the choking dust. The swaying palms of Jericho offered welcome shade, and even the bitter blue waters of the nearby Dead Sea looked inviting. After a night's rest they began the final leg of their journey, following the rugged mountain road up to Jerusalem. They climbed steadily upward, passing dry stream beds and deep mountain gorges, until their legs ached and it seemed as if they had climbed to the skies. Late in the afternoon as the caravan paused to water the animals, Jerimoth scanned the horizon for the first glimpse of Jerusalem.

"Look, Hodesh!" he suddenly shouted. "There it is!"

Squinting into the distance, they could barely discern the golden walls of the Holy City nestled among the green-and-brown hills. They even caught the glint of the Temple's golden roof, perched on the highest hill. This glimpse of their destination seemed to give the tired travelers the extra encouragement they needed to finish their climb, and they continued on, reaching the gates of Jerusalem an hour before sundown. When the sun set, the eve of Passover would begin.

As soon as they entered the city, the caravan disbanded as each family went in search of friends or relatives. In the morning they would begin the preparations for the feast. It was only after he reached the city that Jerimoth realized he had no place to stay during the festival. The crowded city seemed huge and strange to him, the walls confining. He missed the open fields and broad skies of home. He wandered lost through the unfriendly streets, tired and disoriented, searching for a room in an inn until it was almost dark. But pilgrims crammed every available space, and all the rooms were taken. Maacah looked pale and frightened; Hodesh was close to tears.

"What are we doing here, Jerimoth?" she asked. "We don't even know anyone."

"We'll be fine, Hodesh. One of the innkeepers said to try the caravansary in the market square. It means sleeping out in the open, but I guess it's the best we can do."

Hodesh glanced anxiously at Maacah. "Is it safe? Won't there be foreign caravan drivers there?"

"We'll go and see, Hodesh," he said wearily. "I don't know what else to do. Besides, don't we need some things from the market? Come on."

When they reached the square, Jerimoth let Hodesh barter for the food while he searched for an empty place to park his cart for the night. But as he listened to the caravan drivers settling into their places and heard their crude jokes and vulgar language, he realized that the caravansary was no place for his wife and daughter to sleep. He didn't know what to do. He wandered farther down the street, where the shops were more elegant and well-kept, looking for an empty doorway to shelter them.

Suddenly Jerimoth heard jovial laughter drifting from a nearby booth, and he was drawn toward the sound. A round, bald little man and his servant were closing up a shop of elegant, imported cloth and laughing merrily. Jerimoth stopped a few feet from the shop and stared at the man. The merchant turned a beaming face up at Jerimoth.

"And what can I do for you, sir? I'm about to close my shop for the holidays, but if I can help you with anything—"

Jerimoth wasn't interested in the imported cloth. He didn't know what to say. He stared mutely for a moment, kneading his calloused hands, then blurted, "I'm from Israel. I've come to celebrate Passover."

"That's wonderful, wonderful! My name is Hilkiah, and if you're a follower of the Eternal One, then you're already my friend. Did you have a pleasant journey?"

"I have no place to stay," Jerimoth said.

"Ah, I see. Are you traveling alone?"

"No, I came with my wife and daughter." He pointed to his cart standing on the corner by the square. Maacah sat on top of the load, looking tired and forlorn.

"Ah, yes. And what is your name, my friend?"

"Jerimoth."

"Well then, Jerimoth, I'm celebrating Passover with my son, and we'd be honored to have your family as our guests." He grinned so warmly that Jerimoth managed a tired smile. "Then you accept?"

"Yes, thank you. But I've brought a lamb with me from my flock. I'd like to share it with you."

"Then it's settled. I don't live far from here. Give me a moment to finish closing my shop, and we'll be on our way."

Jerimoth hurried back to where Hodesh and Maacah waited beside the cart. "I've found a place to stay. Come on."

"Where? At an inn?"

"We'll be guests of Hilkiah the merchant and his son."

"Who?"

"He owns a shop. Over there. See?"

"A stranger? You accepted an invitation from a stranger?"

"Just come, Hodesh."

"I don't like the idea."

Jerimoth gestured to the caravan drivers in the square around him. "It's better than this. And it's nearly sunset. Where else can we go?"

She followed nervously as Jerimoth led the way to Hilkiah's lavish shop, and they both bowed low in respect. "My wife, Hodesh, and I are so very grateful, my lord—"

"Now, now. None of that. I'm pleased to meet you, but you must both call me Hilkiah. Shall we go? I hope dinner's ready, because I'm starved." He patted his round belly and led the way up the hill to his house.

◈

After the evening sacrifice King Hezekiah sat on the palace rooftop with his grandfather, watching the steady stream of pilgrims flowing into the city for the feast. A pang of hunger rumbled through his stomach, and he thought of his brother Eliab. Hezekiah had eaten nothing since dawn, fulfilling the Fast of the Firstborn in Eliab's memory.

"I was hoping this many people would come," he said to Zechariah as another caravan passed through the gate below them. "But I still can't believe it's happening."

"Yes, it's a wonderful sight, isn't it?"

Hezekiah thought he detected a note of hesitancy in his grandfather's voice. "Is something wrong?"

"Well—it's just that the people are required to consecrate themselves before celebrating the feast and—"

"Meaning what?"

"Well, among other things, all the men must be circumcised."

"And you think some of them aren't?"

"I'm sure many of them aren't, especially the younger ones who were born during your father's reign, when the Temple was closed. And if any of them have come from Israel, they are probably ignorant of the Law. It's not their fault, of course. They were never taught, but—"

"So which is the greater sin—coming to Passover unprepared or not coming at all?"

Zechariah shrugged. "If their hearts are longing to return to Yahweh, surely He is merciful even if the Law isn't fulfilled—"

Zechariah's answer sounded more like a question, and it disturbed Hezekiah. He wanted clear answers from God, precise rules that he could follow with confidence. If Zechariah didn't know the answers, how could Hezekiah know?

The sun sank halfway below the horizon, and still the pilgrims streamed through the city gates. How many were there? How far had they come? He thought of the long, arduous journey many of them had made, and it worried him that Yahweh might reject them because of their ignorance of the Law.

"Isn't there anything we can do for them?" he asked. Zechariah sat in silence for a moment, then stood and lifted his prayer shawl over his head. Hezekiah followed his example, and they stood together on the palace roof.

Praying was still new to Hezekiah, and he was unsure how to begin. But he thought of all the people who had journeyed this far and the problem he had created because of his ignorance, and he began to pray.

"May the Lord pardon everyone who determines to follow the Lord God of his fathers, even though he is not properly sanctified for the ceremony." He prayed with Zechariah long after the sun had set and Hezekiah's time of fasting had ended. By the time they finished, the first stars shone brightly in the heavens.

Hezekiah looked at his grandfather hopefully. "Yahweh hears?"

"He hears. He says in His Word, 'When you and your children return to the Lord your God and obey him with all your heart and with all your soul . . . the Lord your God will restore your fortunes and have compassion on you.'"

Hezekiah looked out over the darkened hills that surrounded his city. "Please, Lord. Have compassion on us."

Eliakim frowned as he stood beside Hilkiah, performing the ritual handwashing before the evening meal. He didn't share his father's enthusiasm for inviting strangers into their house, and he was annoyed with Hilkiah for not consulting him first.

"Where did you say these people are from, Abba?"

"They're from Israel, Son—northern Israel." He tossed Eliakim the towel as if that ended the conversation.

Eliakim grabbed his father by the sleeve and drew him back. "You don't even know them, do you, Abba?"

"Certainly I do. They're followers of Yahweh, blessed be He."

"Abba, you know what I mean. You've invited strangers into our home again."

"They're followers of Yahweh. Why should you need more information than that?"

"Because Micah was a follower of Yahweh, and I remember all the trouble it caused when you invited him into our home."

"Hasn't God paid us back for all our trouble—a double portion?"

"Yes, and I grew to admire Micah, so I suppose it was good that we helped him, but—"

"And I'm sure you'll grow fond of Jerimoth and Hodesh and their little daughter as well."

"Abba, will you listen to me? You have to admit that the soldiers made a terrible mess of our house that night, not to mention nearly slitting my throat." He rubbed the long thin scar on his throat protectively.

"Eliakim, I give you my pledge. Our guests will not slit your throat. OK? Let's eat."

"Abba, will you listen to me?"

"The Torah says it is a great blessing to extend hospitality to strangers at Passover. Amen."

Eliakim cocked an eyebrow skeptically. "The Torah says that?"

"You don't believe me? Didn't the Eternal One heap blessings on us for helping Micah? Aren't you working for the king himself?"

"Well, yes, but—"

"Amen. And you'll see how greatly Yahweh will bless us in return this time too. You can never outgive God. Don't ever forget it." Hilkiah punctuated each word by poking Eliakim's chest with his forefinger; then he smiled, and Eliakim knew the discussion had ended. He followed his father into the house, wondering if the Torah really said it was a blessing to help strangers or if Hilkiah had conveniently made it up.

Their guests were already seated on cushions around the low dining table. "My friends, meet my son, Eliakim," Hilkiah said. "Eliakim, this is Jerimoth, his wife Hodesh, and their daughter, Maacah."

"I'm happy to meet you." Eliakim concealed his shock at how poor they looked, how tired and frightened. Where had his father found them?

After Hilkiah said the blessing, they began to eat. The strangers seemed nervous and ill at ease with the elegant table settings, silken floor cushions, and rich food. Not wanting to stare, Eliakim stole quick glances at them between bites of food.

Jerimoth reminded him of Micah, tanned and muscular with hard, work-callused hands. He had thick, bushy black hair, mottled with gray, and mournful, green eyes. His short, squat wife seemed built for hard work and out of place in Hilkiah's elegant home attended by servants. Their daughter was little more than a shadow, so thin that only her thick braids seemed real to Eliakim, the rest of her a mere spirit. Wherever they had come from, Eliakim decided to make peace with them.

"My father tells me you're from Israel," he said as he passed Jerimoth the bread. "Are you close to the border of Aram?" Jerimoth nodded silently. "I hear that's Assyrian territory now. Do their armies ever come that far south?"

Jerimoth's bread slipped from his fingers, and his hand touched the jagged scar on his forehead. Eliakim saw the pain and sorrow in his guest's eyes and wished he had never asked the question. "Yes, we've seen their armies." Jerimoth's voice faltered as he struggled for composure. "A few months ago they raided our village. They destroyed most of my crops and—and they carried our daughter Jerusha away."

Hilkiah sprang to Jerimoth's side, resting his hand on his shoulder. "I'm so sorry, my friend. So sorry—" But Jerimoth didn't seem to hear him. He gazed straight ahead as if looking into the past, at scenes only he could see.

"The Assyrians have no hearts as we do," he said in a hollow voice. "They can't be moved to pity or touched by pleas for mercy. They flow over our borders like a flood of death, and the earth is red with blood when they leave.

"They're deaf to pain and blind to human suffering. If you beg for mercy, they will cut out your tongue. If you lift your hands to them in supplication, they will cut them off. They rip babies from their mother's arms and toss them beneath their horses' hooves to be trampled. They will torture your loved ones in front of you, then put out your eyes, leaving you to remember the sight forever.

"The more valiantly a village resists them, the greater the punishment that town receives. The more you plead for mercy, the heavier the torture they inflict. They know a hundred ways to prolong death—slowly, horribly—and there are more Assyrian soldiers than there are grains of sand in the desert.

"No city wall is strong enough to keep them out. No army is mighty enough to defeat them. They carry away entire villages, nations full of people, and those who are carried away are never heard from again."

The room was still when Jerimoth finished. Embarrassed and guilt-ridden, Eliakim was afraid to speak again. Even Hilkiah seemed at a loss for words to ease Jerimoth's pain.

But at last Jerimoth groaned softly, almost a sigh, then looked at Hilkiah who still knelt by his side. "Your king has promised—if I celebrate Passover—Yahweh will have compassion, and my daughter will return to me again."

Jerimoth's unrealistic hopes alarmed Eliakim. He didn't believe in such an oversimplified faith. God wouldn't make all your wishes come true if you prayed. His own father was a man of prayer and had enormous faith in God, yet Eliakim had watched his mother and two small brothers die of a fever, one after the other, while his father's useless prayers ascended into the silent heavens. He remembered kneeling beside his father, praying with all his heart that his mother would live. And he remembered her hollow, suffering eyes, her wasted flesh, her feverish moans. Eliakim knew God wouldn't answer Jerimoth's prayer; he would never see his daughter again. It would be better if he faced the truth.

"Listen. I don't think it's realistic to expect—"

Hilkiah cut Eliakim off. "We will join with you in prayer, my friend. Yahweh is merciful and compassionate. And I know that He answers prayer."

"But, Abba—"

Hilkiah silenced Eliakim with a warning look. "My dear friend, tomorrow we will take your Passover lamb to the Temple, and my son and I will pray with you. Yahweh will answer you. I know He will."

Eliakim was furious with his father for making such a rash promise; worse, for involving him. God couldn't answer a prayer as impossible as this one. The Assyrians never returned their slaves from captivity. The girl was probably dead already.

Eliakim stared down at his plate, picking silently at his food while everyone else ate—everyone but little Maacah. Eliakim noticed that she wasn't eating either. While Jerimoth had been speaking she had sat as still as a stone, her eyes wide, as if she saw what her father saw. Eliakim realized with a shock that she had probably witnessed what Jerimoth had described, and he was moved with pity for this slender, haunted child.

When they finished the meal, Hilkiah turned to the little girl, speaking gently to her. "Maacah, I have a very important job to do right now. Do you think you could help me?" She didn't move or respond, but stared silently at her hands, folded in her lap.

"Actually, it's the children of the household who are supposed to perform this job," Hilkiah said, gesturing toward Eliakim. "But as you can see, my child is all grown up. This is the very first part of the Passover celebration and—"

At the mention of Passover, she looked up. "I'll help you," she said softly. "For Jerusha."

Eliakim started to his feet, angry with Hilkiah for dragging this wounded child into his fantasies. She had obviously suffered enough already. "Abba, wait a minute. May I have a word with you, please?"

"Not now, Eliakim. You see, Maacah, Yahweh has commanded us to clean our houses very thoroughly before Passover. We can't leave even the smallest trace of leaven. That's because of our forefathers' hasty journey out of Egypt, when they couldn't even wait for the bread to rise. My servants have been cleaning our house from top to bottom for the last few weeks, but what if they accidentally missed something with leaven in it?"

He tried to look horrified, but his sparkling eyes betrayed him. He nudged Maacah to her feet. "When Eliakim was a child he always helped me search on the eve of Passover, and you know what? I think a child's eyes are just a wee bit sharper than a grown-up's, because he always found something we missed."

Eliakim had fallen for this ruse for years before realizing that the leaven had been carefully planted for his benefit. But Maacah seemed convinced and eager to help. Hilkiah armed her with a wooden spoon and a feather to scoop up the forbidden leaven.

"But first we must say the blessing." Hilkiah closed his eyes and lifted his hands toward heaven. "Blessed art Thou, Yahweh our God, King of the Universe, who has commanded us concerning the destruction of the leaven." Then he and Maacah set off to search the house, and Eliakim was left behind with her parents.

"It seems like a long time since I searched for the leaven like that," he said. "My father tried to keep some of the Passover traditions even though the Temple was closed, and we couldn't celebrate the right way. I guess he's always had a lot of faith in Yahweh." He smiled, but Jerimoth made no response. "You have a lovely little girl," Eliakim said, trying again. Jerimoth finally looked up at him, his eyes mournful.

"Yes. She's all I have left," he said softly. "All I have left."

11

Hezekiah stood alone on the palace roof, gazing at the Temple of Solomon on the hill. He had just returned from the evening sacrifice, where the music and worship had moved him deeply. "My soul finds rest in God alone," the Levites had sung. "He is my fortress, I will never be shaken."

Hezekiah found it easy to believe in a living God, to believe he played a part in His plan, when immersed in an atmosphere of praise and worship. On the Temple Mount, high above the city, God's presence seemed real, and Hezekiah could easily forget the existence of poverty and starvation in his nation. The music and rituals lifted him far above the awareness of those realities. But now the praises had ended, and the crowds had returned to their homes. The daily sacrifice was left to roast slowly on the altar. And as the problems of his nation confronted Hezekiah again, the presence of the Lord seemed to have faded and died with the music.

A week ago he had stood before the cheering crowd on the final day of Passover. He had held up his hand for silence, but a long time had passed before the cheering stopped and Hezekiah could speak. "I wish that the Feast of Passover could go on forever," he had told them, and they had cheered and shouted, "Yes! Another week! Another week of Passover!" Their willing response astonished him.

Zechariah held a hurried discussion with the other Levites, then explained the precedent. The first Passover celebration in Solomon's newly built Temple had been such a success that the king had extended the celebration for a second week.

"Then let's do it," Hezekiah had said. "I'll extend this Passover feast for another week as well."

The rejoicing was so great it seemed as if the heavens had opened and hosts of angels had joined in the praises of the people. It had been easy to believe then. But now?

Alone on the rooftop, Hezekiah felt very far away from God. Why had he started this reform movement, this revival of faith in the God of Abraham? He thought back to his coronation and all the events of that night, and he knew that part of the reason was gratitude. He owed Yahweh a debt for saving him from Molech's fire.

But the primary reason was because he had wanted to restore his nation to prosperity and security. And if he served Yahweh, Hezekiah was promised blessings in return. His selfish motives shamed him.

In the streets below, Hezekiah heard singing and dancing as the second week of Passover drew to a close. What motivated all these people? Why had they traveled great distances to Jerusalem? And why did they dance and sing songs of praise in the streets? Because of the food he provided? Because they hoped Yahweh would bless them too? He thought of Micah and the vicious beating he had suffered for proclaiming Yahweh's message. What motivated him to serve God? And what inspired Zechariah to endure many years of unjust imprisonment for God and then, at his age, to serve Him with the hard work of thousands of sacrifices?

If he asked his grandfather or Micah these questions, he thought he knew what they would say: because they loved Yahweh. But in his heart Hezekiah knew that he didn't feel the depth of love for God that they felt. He felt gratitude for his salvation from Molech, and he felt obligated to serve Him. But he didn't really know God. How could he say that he loved Him?

The song in the street ended, and in the stillness Hezekiah heard footsteps ascending the stairs to the roof. He turned to see Zechariah coming up to join him. How Hezekiah loved this frail giant of a man! They stood side by side in silence for several moments before Zechariah asked, "What's troubling you, Son?"

"Am I that easy to read?" Hezekiah sighed and turned to gaze down at the view again. "I guess I've been thinking about the first law you ever taught me—'Love Yahweh your God with all your heart and with all your soul and with all your strength.' I've been trying so hard to keep all the laws of Yahweh, all the sacrifices, all the sacred observances—yet I can't honestly say that I'm even fulfilling the first law I ever memorized. How do I learn to love Yahweh?"

"You already love Him."

Hezekiah shook his head. His hypocrisy had fooled even his grandfather. "You think because I've restored our nation's covenant that I love Yahweh?"

"Yes. A sign that we love Him is that we keep His command-ments. That's the starting place for all of us. As the psalmist has written, 'The Lord's love is . . . with those who keep his covenant.'"

Hezekiah still couldn't face him. "I've been studying His Law, and I'm trying to obey every letter of it as perfectly as I can. Why doesn't that seem like enough?"

"When you married your wife, you made a covenant with her, but you didn't love her yet. Love will require mutual trust, opening your hearts and lives to one another. It takes work to build a true rela-tionship. The same is true of Yahweh. You've respoken your vows at this Passover feast; now the work begins as you learn to love your God. Love for God is never instant. It has to grow and mature just like any other kind of love. The struggle is always with our will."

"But why do I feel like such a hypocrite, serving a God whom I barely know?"

"God revealed himself to Israel in the Law at Mount Sinai. As you learn to keep that Law, you'll learn to know Him better."

"I don't understand."

"When you brought your sin offering to the Temple and placed your hand on the animal's head, how did you feel at that moment?"

Hezekiah relived the sacrifice, feeling the cold, misty rain on his face and the warm stubble of the animal's fur beneath his hand. "I felt—unworthy."

"Then you do know Yahweh. When we feel unworthy in His presence it's because we glimpse His holiness. You obeyed the Law, and He revealed His holiness to you." Hezekiah nodded slightly, re-membering Isaiah's vision of a holy God. "And now, at Passover," Zechariah continued, "when you ate the Passover lamb in obedience, how did you feel?"

Hezekiah thought for a moment, trying to put into words what he had felt. "I felt like I was part of a much greater plan—a plan that began in the past and continues in the present and will go on into the future. I felt like part of a greater purpose than I can clearly see."

"When you obeyed the Law and celebrated Passover, Yahweh revealed himself to you as the Eternal One, whose plan reaches throughout all the ages. That's why the people wanted to celebrate; Yahweh revealed himself to them, and they hungered for more. As long as you continue to seek Him, Son, your love will continue to grow. And as you express your love for Him through obedience, He'll reveal more of himself to you."

"Will I ever have faith like yours?"

"That's up to you. The only way to grow in faith is to put your faith to the test. You must place yourself in His hands and let Him prove himself faithful. Unless you make up your mind to trust Him, you'll never know that Yahweh is faithful."

"You're talking about trusting God against the Assyrians, aren't you?"

Zechariah didn't answer right away. "Hezekiah, do you remember what Yahweh promised you long ago, in the Valley of Hinnom?—'When you go through deep water, Yahweh will go with you. And when you ford mighty rivers, they won't overwhelm you. When you pass through the fire, you won't be burned. The flames will not hurt you. For Yahweh is your God. The Holy One of Israel is your Savior.'"

Hezekiah stared at his grandfather as the truth struck him. "That prophecy wasn't just for me, was it?"

"No, Son. That promise is for all who believe in Him and trust Him in faith."

The merriment in the street died away as the revelers went home for their evening meals. Hezekiah gazed over the parapet, watching them go. When he turned back, Zechariah was gone. Hezekiah stood in the growing twilight, pondering the decision he had been avoiding. He knew he couldn't avoid it much longer. The time rapidly approached when the tribute payments to Assyria were due.

His people suffered under a heavy burden, even though God had delivered them from slavery once before, at the first Passover. Worse, the Assyrian king was receiving Yahweh's tithe. For both of these reasons, Hezekiah knew it was wrong to send the tribute. But now there was a third reason. If he truly believed that God heard Israel's cries of suffering, truly believed all that the Torah said about Him and His covenant with the nation, then why didn't he trust Yahweh to deliver him from Assyria? Was the Assyrian emperor more powerful than Yahweh? Zechariah told him to put his faith to the test, but did Hezekiah dare test Yahweh if the future of his nation was at stake? Was it fair to risk the lives of his people? Would God really intervene in the political struggles of his nation?

Hezekiah felt as if he balanced on the parapet and one mistake—one misstep would send him hurtling to disaster. No matter whether he decided to send the tribute or not, the effect on his nation was certain to be great. He needed only a push, a gentle shove to help him decide which way to fall—to allow his nation to plunge deeper into poverty and debt, or to let them fall into the hands of God. Again Hezekiah heard footsteps ascending the stairs, and this time he turned to see Shebna walking toward him.

"Your Majesty, the meal is ready, and I told the servants I would summon you. I—I wanted to talk to you."

Hezekiah was surprised to see Shebna struggling for words. It hadn't happened before, in all their years together. "Yes? What is it, Shebna?"

"Your Majesty, I owe you an apology. You know that at first I did not agree with all the religious reforms you were making."

"Yes. I know."

"I am sorry. I was wrong. Now I can see the wisdom in what you have done."

"Does that mean you believe in God?"

"No, my lord. I still cannot say I believe. But in the short time that you have been king, I have seen this shattered nation pull itself together almost miraculously. It is wonderful! I have never seen such strong bonds of nationalism, such a sense of shared history. You used the same strategy that your ancestor King David used. He strengthened his power by returning the ark to Jerusalem. And now, by celebrating Passover, you have unified the nation in support of your reign. It was a brilliant strategy, Your Majesty. No king has been this popular since David. You could do anything now, ask anything of them, and they would follow you."

"Is that what you think? That I started these religious reforms as—as some sort of political strategy? For my own personal gain?"

Shebna didn't need to answer. Hezekiah knew that his friend wasn't far from the truth. His original motives had been self-serving—to save his reign from economic and political disaster. And Yahweh, who knew all men's hearts, knew the truth as well.

"Please, don't let it be true," Hezekiah whispered.

"Pardon, Your Majesty?"

"You're wrong, Shebna," he said quietly. "David brought the ark to Jerusalem because he wanted the reality of the presence of God."

"I do not understand."

"No, of course not," he said to himself. "You couldn't possibly understand unless you believed." Hezekiah felt the push he needed, the gentle shove that forced him off the wall of indecision. "Shebna, I know you've argued against this in the past, and that's why I want you to be the first to know."

He looked alarmed. "To know what, Your Majesty?"

"At harvesttime, when the tribute to Assyria is due, we won't be sending it. Our nation is in God's hands now."

"Your Majesty, *no!* Are you certain you want to do this? You cannot possibly believe that some invisible god will be able to protect you if you rebel against the Assyrians!"

Once again Hezekiah recalled the prophet's words: *"When you pass through the fire, you won't be burned. . . . for Yahweh is your God."*

"Yes, Shebna," he answered quietly. "I do believe it."

------◆------

Shebna looked up from his evening meal as Prince Gedaliah pushed past the servant and barged into his private chambers without waiting to be invited. Gedaliah's face was flushed, and his body bristled with anger. Shebna knew immediately why he had come.

"You can't let him do it!" Gedaliah shouted. "Rebel against Assyria? Are you both crazy?"

Shebna laid his bread down and pushed his plate aside. "I had no choice," he said, controlling his own anger. "The king never asked for my advice. He reached the decision on his own."

"Well, why didn't you send for me right away? We could have gathered a delegation to petition him. There are plenty of men who disagree with Hezekiah. We could persuade him to listen."

Shebna remembered the determined look on Hezekiah's face and shook his head. "I don't think so—"

"Yes! There are plenty of influential people who believe we should stay under Assyria's protection. I know the taxes are high, but we've lived in peace since my father made his alliance with them. Why jeopardize that now?"

"Stop shouting at me and sit down. I am telling you the king would not have listened—not to me, not to you, not to a whole delegation."

"Who brainwashed him, then? My grandfather?"

Suddenly Shebna recalled passing Zechariah on the stairs to the palace rooftop the night Hezekiah had made his decision. "Maybe so."

"I knew it!" Gedaliah cursed. "That old man and his prophets have more power in this government than you do!"

"No. They have no power at all." Shebna's voice grew louder.

"Oh really? Take a little tour of our nation then, if you don't believe me. Those religious fanatics are causing trouble everywhere. I've got one nut named Micah who's been trying to stir things up in Lachish, telling me to tear down our temple to the sun god. My father had the right idea in dealing with these fanatics—he never tolerated any of their religious garbage."

Shebna allowed Gedaliah to ramble and curse until he finally ran out of venom. "Are you finished?" he asked. Gedaliah cursed again and slumped into a chair. "Now listen to me, Gedaliah. I know your

97

brother very well and, believe me—he is not going to listen to reason. This is some sort of a test he is putting himself through to prove he has faith in his god."

Gedaliah bolted to his feet again. "What? He's trying to prove a point by putting our entire nation at risk?"

Shebna moved to within inches of Gedaliah, staring hard at his unreasonable guest. "Listen to what I am trying to tell you. It is impossible to talk him out of it. You had better consider some other options."

Gedaliah sat down again, his brow furrowed, his body tense. "I'm governor of one of Judah's largest cities. Maybe we could organize a coalition of other city-states, persuade them to rebel against the king, and become independent. Then we could pay the tribute to Assyria ourselves—"

"It would never work."

"Why not?"

"King Hezekiah is much too popular with the people. You could never incite the masses to rebel. They would tear you to pieces if you tried. Did you not hear what happened all over the country after the Passover feast—how the men of Judah destroyed all of Ahaz's shrines and high places on their way back to their homes?—in nearly every city, all the way down to Arad."

"I know," Gedaliah said. "I told you they went after my temple in Lachish. But I wouldn't let them destroy it."

"And are you going to try fighting that kind of popularity, that spirit of nationalism, all across Judah?"

"What if we convinced the military to back us up?"

Shebna gave a short laugh. "What military? If you are talking about the palace guard, General Jonadab would lie down and die for his king. He trained you and Hezekiah since you were children—remember?"

Gedaliah cursed in frustration. "Well, if the king's going to go ahead with this suicidal rebellion, then at least we can convince him to make some alliances with other nations. We can't possibly take on Assyria alone."

"That is exactly what I am trying to do," Shebna said.

"And is my brother listening to you?"

Shebna sat down at the table again and toyed with his bread. "It is not that easy. The timing is never right. Besides, I cannot freely offer my advice unless the king asks for it."

"You're stalling, Shebna. You don't want to lose your precious job, do you?"

"It has nothing to do with—"

"Are you going to stand up for what you believe, or are you going to sell out, just to keep your fancy lifestyle?"

Shebna leaped from his seat. "I do not know why I am even listening to you. I know what you are really after—you want to be the king. Well, I have no intention of helping you. Your brother is doing an outstanding job, considering the mess he started with. And who knows? Maybe he will succeed in this too. Maybe he *will* rebel against Assyria and get away with it."

"And maybe he won't!"

"Assyria has other problems with her empire. She is too busy to be concerned about our puny country. And it will certainly be in our best economic interests if we do not send the tribute."

"So, I see they've brainwashed you, haven't they?" he said bitterly. "Next thing I know you'll be spouting faith in God."

"No, but I do have faith in King Hezekiah. And our nation is certain to benefit if he succeeds in this rebellion."

"Yeah, and we're certain to be annihilated if he doesn't!"

12

Jerusha awoke as the first rays of dawn soaked through the seams of the heavy tent. An unbearable atmosphere of tension hung over the camp, and she had slept poorly. The powerful Assyrian battering rams were poised to break through the walls of the besieged city. Today would be the day. And the lust for battle, the scent of spoil intoxicated the restless soldiers. Like wild animals who know their prey is cornered, the warriors prowled around the camp waiting for the signal to pounce and kill.

As Jerusha lay on her mat, her baby thrashed and kicked restlessly inside her. She gently stroked her abdomen, trying to soothe the child back to sleep, but the activity inside her increased. Was it part of the Assyrians' nature, even before birth, to fight and struggle? Would her baby, born into this atmosphere of death and destruction, be cursed into becoming like them? She shuddered at the thought of giving birth to a son in Iddina's image.

Iddina. The name alone had the power to terrify her. Everything about him seemed more animal than human; his powerful muscular stance, his stealthy catlike movements, his fierce brutality. He could torture and kill another human being as casually as a boy pulls the wings off a fly.

Jerusha no longer dreamed of escaping. Some of the male slaves had tried it, but the soldiers quickly recaptured them. The Assyrians loved the challenge of a hunt, and they tracked runaways as a gleeful sport, wagering among themselves on the success of their pursuit. The Assyrians always recaptured their slaves. No one ever escaped. And the brutal punishment that awaited runaways was horrifying as the Assyrians prolonged their victim's agony for days and weeks. Jerusha would never attempt to escape. There were much faster ways to die. She finally rose from her mat and began preparing the morning meal, dragging the heavy clay pots from the tent, rekindling the fire, grinding grain between the stones to make flour.

Marah remained huddled inside the tent, mute and staring, paralyzed with fear. Jerusha would have to do the work alone. Iddina and the other officers had risen earlier to meet with the priests and consult the gods for omens. Jerusha could hear the distant pounding of the barus' drums and the faint drone of their incantations as she worked.

Before long the drumming stopped, and when Iddina returned for his breakfast a few minutes later, Jerusha knew the omens had promised victory. The great walled city was doomed. Aroused to a near frenzy, Iddina's dark eyes glittered with hatred and with lust for battle. Every muscle twitched with readiness to kill. Jerusha had seen him in this state before and had watched as he killed a slave for committing a minor mistake, snapping the man's neck with his bare hands. The sight of him now made Jerusha's hair stand on end, and her hands trembled uncontrollably as she served his meal. When he finally left, she wept with relief.

All day Jerusha had to listen to the distant sounds of battle. As she hauled fresh water from the spring, she heard a thundering rumble as a portion of the breached wall finally toppled. As she washed the dishes and serving platters, the Assyrians' piercing war cries and the first sounds of torture drifted to her on the wind. She tried not to think about what it would be like to be one of the victims trapped inside the city with no hope of escape. All day Jerusha's baby thrashed inside her as if longing to join the battle. The stench of fire and death grew so overpowering it gagged her, and she wondered if the child could smell it too; if it would poison his soul, even in the womb. The sky turned black with vultures, like dark-robed pilgrims flocking to a great feast. Jerusha watched and listened all day, then the next day, and the next. The soldiers didn't return from their sport, and she was alone. Marah hadn't moved from her place inside the tent.

The brutality and violence Jerusha witnessed as the days passed reached nightmarish proportions, with every kind of inhumanity imaginable. She envied Marah's uncomprehending trance. The conquered inhabitants, already half-starved, were being tortured, dismembered, impaled, beheaded, flayed alive. Orphaned children, lost and terrified, cried pitifully for their parents. The moans and screams and cries of the condemned rang endlessly in Jerusha's ears, day and night, as she worked and as she lay in her tent, until she begged God to strike her deaf. Where was He? Didn't He hear their cries anymore? Didn't He care?

On the third night Iddina and the other officers finally staggered home to their tents, intoxicated by the thrill of their conquest, soaked in the blood of their enemies. Iddina carried two trophies of war, the severed heads of enemy noblemen, which he hung from the branches of the tree beside his tent. He believed they contained powerful magic.

Suddenly Jerusha thought of her father, remembering how he would return from his vineyards on a summer day beaming with pride as he carried the first ripe grapes from his vines as a gift to his family. Her life had become a mockery of real life, a twisted nightmare she couldn't awaken from. Jerusha was weary of death—the sight of it, the smell of it, the sound of it. She didn't know why she struggled to live anymore, except that the only way to conquer her Assyrian captors was to cheat them out of her death. Life became very precious to her, her own life and the one that struggled inside her. Somehow she would defeat her captors. She would go home again. She would find a way to rejoin the world of the living.

—∘→ **13**

Perspiration dripped off Hezekiah's brow and splashed on the scroll unrolled before him. He mopped his face and poured a drink of water from the pitcher. As soon as the rains ended, a khamsin had blown into Jerusalem from the Arabian desert, bringing oppressive heat and clouds of fine dust that seemed to penetrate every shuttered window and doorframe. Two days ago the land had been green, the wildflowers in full bloom, but then the khamsin had begun to blow, and suddenly the air was stifling and the earth was baked brown and coated with a layer of gray dust.

Hezekiah glanced up at his grandfather. He looked unwell. For weeks he had begged him to slow down, without success. Hezekiah leaned back in his seat and stretched.

"Why don't we quit for today?" he said. "It's too hot to work."

"If you keep going, you can finish the fifth Book of Moses." Zechariah didn't even look up.

"Wouldn't you rather rest?" Hezekiah asked.

Zechariah gestured impatiently, and Hezekiah returned to his work, carefully copying Moses' final commands to the Israelites. He worked as quickly as he dared, barely noticing what the words said, and when he finished, he started to roll up the scroll. Zechariah stopped him, placing his hand on top of Hezekiah's.

"Son, I want you to keep these words of Moses very close to your heart. They were Yahweh's promise to Joshua as he prepared to lead His people. And they will be God's promise to you too: 'Be strong and courageous . . . Yahweh himself goes before you and will be with you; he will never leave you nor forsake you. Do not be afraid; do not be discouraged.'

"There have been times in my life when I have been very discouraged," Zechariah said, "and even a time when I turned away from

Yahweh altogether. But one truth I know—He never abandoned me. You have a huge task ahead of you as you lead this nation back to God, and you'll be forced to make some difficult and dangerous decisions. Yahweh never promised that your life would be without problems. But meditate on what He has promised; let it be your strength: God will never leave you or forsake you. He commands, 'Do not be afraid,' so to be fearful is to doubt God. And that is a sin."

Hezekiah gazed down at Zechariah's wrinkled hand resting on his own, remembering his warm, reassuring touch from childhood. He trusted his grandfather as he trusted no other person on earth, and he knew he would give an honest answer to the question that haunted Hezekiah's mind like an endless refrain. His eyes met Zechariah's clear, keen eyes and held.

"Am I making a mistake in not sending the tribute to Assyria?" Zechariah studied him gravely for a long time without answering. "Am I?" Hezekiah repeated.

"No, Son. You're not making a mistake. It's never a mistake to trust God." He squeezed Hezekiah's hand reassuringly, then gathered his scrolls together. "Sometimes you may feel like you're all alone, especially after I'm gone. But Yahweh will be with you. He will never leave you."

Hezekiah knew his grandfather's words were meant to comfort him, but they gave him an unsettled feeling, as if they were Zechariah's parting words instead of Moses'.

"But do you think I should—"

"You're right, Son. It's too hot. Let's quit for today."

Reluctantly, Hezekiah walked Zechariah to the door. "Thanks for all your help." When they embraced, Hezekiah was aware that he held someone very precious in his arms.

———◆———

Zechariah paused to catch his breath several times as he walked up the hill to the Temple. It was hard to breathe the stifling air, and the dust burned his lungs. When he reached his room he felt dizzy, and he lay down on his bed to rest for a few moments.

Hours later his friend Shimei shook him awake. "Zechariah—it's time for the evening sacrifice."

"Evening? You mean I've been asleep that long?" He felt groggy and disoriented.

"It's the heat, my friend. Don't worry about it. Besides, it's too hot to do anything else but sleep."

"Thanks, Shimei. I'll be right out." Zechariah closed his eyes for a moment, marshaling his strength for the tasks ahead. He remembered a time when his body felt vigorous and strong, a time when his life stretched before him and his beloved wife stood by his side, a time when he had important work to accomplish for King Uzziah—a lifetime ago.

The heat was still oppressive as evening drew near and Zechariah washed at the brazen laver in the Temple courtyard. The sun perched on the crest of the mountains west of the city, but as soon as it set the Sabbath would begin, and he would have extra duties to perform in preparation.

He helped Azariah with the evening sacrifice, feeling as if he were floating, every movement dreamlike. When the service ended, he fetched the fresh loaves of bread along with a jug of olive oil to replenish the lamps. The other Levites helped him wash his hands and feet before he entered the holy place, working quickly as the sun set. The symmetry and perfection of Yahweh's holy place struck Zechariah as he entered the holy sanctuary. Everything had been built according to God's design, and now that it was restored, Yahweh's order and beauty shone everywhere.

Zechariah turned to the golden lampstand first, trimming the wicks and replenishing the oil so that the flames would burn all night. Then he replaced the bread with the fresh loaves, working by the light of the flickering lamps.

As he prepared to leave, he thought he heard a fluttering noise coming from behind the holy veil, and he stood still to listen. Had a bird gotten inside the holy of holies? In the hushed silence, the room slowly grew brighter, as if the sun were emerging from behind a cloud. But the sun had already set. Zechariah heard the fluttering sound again, a soft whisper. He was certain that none of the priests had gone inside the holy of holies, but that was where the whispering sound came from. The Law forbade him to enter the holiest place. If something was amiss, the high priest would have to investigate.

Zechariah stood near the thick veil and listened again. The room had grown noticeably brighter now, and the light was emanating from beyond the veil. Zechariah shivered. He heard the noise again, like the sound of rustling silk.

"*Zechariah. Yahweh has remembered.*" It was the meaning of his name in Hebrew.

He fell to his knees, trembling. The room grew brighter and brighter until the light forced Zechariah to close his eyes, shielding them from its glow. It shone brighter than the sun, brighter than 10,000 suns. He felt the light soak through his robe and touch his skin, washing over him, engulfing him in wave after wave of brilliance and love.

Overwhelming love. He never could have put that love into words. It was the love he felt for his children and grandchildren. It was the tender intimacy of his wife's embrace. It was the love he had felt as a child, wrapped in his mother's bosom or sheltered in his father's protecting arms. It was all of these and more.

Yahweh. Wave after wave of Yahweh's presence washed over him until he felt completely consumed. He bowed his forehead to the floor, aware that he was unworthy of such love. He reached out for something to hold on to and grasped the hem of the holy veil. He wanted to look up, to see his God face-to-face, but he was afraid.

"Zechariah."

Another wave of love washed over him.

"Don't be afraid, Zechariah. Look up."

Zechariah's fear dissolved. Slowly he raised his head and opened his eyes.

—◆—

When the Sabbath meal ended, Hezekiah led Hephzibah up the winding stairs to the palace roof. The day had been unbearably hot, but he hoped the roof would catch a cool evening breeze from the Great Sea now that the sun had set. A faint light shone in the west, but above the Mount of Olives the first stars already twinkled in the darkened sky.

"Have you ever been up here before?" Hezekiah asked.

"No. It's magnificent!"

He studied Hephzibah as she looked around in wonder, loving the way the tiny tendrils of her hair curled around her face, the way her tawny skin glowed like ivory in the pale starlight. She gazed in awe at the canopy of sunset sky, at the square houses with lamplight flickering through their windows, at the distant hills fading away like specters into the night. Hezekiah was glad he had decided to share his favorite place with her.

"I come up here a lot, just to think—or sometimes to pray. And I'm always reminded of my ancestor, King David. He liked it on the rooftop too."

She looked up at him, her dark eyes luminous. He put his arm around her slender waist and drew her close to his side. "Look up! Sometimes the stars seem so close I could touch them."

They stood together, enjoying the infinite sky and the ever-increasing number of stars. "I always feel so small when I look at the stars," she said.

"'When I consider your heavens, the work of your fingers, the moon and the stars, which you have set in place, what is man that you are mindful of him?'" Hezekiah quoted. "I always think of those words when I look at the stars. Maybe David wrote that psalm on a night like this, when he was up on this rooftop."

He wrapped his arms around her and held her close, resting his cheek on her fragrant hair.

"I want to tell you something," she murmured.

"Hmm?"

"I wasn't going to say anything until I was sure—but—"

"Tell me anyway." Hezekiah smiled in anticipation.

"Well, I think that I—we—are going to have a baby."

He hugged her tightly. "Didn't I tell you Yahweh would give us an heir?"

"Well, I think He had a little help from you."

As he kissed her, Hezekiah heard a rustling in the shadows by the stairway and the sound of approaching footsteps.

"Excuse me—Your Majesty?" a voice called hoarsely. It was too dark to see who had spoken.

Hezekiah released Hephzibah and walked toward the shadowy figure. "Yes? Who is it?"

"It's Shimei the Levite. I'm sorry to disturb you, my lord."

A knot of dread tightened in Hezekiah's stomach at the sound of Shimei's faltering voice.

"Yes? What is it, Shimei?"

"Your Majesty it's Zechariah . . ."

Hezekiah closed his eyes and waited. He heard Shimei draw a shuddering breath.

"I woke him before the evening sacrifice. I even talked to him, *but he never came out to the courtyard. We had to hold the sacrifice without him.* When it was time for Zechariah to perform the Sabbath duties afterward, I went back to his room again to find him. At first I thought he was still asleep. I called to him . . . but he didn't move."

Hezekiah wanted to cry out, to call Shimei a liar, but he waited in silence for him to continue.

"He was dead, Your Majesty . . . just lying there peacefully. He must have died in his sleep before the evening sacrifice. But his face . . . when I saw the radiance on his face—" Shimei couldn't finish. He covered his own face and wept.

Hezekiah stood in agonized silence, unable to speak, unable to cry out. Zechariah was dead. His beloved grandfather, gone. It couldn't be true. He needed Zechariah. There were so many questions he needed to ask him, so many things he needed to learn—and so much he wanted to tell him. Now he would never have the chance. Hezekiah knew he was to blame. He had convinced Zechariah to come out of retirement to serve in the Temple again. But it was God's fault too. Zechariah had labored too hard for Yahweh.

Suddenly Hezekiah wanted to rage at God, question Him, lash out at Him for stealing Zechariah away now, when he needed him the most. How could God let this happen?

"Thank you for coming, Shimei," he finally managed. His voice was strained as he struggled with his rising grief. "You may go."

As Shimei crept quietly down the stairs, Hezekiah grabbed the front of his tunic with both hands and tore it with all his strength, ripping the fabric over and over until it hung in tattered shreds.

―――◈―――

Hephzibah hesitated, holding her breath, not certain if she should go to Hezekiah or not. He stood a few feet away from her, unmoving, the front of his beautiful robe ruined. He still hadn't opened his eyes, and it hurt Hephzibah to watch him struggling with his pain and grief. He had been so happy a moment ago when she had told him about their baby. Now that joy was forgotten. She wanted to hold him, comfort him, and she waited for him to call to her, certain that he would. But several minutes passed, and he still hadn't moved, a statue frozen in sorrow and despair.

"I'd like to be alone now," he said at last.

Hephzibah turned away. As she slipped silently down the stairs, she heard his anguished cry in the darkness behind her.

Searing pain tore through Jerusha, blotting out everything else. She gripped Marah's hand and groaned.

"Go ahead and scream. Everyone does," Marah said. But Jerusha gritted her teeth and stifled her cries, unwilling to show weakness in front of her enemies. "It won't be much longer now," Marah told her.

The resting times between Jerusha's pains became shorter and shorter, and in the brief rests, while Marah splashed cool water on her face, she saw stars through the tent door, sprinkled across the sky. Her labor had begun after breakfast and seemed as if it would last forever as she neared the end of her strength. Then the pain became a constant fire, and Jerusha could no longer stifle her cries. With a final burst of strength she didn't know she had, it was suddenly over. And, blending with the sounds of hyenas' screams and soldiers' voices around their campfires, Jerusha heard a tiny, pitiful cry.

"My baby," she whispered. Tears of joy and triumph welled up in her eyes. "Let me see my baby." Marah briskly washed the squalling child and rubbed it with salt. Her face was harsh and unsmiling.

"It's a girl," she told Jerusha. She made it sound like a curse.

"Let me see her—let me hold her."

She reached out longingly. Marah wrapped the baby in an old torn blanket and reluctantly placed her in Jerusha's arms. The tiny child cried pitifully, as if outraged by the indignities she had suffered. "Shh—don't cry, little one; don't cry," Jerusha soothed.

She had long silky black hair that curled softly around her face, and she looked Assyrian. The baby's hair, her eyes, her dusky complexion resembled Iddina's. Jerusha picked up her tiny, perfect hand, and as the dainty fingers wrapped around her own, Jerusha began to weep. They were Mama's hands, sturdy and square. She traced her delicate, upturned nose and saw her sister, Maacah. How was it possible? How could this helpless, innocent child be such a perfect blend of her beloved family and her dreaded enemies? How was it possible to create a flawless new life from violence and hatred? Jerusha put her daughter to her breast, and she stopped crying and began to suck.

"Don't do that," Marah said sharply.

Jerusha held her baby close. "But she's hungry."

Marah shook her head. "You'll only grow to love her if you do that." She stormed from the tent to empty the basins.

Jerusha stroked the downy, black head. "I already do love you," she whispered.

Jerusha lay in her tent for hours, exhausted but unable to sleep. She stared at her baby by the fluttering light of the oil lamp, marveling at this miracle of perfection. It had been a long time since she had felt the power of love, and the emotion overwhelmed her as if she felt it for the first time. For more than a year her life had been mere existence, with no emotion except fear and hatred. Now, as if raised from the dead, Jerusha had a reason to live. She had someone who needed her, someone to love and who would love her in return. Her baby brought her family back to life, and she offered Jerusha a future as well. At last she slept, hugging her baby close to her side.

———◈———

A sudden flood of light through the open tent flap awakened her. Groggy with sleep, Jerusha squinted into the glare and saw Iddina standing over her. But before she could react, he bent down and snatched her sleeping baby from her arms, then left.

"No!" she screamed. "Oh, please, God—no!" She tried to scramble off her pallet, tried to run after him, but Marah stood in the doorway of the tent, blocking her path.

"Get out of my way!" Jerusha screamed. She beat Marah with her fists, trying in vain to push past her, to save her baby, but Marah was as immovable as stone. "My baby! He took my baby! Make him bring my baby back!"

"Stop it!" Marah slapped Jerusha, and she slumped to her knees, trembling and weak from shock. "Shut up or he'll come back and give you a beating to remember."

"I don't care! My baby—he took my baby! Dear God, where did he take her? What's he going to do with her?"

"Don't ask. You don't want to know." Marah's harsh face betrayed no sympathy. She shoved Jerusha backward toward her bed.

"O God, please—not my baby! Make him bring my baby back!"

"Shut up!" Marah slapped her again, and Jerusha collapsed. "Your baby is *gone!*"

"No—no—" Jerusha buried her face in the baby's blanket, which Iddina had left behind. It was empty, but it still carried her soft, sweet scent.

"My little girl—my baby—" Jerusha wept in anguish, pouring out all her grief and hatred. For one brief night she had felt love again, only to have it snatched away. God hadn't come to her baby's rescue, and now Jerusha knew that there was no God. She would never pray again.

Hours later Jerusha had no tears left to shed, and it seemed as if her heart had stopped beating, leaving only a dull ache in her chest. Gradually she became aware of Marah sitting beside her, stroking her hair. Jerusha turned to look at her, and the harsh lines of Marah's face seemed softer, her eyes moist.

"Little fool," she whispered. "Did you really think they'd let you keep her? Look around you. Do you see any children in this place? Any love or compassion? Any joy or happiness? No, only hatred and killing, brutality and destruction and death. That's all they know. That's why I destroy my babies before they're born into this god-forsaken place. I tried to tell you. I offered to spare you from this, but you wouldn't listen."

Marah swiped impatiently at her eyes as if sorry for showing emotion. She rose to leave, then paused at the tent door. "We'd better start their noon meal. They'll be wanting it soon."

Jerusha watched Marah go. She didn't care about their noon meal. She didn't care about anything. In the stifling semidarkness, Jerusha crawled like a beaten animal into the farthest corner of the tent and crouched into a tight ball. Hugging her knees to her chest and clutching the tattered blanket to her face, Jerusha rocked slowly back and forth, staring through vacant, unseeing eyes.

15

Hezekiah mourned deeply for his grandfather, dressing in sackcloth day after day, trudging up to the Temple in a daze of grief to recite prayers for the dead. The daily sacrifices became a painful ordeal for him. Zechariah had played such a visible role in them that Hezekiah expected to see his grandfather there, like the sacrificial altar or the brazen laver. His absence was conspicuous, the void he left unfillable. Zechariah's deep love for God had been the spark that had set the Temple worship ablaze, and without him the ritual seemed empty and flat.

Hezekiah knew he was angry at God. Why hadn't God given him more time with Zechariah after separating them for so many years? He needed his grandfather's strong, reassuring faith more than ever, now that he had taken the dangerous step of rebelling against Assyria. He felt as if God had cut him adrift, condemning him to sink helplessly below the rising tide of Assyria. He had relied on Zechariah's support in order to govern. Now he had no one. Even Isaiah was too busy doing Yahweh's work.

Yahweh's work. First it had caused his grandfather's long imprisonment, and now it had killed him. Zechariah had labored too hard for a man his age, restoring Yahweh's Temple, organizing all the sacrifices and feasts. Now God hadn't even allowed him to enjoy the fruit of his labors. Death seemed an unjust reward. Hezekiah raged at God and asked, *Why?*

More than a week passed before Hezekiah returned to see Hephzibah. When he did, he was unable to share his staggering burden of grief with her. Even her singing couldn't comfort him. As he plodded through his daily routine, he knew his leadership was faltering, but there was little he could do except hand the burden of government to Shebna. The Egyptian quietly took over, covering for Hezekiah's paralyzing grief and helping him hide the truth of how serious his depression really was.

Several weeks after Passover, Hezekiah stood in his private chambers, staring sadly through an open window as streams of pilgrims flowed into Jerusalem for the Feast of Pentecost. He knew he would never be able to take a leading role in this joyful feast of thanksgiving. He had no reason to be thankful. He glanced over his shoulder as Shebna entered, then gazed out the window again.

"What is it, Shebna?" he asked dully.

"There seem to be even more pilgrims for this feast than for Passover."

"Maybe so."

"That should please you, my lord."

"I wish my grandfather could have lived to see it."

Shebna sighed, then drew a deep breath. "Your Majesty, at the risk of angering you, I have something I need to say."

Hezekiah turned to his friend and saw anxiety in Shebna's dark eyes. "What's wrong, Shebna?"

"You have brought this nation a long way in a short time, but now I am afraid it will all be in vain. All your reforms may be lost unless you begin to put your grief aside."

"The government is functioning smoothly enough. What's your point?"

"I have taken over many of your duties these past few weeks, but I cannot take your place at the festival. You know that I am forbidden to go beyond the Court of the Gentiles. Your Majesty, you must lead these pilgrims in thanksgiving."

Hezekiah turned away from Shebna to stare out the window again. Shebna's tone had been that of the tutor admonishing his pupil, and it irritated Hezekiah. Yet in his heart he knew that Shebna spoke as a friend.

"I'm not sure I can do that," Hezekiah said at last.

"But you must. You led these people to discard their idols and renew the covenant with Yahweh. You reminded them of their history at Passover and urged them to follow the laws of your God. Now they have come in obedience to those laws, bringing their tithes and offerings. You have led them this far, Your Majesty. You have brought them to this day, a day of great rejoicing for your people. If you do not lead them and encourage them in what they are doing, then all that your grandfather worked for will be lost."

Hezekiah knew Zechariah would want him to continue leading the spiritual revival. But how could anyone expect him to lead a feast of joy and thanksgiving with anger and bitterness toward God in his heart? Hezekiah had the overpowering conviction that he didn't owe

God a thank offering. Instead, God owed him a debt for taking away his grandfather a second time.

"I can't do it, Shebna. It would be a lie."

"Very well," Shebna said quietly. "But will you come for a short walk with me, please? There is something I need to show you at the Temple."

"At the Temple?" Hezekiah recognized the bitterness in his voice. "Is this really necessary?"

"Yes. Please."

Neither of them spoke as they climbed the steps of the royal walkway to the Temple mount. When they reached the Court of the Gentiles, Shebna stopped. "I can go no farther, but look."

He pointed beyond the Temple to the side chambers and storehouses. Hezekiah shaded his eyes in the brilliant sunlight and saw several huge piles of sand, heaped in mounds near the storehouses.

"What is all that?"

"Please—I urge you to go look, Your Majesty. I cannot go with you."

He left Shebna behind and strode impatiently across the courtyard toward the mounds. As he got closer, he saw a huge layered pile of clay storage jars and more golden piles of sand behind the first ones. Suddenly he realized that it wasn't sand but grain. Azariah and several other Levites stood near the mounds, taking inventory.

"Where did all this come from?" Hezekiah asked.

"These are the tithes, Your Majesty," Azariah said. He seemed equally amazed. "We have been eating from these stores of food for many weeks, and still they grow bigger. God has blessed our land with a bountiful harvest, and He has moved the people's hearts to give Him the tenth portion."

"And this isn't all of it, Your Majesty," Conaniah added. "Not only have the people given a tenth of their grain, but also their new wine, olive oil, cattle, sheep, silver, and gold. We can't keep track of it all."

"And since it isn't going to Assyria any more, the people are giving more than their tithes. They're giving freewill offerings too," Azariah said. "I've never seen anything like it—certainly not during your father's reign, or King Jotham's reign either. This is just like the golden age of King Uzziah."

Hezekiah carried an awareness of his loss with him wherever he went, but suddenly it became an acute pain as he remembered sitting in the olive grove near the Gihon Spring with Zechariah, discussing the kings who had reigned before him. *"There's a lot of Uzziah in you, Son,"* his grandfather had said. But then he remembered what else Zechariah had said. King Jotham had been destroyed by his bitterness.

Slowly Hezekiah began to see what Shebna had been desperate to show him. All his religious reforms, all the economic prosperity he saw before him stood at risk of being lost because of his own bitterness. He was doing exactly what King Jotham had done, allowing resentment toward God to bring his reign to a standstill. Hezekiah still didn't understand why Zechariah had to die, but he suddenly knew what these heaps of tithes really meant. This was the beginning of God's blessings on his nation. God had renewed his nation's prosperity as His part of their covenant, just as Zechariah had assured him. The evidence of Yahweh's fulfilled promises lay before him, too plentiful to fit into the storehouses.

Then Hezekiah remembered what else he had talked about with Zechariah that cold, wet morning—taking back the land that Ahaz had lost to the Philistines and Ammonites. *"With God you can do anything,"* Zechariah had said. *"Anything at all."* If Hezekiah was forced to accept Zechariah's death as God's will, then he believed God owed him victory over his enemies in return. And Hezekiah was ready to claim that debt.

As if suddenly awakening from a long sleep, Hezekiah turned to Azariah with renewed vigor and authority. "Start building more storehouses," he said to him. "Eliakim can plan their design and supervise construction. Conaniah, you and your brother Shimei will be in charge of all the storehouses. See to it that the tithes are evenly distributed among the priests and Levites throughout Judah."

The men appeared startled by the sudden change in him. "Yes, Your Majesty," they murmured.

Then, without a further word, he strode back across the courtyard to where Shebna waited. As they walked down the hill, he told Shebna about his plans for the storehouses and saw surprise and pleasure on his friend's face.

"Find General Jonadab and bring him to my chambers for a conference at once," Hezekiah said when they reached the palace. He saw a broad smile spread across Shebna's face as he turned to leave.

"Oh, and Shebna—"

"Yes, Your Majesty?"

"Thanks."

Hezekiah wasted no time. As soon as Shebna returned with Jonadab, he began to plan his military strategy, pacing restlessly in front of them and gesturing forcefully as he talked. "The three of us are going to plan a campaign against the Philistines to win back our territory in the Shephelah and the Negev. It's time we took back what's rightfully ours."

Shebna appeared surprised, Jonadab pleased. "Shebna, you know how badly we need that farmland if we hope to be active in world trade again. And you both know how important those fortified cities are to us. If we win them back, we will control the main routes from Jerusalem to the Way of the Sea. Do you think we can do it?"

"Yes, sir—I'm ready," Jonadab said. If he had been wearing a sword, he would have unsheathed it.

The corner of Shebna's mouth twitched as if suppressing a smile, and he gave a slight bow. "Yes, Your Majesty. I am sure you can do it."

"Good. Now—the storehouses and treasuries are starting to fill up with tithes from what formerly went to Assyria. We will use those resources to secretly purchase weapons and supplies for our armies. Jonadab, over the next few months I want you to mobilize an army for me, all volunteers. Train them and arm them—then let me know when they're ready. Lachish is the strongest fortified city in the area. We'll use it as a staging point for attacks on the Philistines in the Shephelah and on the Ammonites in the Negev. It'll be my headquarters."

"You are going into battle yourself?" Shebna asked.

"Yes, as field commander. Now, I want you to move supplies down to Lachish a little at a time. Jonadab, train your army as secretly as possible. The Philistine army undoubtedly outnumbers ours, so we must achieve surprise at all costs."

Hezekiah's enthusiasm became contagious, and Jonadab could scarcely stay seated. "Your Majesty, we can do it! We can take back those cities and fortify them as Jerusalem's perimeter defenses. The Philistines will be easy prey."

"If we could win back all that rich, fertile farmland," Shebna said, "we could begin to export goods—which would mean an increase in the goods we could import."

"Exactly. Jonadab, send your best men out on a scouting mission. Have them report directly to me. Then we'll plan our battle strategy."

—◆—

The planning in the weeks that followed rapidly consumed each day, diverting Hezekiah's thoughts from his grief. Gradually the military campaign began to take shape. The scouts returned with their reports, and Shebna stockpiled supplies at Lachish. Jonadab procured weapons and trained a strong corps of volunteer soldiers.

When everything was ready, King Hezekiah led the army into battle. His forces quickly routed the startled Philistines from Judean territory and chased them as far as the city of Gaza on the Great Sea. It was a stunning victory for Hezekiah and the Judean army. Their losses were minimal compared to the tremendous gains they made in taking back the cities in the Shephelah and the Negev that had once belonged to them.

The Philistines abandoned many of the cities without a fight, and destruction of the fertile countryside was kept to a minimum, with olive groves and vineyards left untouched. It seemed to Hezekiah that his victory was taken from the pages of the history books in which the Philistines had fled before the armies of his childhood hero, King David. He felt tremendous satisfaction that the campaign he had planned and commanded resulted in such a resounding victory.

When it was over and the territory was secured, he returned to Jerusalem with the Judean army and the spoils of war, assured of his sovereignty and confident in his abilities. His monarchy was firmly established, his authority honored both in his own nation and by his neighboring states. He no longer feared a rebellion from among the nobility, for he had won their respect and homage.

On the Sabbath day, Hezekiah climbed the hill to the Temple to worship for the first time in many weeks. As he stood before the brazen altar, celebrating his victory, he realized that he had tested his God and found Him faithful to His covenant, just as Zechariah had promised. As the priests slew the sacrifices and the praises of the Levite musicians reached their crescendo, Hezekiah entered into the praise and worship freely, his anger against Yahweh gone, his grief assuaged.

＊

That night when Hezekiah came to her chambers, Hephzibah thought he seemed happier than he had for a long time. The oppressive cloud of depression he had suffered under had finally lifted. Hephzibah studied him as he lay stretched out comfortably on the ivory couch with his long legs propped on a footstool. His skin was deeply tanned, and his dark, curly hair and beard reflected glints of copper in the lamplight. He seemed changed since returning from battle, as if the war had hardened him, making him tougher, more decisive. Hephzibah was awed by these changes, and sometimes it was difficult to think of him as her husband instead of as the king of Judah.

Each day Hephzibah had grown more excited about their baby, but she hadn't mentioned it to Hezekiah since the night his grandfather had died. She wished they could talk about it together and that he would share her excitement, but she wondered if Hezekiah even remembered. Perhaps the tragic news of his grandfather's death had erased it from his mind. Tonight, when she saw how happy he was and felt the faint, fluttering movement of his child inside her, she decided the time had come to share her joy with him again.

"I want to sing a song for you, my lord."

"I'd like that. I missed your singing while I was away."

Hephzibah picked up her lyre and sang a lullaby, one her mother had sung to her when she was a child. "Mmm—that was lovely," he said when she finished.

She put the lyre down and curled up beside him, resting her head against his chest. "Do you think our baby will like it too?"

"Yes, I'm certain he will." Hezekiah played with a lock of her hair. "I'm very happy about the baby, Hephzibah. I know it must have seemed like I'd forgotten, but I didn't forget."

She hesitated, not sure if she dared to bring up the next subject, but at last she sat up to face him. "If it's a son, I think we should name him Zechariah—if that's all right with you." She held her breath, waiting for his reaction to his grandfather's name, but Hezekiah's expression of quiet contentment never changed; his warm, brown eyes showed neither anger or sorrow.

"Yes," he said. "I'd like that very much."

16

Jerimoth returned home from the Passover feast convinced he would find Jerusha waiting for him. He flung open the door of his house calling her name, but only his startled servant answered. Throughout each day Jerimoth would pause from his labors and scan the horizon, no longer looking for the dreaded Assyrian soldiers, but for his daughter, walking up the road toward home. Before retiring each evening, he gazed longingly in the direction the soldiers had carried Jerusha, watching for her long after the sun had set and the dim light of the flickering stars made visibility beyond the borders of his vineyard impossible. Jerimoth would lay awake late into the night, listening in the darkness for the sound of Jerusha's footsteps on the hard-packed road. The first rays of dawn would find him hurrying to the highest point of his land, scanning the horizon for a glimpse of his daughter.

When harvesttime ended and Jerimoth had stored away the last of his crops, he and his family traveled to Jerusalem again for the Feast of Tabernacles, bringing as a sacrifice for Yahweh the tenth portion of all he had reaped. Once again they stayed with Hilkiah, and, like the other pilgrims, they slept outside on the rooftop in rustic booths to celebrate the long wanderings of their forefathers in the wilderness. The Feast of Tabernacles was a joyful feast, and on the last night the men sang and danced and waved branches in joyful praise to Yahweh.

But Jerimoth couldn't rejoice as the other men did. He was eager to return home, to be reunited with his daughter. He knew she would be waiting for him. And as his feet moved in rhythm beside Hilkiah's, Jerimoth's dance became an endless, silent plea to God for his daughter Jerusha.

On the last night of the feast, Eliakim returned home from the festivities with his father and Jerimoth long after sunset. His feet hurt from dancing in new sandals, and he was ready to sleep. But the other two men seemed oblivious to the late hour. Instead of heading to bed, they settled down in the large main room of Hilkiah's house, lighting all the oil lamps, talking together.

"It's hard to believe that the festival is over already," Jerimoth said.

"Yes, it's gone quickly, hasn't it?" Hilkiah agreed. "Tomorrow is the final convocation already. I suppose you'll need to start for home afterward?"

"That's when our caravan is leaving."

"I hate to see you go, my friend. I can't tell you how much I enjoy our visits together." Hilkiah's eyes twinkled warmly in the lamplight. "Naturally, Eliakim and I will look forward to seeing you again in the spring, for Passover. Right, Son?"

"Absolutely!" Eliakim replied. As much as he hated to admit it, his father had been right again. Eliakim had grown very fond of Jerimoth and Hodesh and their little girl. Only the ghost of their lost daughter, Jerusha, who intruded into every conversation, made Eliakim uncomfortable.

"Then it's settled, yes? You will come to see us again in the spring," Hilkiah said.

Jerimoth gave a tired smile, a rare sight on his mournful face. "Thank you. I'm honored to stay in your home. And in the spring you will meet my other daughter, Jerusha."

"She will be our guest of honor! We will bring our thank offerings to the Temple and hold a huge feast, won't we, Son?"

Eliakim didn't answer, but the two men didn't seem to notice as they talked on, making elaborate plans to celebrate Jerusha's homecoming. Eliakim wanted to go to bed, but as he listened to their nonsense, he determined not to sleep another night until he had a serious talk with his father about Jerimoth's unrealistic expectations. He didn't want to belittle his father's faith in Yahweh, but discussing Jerusha had become unbearable for Eliakim. It was time Hilkiah admitted the truth. With his head in his hands, Eliakim gazed sullenly at the floor until finally Jerimoth bade them goodnight and retired to the roof.

Hilkiah yawned and stretched. "My—it's late. I guess I'll go to bed too."

"Abba, wait. There's something we need to talk about."

"Son—what is it? What's wrong?"

"Abba, I don't know how to say this. I don't want to hurt you, but we can't say good-bye to Jerimoth tomorrow until we straighten a few things out."

"Straighten out—? What's to straighten?"

"I can't sit through any more evenings like tonight, Abba. I just can't."

"What are you talking about? We had a wonderful evening."

"Don't you understand? I can't bear to hear you talking to that poor man about this fantasy you've created and nurtured for so long. You keep encouraging Jerimoth as if—as if Jerusha could walk through our door any minute."

"Fantasy?"

"Yes, that's what it is—a fantasy. Jerusha's not coming back, Abba—not now, not next spring, not ever."

Hilkiah wore a look of incomprehension and confusion, as if Eliakim spoke a foreign language. "How can you say such a thing?"

"No, Abba. The question is—how can you keep saying such a ridiculous thing? Jerimoth will never see his daughter again. Surely you know that in your heart." Eliakim rested his hand on his father's shoulder.

Hilkiah appeared stunned. Then the laughter always present in his eyes turned to anger, a rare emotion for Hilkiah. He shrugged Eliakim's hand away. "I know nothing of the sort. What I know in my heart is that Yahweh answers prayer!"

"Yes, yes. Yahweh answers some prayers—but not all prayers. Not 100 percent of the time. Surely you know how impossible this situation is, Abba. You're asking for a miracle."

"And surely you know that Yahweh is the God of miracles! Haven't I taught you anything at all about faith?"

"Abba, be reasonable. Think about it. She was captured more than a year ago. The Assyrians killed all the other girls—"

"But not Jerusha. They never found her body."

"Yes, but even if she's still alive, the Assyrians never set their slaves free. Never! And no one has ever escaped and returned home, least of all a woman. How can Yahweh possibly answer your prayers?"

Hilkiah's face was flushed with controlled fury. "I don't care if no one has ever escaped from the Assyrians before! There's a first time for everything! And as the Torah says, 'Is anything too hard for Yahweh?'"

"But you're not being fair to Jerimoth. If you're his friend, you should help him face the truth so he can get on with his life. It's not fair to encourage his irrational hope that—"

"And you think it's fair to deprive him of that hope? Is that what you're asking me to do?"

"No, Abba, but—"

"What, then?"

"Jerimoth has a fine wife and another daughter to live for. I'm saying we should help him see that, help him accept the truth that Jerusha is gone. She's dead. He needs to admit it and get on with his life."

"Jerimoth has a right to have faith in God!"

"All right, then! All right!" Eliakim shouted. "Let Jerimoth believe what he wants to, no matter how irrational it is! But you don't have to encourage him, Abba. You can't honestly believe he'll ever see Jerusha again, so how can you go to the Temple with him all the time and offer a bunch of stupid, pious prayers? You're a hypocrite!"

The expression of rage and shock on Hilkiah's white face was frightening. He drew his hand back as if to strike Eliakim, the first time he had ever done so in his life; then he stopped. He could barely speak through his fury. "I offer my prayers for Jerusha in faith! Because I *believe* that Yahweh answers prayer! And if there's any hypocrisy in this household, Eliakim, I might ask why *you* attend morning and evening prayers every day if you don't believe any of it!"

"Then why did Mama die? We both prayed, we both believed, but she died anyway, Abba! She *died!* And so did my brothers! Where was Yahweh then? Why didn't He answer our prayers?"

Eliakim stopped, stunned by the bitterness in his voice, alarmed at the look of horror and pain on his father's face. Things had gone too far. They had both said things to hurt each other, words that could never be taken back. But before Eliakim could speak again, he heard Jerimoth's trembling voice behind him.

"Please—don't let there be angry words and discord in this household because of me."

Eliakim's stomach knotted in shame. "Jerimoth, I—"

But Jerimoth held up his hand to silence Eliakim. "Forgive me, my friends. I never intended to eavesdrop. I came back for something and heard you shouting." He sighed heavily, and his melancholy green eyes seemed more sorrowful than ever. "If I'd known I would cause a rift between father and son, I would never have set foot in your house. So listen to me, please.

"Eliakim, I'll go to my grave believing that God is able to answer my prayer. Somehow, someday, He will do the impossible and bring

Jerusha home to me. Even if Hilkiah agreed with you—and I know that he doesn't—he could never talk me out of this conviction. Never.

"And, Hilkiah, my dear friend—I beg you not to be so hard on your son. Let him question his faith. Let him voice his doubts. You've taught him well, both with your words and by your example. His questions will make his faith stronger in the end. I know that his love for you is very, very deep. How I envy you, Hilkiah! How I wish that Eliakim were my son."

Agonized silence filled the room. Eliakim stared mutely at the floor. Never in his life had there been such a terrible, unbreachable rift between him and his father. Hilkiah's faith was the most important thing in his life, and Eliakim had challenged that faith. Worse, he had called him a hypocrite.

Again Jerimoth broke the silence. "Please—forgive me for interfering—but I beg you to reconcile, for my sake."

Eliakim slowly looked up, afraid to face his father, afraid to ask for the forgiveness he didn't deserve. "Abba—I'm so sorry—," he began, but Eliakim's words were silenced by the strength of his father's loving embrace.

——◆——

Hephzibah awoke while it was still dark, and at first she wasn't sure what had awakened her. But then she felt the dull, cramping ache inside and drew her knees up to her chest to ease the pain. When it died away, Hephzibah lay still for a moment, listening in the darkness to Hezekiah's breathing as he slept beside her. A few minutes passed; then suddenly the pain returned, stronger than before. The baby shouldn't come this soon. Fear overwhelmed her.

As the pain eased, Hephzibah slipped quietly from the bed. Then, as she paused to pull the covers over her sleeping husband, she saw blood soaking the sheet. She cried out and sank to the floor beside the bed, sobbing.

"Hephzibah, what is it? What's wrong?" Hezekiah asked. Another pain twisted through her before she could answer, and she cried out again. Hezekiah bounded out of bed and ran to her. "Merab! Somebody—come quickly!" he shouted.

Merab tottered from her room, wrapping herself in a robe. When she reached Hephzibah's side she gasped. "Oh, no—my lady—my lady!" More servants rushed into the room and lifted Hephzibah onto her bed. Hezekiah stood over her, looking shaken and stunned.

Then Merab took his arm and hustled him to the door. "You'd better leave now, Your Majesty." Hephzibah felt another pain intensifying, and she began to scream.

―◆―

Hezekiah returned to his chambers, but he couldn't sleep. "Dear God, please—not Hephzibah too," he whispered.

He stared out of his window into the dark night, worrying about her, remembering the blood, pleading with Yahweh not to take her from him too. Adjusting to Zechariah's death had been so difficult that he couldn't bear to think about losing Hephzibah. She was so much a part of his life now that he wouldn't be whole without her. Hephzibah was more to him than any other person had ever been—confidante, companion, lover, friend. How could he live without her laughter, her songs, her beauty, her love? He loved her. He had never acknowledged it before, but he knew it was true. And he was seized with the terrifying thought that she might die. With his hands bunched into fists, Hezekiah fell to his knees and prayed.

As the sun rose, he could no longer bear the agony of waiting. He returned to Hephzibah's room and tapped on the door. Merab opened it a crack.

"Hephzibah? Is she all right—?"

"Yes, my lord. She's asleep. She'll be fine in a few days."

"Oh, thank God." His knees went weak as relief surged through him.

"But the baby is gone. I'm so sorry, Your Majesty."

For a moment Hezekiah didn't comprehend what Merab had said. In his concern for Hephzibah, he had never thought of their baby. Suddenly he understood.

"Let me see her, Merab. I won't wake her."

Hezekiah crept into the room and stood beside the bed. Hephzibah looked so fragile and pale as she lay against the pillows that he had to remind himself of Merab's words. Hephzibah would recover. She wasn't going to die. Yet the terrible fear that he might lose her was still too real.

He touched her hair. "I love you," he whispered. He was surprised to realize how deeply he loved her. Hephzibah's eyelids fluttered open; then tears began to flow silently down her cheeks.

"I didn't mean to wake you—I'm sorry—"

"No—I'm glad you're here."

"How do you feel?" It was an absurd question, but he didn't know what else to say.

"Empty. I feel so empty—as if all the life has drained out of me and I'm just a hollow shell."

"Don't cry—there'll be others—we'll have more—" His words sounded glib and artificial. He groped for better ones but couldn't find them.

"I can't stop thinking about our baby—wondering what he would have looked like—if he had your hair—your eyes—"

"Hephzibah, don't—"

"They told me it was a boy."

Her words stunned him. For the first time he understood that the child had been a person, a living baby boy, his son. Now he was dead. Hezekiah knew that Hephzibah's grief far surpassed his own, but at that moment he shared a small part of it with her. Their son was dead.

"Can I—do anything, Hephzibah?"

"Please hold me." She held her slender arms out to him. She looked so sorrowful, so lost in the piles of pillows and covers, that Hezekiah's heart twisted inside him. He could see how much she needed him. But he hesitated, remembering something else.

"Hephzibah, I can't. I'm sorry."

"Why not?" Her eyes pleaded with him, and he had to turn away.

"Because the Torah forbids it until—until you're better. Then for seven more days after that." He was aware of how much his words hurt her. They sounded cold and unfeeling to him as he spoke them. "Afterward, you must go to the priest and offer two doves, one for a sin offering, the other a burnt offering."

"But why? How have I sinned? Is wanting our baby to live a sin?"

Hezekiah didn't know why the Torah required it. He only knew what was written. "The Torah says—"

"Our baby is dead and you're telling me I've sinned? Is that the kind of God you worship?" The anguish in her voice cut him deeply.

"No, Hephzibah. Yahweh's not like that."

"Then why did He let our baby die? Can you tell me why? And why does He want more blood from me? How have I sinned?" Hezekiah couldn't answer. He didn't know. "I won't bring a sin offering," she said bitterly. "I have not sinned!"

Hezekiah's stomach churned as he wrestled with his own doubts. He still didn't understand all of Yahweh's laws, and he knew how it felt to be angry with God, to have someone very precious snatched away by death. But he had finally adjusted to his loss and had accepted it as the will of God whether he understood it or not. Hephzibah would have to do the same.

He stared at his feet, ashamed to face Hephzibah, afraid she would see through his facade of legalism and discover the doubts and questions beneath it. He ached to go to her, to take her in his arms and comfort her, but if he held her he would become unclean until evening and would not be able to worship in the Temple. As king he had the responsibility to lead the final convocation of the Feast of Tabernacles. He stood beside her bed, torn between love and duty. Then, as the distant shofars trumpeted the call to worship, Hezekiah turned and left the room.

So the Lord was very angry with Israel and removed them from his presence. Only the tribe of Judah was left, and even Judah did not keep the commands of the Lord their God. They followed the practices Israel had introduced. Therefore the Lord rejected all the people of Israel; he afflicted them and gave them into the hands of the plunderers, until he thrust them from his presence.

—2 Kings 17:18-20

17

Darkness settled over Hephzibah's soul as night fell and the pale light of oil lamps flickered to life in the houses below her palace window. She recalled tender family scenes from her own childhood and imagined them taking place in homes throughout the city. Families would gather for the evening meal, and their faces would glow in the lamplight as they shared the day's events with each other. Then the children, scrubbed and sleepy, would be tucked into their beds for the night.

If her baby had lived he would be nearly three years old, and perhaps she would be rocking him to sleep, singing him a lullaby. But her baby was dead, and Hephzibah's arms remained empty.

"My lady, that cool evening air isn't good for you," Merab said. "You'll catch a chill. Here—let me light a fire for you."

Hephzibah closed the shutters and turned away from the window. She watched her handmaiden fuss with the charcoal brazier, blowing noisily on the coals until they caught fire. "There. Maybe it'll warm up in here before the king arrives." She bustled around the room, plumping pillows and straightening rugs, then stopped when she glanced at Hephzibah. "What is it, my lady? What's wrong?"

"Oh, Merab, I hope he's too busy to come tonight."

"My lady! Why would you wish for such a thing?"

Hephzibah's grief spilled over in tears. "Because my monthly time has come again."

"Oh, don't start crying, honey. Your eyes will be all red and puffy. And he'll be here any minute—" Merab dabbed at Hephzibah's eyes with a handkerchief.

"I don't want to tell him, Merab. I'm so afraid."

"Afraid of what?"

In her despair Hephzibah voiced her greatest fear. "What if he divorces me?"

The little handmaiden stared at her in disbelief. "What—? Divorce you? But the king is in love with you! Can't you see the way he looks at you—the way his eyes never leave your face? He'd sooner cut off his right arm than divorce you!"

Hephzibah knew Hezekiah loved her. In the three years since their baby died she had felt his love grow stronger and deeper. Hezekiah was hers. But she also knew the strength of his devotion to Yahweh's laws.

"He'll have to divorce me because I'm barren. I can't give him an heir."

"You're not barren! Don't even think that!"

"Then why can't I get pregnant? After all this time?"

Merab wrapped her arms around Hephzibah, comforting her like a child. "Shh—never mind, honey. You'll get pregnant again—I know it. And King Hezekiah loves you too much to divorce you."

"But if I don't give him a son he'll *have* to divorce me. It's a terrible disgrace if the king has no heir to the throne."

"He can always take another wife or a concubine—"

"But he won't do that. Yahweh's Law allows him to have only one wife. And the royal line of David must continue."

"You mean more to him than a silly old law," Merab said as she dabbed at Hephzibah's eyes. But Hephzibah remembered the night her baby died, and she knew that wasn't true. "Now—it's time to stop all this nonsense. Your husband is coming. Your face will be a frightful mess."

Hephzibah tried to compose herself, fighting back her terrible fears. She splashed cold water onto her face, then let Merab comb her long, thick hair. A few minutes later she heard Hezekiah's familiar knock and looked up to see his tall frame and broad shoulders filling her doorway. He looked so regal in his gold-and-purple robe, so handsome as he stood smiling at her, that she longed to run to him, to feel his strong arms surrounding her, comforting her.

Instead, she turned away. "It is unlawful to touch me, my lord." She hated Yahweh's Law for making her feel like a leper, for forbidding the very thing she needed the most. The law caused a separation from her husband, and Hephzibah feared that someday it would be permanent.

"It's not unlawful to talk," Hezekiah said.

Hephzibah saw the love in his eyes just as Merab had said. "I'm sorry for failing you, my lord."

"I've told you before, Hephzibah—it doesn't matter to me. We have the rest of our lives to bear children. Yahweh has promised us a son."

Hephzibah cringed. She had never brought Yahweh the required sin offering, blaming Him for her baby's death. She worried that her barrenness was His punishment for breaking the law, but she stubbornly refused to offer more blood. Yahweh had taken her baby; that was enough. Hezekiah sat down beside the charcoal brazier and spread his hands before the coals to warm them. When he looked up, his expression was strained with worry.

Forgetting his reassurances, Hephzibah felt certain that he contemplated divorce. "What's wrong, my lord?"

"I'm worried about a report I received from Israel this afternoon. The Assyrians may be on the march again. Every year their empire expands, and it looks like they won't be content until they've conquered Egypt. The problem is, our nation straddles the road to Egypt."

"What will you do if they invade us?"

"Well, I'll have two choices. I can try to fight them off or appease them by joining their empire as a vassal nation again."

"Which will you do?"

"I don't know—neither one until I have to. They haven't begun to march yet, but the rumors say it's inevitable." His hands knotted into fists as he talked.

Hephzibah saw the deep creases in his face and knew the threat must be serious, but she was incapable of worrying about a vague, future invasion from a distant enemy. Her thoughts focused only on her empty, aching arms.

"I'm sorry, Hephzibah," he said, looking up at her. "I didn't mean to burden you with all my problems. Maybe the rumors are wrong. Maybe the Assyrians will turn around and march home."

"You didn't burden me, my lord. I wasn't worried about that."

"What is it, love? Why are you are so sad tonight?"

Her eyes glistened with tears. "I'm just—disappointed, that's all. I thought maybe this time—this month—"

Hezekiah moved as if to go to her, and she thought for a moment that he would take her in his arms and willingly become unclean for her sake. But he stopped before he reached her, and his arms hung limply by his sides.

"Isn't there anything I can do?" he asked helplessly.

She would not ask to be held, knowing that if she forced him to choose between her and his God, she would never win. She hastily wiped her tears. "No, my lord."

"Are you sure?" He looked as if the burden of his reign weighed heavily on him, and guilt stung her. Hezekiah came to her for comfort, not the other way around.

"Shall I sing for you, my lord?" She tried to smile.

"Yes, I'd like that."

She picked up her lyre and began to sing one of his favorite songs. But as she lost herself in the words and the melody, a flood of grief and disappointment suddenly overwhelmed her. She stopped, unable to finish, and covered her face.

"Hephzibah, would it be easier for you if I left?"

She longed to cry out, *"No, don't go! Hold me in your arms!"* But she didn't. "Yes, my lord," she said instead, and she heard him get up and quietly leave, closing the door behind him.

—◆—

Jerusha knelt before the simple hearth, slowly grinding grain into flour between the stones. On the horizon the sun rose with delicate shades of muted pink and mauve, but Jerusha never noticed as she ground out her sorrow and hatred along with the grain. Today would be her last day in this camp. The city the Assyrians had besieged for more than two years had finally fallen. As if in a dream, Jerusha had again witnessed thousands of helpless men, women, and children being clubbed to death, beheaded, tortured, impaled, flayed alive, or carried away into slavery.

Jerusha knew she couldn't live with this brutality much longer and stay sane. The first signs of madness had already appeared as her soul splintered and disintegrated like a rotted log. She hadn't smiled or laughed or felt any emotion besides fear and hatred since Iddina took her baby. She thought of Marah's icy bitterness, her harsh, unsmiling features, and knew she was becoming like her. Jerusha wasn't a human being to the Assyrians—she was their possession, a plaything, to use and discard. More than anything else, Jerusha feared becoming pregnant again. She couldn't kill her child in the womb, like Marah did, nor could she bear the agony of having her baby snatched from her arms again. It was only a matter of time before she would be forced to choose, but both options horrified her.

She poured the finished flour into the kneading trough, scooped another handful of grain and placed it between the grinding stones, and continued to grind. Tomorrow the tents would come down, and the army would march relentlessly forward to destroy another nation, enslave another helpless population. And Jerusha's life would also grind hopelessly on, with no choice but to submit or die. She could no longer remember why she had wanted to live, and she often recalled Marah's words that first day in camp: *"Die, little fool! Die while you still have the chance to die quickly!"* Why hadn't she listened to her?

When she finished the second batch of flour, Jerusha poured it into the trough. She had enough to make the dough as soon as Marah returned with the water. But as Marah hurried back from the spring with the water jug, she appeared agitated.

"What's the matter?" Jerusha asked.

"I've just heard them talking. I know where the Assyrians are marching next." Marah set the jug down and sank to her knees, pausing as if unable to speak the words. "They're going to invade Israel."

Jerusha didn't respond. The news that she would witness the brutal destruction of her homeland and her people came as a blow to a soul too numb to feel more pain. For a moment she pictured the rolling green hills of Israel, the beautiful Jordan Valley, the shimmering Sea of Galilee; then she quickly closed her eyes against the vision of what the Assyrians would do.

All these years, against all reason, Jerusha had nurtured hope in her heart like a fragile seed—hope that someday she would go home, that she would see her family again. That hope had fueled her overwhelming drive to survive. But now the Assyrians had pronounced a death sentence on Israel. Her home and her family would no longer exist. Jerusha's delicate sprout of hope withered and died, and her will to live died along with it. She had managed to exist without love, but she could never survive without hope. They had finally destroyed the only thing she had left.

Silently, Jerusha made a well in the center of the flour, mixed in water and olive oil, and began to knead. As the dough took shape beneath her fingers, a firm resolve took shape in Jerusha's heart. She wouldn't live to witness the destruction of Israel, the enslavement of her people. She wouldn't endure another day of hopeless existence.

As the sun climbed higher in the sky, Jerusha moved through her routine on instinct, unaware of her surroundings. Instead, as she packed dishes and food supplies, then swept out her tent, she searched for a way to end her own life.

By evening, when she had loaded everything onto the carts except her tent and bedding, Jerusha had formulated her plan. She would die tonight when one of the officers came to her tent. They always brought their weapons with them and kept them close at hand, as if not even trusting each other's treachery. If she acted swiftly, she could grab one of their knives and kill herself before they had time to stop her.

She helped Marah prepare the evening meal, but she couldn't eat. Waves of terror washed over her as she faced the unknown. She had witnessed thousands of deaths, but now that it was her turn she wondered what it would be like. At last she decided that dying couldn't possibly be worse than living.

Her hands shook uncontrollably as she helped Marah wash up after the meal and pack away the cooking pots. Then Jerusha went into her tent and sat alone to wait. For the first time since Iddina had captured her, she hoped that one of the officers would come to her tent tonight. The long wait felt like hours, and the dark canopy of the tent hovered over her like a shroud. She held her baby's blanket against her cheek for courage. Soon she would join her daughter in death.

Finally Jerusha heard footsteps approaching. She held her breath. The flap opened, sending a gust of cool air into the suffocating tent. Then Iddina stood in her doorway, his powerful, muscular stance unmistakable.

She thought it fitting that Iddina would watch her die, since he was the one who had captured her so long ago. She only wished she had let him end her life long ago instead of needlessly prolonging it all these years. He ducked inside the tent and staggered toward her. His wavering, uncertain movements revealed that he had been drinking, and she was glad. The alcohol would slow his reflexes, making it difficult for him to stop her in time.

Jerusha gazed longingly at the dagger strapped to his belt. Every morning Iddina honed it on his whetstone to keep it razor sharp, and she hated the dull, rasping sound the metal made against the stone. Now she was grateful for his diligence. She wished he would hurry and take it off. She was ready. Her courage had reached its peak. If only he would lay it within her reach.

She reminded herself not to hesitate, but to plunge the knife hard and deep. Her suicide would make Iddina furious, and if she didn't die immediately he would prolong her death to torture her. Jerusha had no right to kill herself—that privilege was his.

But Iddina was in no hurry tonight. His black eyes had a malicious gleam as if he laughed at a secret joke. He sank down beside her, moving so close she felt his moist breath on her face and smelled the fruity wine he had drunk. Jerusha felt as if she was suffocating. Determination pounded through her veins until her ears rang, but she forced herself to be patient. She could never get her hands on the dagger unless he laid it down. Why didn't he take it off? She was afraid to look at him, afraid he would peer into her eyes and read the contract she had signed with death.

"I have a surprise for you, my little dog," he said at last.

Jerusha thought of his bloody trophies hanging outside on the tree branches, and she shuddered. He seized her face in his rough hands, forcing her to look at him.

"I don't know if I should tell you about my surprise tonight or make you wait until tomorrow."

Jerusha would never see tomorrow. She looked into his pitiless black eyes, and when she spoke, the defiance in her own voice surprised her. "Tell me now."

Iddina smiled. His yellow teeth were sharp and pointed, like a wolf's. "You'd better enjoy your last night with me . . ."

Last night? He knows! Oh, God—he knows! Somehow he had read her thoughts! That's why he still wore his weapon!

". . . because tomorrow I'm setting you free."

For a long moment Jerusha's heart seemed to stop beating. She must have misunderstood. She didn't speak his language very well. It had to be a mistake.

"What did you say?" she managed to whisper.

"You heard me—you're going free. Free, like a little birdie, to fly away to your nest."

Jerusha stifled a scream. He was lying. It was a trick, a horrible, cruel joke. He would never set her free. Somehow he had discovered her plan and had invented this deception to stop her from doing it. The ringing in her ears grew so loud she could hardly stand it. Then slowly, with almost deliberate boredom, Iddina removed his belt and lay the dagger beside the sleeping mat. The polished handle gleamed. At last it was within her reach. All she had to do was grab it. But what if Iddina told the truth? What if tomorrow morning, for whatever reason, she would really go free?

Iddina stroked her cheek with his rough hand. "Why are you so serious, my pretty dog? Doesn't my news make you happy?" She shook her head. "Why not? Would you rather stay here with me?"

Jerusha's stomach rolled over in revulsion. Unwillingly, she glanced at the dagger, assuring herself that it was still there. "I don't believe you'd really set me free," she said.

Without warning, Iddina's fist slammed into her face, and she tumbled backward into the side of the tent. She lay stunned, her face throbbing with pain. "How dare you call me a liar?" He raised his fist again.

"No! I—I'm sorry—" She could barely force her aching jaw to move. "I didn't mean it that way—I only wondered why. Why are you setting me free?"

Iddina lowered his arm and studied her as if debating whether or not to tell her. "Because you're going to help me earn a promotion, you stupid dog." He offered no further explanation as he grabbed her by the arm and pulled her toward him.

Hours later, Jerusha lay in the darkness thinking about his words, wondering what he had meant by them, wondering what to do. Iddina finally slept beside her, and his knife lay beyond him if she still wanted to use it. It was time to carry out her plan. But suppose he had told her the truth? Suppose she would really know freedom again in a few short hours? She lay awake throughout most of the long night, wondering what Iddina had meant and what she should do.

Then, as the eastern sky began to grow light and the snarling jackals crawled away to their lairs, Jerusha realized that the slim thread of hope Iddina had dangled before her had been enough to hold onto. Her will to survive had come tentatively to life again. She would live for one more day.

———◈———

Jerimoth paused in his labors and leaned against his hoe, watching another caravan of refugees rumble down the road past his land. He counted four—five—six carts loaded with tools and children and household goods, and six weary farmers and their wives, trudging alongside.

Then Jerimoth gripped his hoe once again and attacked the weeds sprouting in his garden plot. He no longer bothered to cross his fields to the roadside to talk to the passing travelers. He would hear the same story from these refugees that he had heard from all the others during the past few weeks: the Assyrians were mobilizing to invade Israel. Everyone was fleeing to escape, some to the fortified capital of Samaria, others leaving Israel altogether, going south to the nation of Judah. If he spoke to them, they would urge him to join them, to escape while he still had a chance.

As his nation writhed in a state of upheaval, Jerimoth watched the quiet days of planting and reaping on his ancient plot of land draw to a close. Like a tremor before the earthquake, the masses of refugees would soon be followed by an even greater horde. No hope remained for Israel. Jerimoth would have to decide what to do. He was born on this land, and if he stayed he would probably die here as well.

Eventually the mournful caravan passed, but then in the trailing wake of dust Jerimoth spotted a solitary figure walking slowly up the road from the south. He watched as the figure drew near, then recognized his younger brother Saul. He hurried over to the well to meet him and drew a fresh bucket of water.

"Ah, thank you," Saul said wearily. He held the drinking gourd awkwardly between his right hand and the ugly stump of his left. With his thirst quenched, he tilted his dusty head back and poured water over it. Jerimoth guessed why Saul had come. They stood in silence, neither of them in a hurry to begin this conversation.

Finally Saul gulped more water, then wiped his lips. "We can't wait any longer, Jerimoth. We have to leave before it's too late."

"Just one more week."

"You said that last week and the week before. Now we can't wait any longer." He rubbed his stump nervously as he talked.

"But Jerusha—maybe she—"

"No! Jerusha is dead. Don't you realize that yet?"

He didn't reply. It was what Eliakim insisted as well, but Jerimoth didn't believe it. He knew she was alive. He knew it.

Saul sighed heavily as if tired of repeating this useless conversation. "Listen—the Assyrians will kill us, too, if we don't get out soon and go someplace safe."

"But how will Jerusha ever find me again if—"

Saul didn't wait for Jerimoth to finish. With a weary groan, he turned and walked up the little rise to Jerimoth's house. Hodesh came to the door to meet him.

"We can't wait any longer," Saul told her. "Please make him listen to reason, Hodesh."

"Take my wife and daughter with you, then," Jerimoth said, following Saul up the hill to the house. "I've decided to wait here for Jerusha."

"Even if the Assyrians have Jerusha, even if she's still alive, how could you possibly rescue her? Be reasonable, will you? Think about it. There are thousands and thousands of them."

"God has promised—"

"Enough! I've heard it all before. Now it's time to flee to safety. Come with me and save what's left of your family!"

Jerimoth didn't reply, torn between his concern for Hodesh and Maacah and his fear that Jerusha would return to an empty house.

"Yes or no?" Saul said. "For heaven's sake, don't you know enough to give up?"

"How can I give up on my daughter?"

"I lost both of my daughters! You still have one left! Don't you want to save her?"

Maacah suddenly appeared out of the shadows of the darkened house and wrapped her thin arms around Jerimoth's waist. She was almost 15 and rapidly approaching womanhood, but she remained slender and wraithlike.

"We can't go yet, Abba. We have to wait for Jerusha."

Saul groaned and gestured in defeat. "Listen—I'll wait two more days, Jerimoth. Two days, but that's all. Whether Jerusha comes home or not, we must leave in two days. That'll give you plenty of time to load everything and meet me in Dabbasheth."

"Yes. Yes. All right." Jerimoth tugged on his beard as he looked into his brother's sorrowful eyes. "Have you thought about where we should go?"

"We have to get out of Israel. Even Samaria won't be safe if the Assyrians attack. I think we should go south to Judah."

"I have friends there—Hilkiah the merchant and his son. Maybe they can help us resettle out in the countryside."

"Yes, you've spoken of Hilkiah before. It's a good plan." Saul reached out to stroke Maacah's cheek tenderly as she stood with her arms around her father. "I miss my girls," he whispered. Then his eyes met Jerimoth's as he pleaded with him: "Two days, Jerimoth. If you don't come to Dabbasheth in two days, I'll have to leave without you."

As the first rays of daylight seeped through the seams of the tent, Iddina stirred in his sleep, then sat up. In one swift movement he reached for his dagger and strapped it to his waist, and Jerusha knew that her chance to die quickly had passed. Exhaustion numbed her. She had stayed awake most of the night, wondering what Iddina's words meant, trying to imagine why he would set her free.

Now she rose from her pallet and began preparing the morning meal, grinding grain into flour and kneading the sticky dough. She felt dazed, and her bruised jaw ached from where he had struck her. A great flurry of activity swept through the camp as the army prepared to march toward Israel, but Jerusha barely noticed. The tantalizing prospect of freedom danced through her mind as she watched the round, flat loaves of bread bake on the fire stones. Perhaps Iddina had invented this lie as more of the warfare the Assyrians loved to wage in their victims' minds. It was their cruelest form of torture. Jerusha steeled herself for disappointment, vowing not to let Iddina see her suffer because of his lies.

When the meal was ready, Jerusha helped Marah spread the mat on the ground beneath the tree and lay out the officers' food. Then she squatted beside it, fanning away the black flies that hovered everywhere. As Iddina and the other officers approached, Jerusha saw them laughing and whispering behind their hands and casting odd glances at her.

Marah stopped swatting flies, and her hand froze in mid-air. "They're plotting something," she said. "Something evil."

Jerusha's heart pounded in her chest as if trying to escape, but she determined not to let them see her fear—or her hope. The officers sat down, and as Jerusha placed Iddina's food in front of him, he grabbed her roughly by the wrist.

"Are you ready to fly away, my little bird?" he grinned.

Jerusha nearly cried aloud. Abba had always called her his happy little bird. How dare Iddina use those words? She swallowed back her hatred and stared down at her bare feet. "Yes, my lord—I'm ready," she said.

Iddina and the others burst into loud, mocking laughter, and Jerusha felt a sob rising in her chest. Iddina had lied. They would never set her free. She should have died last night while she had the chance. She looked up at him.

"Go pack your things then, little bird," Iddina said, gesturing toward her tent. "Soon it will be time to fly." One of the officers muttered something, and they all laughed again. Why did they torment her like this? Why tantalize her with the hope of freedom if they had no intention of granting it? They were masters of torture, delighting in their game.

Jerusha fled into her tent to avoid their mocking stares, then looked around, wondering what to pack. This was part of their game too, to force her to get ready and then laugh at her again. Besides, what did she have to pack? She owned only the coarse, shapeless dress she wore and the tattered blanket that had once swaddled her daughter. But she knew they would force her to play their sadistic game to the end.

She carefully unfolded the blanket and wrapped some food inside it: yesterday's bread, a chunk of cheese, a cake of dates, some dried smoked meat, a handful of figs, a small skin of water. It was enough to last three or four days, a week if she rationed it. Then she stepped outside again to face her tormentors. They were no longer laughing. They were arguing fiercely.

"Do you want to part with even more of your precious gold?" Iddina shouted.

"Make the stakes as high as you want, Iddina. But if you wager it all, you'll lose it all!"

"Then I'll raise your bet! Because I know I won't lose!" Iddina turned to face Jerusha. "Isn't that right, my pretty one? You're my little good-luck charm, aren't you?"

Then the men rose to their feet and led Jerusha down through the encampment to where the infantry divisions had their tents. In a gruesome procession, the officers spent the next half hour parading her before their assembled ranks.

Confused and disoriented, Jerusha couldn't imagine what cruel game they were playing. She felt thousands of cold, black eyes studying her, examining her, as if trying to memorize her face. Then all at once it made sense, and Jerusha nearly cried aloud at the terrible realization of what they had planned: they were setting her free to hunt her down again. She was the object of their wagers. Whichever officer recaptured her would probably receive the promotion Iddina had mentioned last night.

Jerusha felt herself sinking in cold, black waters. They would pursue her, track her down for sport like a wild animal, then take her captive again. How long could she hope to stay free with four divisions of Assyrian infantrymen following her, searching for her? She wanted to scream. Why hadn't she ended her life last night as she had planned? Why hadn't she realized that Iddina would plot something horrible? Didn't she know that mercy played no part in his vicious nature? But before she could recover from her shock at what they were doing to her, they reached the edge of the camp, and the main road that led south toward Israel.

Iddina gave her a rough shove into the middle of the road. "Go on, little birdie! Fly away home! I found you the first time, and I can find you again."

She turned to face him, longing to throw herself at his feet and beg him not to do this to her, but he grinned like a wolf and flapped his arms crying, "Fly! Fly! You're free, little birdie! You've got fire, my pretty one, and a strong will to live. I know you'll provide a good hunt."

The watching soldiers dissolved into laughter at his words. As if in a daze, Jerusha turned and stumbled blindly down the road, clutching her bundle to her breast as the sound of their laughter rang in her ears. Running was useless. She wasn't free from them, and she never would be. She would wander through an unknown land alone and barefoot while they pursued her with chariots and horses and thousands and thousands of men. She wanted to sink down in the dust and wait for them to come for her, refusing to play their sadistic game. But she knew Iddina would be furious, and he would torture her without mercy. She had to play along.

The Assyrians wouldn't break camp and follow her for a few more hours, but once they did, Jerusha knew the well-disciplined soldiers could travel at an exhausting pace. She could never outrun them. Why should she try? She had no reason to keep walking, except that Iddina expected her to, and so she plodded hopelessly on, not caring where the road led.

Jerusha had walked for more than an hour, never once looking back, when suddenly she became aware of a deep, eerie stillness all around her. The strangeness of it made her stop. For the first time in years she no longer heard the low rumble of the army camp, the raucous cries of the vultures, the dying moans of the condemned. Instead, in the echoing silence, she heard the hum of bees and insects, the sweet chirp of songbirds, the soft swish of the wind as it brushed through the treetops. She hadn't heard those sounds in such a long time that they seemed like music to her.

Jerusha sank down in the middle of the road to listen as tears streamed down her face. She drew a deep breath and smelled the magnificent fragrance of the earth—clean and fresh, free from the stench of smoke and rottenness and death. Dazzling colors replaced the black she had grown so accustomed to—the deep velvety blue of the sky, the rich green of the trees and waving grasses, the snowy white of billowing clouds, the mauve and scarlet of dainty wildflowers. Jerusha had forgotten that such a beautiful world existed. This was freedom, and this was torture. They would let her taste it and smell it for a while, then snatch it from her again.

"No!" she cried aloud. "Never!" If only she could call upon God for help, if only He would deliver her. But Jerusha knew there was no God. He hadn't answered her other prayers, and if she wanted freedom she would have to win it herself. Suddenly she realized how desperately she wanted to remain free. She wanted to beat Iddina at his game or die trying. She hated him, hated what he had done to her, and she vowed that no matter what, she would never return with him to that hell.

Jerusha scrambled to her feet, her heart pounding with determination. She must get away from him, but how? The chariots and horses would overtake her first. Her only hope was to leave the road and climb the rocky hillsides where the horses and chariots couldn't follow. Immediately she left the road and began blindly running and stumbling across the rugged terrain toward the safety of the steep hills and barren rocks. She imagined Iddina crouching by the side of the road, studying her trail as it cut toward the foothills, and smiling to himself. She hadn't disappointed him.

"All right, Iddina," she said fiercely. "You'll have your hunt."

———◈———

King Hezekiah sat in his private chambers with Shebna, reading the daily reports. The sun had set more than an hour ago, and his servants lit all the oil lamps, moving the tall bronze stands closer to him for more light. Reading the tiny lettering made Hezekiah's head ache, and when Shebna handed him a scroll with a long list of numbers, he leaned back and closed his eyes.

"Read it to me, Shebna."

"It is a report on the wheat harvest, Your Majesty, with record-breaking figures once again."

"Enough to export and trade?"

"More than enough. More than last year."

Hezekiah opened his eyes and leaned forward, scanning the list with growing excitement. "That's three years in a row! Think of the goods we can import with profits like these!"

"Our economy continues to prosper, my lord."

"Yes, and do you know why?"

"Certainly. It prospers because of your brilliant economic policies. First you won back valuable farmland where most of this surplus is grown, then you decided not to pay tribute to—"

"That's not why, Shebna."

"I know—I know—you are going to say it was because of your God."

"How else could we conquer that territory when the Philistine army outnumbered our inexperienced troops 10 to 1? And all that farmland would be worthless without rain to make the crops grow. You hold the proof right in your hands, of how God has blessed this land since we renewed our covenant with Him, and you still refuse to believe it?"

"I am sorry, Your Majesty."

"But the evidence is so clear!"

"I interpret the evidence differently than you do."

Hezekiah's head pounded painfully, but he continued to argue, frustrated by Shebna's stubbornness. "How do you interpret it?"

"You are a bold, decisive leader, willing to take enormous risks, such as attacking the Philistines and rebelling against Assyria, and your risks have reaped astounding benefits."

"If I didn't know you better, I'd say you were trying to flatter me."

"Not true."

"Then how did my bold leadership bring three years of abundant rainfall and cause the crops and herds to multiply in record-breaking numbers?"

"I would have to evaluate the rainfall in nations that have not served your God and examine their crop yields before I would be willing to eliminate the possibility of a coincidence."

Hezekiah sighed and rubbed his tired eyes. "Time to quit, Shebna."

"Have I offended you, Your Majesty?"

"The question is—have you offended God?"

Shebna appeared unconcerned. "Shall I read you this next report, Your Majesty?"

"No, I really want to quit for the day."

"So early? Are you unwell?"

"Just very tired, and this headache is making it difficult to concentrate."

"Well—there is one more issue that I have been wanting to discuss with you for some time."

"Is it important?"

"Yes. It is of vital importance."

Hezekiah closed his eyes. "Go ahead, then."

"The potential for a crisis in our nation is growing worse now that the Assyrian army has invaded Israel. They are only 150 miles from our borders, and—"

"I'm very aware of that fact."

"—and they may invade our nation next. I would strongly advise you to organize a defensive treaty with some of our neighbors. No single nation can mobilize an army the size of Assyria's, but if we formed an alliance—"

"Shebna, are you forgetting that Israel attempted to do that very thing, which is why the Assyrians are invading them?"

"We would be more subtle about it than they were, Your Majesty." He smiled slightly and folded his arms across his chest, looking very pleased with himself.

Hezekiah exhaled wearily. "What are you talking about?"

"As you know, we already have trade agreements with all our neighbors—"

"Yes—so what?"

"So, the foundation for a military alliance is already in place. The diplomatic ties, the network of roads, the economic interdependence and cooperation—they are all there. I am only suggesting that we take those trade agreements one step further."

"How?"

"By establishing family links."

Hezekiah glared at Shebna. "You're talking about marrying the daughters of foreign kings, aren't you?"

"Just consider it for a moment, Your Majesty. Suppose you married Pharaoh's daughter; if the Assyrians threatened Jerusalem, he would send his armies here to defend her and his grandsons."

"Shebna, I'm ruling this nation by God's Law, and that Law says the king should have only one wife. I won't even discuss marrying another one."

"Just a minute, please. I have reread that passage, Your Majesty, and it says, 'the king must not take *many* wives.' It does not limit you to one."

"But I remember copying that portion with my grandfather. I'm sure he told me it meant *one* wife."

"It says *many*. You may read it for yourself. Even King Solomon formed an alliance by marrying Pharaoh's daughter."

"Yes, and it led to his ruin. Did you read that part too?"

Shebna's calm facade began to crumble. "Your Majesty, international politics are very complex. Marriage alliances are a modern necessity. You cannot govern this nation with a set of laws that are a thousand years old."

"I can and I will."

"But—"

"Foreign wives bring foreign gods with them, Shebna. They encourage their sons, *my* sons, to worship those gods. How would Pharaoh respond if I refused to let his daughter worship Isis or Ra or any of her other idols? I won't do it!"

"If you refuse to marry a foreign king's daughter, it might collapse the whole agreement. And the day may come when you will need the support of your neighbors."

"Well, you'll have to find another way to win their support, because I won't do it."

The throbbing pain in Hezekiah's head seemed worse than before. Shebna stood abruptly and gathered his scrolls and tablets in icy silence, his dark eyes brooding. Then he stopped and looked up at Hezekiah in stubborn anger.

"I am sorry. But I still do not understand your refusal. I do not see how the Torah would be violated."

Hezekiah faced him with a steady gaze, carefully controlling his own anger. "This may come as a great surprise to you, Shebna, but I love my wife very much. I don't want to marry anyone else— not for Pharaoh, not for politics, not even for pleasure. I don't care if the Torah grants me a hundred wives."

Shebna looked away. "I see. However, I doubt that there are many kings in the world who would agree with you."

"You're probably right about that, Shebna. I doubt it too."

19 ◄—

For hours Jerusha trailed through the rocky underbrush until her feet bled, yet the mocking foothills appeared no closer than when she first left the road and started toward them. By noon the sun blazed in the sky, a fiery enemy determined to defeat her. The skin of water was already half empty and she desperately needed a drink, but the bleak, arid countryside offered no water. It seemed useless to go on. She could never survive out here.

Dizzy and nauseated from the heat, she rested for only a moment and made sure she still headed south, then plodded forward. She could no longer see the road, but she kept the sun's rising point on her left and setting point on her right, knowing that would take her in the right direction. Occasionally she nibbled on some of the food for strength, rationing it carefully.

By dusk, a gradual upward slope in the terrain told her she had finally reached the foothills. She could no longer see the mountains through the thick forest ahead of her. She yearned to lie down, to close her eyes and sleep, but she forced herself to keep going. Her enemies would stop at night, but every hour that she walked put more distance between them and her.

Shortly after dark she stumbled upon a shallow stream trickling down the rocky slopes of the mountain, and she sank down beside it to drink. With her thirst quenched, she refilled her water skin, then sat for several minutes soaking her tired feet, searching for a way to carry more water. Her exhausted mind found no solution. Her eyes burned with the need to sleep, her legs trembled with fatigue, but she thought of Iddina and scrambled to her feet. She glanced behind her, half expecting to see him, and saw her own trail of crushed weeds winding through the thick brush. Iddina could follow her tracks effortlessly.

146

"Oh, no!"

Her voice seemed to echo like a thunderclap through the silent woods. An inner voice of fear and despair urged Jerusha to quit. She could never escape from Iddina. She may as well give up. But another voice, just as clear, urged her to go on. She had given in to fear before, choosing to live as a slave, but now something more powerful than fear motivated her—hatred. She would rather die than help Iddina win his evil wager, rather collapse from hunger and exhaustion than return with him to hell on earth.

Jerusha sloshed into the frigid water. It would hide her tracks and if she waded ashore carefully, she might lose him. She made slow progress in the knee-deep water and the rocky stream bed bruised the soles of her feet.

Near midnight, when her feet were numb with cold, Jerusha began shivering uncontrollably. She stopped to rest on a large boulder, swaddling her icy feet in her blanket, hugging her knees to her chest. Bears and lions no doubt roamed these mountain heights, but Jerusha felt strangely unafraid. No savage animal seemed as fierce and brutal as Iddina. At least she would die free.

As sleep bore down on her, Jerusha stood and trudged on. She had to reach the top of the mountain before dawn; they might spot her on the barren upper slopes once daylight came. She waded into the icy water again, following the stream until the current grew too swift. Then, choosing a rocky bank to hide her trail, she abandoned the stream to climb the craggy slope to the summit. As the eastern sky grew light, she struggled over the jagged rocks, her hands and feet bloody and aching. Then, as the pale stars faded, she reached the summit and scrambled over the top, out of sight. She had done it!

Weeping with joy and pain, Jerusha collapsed among the rocks. She had accomplished much more than scaling a mountain. She had conquered a private mountain as well, climbing out of the emotionless wasteland she had inhabited so long, feeling joy and victory for the first time since giving birth. Even her pain told her she was alive again, not one of Iddina's lifeless possessions.

But as the sun burned away the morning haze, Jerusha glimpsed the terrain that lay ahead. Her triumph evaporated in defeat. She had merely scaled one of the foothills; a huge ridge of mountains loomed ahead, directly south. She couldn't possibly climb them.

Tears blurred her vision as she gazed at the cruel peaks blocking the path to freedom. If she returned to the road to find a mountain pass, she would never escape the horse patrols. But how else could she navigate such forbidding terrain? Despairingly, she counted the layers of mountains she would have to traverse. Then, on the farthest peak, Jerusha spotted a patch of white. She leaped to her feet, squinting at the horizon, then cried for joy. It was Mount Hermon!

Back home she could see the snowy peak on a clear day. Abba said Mount Hermon was the only mountain in Israel with snow. Fear argued that she was wrong, that it wasn't Mount Hermon, that she couldn't walk that far. But glimpsing the familiar landmark had renewed her hope.

Jerusha clambered down the rocky slope toward home. Descending seemed harder than ascending as Jerusha's aching legs continually buckled on the steep gradient, but she persevered, yearning to remain free, to go home. Three times the pitiless sun sank beneath the horizon on her right and three times it quickly rose to become her enemy again, blazing in a cloudless sky, sucking moisture from her body until her tongue swelled and her lips cracked. She rested or slept only minutes at a time, then struggled to her feet to push on, never looking back.

On the fifth day she spotted a road, threading out of the foothills, crossing a broad valley, then disappearing into the steep mountain range ahead of her. She sat down to eat her last bite of food and to decide what to do. Traveling would be easier on the road, but what if it was the same road she had left days ago? Then her exhausting journey through the wilderness would have been in vain. They would find her again. Fatigue turned her limbs to lead, and she had crossed only the first ridge. Rows of steep mountains still stood between her and Mount Hermon's snowy peak. If it *was* Mount Hermon.

Suddenly a flicker of movement on the distant road caught Jerusha's eye. *The Assyrians.* Somehow they had overtaken her, even though she had walked nonstop. Motionless, she strained to watch the tiny figures and saw splashes of color instead of black. Then she noticed the slowly plodding camels: a caravan.

Tears of relief sprang to her eyes, and without thinking, Jerusha ran down the slope toward the road, tripping and stumbling, exhausting her last reserve of strength. She must reach them. They would help her get home.

But by the time Jerusha staggered onto the road, the caravan had disappeared. The flaming sun, now at its zenith, made her nauseated. Disappointment and fatigue left her defeated. Her food and water were gone. She couldn't will her quivering legs to take another step. She crawled under a clump of bushes along the side of the road to rest, to think, to escape the blinding sun for a moment. Then she would go on. But her eyes drifted closed in total exhaustion, and she collapsed into a deep, dreamless sleep. She awoke hours later to the sound of breathing. She focused on a dark figure bending over her—a face, a bushy beard, a pair of dark eyes.

Jerusha screamed.

———◆———

Jerimoth watched as Hodesh folded their bedding and tied it to the loaded cart outside their door. The family had eaten breakfast in silence, and when Maacah finished washing the dishes she added them to the cart as well. Jerimoth gazed up the deserted road again, then reluctantly led his team of oxen from the stable and hitched them to the cart. For the past two days his agonized wait for Jerusha had been unbearable. He couldn't sleep or eat, and his eyes ached from the strain of watching for her. Day and night he had never stopped pleading with God for her safe return. But when she hadn't returned by the third day, he knew his brother wouldn't wait any longer.

Jerimoth looked north one final time. The pale dawn sky was clear, and the snowy peak of Mount Hermon perched on the horizon. It was time to go. They had to flee Israel. But Jerimoth knew he could never leave. He couldn't abandon Jerusha.

Tears slowly coursed down his face as he turned to his wife. "Hodesh, listen to me. Take Maacah and go with Saul. I can't go without Jerusha." Hodesh didn't move or speak. "Saul will take you to Jerusalem, where you'll both be safe. Hilkiah will look after you until Jerusha and I come."

Hodesh touched Jerimoth's cheek. "I'm not going anywhere without you. Saul can take Maacah to Jerusalem, but I'm staying with you."

Jerimoth looked at his wife's determined face and knew it was useless to argue with her. He drew her into his arms. "All right Hodesh. All right." His voice was thick with emotion. "I'll take Maacah into town so she can go with Saul."

"Abba, no! Don't make me go with Uncle Saul—please!"

"Your mother and I will come later, with Jerusha."

"I want to wait for her too! Please don't break our family apart again. Please, Abba!"

Jerimoth groaned and leaned against the cart, praying that Jerusha would miraculously appear and end the agonizing choice he faced. He understood the danger of remaining in Israel as the Assyrians marched closer, and he longed to send his wife and daughter to safety. But he didn't know how to force them to go against their will. Nor could he leave without Jerusha. The decision overwhelmed him.

As Jerimoth wrestled with his dilemma, Maacah quietly unloaded her bedding and an armload of cooking pots from the cart and carried them into the house. Hodesh watched their daughter disappear through the door, then picked up the bedroll she and Jerimoth shared and followed her inside.

On the horizon another caravan of refugees rumbled down the road from the north, and Jerimoth watched in mournful silence as they streamed past his land—six wagons—seven—eight. He counted 19 children perched on towering loads, carried on shoulders or walking wearily alongside. Then, as the caravan disappeared into the trailing cloud of dust, Jerimoth unhitched his team of oxen and led them out to pasture.

—◆—

Jerusha scrambled backward through the bushes, scratching her arms on the branches, desperate to escape from the man bending over her. But instead of pursuing her, he offered her a cup of water. He was her father's age and was dressed in a homespun tunic and sandals. His brown eyes seemed kind, and he spoke soothingly, as if to a frightened animal, but Jerusha couldn't understand what he said.

Her mouth and throat felt parched, and suddenly she didn't care what he did to her. She gulped the warm water greedily, then glanced up at him again. He extended his palm, offering a handful of dates. Jerusha's stomach ached from hunger; she devoured the sweet fruit.

"Thank you," she murmured.

He looked surprised. "Israel?" he asked, pointing to her.

"Yes, I'm from Israel."

He beckoned to her, then walked toward the road. Jerusha slowly rose to her feet and saw that he traveled alone with a cart and a team of oxen. When he reached them, he beckoned again, then pointed to the cart. What did he want with her?

Jerusha considered all the possibilities from slavery to rape, then realized that he couldn't do anything to her that hadn't already been done. Even if he killed her, she would still escape from the Assyrians. Besides, his cart headed south. With nothing to lose, Jerusha walked toward the road.

But the sun felt so hot, her legs so weary, that the earth began to sway, and she collapsed a few feet from the road. The stranger hurried over and gently lifted her into the cart. He flicked his short whip over the oxen, and the cart jolted down the road with Jerusha's new captor walking alongside it. Before long, the warm sun and slowly swaying cart rocked her into an exhausted sleep.

The sun hung low in the afternoon sky when she awoke. Furrowed fields and vineyards dotted the rolling hills beside the road, but the country appeared deserted and strangely quiet. The Assyrians were coming. Everyone had fled. As the oxen plodded sluggishly down the road, Jerusha silently begged the cumbersome beasts to move faster.

She studied the stranger as he walked patiently beside them. She thought of him as her captor even though he hadn't taken her by force. His clothing and features were not Israeli, and Jerusha guessed from his deep tan and brawny shoulders that he was a farmer or a laborer. Why had he helped her? What did he want with her? And what would happen if she tried to run away from him now? But Jerusha was much too tired to run, much too grateful for a chance to ride, even if the pace was maddeningly slow.

The snow-capped mountain loomed closer now, and although she couldn't be certain, it did resemble the familiar peak of Mount Hermon. Once, when the man turned around, Jerusha pointed to it, asking, "Is that Mount Hermon?" But he shrugged and shook his head, muttering in a language she didn't understand. She tried saying a few words in the Assyrian tongue, but he didn't understand that either.

Who was he? Why did he travel this road all alone when everyone else had obviously fled before the approaching Assyrians? As the sun set, the stranger led the oxen down a side road to a tiny village tucked between the shadowy hills. Its thin walls would be pitifully inadequate against the Assyrian battering rams. Inside, the streets were nearly deserted, no oil lamps glowed through the shutters of the houses, no smoke rose from the hearths.

Jerusha knew what the Assyrians would do to this village, and she wanted to run through the streets and warn the remaining inhabitants to flee for their lives. But they spoke a language she didn't understand, nor did they understand hers. When the huge iron gates swung shut for the night, Jerusha felt trapped.

"Wait! Let me out," she cried, but no one listened. She didn't want to stay locked in this village, even for one night. But once they had barred the gates she was their prisoner. Trembling, Jerusha followed the stranger through the narrow, twisting streets. She hadn't been in a town since she had been captured, and the houses and walls seemed about to tumble in on her, suffocating her. She would never be able to sleep in one of these terrifying buildings.

But her captor led her to the open market square, which was tightly shuttered and deserted except for a few weary travelers like themselves. He unhitched his oxen to feed and water them, then prepared a simple meal, offering half to Jerusha. When she finished, the stranger gave her his heavy cloak and prepared a bed for her in the cart while he slept on the ground nearby, protecting her.

Why was he doing this? What did he want in return? He reminded Jerusha of her father, and suddenly she realized that if Abba had found a hungry stranger, lost and alone, he would help her too, expecting nothing in return. Could it be that simple?

Jerusha lay awake for a long time, staring at the starry sky, weeping in wonder at the stranger's unexplainable kindness until she fell into a fitful sleep.

20

Eliakim touched the mezuzah on the doorpost, absently performing the ritual before entering his house. Inside, his father paced anxiously, head bowed, hands tightly clasped, lips moving in silent prayer. As Eliakim entered, he looked up.

"There you are, at last! Any news?"

"News? About Jerimoth, you mean?" Exhaustion numbed Eliakim and slowed his thoughts. He stumbled to a bench and sank down.

"Yes—have you heard anything?"

"No, Abba. No news."

"Jerimoth wasn't with this latest group of refugees?"

"I didn't see him. But there are so many of them." Eliakim sighed and bent to untie his sandals.

"God of Abraham, keep our friends safe!" Hilkiah's face looked strained, with no trace of his usual merry humor. He twisted his fingers as he paced the length of the room again, then stopped when he glanced at Eliakim. "What happened to you, Son?"

"What do you mean?"

"You look like you've been run over by a caravan."

"I feel like it too." He slumped against the wall and closed his eyes. "I've never worked so hard in my life, Abba. And the refugees still keep pouring in. Israel must be deserted by now. We're running out of room to house them all."

"King Hezekiah must know you're capable, Son, or he wouldn't have placed you in charge of such a big project."

"I don't think he realized it was going to be this big when we started. None of us did. We're building permanent housing for them as fast as we can, but we can't keep up with the demand."

"You look exhausted. Why don't you wash up and rest a bit before the evening sacrifice?"

"Sounds wonderful." Eliakim gripped his father's hand and pulled himself to his feet. Carrying his sandals, he went out to their courtyard to bathe in the mikveh. The cool water rejuvenated him, and after changing into clean clothes, Eliakim felt refreshed and hungry.

As he entered the house, a servant met him. "There's a stranger at the gate asking for your father."

"Did he say what he wanted?"

"No, my lord. But he looks like one of those refugees."

"Where's Abba?"

"He's still resting."

"Let the stranger in quietly and don't wake my father, or we'll probably be stuck with a houseful of strangers for dinner."

Eliakim stood in front of a bronze mirror and smoothed down his curly wet hair as he waited. The servant returned shortly, followed by a bewildered-looking man in ragged clothing and blistered, dirt-caked feet. Eliakim had labored to resettle and house thousands of refugees the past weeks, and here stood another one. He was glad that Hilkiah still slept.

"I am Eliakim, son of Hilkiah," he said just above a whisper. "How can I help you?"

The stranger's mouth opened but no sound came out. He stared at Eliakim, then glanced around the luxurious room and backed up a few steps as if he had made a terrible mistake and come to the wrong house. Eliakim looked him over, then gaped in shock when he saw that the stranger's left hand had been amputated.

The man thrust his hand behind his back. "I—I'm sorry."

"No, forgive me. I was rude to stare. Please, have a seat."

"I can't stay. I'm sorry for bothering you, my lord. I—I never would have come if I had known—I mean, my brother never told me—" He glanced around the room nervously, and Eliakim began to lose patience.

"Told you what? Who's your brother?"

"I saw you today in the refugee camp, my lord. You're King Hezekiah's representative, aren't you?"

"Yes, that's right." The man edged toward the door. "Forgive me for troubling you. Jerimoth never mentioned that you were a man of such importance."

Eliakim forgot about his sleeping father. "Jerimoth! Is he here with you?"

"No, my lord—"

"Well, where is he, then?"

"He's still in Israel."

"*No!* Why hasn't he left? Doesn't he realize he's in danger?"

"I begged him to leave, my lord. Then I waited for him as long as I possibly could, but he wouldn't come with me."

"What about his family—Hodesh and Maacah?"

"I offered to bring them with me, but they wouldn't leave without him."

Eliakim saw Jerimoth's features mirrored in his brother's mournful face. He remembered the story of the day the Assyrians captured Jerusha and how Jerimoth's brother had lost his hand attempting to save his daughters. When he imagined Jerimoth and his family enduring another brutal invasion he was overwhelmed. He stumbled to the seat he had offered his guest and sank down.

"Go wake my father," he told the servant; then he looked at the stranger again. "I'm sorry—what's your name, my friend?"

"Saul. I—I'm from the village of Dabbasheth. Jerimoth is my older brother." He massaged his stump nervously as he talked. "Jerimoth inherited our father's ancestral land, and so I became—I was—a potter, by trade." He hid his hand behind his back.

"Don't return to the refugee camp, Saul. You're welcome to stay here as our guest. We'll be eating dinner in a little while, and I'm sure my father will want to talk to you. He's been worried about Jerimoth and his family. We're both very fond of them."

As Eliakim spoke, Hilkiah wandered into the room, blinking sleepily. "What—? Is there news of Jerimoth?"

"Abba, this is Jerimoth's brother Saul."

Hilkiah gripped Saul's shoulders. "What's happened to him? Where is he?"

"Still in Israel, my lord—"

"But he's coming soon, isn't he? Tell me he's planning to get out of there!"

"I begged him to leave. I waited as long as I could. He—he wouldn't go."

"Why?" Eliakim cried. "Why won't he leave?"

Saul stared at the floor. "He's waiting for his daughter, my lord. He still thinks Jerusha's coming home."

"Oh no," Eliakim groaned. "How could he be such a *fool?*"

"Eliakim!" Hilkiah said sharply.

"I warned you, Abba! I tried to tell you not to encourage Jerimoth's hopes! I told you to make him see the truth but—"

"Saul, I'm sorry," Hilkiah said. "My son doesn't understand."

"My daughters are already dead, or maybe I would have stayed too. But we never found Jerusha, and that makes Jerimoth think she's still alive."

"I know, Saul. I know. But please forgive my son. He doesn't have children of his own. If he did he would understand why Jerimoth—" Hilkiah's voice broke. He swallowed hard. "He would understand the strength of a father's love for his child."

"I'm sorry—," Eliakim muttered.

"And if he understood that," Hilkiah continued, "he would understand why Jerimoth has faith in his Heavenly Father's love as well." He drew Saul into his embrace. "Ah, my poor friend. How you have suffered! Thank God you made it here. All we can do now is pray for your dear brother and his family." He released Saul as a shofar sounded from the Temple mount.

"They're announcing the evening sacrifice. Will you come with my son and me? We'll pray for their safe return."

Slowly, Eliakim rose to his feet. "I'm sorry, Abba, but I can't pray with you."

"*What?*"

"I can't pray that prayer. I don't believe it's possible for God to help Jerimoth and his family anymore."

—◈—

Thousands of stars sparkled in the sky when the man shook Jerusha awake. Terror prickled through her veins, and she bolted out of the cart, ready to run. But the stranger whispered soothingly as he yoked the oxen, telling her it was time to leave. The wagon wheels rumbled like thunder on the cobblestone street, and when Jerusha saw that the city gates stood open she sobbed with relief. Neither of them glanced back at the doomed village as they headed south once again. They traveled for an hour before the sun rose, then stopped to rest and to eat some dry bread and parched grain from the cart.

When they started down the road again, Jerusha felt restless and impatient with the oxen's lethargic pace. She had regained her strength and yearned to run ahead, knowing the Assyrians would quickly overtake the plodding oxen. Yet she was reluctant to leave this man who had saved her, as if she owed him loyalty in return for his kindness. He had not only provided food and rest, but he had been a bridge between the world of the Assyrians and a world of trust and compassion.

When they came to the top of a rise, she glanced anxiously over her shoulder. They were so close to the snow-capped mountain now that the foothills hid it from view. The road climbed steadily upward, and Jerusha walked to lighten the load. When the sun stood directly overhead and the roadbed burned beneath her bare feet, they reached a crossroad. The man headed toward the right fork, but Jerusha stopped, seeking her bearings from the sun, scanning the horizon for a glimpse of Mount Hermon.

The stranger halted his oxen and watched her, then tried to convince her to take the right fork by pointing and chattering. But his route headed west, toward the setting sun and the Great Sea; Jerusha's home lay down the other path to the south.

"Israel?" she asked, indicating the left fork.

He studied her gravely, and she saw his concern for her safety. Finally he nodded. But then he gestured to the way they had come and pleaded with her, jabbering urgently. Tears sprang to Jerusha's eyes as his compassion overwhelmed her.

"I know they're coming," she said. "But I want to go home, to Israel."

He gazed at her, biting his lip, then he turned and rummaged through his cart. Panicked, Jerusha had the urge to run, imagining that he would brandish a weapon and force her to stay with him. But a moment later he handed her a skin of water and her tattered blanket, filled with food.

The tears flowed silently down her face. She wanted to thank him but didn't know how. She didn't even know his name. He mumbled something as he pushed the provisions into her hands, and Jerusha felt the tender stirrings of love for the first time since her baby died.

"Thank you," she whispered. "Shalom."

He smiled sadly and raised his hand in a little wave. "Shalom." Then he snapped his whip, and his cart headed west, leaving Jerusha alone in the middle of the road.

21

When the morning sacrifice ended, Hezekiah lingered on the royal platform for a moment, reluctant to leave the atmosphere of worship that permeated the Temple. The stirring music and daily confession of his sins left him with a quiet sense of Yahweh's presence that he wished would last all day. It seldom did.

The Temple courtyards emptied slowly, crowded with refugees fleeing the Assyrian invasion. Their presence unsettled Hezekiah, making him question his decision to rebel against Assyria, and he wished he had his grandfather's unshakable faith in God. He sighed and started down the royal walkway to the palace.

"Your Majesty, wait! Please!" Eliakim sprinted toward him with his robes flapping in the wind and leaped over the barrier that separated the royal dais from the courtyard.

"Your Majesty—may I have a word with you, please?"

"This is neither the time nor the place, Eliakim. You may petition me at the palace through Shebna." He walked away, irritated at Eliakim's presumption, but Eliakim kept pace alongside.

"Please, Your Majesty. I've tried to go through the proper channels, but Shebna refused my request."

"Shebna has the authority to speak on my behalf. If he refused your request, then I can't help you." Hezekiah continued walking, hoping Eliakim would have the sense to retreat.

"But, Your Majesty, Shebna doesn't understand God's Law."

Hezekiah glanced at Shebna waiting in the Court of the Gentiles. He was watching them from behind the barrier he was forbidden to cross, and his dark face smoldered with rage.

"Is this matter worth risking my anger?" Hezekiah asked.

"Yes, my lord—that's why I did it this way. I'm sorry."

"Come with me, then." He led Eliakim down the royal walkway until they reached the Court of the Gentiles, then held up his hand, cautioning Shebna to remain silent while he spoke. "I'm going to hear your petition, Eliakim, only because you've worked hard and served me faithfully. Don't use this as an excuse to bypass Shebna in the future. I've already warned you that he has the authority to speak for me."

"I understand." Eliakim drew a deep breath and pushed his hair off his forehead. "Your Majesty, I would like to request more funds for the refugees. The money you've allotted for housing has run out. I submitted the request formally but—"

"I refused," Shebna said. "And I will continue to refuse it."

"But the flood of immigrants hasn't even begun to crest! They're pouring in by the thousands, every day, and they need housing and food and—"

"It is not in the economic interests of our nation to spend any more funds on the refugees," Shebna said.

"But it is! These people will become assets to our economy!"

Shebna gestured to the outer court, where a ragged knot of refugees begged alms from the Judeans as they filed through the Temple gates. "These are not assets," Shebna said. "They are worthless beggars looking for a free handout."

"They wouldn't have to beg if you'd give me the funds to help them!" Eliakim turned to plead with Hezekiah. "Your Majesty, they're forced to beg because they're desperate. But most of them were once farmers or potters or tanners or other craftsmen. They'd be willing to work if we gave them a chance."

Hezekiah watched as the refugees continued to beg, ignored by the wealthier Judeans. "What are you proposing, Eliakim?"

"Give me the funds to feed them and help them get a new start in our nation. I promise you they'll be willing to work for it."

Shebna exhaled angrily. "I have offered him government loans, Your Majesty, but he refused them. He wants a free handout. I did everything I could short of making these people a huge financial drain on our nation, but it was not enough for him. That is why I refused to pass his request on to you."

"Wait a minute," Hezekiah said. "Let me get this straight. If you requested funds, Eliakim, why did you refuse the loans?"

"Because they violate the Torah."

"And I suppose you are also an expert on the Law, as well as an engineer?" Shebna asked.

Eliakim grinned sheepishly. "I should be an expert—my father has been quoting it to me all my life."

"Then how does accepting a loan violate the Law?"

"In the third Book of Moses it says that 'If one of your country-men becomes poor and is not able to support himself, help him so he can continue to live among you. Do not take interest of any type from him, but fear God—'"

"They are not our countrymen," Shebna interrupted.

"We're all sons of Abraham. And it also says 'If you lend money to one of my people who is needy, charge him no interest—'"

"That is absurd!"

"No, he's right," Hezekiah said. "The Torah says, 'For you were also slaves and the Lord redeemed you . . .'"

"But an interest-free loan is the same as a free handout! You know we will never see that money again."

"Yes, we will," Eliakim insisted. "The Torah says, 'If you fully obey the Lord your God and carefully follow all his commands . . . you will be blessed in the city and blessed in the country. However, if you do not obey the Lord your God, . . . all these curses will come upon you and overtake you—'"

"Enough," Hezekiah said. "I know the rest: 'cursed in the city . . . cursed in the country . . . your basket and your kneading trough will be cursed . . . ' and so on. I'm sorry to overrule your decision, Shebna, but he's right." Eliakim exhaled in relief, but Shebna's anger and humiliation smoldered dangerously.

"Continue your work with the refugees, Eliakim, and I'll see that arrangements are made for some interest-free loans."

"Thank you, Your Majesty. You won't regret it—I promise." Eliakim bowed and quickly disappeared.

All that day and late into the night, one question continued to nag at Hezekiah. What if Eliakim hadn't been willing to speak up for the refugees? What if he had given up after Shebna's refusal? By not helping his brethren, Hezekiah would have violated God's Law, and that worried him deeply. Shebna's decision seemed to make sense, and Hezekiah had agreed with it at first, but God's Law often disagreed with human reasoning. By ignoring that Law, Shebna could have triggered a disaster, and Hezekiah's confidence in him had been seriously shaken. As much as he hated to do it, Hezekiah would have to monitor Shebna's decisions to make sure this never happened again. Eliakim had risked a lot for the refugees' sake and had earned Hezekiah's respect. But as Hezekiah lay awake that night, he found that he envied Eliakim. The engineer's integrity and compassion sprang from a source that Hezekiah had never known—the loving discipline of a godly father.

Iddina crouched by the fork in the road and studied the footprints lightly etched in the dust. "It's her. I know it is." Three of Iddina's best trackers stood around him, observing him with cautious respect.

"Do you want one of us to keep following the oxcart, sir?"

"No. She turned south. A little birdie, flying home to her nest." He stood up, brushing the dust from his hands, and studied the rutted road until it disappeared behind a small rise. "An excellent hunt," he said. "She provided a good chase. But she's close to home now, and she's growing careless. This is almost too easy." He twisted his sandal in the dirt, erasing the delicate footprint.

As the sun bore down with relentless heat, Iddina strode over to his horse and untied a skin of water. He gulped noisily, then wiped his lips with the back of his hand.

"She made it farther than I thought she would, sir," one of the trackers said. "The way she started out that day, I figured we'd have her back by nightfall."

"She didn't surprise me. She has a strong will to live—though only the gods know why!" Iddina laughed, a rumbling, mirthless sound. "I wonder if my fellow officers have captured their pitiful village yet? They can sift through the rubble with a sieve, but they won't find her."

"Sir, with all those wagon tracks going in and out, how did you know she'd left the village?"

Iddina removed his dagger from his belt and held it in his teeth while he unwound his long, fringed sash and used it to wipe the sweat from his forehead. He glanced at the soldier who had asked the question, and the corners of his mouth curled up in a grin around the knife.

"Because I know her." He refastened his belt and tucked the weapon in place. "That's the first rule of any hunt—know your prey, what they would do, how they would think."

He stroked his lower lip as he studied his three trackers, pleased with their admiring gazes. "I know her," he repeated, "and she wouldn't like to be locked behind city walls."

Iddina mounted his horse in one swift, muscular leap, and the other men hurried to follow him. "We're close now—very close," he said. "Search inside every house and barn, under every rock and bush, until we get her back, understand?"

"Yes, sir."

"She's mine. She belongs to me. But when we find her you will all have a share."

———◆———

Jerimoth awoke before dawn and lay on his mat, listening. Something had jolted him awake. He had waited for so many years to hear Jerusha's soft footsteps on the dusty road that he had imagined them many times. Was he imagining them now? He raised up on his elbows and cocked his head, straining to listen. He heard something. He tossed the covers aside and leaped to his feet, startling Hodesh.

"What is it?"

"Shh! Listen!" He ran to the window overlooking the road and flung open the shutter, but it was too dark to see anything.

"You were dreaming, Jerimoth. There's nothing—"

But before she could finish, Jerimoth bolted from the house and ran down through his vineyard toward the road. He waited in the semidarkness behind the leafy vines, his eyes straining for his first glimpse of her.

At last a lone figure came into view, a pale specter, a shade darker than the gloom around him. But even in the dim light before dawn Jerimoth knew her at once.

"Jerusha! Oh, God—my Jerusha!" He raced toward her, stumbling down the rutted road. The runner froze, startled by Jerimoth's sudden appearance, then ran toward him, arms outstretched.

"Abba! Abba!" Jerimoth clasped his beloved daughter fiercely, holding her like he would never let go.

"Praise God! Oh, praise God!" Jerimoth wept. As he held his precious daughter in his arms he wanted to dance and leap and shout for joy. "Oh, thank You, God! Thank You for my Jerusha!"

She was alive! Yahweh had brought her home again. He leaned back to gaze at her beloved face and saw how thin she was. He held a mere skeleton in his arms instead of his vibrant, healthy daughter. She looked old, as old as the trees that had shaded his land for centuries—not in appearance, but in her spirit. He saw death in her vacant eyes and in her tattered soul.

"Dear God, what have they done to you? What have they done to my little girl?"

He lifted her into his arms and carried her up to the house, stumbling over vines in the path, his vision blinded by tears.

"Hodesh, look! She's home! Jerusha is home!"

Hodesh moaned and clung to her daughter, too overwhelmed to speak.

"Jerusha, is it really you?" Maacah cried as she scrambled down the ladder from the loft. "Oh, God—it is! It really is!" She threw her arms around her sister and wept.

"I never thought I'd see any of you again," Jerusha sobbed. "I never thought I'd come home!"

"But you're here! Oh, God, thank You! Thank You!" Jerimoth murmured it over and over as he rocked her in his arms. Yahweh had answered his prayers. He had done the impossible. God had brought his beloved daughter back from the dead.

22

"Mama—Abba—," Jerusha wept. She had dreamed of this moment for so long that she could scarcely believe it was real. But she felt Abba's strong arms crushing her to his chest, smelled the sweet out-doors smell on his clothes, felt his warm tears on his beard. Mama's sturdy hands stroked her hair, caressed her face, dried her tears. It wasn't a dream.

"I never thought I'd see you again!" Jerusha sobbed.

She was home. She had made it home again. Everything seemed smaller to Jerusha, yet unchanged—the simple, handmade furnishings, the oxen in their stall opposite the living quarters, the soot-smudged cooking pots, even the clumps of fragrant herbs hanging from the ceiling beams seemed the same.

Abba appeared older, thinner, and his broad shoulders hunched as if carrying a heavy burden. She saw the jagged scar on his forehead, too white against his tanned face, and remembered the last time she had seen him. Strands of gray streaked Mama's ma-hogany hair, and she seemed shrunken and small. Maacah was no longer a wispy 11-year-old, but had grown into a handsome young woman. Jerusha recognized her by the freckles sprinkled across her delicate, upturned nose. How she loved her family! She would nev-er let them out of her sight again.

Jerimoth stroked her swollen, blistered feet. "Look at you! Look at your poor feet! Did you walk all the way from Nineveh?"

Hodesh fetched a jug of olive oil and massaged Jerusha's feet. "No, Abba. I lived with the army that's been fighting in the land north of here all this time. I walked part of the way home, over the mountains, until a stranger let me ride in his cart."

"An angel—God sent His angel," Jerimoth murmured. "I knew you were alive. When we didn't find your body with the others—"

Jerusha turned away, ashamed. What would her family think of her if they knew how she had survived? She could never tell them what she had become. Jerusha shivered, but it wasn't the damp air inside the house that chilled her. The coldness crept out from her soul as she lied to her parents.

"They kept me alive to cook for them—for their officers."

"And you escaped?" Jerimoth asked.

"No, Abba—they let me go. This is a game for them, a sport. They set me free so they could track me down again."

"They would hunt my daughter like an animal?"

Jerusha knew Abba could never comprehend how evil they were, how brutal and vicious. Jerusha shivered again as she remembered her pursuers. Home was not the end of her journey; it was only the beginning. She scrambled to her feet, tugging on his hands.

"Abba, we've got to get out of here! They're coming!"

Jerimoth clasped her tightly to his chest. "I will never let them have you again. Never!"

"But they're right behind me! I can't stop!" She struggled out of his embrace. "We've got to get out of here, Abba. I don't want to go back with them! I'd rather die!"

"The Assyrians are tracking you?"

"Yes, Abba! Please! We can't stay here! We've got to hurry!"

But Jerimoth stood paralyzed. Why didn't he run?

"We'll stay right here," he said at last. "There's a hiding place under the house." He kicked the rug aside and lifted the flagstone to show her the empty cistern. "When they come you can all hide in there. They won't find you—you'll be safe."

"You don't understand!" she wept. "All those other times when the Assyrians came, they were only idle soldiers on a binge for fun. This time their entire army is invading us! They won't leave us here. They'll kill us all, or worse—they'll make us slaves! Nothing will be left of Israel when they're through!"

"I won't leave my land," Jerimoth said quietly. "If what you say is true, then there is no safe place. I'll die here, on the land of my fathers."

Despair overwhelmed Jerusha until she felt as if she was drowning. She turned to her mother, gripping her hands. "Mama, please talk to him, make him listen to me! We can't stay here!"

Hodesh nodded toward Jerimoth who stood in the doorway, gazing at the fields and vineyards he had tended all his life. "I could never persuade him to leave. Where could he go? This is his land. He is rooted here, like his vines and olive trees."

Jerusha covered her face and wept. "How can I make you understand? I've struggled for so long to survive, to come home and see you again! We can't let them win now—we can't!"

Suddenly Jerimoth stiffened. "It's too late," he said, staring at the horizon. "They're coming. I can see the dust cloud on the horizon and a few riders out in front."

Jerusha began to scream. The Assyrians had caught up with her. They had found her. She bolted for the door, desperate to escape, but Jerimoth blocked her path. She screamed hysterically, beating her father's chest, struggling to push past him, to flee from the house, to run and run forever. It took all three of them to subdue her and keep her inside the house.

Trembling and weeping, Jerusha finally collapsed. Then she drew her knees to her chest as her mind splintered into madness. Dimly, she heard her father's voice calling her back.

"I'll hide you from them, Jerusha. I'll keep you safe. I won't let them find you again. Yahweh is merciful. He'll let me die on my land, and He'll keep the rest of you safe underground."

Jerusha looked up, slowly comprehending what he was telling her. She saw the open cistern and clutched him desperately, "You hide, too, Abba."

"There isn't enough room. Besides, I don't want to live to see what they do to my land."

"Abba, please—," Maacah begged.

"We have Jerusha back. Yahweh answered our prayers; that is enough for me. Yahweh will protect all three of you."

"I'm staying with you, Jerimoth," Hodesh said. "I'm your wife, and my place is with you."

"Don't be foolish. Who will take care of our girls?"

"Look," Hodesh said pointing to the cistern. "There's no room for me either. Please let me stay with you."

Jerimoth pulled her into his arms. "All right, Hodesh."

Jerusha could barely comprehend that she was losing Mama and Abba again. She fell into their arms, clinging to them in sorrow, memorizing their faces for eternity. The life they had shared in this ancient stone house was coming to an end, this time forever.

At last Jerimoth wiped his eyes. "Enough. It's time. God has helped you survive, Jerusha. Promise me that you'll take care of your sister now."

The room seemed to whirl. "I promise, Abba."

While Hodesh lowered dried fruit, cheese, and bread into the cistern, Jerimoth tenderly laid his hands on Jerusha and Maacah and prayed for them. "Ah, Sovereign Lord—keep them in the hollow of Your hand—take care of my precious girls for me. You saved Jerusha for a reason, Lord. May she find that reason and be a living testimony to Your goodness and grace."

Then Jerimoth wrapped his arms around them, crushing them to his heart. "My beloved daughters! I wanted to recite the blessing for each of you on your wedding day, but it can never be. Someday—somehow—God will turn your tears of sorrow into joy again. In faith that such a day will come—in faith that one day you will laugh and sing and hold my grandchildren in your arms—yes, in faith I will bless you now: May Yahweh bless you and keep you. May Yahweh cause His face to shine upon you and be gracious to you. May He make you as Sarah and Rebecca. May He bless you with His love and grant you His peace. Amen."

He kissed Jerusha, then pushed her away. Mama helped her climb into the cistern, and Maacah slid in beside her.

"I love you," Abba whispered. "Shalom."

A moment later he moved the stone into place, covering the hole and plunging Jerusha into total darkness.

━━◆━━

Jerimoth wiped his eyes and peered out the door again. The dust cloud on the horizon loomed larger than before, and he heard a rumbling sound, like summer thunder. Four Assyrian soldiers had stopped beside his vineyard and were dismounting. Jerimoth ducked inside the adjoining stable and unlatched the outside gate, then slapped his oxen on their rumps, setting them free to fend for themselves.

When he returned, he drew his wife into his arms, clinging to her in silence. Finally he tilted her face up and looked into her eyes, gently wiping her tears with his calloused hand.

"I love you, Hodesh. Don't be afraid. Yahweh is with us."

"I know," she nodded.

"Our girls will live. Yahweh will keep them safe."

Then, holding his wife by the hand, Jerimoth walked outside into the sunlight and down through his vineyard, silently praising God as he faced the approaching holocaust.

━━◆━━

Iddina dismounted beside Jerimoth's vineyard and stooped to examine the footprints he had been following. The trail halted abruptly in the middle of the road as if the girl had floated away. But then he saw a larger set of prints leading up the path through the vineyard. Of course. Someone had carried her.

As Iddina stood, he heard the soft whoosh of an arrow and a dull thud as it struck flesh, followed by a startled, agonized cry. In quick succession, another arrow swished from a bow, another thump sounded as it hit its mark, and another victim moaned in pain and surprise. Two bodies lay sprawled in the vineyard, and Iddina whirled around in time to see one of his men sliding his bow back into its quiver.

"Why did you shoot them?" he asked angrily.

"They were coming toward us, sir. They might be armed."

Iddina lifted the soldier by his tunic and hurled him to the ground, then pushed his face into the dirt. "Look at that trail, you fool! She was here! Those people probably knew where she is. And now you've killed them!"

Iddina kicked the soldier onto his back, drew a dagger from his belt and slit his throat. As the soldier lay dying, Iddina turned to face his other two men.

"No more stupid mistakes! Spread out and search every inch of this place until you find her."

Iddina followed a well-worn path through the vineyard, which led to the stone house on the rise. He paused beside the two bodies—a man's and a woman's—that lay sprawled side by side in a spreading puddle of blood. He rolled them over, then braced his foot on each chest in turn, jerking the arrows out and placing them in his own quiver. He felt a momentary, grudging respect for the soldier he had just killed—the man had shot his arrows straight through their hearts, killing them instantly.

From the doorway of the house Iddina saw the infantry advancing down the road. He would have to hurry before hordes of tramping soldiers wiped out every trace of the girl's trail. He stormed into the house and began ripping it apart, smashing cooking pots and storage jars, kicking at piles of hay and manure in the stable, slashing through straw pallets and bedding with his dagger. The fire on the hearth was warm, the food fresh, the house recently inhabited, unlike the hundreds of other houses they had searched along the way. Again he cursed the foolish soldier for killing the two occupants.

Suddenly Iddina froze. *Two* occupants. Yet he had just ripped open three sleeping pallets, two down here and one in the loft. All three had been rolled out on the floor, recently used. With deliberate patience, Iddina searched every inch of the house, examining every crack, testing every stone, looking for a missed clue or secret hiding place. He would find her. The game had become challenging to him again, and he sniffed the air for her scent, smiling with anticipation and delight.

―◆―

Jerusha huddled in the cramped hole beside her sister and sobbed. Not even a pinhole of light penetrated around the edges of the stone lid or through the plastered walls of the cistern, and she felt the stark terror of blindness. She couldn't tell if her eyes were open or shut. The darkness and confining space terrified her. She whimpered, trying not to scream. She was buried alive!

As if sensing Jerusha's terror, Maacah squeezed her hand, whispering, "It's all right—no one will find you here."

It wasn't true. Iddina would find her. He never lost his prey. Jerusha wanted to stop running and die with her parents, but she knew what Iddina would do to Maacah. For her sister's sake, Jerusha had to survive. She had promised Abba.

Exhaustion numbed her. Dazed by grief and shock, surrounded by inky darkness, Jerusha longed to sleep. But then she heard the rumbling sound and felt the earth trembling beneath her. "They're here," she whispered. "The Assyrians are here." The noise grew louder and louder until the ground shook like an earthquake.

"There must be hundreds of them!" Maacah said.

"Not hundreds, thousands. *Tens* of thousands."

She remembered the numberless hordes of Assyrians—foot soldiers and cavalry, chariots and war machines, stretching across the horizon as far as the eye could see—and Jerusha trembled along with the earth. The noise grew louder still, until it seemed as if the earth would shake apart. She heard the distant whinny of horses above the din and an occasional shout.

"Please, God—please, God," Maacah sobbed.

Sticky with sweat and tears, Jerusha clung to her sister, weeping for their parents. As they huddled together in the darkness, buried alive, she tried not to envision the horrifying scene above her head.

23

Iddina knelt to examine the flagstone floor of the house, his eyes patiently scanning the stones, searching for the lid to an underground cistern or root cellar. Perhaps they had hidden her. The ground shook from thousands of trampling feet as his army approached, but Iddina barely noticed. Clamping his dagger between his teeth, he continued to study the stones.

He hadn't gotten very far when something heavy struck the roof, and he heard a whoosh of flames as the ceiling beams caught fire above his head. Another torch flew through the open window and landed at his feet. The straw pallet he had ripped apart burst into flames, singeing the hair on his legs. A third torch ignited the hay on the stable floor, and within seconds flames engulfed the house.

Iddina staggered backward through clouds of choking smoke, groping for the door as flaming beams crashed to the floor. He stumbled from the burning house, his eyes watering, his lungs heaving from the suffocating smoke.

"What fool set fire to this house?" he bellowed. But no one heard him above the deafening roar of horses and troops.

Two trackers hurried up the hill toward him. "Are you all right, sir?"

Iddina coughed more smoke from his lungs. "Did you find any trace of the girl?"

"Nothing, sir."

Iddina cursed. "She was here—I know she was!"

Heat from the flaming house warmed his back, and he moved down the hill away from the inferno. The storehouses had ignited too, and flames from the burning olive press spread to the ancient olive trees. Smoke swirled around him as he stalked down the path through the vineyard, walking over the bodies in the path. He couldn't wait around until the fire died out; he was supposed to stay in front of the advancing troops. He'd have to come back later and complete his search.

He remounted his horse, furious with the stupid fool who had killed the two witnesses and with the incompetent archers who had set fire to the house before he had finished his search. He spurred his horse, signaling impatiently to his two men.

"Let's go. Maybe we'll pick up her trail down the road."

◆

The noise surrounding Jerusha thundered on, and it seemed as if the sun should have set by now. But the rumbling grew no fainter and the ground continued to shake.

Suddenly Maacah stiffened. "Jerusha, I smell smoke! Will they burn the house?"

"Yes! They'll burn everything!"

"But we'll die in here if they burn the house!"

Jerusha groped for the water skin, then soaked their clothes. "Hold the wet part over your face, and breathe through it."

The crackling of flames and scent of smoke grew stronger. At first they tried to stifle their coughs, but as the cistern filled with smoke it became impossible. Jerusha could scarcely breathe. The heat was unbearable.

Maacah struggled to stand up. "We've got to get out of here! We're going to die—we've got to get out!"

"No, Maacah. Stay here. We can't escape if the house is on fire. We have to stay here."

Jerusha held her sister down, fighting her own terror as the dark, airless hole filled with smoke. Fire raged above them, turning the cistern into an oven, slowly roasting them alive. But it was better to die in this stifling pit than to be recaptured.

"Please help us, God—don't let us die," Maacah whispered.

"There is no God," Jerusha said. "Save your breath."

"Please, God—I don't want to die—please—"

Jerusha held her sister in her arms, rocking her gently, waiting to die.

◆

Slowly, almost imperceptibly at first, the noise and the heat and the rumbling of the earth began to fade. Jerusha was still alive, but her lungs strained to breathe. She had to let fresh air into the cistern soon.

Suddenly she realized that Maacah hadn't moved for a long time. Jerusha panicked. She had promised Abba that she would take care of her.

"Maacah! Don't die! Please don't die!"

Maacah stirred and coughed weakly. Jerusha laid her sister down and felt for the stone lid above their heads. She would have to gamble that the Assyrians were gone. But the stone was too heavy for her, and she couldn't gain leverage from her cramped position. She shook her sister again.

"Maacah, you have to help me. How do we get out of here?"

"Abba—" she mumbled. "Abba will let us out—"

Tears sprang to Jerusha's eyes. "Abba can't come this time," she said gently. "You have to help me. Please try?"

Jerusha lifted her sister up, and they groped above their heads until they felt the stone. "Now, *push!*"

The stone shifted slightly, and a shower of dirt and soot rained down on them. Pale, smoky sunlight streamed in through a crack, and Jerusha saw her sister's dirt-streaked face. She appeared too tired to push again.

"At least we'll get air and a little light," Jerusha said. She found the water and made Maacah take a drink, then broke off two pieces of bread. "We'll wait until night. It'll be safer after dark. Let's try to get some sleep." She gathered her sister in her arms, and they soon slept, clinging to each other and to life.

———◆———

Jerusha awoke to total darkness and to the suffocating panic of being buried alive. She clawed her eyes to see if they were sealed shut and saw the dim outline of her hands. It was night. She moved closer to the crack of light and peered out. The roof of their house was gone, and stars shone through a haze of lingering smoke. She listened, but the night seemed eerily silent. The stone lid wouldn't budge.

"Maacah—Maacah, wake up. Help me move this stone."

Maacah stirred and tried to sit up. "Why is it so dark?"

"It's night. The soldiers are gone. I think it's safe now."

"What about Mama and Abba?"

"I—I don't know. Come on—help me push the lid off." They shifted the stone, and Jerusha crawled out; then she helped Maacah. They stood in the center of their gutted home, mute with shock.

Only the outer stone walls remained standing among the smoldering ruins. Jerusha looked up to see a pale sliver of moon and thousands of flickering stars shining in the sky. A gentle breeze stirred warm ashes beneath her feet. How could the night be so beautiful when the world around her had been so devastated?

"Stay here until I'm sure it's safe," she told Maacah.

"No—I'm going with you."

Beyond the gaping hole where the door once hung, the ruins of their father's land lay naked in the moonlight. A charred pile of stones marked his emptied storehouses; his slaughtered oxen lay strewn in a heap of bones and entrails; his ancient olive grove with its centuries-old vines lay trampled and burned. They had torn his stone winepress apart and left it in a smoldering ruin. His farmland and all his crops lay black and smoking.

"Jerusha—over there." Maacah pointed to a shadow sprawled along the vineyard path.

"Stay here," Jerusha said, but Maacah shook her head.

Together they walked through the vineyard in the pale starlight. Jerusha knelt beside her mother's body. A ragged hole pierced her heart. Abba's body looked the same. She closed their staring eyes, then cradled her mother's head in her arms and sobbed. She had thought she had no tears left to shed, but Mama and Abba lay dead in her arms, and she mourned for them until the sliver of moon sank below the horizon and the stars faded.

"Abba would want to be buried on his land," Maacah said.

They dug a shallow grave beside the vineyard and buried Hodesh and Jerimoth side by side, then piled stones from the winepress to mark the grave. When they finished, the sky was light.

Jerusha sat on the stone steps of her house and stared at the desolation before her. The Assyrians swept across the face of the earth like a merciless plague, killing everyone in their path, leaving a legacy of destruction and death, a holocaust, behind them. Now Jerusha longed for her life to end as well.

"What are we going to do now?" Maacah asked quietly.

"I don't know." Just survive—it had been Jerusha's goal for as long as she could remember, but she no longer knew why. She wished the blackened earth would open up and swallow her.

"Maybe we can plant next spring," Maacah said. "We can grow enough food to live on and—"

"I don't want to live anymore. I'm sick of struggling to survive—sick of it all! Mama and Abba are dead, and I wish it were me. I wish I were dead."

Maacah turned on her fiercely, grabbing Jerusha's shoulders and shaking her hard. "Don't say that! Abba and Mama prayed for you! They refused to leave and go where it was safe because they were waiting for *you!* They died so we could live! You owe them your life, Jerusha! Don't you ever talk like that again!" She stopped shaking Jerusha and threw her arms around her neck, sobbing. "Please—please live for them and for me. I don't want to die."

"All right," she whispered. "Don't cry."

She had promised Abba. Somehow she would figure out a way to keep the two of them alive. They still had each other, and that was reason enough to live.

Iddina stood beside the road and stared at the well-worn path that led through Jerimoth's vineyard. The body of the soldier he had killed still lay beside the road, but the other two bodies had vanished. Dried blood marked the place where they had fallen. He had found no sign of Jerusha farther down the road, and after the army passed, he returned with his men to where they had lost her trail, hoping for a clue they had overlooked. Instead, Iddina discovered the bodies were missing. If the bodies had burned, some evidence would remain. There was none. Nor were there signs of scavengers. Iddina peered closer and saw a flattened trail, as if the bodies had been dragged, leading through the burnt stubble. When he reached the end of it he found the grave near the winepress, heaped with stones.

Every muscle in his body tensed. "Spread out. Search every inch of this farm. Someone lived through this."

With mounting anger, Iddina hurried up the hill to the gutted house, guessing what he might find. Charred beams and rubble lay scattered over the flagstone floor, but in the center of the room a stone had been pushed aside, revealing an empty cistern.

Iddina howled in rage. The veins on his neck and forehead pulsed with anger. The little dog had beaten him. And Iddina hated to lose. He no longer cared about his promotion. This was no longer a hunt for sport. He wanted revenge.

As the day grew late, Iddina knew he had to catch up with his troops. He had soldiers to command, the city of Samaria to besiege. For now, he couldn't waste any more time on her. But he would find her again and get her back if it took the rest of his life.

Corpses—bloated, stinking corpses so numerous that they would never all be buried. Jerusha and Maacah had wandered the countryside for days, scavenging for food, sleeping in gutted ruins and in caves, searching for signs of life, for someone who had survived the holocaust along with them. But all they found were smoldering ruins, desolate, blackened land, and the eerie silence of death. They were the sole survivors.

With every step she took, with every dead body she saw, Jerusha's guilt deepened. She didn't deserve to be alive. Why had she survived when so many others had perished? Eventually they wandered into Dabbasheth, where Jerusha's long nightmare first began. The village lay flattened and burned as if crushed beneath God's heel. As the wind blew soot through the quiet, rubble-strewn streets, even the birds were silent.

Jerusha sat on the foundation of Uncle Saul's house, trying not to stare at the pitiful bodies impaled on stakes around the village, trying not to look into their faces in search of a familiar one. Her cousin's wedding seemed a lifetime ago, part of another world of laughter and song, a world forever lost.

"I don't know where else we can go," she said to Maacah. "We've tried all our relatives—all our friends—"

Maacah said nothing. She had also run out of tears to shed at the horror all around them. She bowed her head and closed her eyes. The futility of her prayers angered Jerusha, and she exploded.

"Are you out of your mind, Maacah? How can you still believe in God? Was He deaf to the cries of all these people? Is He blind to what's happened to His promised land? Doesn't He care?"

"Jerusha, don't talk that way—"

"Have you gone insane, or have I? Maacah, how can you pray to God after seeing all this?"

"But Abba believed, and—"

"Abba didn't have to see dead bodies piled up like cordwood! He didn't have to smell the stench of death and decay, day after day, or cry out to God to deliver him from this hell! Go ahead and pray if you want to, but believe me—it won't do any good!"

Jerusha turned her back on Maacah, then stooped to sift through the debris of her uncle's house until her hands were black and gritty with soot. She found the blade of a flint knife and a clay storage jar of grain. Most of the wheat kernels were too charred to eat, but she sorted out a few edible grains.

Maacah squatted beside her. "Jerusha, I know where we can go."

"Where?"

"To Jerusalem. We'll be safe there. I know the way and—"

"Maacah, you do not!"

"—and we can stay with Hilkiah and Eliakim."

Jerusha stared at her as if she had spoken gibberish. "Who?"

"Abba took us there for all the festivals, to pray for you. I know the way. We have friends in Jerusalem who will help us."

Jerusha felt a crushing weariness, not only from the thought of another long journey, but also from the hopelessness of it all. How could they travel that far? How could they avoid the Assyrians who were camped between here and Jerusalem? It seemed useless to try. It would be better to die here and get it over with. If only she hadn't promised.

"Is that what you want to do?" she asked wearily.

"I know we can make it."

"All right, then. We'll go to Jerusalem. But don't ask me how." She stared down at the kernels of grain in her hand, then held them out to her sister. "Here. You need to eat."

"So do you."

"Then we'll share." They tasted burnt and bitter.

"What else did you find?" Maacah asked. Jerusha gave her the broken knife blade, and Maacah began to draw a map in the dirt with it, twirling her thick braid around her finger as she drew.

"First we follow the road to the Sea of Galilee—"

"Maacah, we have to cut our hair."

Maacah stopped drawing and stared at her. "Why?"

"We have to look like boys. We'll be safer that way." She took the knife. "Do you want to go first?"

"No! I don't want to cut my hair!" She clutched her braids protectively.

"You have to," Jerusha said gently. "It's for your own good. It'll grow back. Here—cut mine first, then."

Reluctantly, Maacah started cutting. Jerusha watched her long, brown hair fall in thick clumps at her feet, some of it blowing away with the breeze. She felt relieved, unburdened, and she reached up to feel her head. "Make it shorter, like a man's."

"But, Jerusha—"

"We'll wear men's clothing too. Maybe from one of those corpses." Maacah shuddered. "Just do it. Then you can show me how to get to Jerusalem."

Sunlight glared off the white stones as King Hezekiah climbed the narrow stairs to the top of the city wall. General Jonadab sprinted up the steps ahead of him, familiar with their sloping unevenness and the dizzying, unguarded view of rooftops below. Shebna and Eliakim followed behind, mindful of their footing, hugging the wall to avoid the 40-foot drop.

When he reached the top, Hezekiah shaded his eyes to gaze at the sprawling new city under construction for the refugees. The area crawled with activity as men labored to lay foundations, plaster mud-brick walls, or tamp earthen roofs with heavy rollers.

"I had no idea we'd take in this many refugees," he said. "You've built an entire city down there."

"And many more refugees have relocated in the Negev," Eliakim told him. "They wanted farmland and seemed grateful to get it, even though they'll have to struggle to raise crops."

General Jonadab wiped the sweat off his forehead. "But these houses are outside the walls. They have no protection."

"We ran out of room inside the walls," Eliakim said, shrugging.

"These people are working so hard to rebuild new lives in our nation," Hezekiah said. "Couldn't we extend the city walls to surround this new section of the city?"

"It would be very expensive," Shebna answered quickly, "and accomplish very little. These people are transients who might pack up and leave Jerusalem as quickly as they came."

"They'd be more likely to stay if we offered them protection," Eliakim said.

"What do you think, General?" Hezekiah asked.

"Well, I don't care much about defending the refugees, but from a military standpoint, double walls would be an excellent defense. And this northwest approach to Jerusalem has always been too vulnerable to an attack."

Hezekiah quickly grasped Jonadab's strategy. "When the enemy breaches the first wall, we retreat behind the second."

"That's right, Your Majesty. Then they have to start all over again on the second wall, adding years to their campaign."

Hezekiah turned to his engineer. "Can it be done, Eliakim?"

"Sure. See the contour of that western ridge? That's where I'd build the wall—around the end of that valley—and join it to the old wall there—on the northern side of the Temple Mount."

Hezekiah followed Eliakim's finger as he drew a wide arc. "That would double the size of Jerusalem!"

"That's right, leaving us plenty of room for growth."

Jonadab frowned. "Wait a minute. I think we should repair the old walls first. There are some places where—"

"Why can't we do both?" Eliakim asked.

"Because we do not have unlimited resources," Shebna said. "You are talking about thousands of hours of work."

"Well, there's your manpower!" Eliakim gestured to the refugees in the valley. "I'm sure they'd be motivated to protect their new homes."

"And it has to be done," Hezekiah sighed. "These old walls couldn't possibly withstand an Assyrian siege. The sooner we start, the better prepared we'll be if they decide to invade us next. I want to start on both projects as soon as we can."

"Yes, Your Majesty," Shebna said. "I will look for an engineer to assign to each project."

"But two engineers will have to compete with each other for manpower and materials," Eliakim said. The bickering between Shebna and Eliakim frustrated Hezekiah. He wondered what lay at its source and how he could resolve it.

"I want you to work together on this. Shebna, prepare a reasonable budget, and allot funds. Eliakim, you'll be in charge of both projects. How soon can you finish your work with the refugees?"

"Immigration has dropped off, now that the Assyrians have overrun Israel. But we can probably expect a few hundred more."

"Do you have someone who can take over for you?"

"Yes—my assistant knows what to do."

"Good. Then draw up plans for the new walls as well as for repairing and reinforcing the old ones. Inspect the entire perimeter. General Jonadab will work with you and advise you from a military standpoint. Have you two worked together before?"

As the two men exchanged glances, Hezekiah saw a look of recognition pass between them—and something more: wariness on Eliakim's part, embarrassment on Jonadab's.

"You *do* know each other, then?" Hezekiah asked.

Jonadab wiped his forehead again. "Yes, we've met. I'm responsible for that scar across his throat."

"No hard feelings," Eliakim assured him. "You were following orders."

"Uriah's orders," Jonadab said. "I didn't know—"

"Just keep it in the past, all right?" Hezekiah said. "I need you to work together."

Eliakim extended his hand to the general. "I have no problem with that." He managed a wary smile as Jonadab grasped it.

"The three of you must work together on our nation's defenses. We must be prepared to withstand an Assyrian attack. Any suggestions?"

"We should build fortified cities and army outposts throughout Judah to defend the borders and the main routes to Jerusalem," Jonadab said.

His nation's weakened condition angered Hezekiah; he was determined to remedy it, regardless of the cost. "I agree," he said. "Finish surveying Jerusalem's defenses; then you and Eliakim can do the same thing throughout the nation."

"We'll also need a communication network," Eliakim said. "I'd like to build watchtowers with signal fires to relay information."

"Excellent. Let's get to work." Hezekiah knew he had found three outstanding men, and he greatly admired each of them for their unique strengths. But as he glanced at the faint scar on Eliakim's neck and at the silently brooding Shebna, he wished he could be sure they felt the same respect for one another.

It took Eliakim more than a month to inspect Jerusalem's walls and supporting terraces with General Jonadab. Before they had completed their circuit, the Assyrians laid siege to the northern capital of Samaria. Eliakim knew they would have to hurry if they hoped to make Judah secure before Samaria fell.

Late into the night Eliakim sat at his worktable, searching for ways to save time and improve efficiency. He worked by lamplight, barely able to see what he was doing. His clay tablets and scrolls were scattered everywhere. As he bent over his drawings, he heard footsteps and looked up to see Hilkiah dressed in his nightclothes, carrying an oil lamp.

"Such an hour to be working!" his father scolded. "How can you see what you're doing? Must you finish it tonight?"

Eliakim leaned back and rubbed his eyes. "I'm almost finished, Abba. And yes, this has to be ready by tomorrow. General Jonadab and I are presenting our plans for the city walls to the king's advisory council. Have a look." Hilkiah leaned over his shoulder as Eliakim pointed to his drawings. "See? These are the city walls as they currently stand. But the king wants me to expand them like this—"

"Around the new city?"

"Right. Ever since the Assyrians laid siege to Samaria, King Hezekiah has been anxious to start on these double walls." Neither of them mentioned Jerimoth and his family, but Eliakim knew their friends filled his father's thoughts and prayers. "Now you know what keeps me up so late."

"My son—such an important man. Working for the king's advisory council, no less! Who would have ever believed it? You should thank God every day for such a blessing as this!"

Eliakim frowned. "I've worked hard to get where I am."

"I know, Son. I know you have. But remember what the psalmist has written: 'Promotion does not come from the east or west, but from God. He puts down one and sets up another.'"

Eliakim wasn't persuaded. He believed God could do a lot of things, but he also believed in himself. The fact that his father gave God all the credit irritated Eliakim. But before he could argue further, a sleepy servant appeared in the doorway.

"Master Hilkiah, two young boys just came to your gate. They look like beggars, sir, but they asked for you by name."

Eliakim rolled his eyes. "Another charity case. You are hopeless, Abba—trying to feed the whole world." He tried to scowl but finally broke into a grin. "You're a pushover!"

"Remember: 'Whoever is kind to the needy honors God,'" Hilkiah muttered as he shuffled toward the door. "But I honestly can't imagine who this could be. I don't remember any beggar boys."

Eliakim returned to his work. Then, worried that his father might invite the strangers to stay, he picked up a lamp and hurried after him. Two ragged youths stood in the shadows, their hair matted and dirty, their filthy bodies as thin as cadavers.

"You poor children!" Hilkiah cried.

One of the youths began to cry. "Oh, Uncle Hilkiah! Eliakim! It's me—Maacah!"

"God of Abraham!" Hilkiah's lamp slipped from his hand and crashed to the floor. He swayed and nearly fell over before Eliakim caught him. Eliakim recognized Maacah now, even without her thick braids, but she looked haggard and exhausted.

She motioned to the taller youth standing beside her. "This is my sister Jerusha."

"*What?*" Eliakim cried. "That's not possible!" The shock paralyzed him, as if his dead mother had returned to life and stood in his doorway. He stared at her. It couldn't be Jerusha. No one escaped from the Assyrians. It was impossible!

"This—this must be—a joke," he stammered. "It can't be—" He fought the urge to laugh out loud. He had argued with his father over the impossibility of Jerusha's return. He had insisted that Yahweh would never answer their prayers. He had begged Hilkiah to accept the fact that Jerusha was dead. Yet here she stood in his doorway, gazing at him with haunting green eyes—Jerimoth's eyes. It simply couldn't be true. But it was.

Hilkiah recovered his balance and pulled Maacah into his arms. "Oh, my sweet child! Praise God—you're alive! Come in, come in!" He bustled her into the house, shouting, "Wake all the servants! Fix these poor girls some food! They're half starved!"

Eliakim stared at Jerusha as she trailed after Hilkiah into the sitting room. She had an inhuman wildness about her; not the fierceness of the hunter, but rather the pursued look of the prey, wary and alert. She walked hesitantly, gazing in awe at the thick carpets and bronze lampstands, the scented incense burners and lavish ivory furnishings. She seemed reluctant to sit down in her filthy condition and chose a spot on the cold stone floor, not quite on the carpet. Eliakim took a seat near her, aware that he was gaping at her but unable to stop himself.

The servants scurried around the room, lighting all the lamps, stoking the fires in the charcoal braziers, carrying in trays of fruit while Hilkiah called for more food and warm broth. Eliakim felt lightheaded, unable to comprehend why his father called for food. Ghosts didn't need to eat, and these two skeletons had to be ghosts.

"You're really Jerusha?" he asked. He had the urge to touch her to see if she was real. "Where's Jerimoth? And your mother?"

"My parents are dead." She closed her eyes, and Eliakim saw how utterly exhausted she was.

"No!" Hilkiah cried. "My dear friends? Oh, Maacah! I'm so sorry!" He pulled her into his arms and wept, heartbroken. "God of Abraham, hold them close to Your bosom," he sobbed. "Jerimoth was such a good man. Thank You for rewarding his faith."

Eliakim swallowed the lump of grief in his throat. "I—I'm sorry, Jerusha."

But she showed no emotion as she stared silently at the floor. He wanted to hold her and comfort her like his father comforted Maacah, but he hesitated, remembering that he was a stranger to her.

"How did you get here?" he finally asked.

She raised her head proudly, almost defiantly. "We walked."

"But—how did you escape from the Assyrians?"

She met his gaze, and her haunting, lifeless eyes startled him. "They let me go."

"But that's impossible—they never let anyone go—"

"Well, they did—so they could hunt me down again, like an animal." Her eyes glittered with hatred. "My mother and father died hiding us from them."

"But how—"

"Not now, Son," Hilkiah said. "Let her eat something first and rest. Ah—here's some warm broth."

As Eliakim watched Jerusha eat, he forced himself to keep quiet instead of barraging her with the hundreds of questions collecting in his brain. She sat tensed and alert as if ready to flee, but in spite of her hunger, she ate slowly and carefully, her long limbs moving gracefully as she reached for the food, like a palm tree swaying in a gentle wind. Her slender hands were calloused but still elegant, and when she held her head high and lifted her chin as she had done a moment before, her long, graceful neck was stunning. Eliakim saw rounded curves beneath her shapeless clothes; in spite of the short hair and men's clothing, she was indeed a woman.

Before long, the unanswered questions burned inside him until he couldn't stop himself. "You actually lived with the Assyrians?"

"Yes—with their army."

Her vacant stare unnerved him, and she seemed to shrink away, as if drawing inside herself. He had never met a human being so empty and haunted before. Whatever they had done to her had robbed her of her humanity and ripped her soul from her.

Suddenly Eliakim had another thought. "Have you actually watched how they lay siege to a city and wage war?"

"Yes. I lived with their army for more than three years."

"You could be a tremendous help to me, Jerusha. I work for King Hezekiah and—"

"Eliakim—let it wait," Hilkiah said.

"OK, OK—but would you be willing to talk about it with me sometime, Jerusha? After you've rested? Maybe in a couple of days?"

"Son, drop it," Hilkiah warned.

But Eliakim knew how important her experiences were, and he held her gaze until she finally nodded in agreement. "Thank you. Your experience could prove invaluable to us."

"You poor, sweet girls," Hilkiah murmured. "I can't imagine what you've been through, how you must have suffered! But it's over now. You're here, and I promise to take good care of you."

"We had no place else to go," Maacah said. "Everyone is dead—all our friends—all our relatives—"

"Not all your relatives," Eliakim said. "Your Uncle Saul came here."

"Where is he?" Maacah asked.

"We wanted to help him," Eliakim said, "but your uncle is a very proud man."

"Yes, I offered him a job in my shop," Hilkiah said, "but he told me he couldn't accept charity."

Eliakim shrugged. "He left for the Negev, and we haven't heard from him since."

"This is your home now," Hilkiah said. "We are your family. It's the very least I can do for your dear father. Ah, God of Abraham, how I will miss him—" Hilkiah's voice broke. "I can't believe he's really gone."

Eliakim grieved for their friends too. He knew that every feast day, every holiday, he would be reminded of Jerimoth and his unshakable faith in God—a faith that magnified his own unbelief. God had finally rewarded Jerimoth's faith. Jerusha sat a few feet away from Eliakim as if resurrected from the dead.

"I have prepared a hot bath for your guests, Master, and clean beds," a servant announced.

They all stood, and when Eliakim hugged Maacah, he felt every one of her bones through her thin clothes.

"Thank you both," she said tearfully. "We had no place else to go."

"You don't need to thank us," Hilkiah said. "This is your home now. I just praise God that you're safe. Good night, and sleep well. We'll talk in the morning, after you've rested."

When they were alone, Eliakim rested his hand on his father's shoulder. "Are you all right, Abba?"

Hilkiah blinked back his tears. "We must go to the Temple together—to recite prayers for the dead."

"Yes, of course, Abba." He wondered if his father would remind him of Jerimoth's faith or chide him for his stubborn unbelief. Now was the appropriate time to say, "I told you so." But instead, Hilkiah wandered slowly to his room without uttering another word.

Eliakim returned to his workroom, thinking how much easier it would be to prepare for an Assyrian assault knowing their strengths and weaknesses. Using Jerusha's experience, he could make sure Judah would be secure. Jerusha! Jerusha had returned from the dead. It was incredible. Impossible. Tonight Eliakim had witnessed a miracle.

———◆———

Jerusha awoke enveloped in a cloud. She bolted upright and stared fearfully at the strange surroundings. The elegant room was like a palace, with polished bronze mirrors and lampstands, woven rugs and tapestries, ivory beds with creamy sheets and soft cushions. Everything felt wrong. She didn't belong here.

"What's the matter?" Maacah asked sleepily.

"Nothing—for a minute I forgot where I was; that's all."

"I know what you mean. I can't believe we made it here."

Jerusha caressed the soft sheets, marveling at the way they felt next to her clean skin. The hot bath she had taken last night seemed like a dream; she hadn't felt this clean in a long, long time. But a sense of foreboding hovered over her, a feeling of wariness and mistrust, as if Iddina might burst through the door any moment and snatch her away.

"We can't stay here," she said.

"Why not?"

"They're so rich. Are they royalty?"

Maacah laughed. "No, Uncle Hilkiah is a merchant, and Eliakim builds things for King Hezekiah."

"Will their wives mind if we stay here?"

"Uncle Hilkiah's wife died a long time ago, and Eliakim isn't married yet."

"But we don't belong here, Maacah. Look at this place. It's like a palace." She tried to rake her fingers through her hair but found only short stubble.

"Uncle Hilkiah says this is our home, now. He wants us to stay."

"'Uncle'? Maacah, these people aren't our relatives."

"Yes, they are. Well, they're almost family."

Jerusha shook her head. "I'll stay only if they let us work as servants."

"Jerusha, listen to me. Abba loved Uncle Hilkiah. They were like brothers. And we always stayed here whenever we came to Jerusalem for the feasts." Jerusha couldn't comprehend Maacah's words. While she had suffered through hell, her family had stayed here with these strangers. This home represented a time in Jerusha's life she longed to forget.

A servant knocked on the door, then entered, carrying two bundles. "Master Hilkiah asked me to find you something to wear, so I bought you these."

Jerusha stared as she unfolded two dresses and laid them onto the bed. The gowns, made of deep blue linen, looked soft and silky; exquisite gold embroidery decorated the long sleeves and neckline. Jerusha had never seen such beautiful dresses. She couldn't speak.

"I hope they're all right," the servant said.

"They're beautiful!" Maacah cried. "Where's Uncle Hilkiah? I want to thank him."

"He and Master Eliakim went to the Temple for the morning sacrifice. They'll be home soon. I'll call you for breakfast when they return."

After the servant left, Maacah scrambled out of bed and held up the dress, admiring herself in the tall bronze mirror. "It's so beautiful! Oh, Jerusha, feel it!"

The dresses and veils were designed for unmarried women, virgins. Jerusha remembered Iddina and the other officers, and shame overwhelmed her. The dress was a lie. She wasn't a virgin. The rape wasn't her fault, but what followed afterward had been her choice.

"I can't wear that dress, Maacah. I can't accept such a gift."

Maacah's smile faded. "Why not?"

Jerusha couldn't find words to express how she felt. *Because I'm not worthy!* she wanted to scream. The bath last night had cleansed her on the outside, but nothing could ever purify her on the inside. She had chosen to prostitute herself. How could she live with the shame?

"Jerusha—why not?" Maacah asked again.

"Because—because—oh, what am I doing here?" she wept. "I don't belong here!"

Maacah sat down beside her and held her close. "Abba brought us to Jerusalem for Passover so we could pray for you. God led us here, to this house, and Uncle Hilkiah always prayed for you too. He loved Abba as much as we did. He'd do anything for Abba's sake. This is our home now."

Jerusha heard her sister's words, but they didn't explain why she deserved to live—or how she could live with her shame. Finally, Maacah grasped Jerusha's hands and pulled her out of bed.

"Come on—try on your dress. Please? You have to wear something."

Reluctantly, Jerusha allowed Maacah to help her dress. The fabric felt soft and smooth as it draped around her body in gentle folds. She tied the sash around her waist, then helped Maacah dress.

"We made a terrible mess of our hair," Jerusha said as they stood in front of the mirror.

"Like you said—it'll grow. You still look beautiful, Jerusha. Be glad you don't have my horrible freckles."

Someone knocked on the door, and Jerusha pulled it open, expecting to see the servant again. But Eliakim stood in the doorway wearing an embroidered skullcap on his tousled hair and a prayer shawl draped over his shoulders. He stood a head taller than her, with the confident posture of a man of wealth and authority. Jerusha fought the urge to bow. His mouth opened in surprise as he appraised her in obvious admiration.

"Isn't she beautiful?" Maacah said.

"Yes—yes—she is," he stammered. He swallowed hard, and Jerusha noticed the long scar that stretched across his throat. Then she looked away, embarrassed by his lingering gaze. "You're both beautiful," he said. "Please, excuse me for staring, but I can't believe the transformation!"

"Your father bought these dresses for us," Maacah said.

"Abba did? They're lovely." He cleared his throat. "Listen, Jerusha—I need to ask a big favor of you."

She looked up at him again, and his eyes were warm and kind. He was unlike any man she had ever known. Abram had been rugged and robust, a man of the land, like Abba; Iddina had been vicious and brutal. But handsome Eliakim was sophisticated, refined, well-educated. Once again, Jerusha felt the urge to bow.

"It's a really big favor," he said. "I know you've been through a terrible ordeal and that you probably need time to rest, but you could be such a tremendous help to me. I'm meeting with the king today to plan the defense of the nation. If you could come with me and—"

"Absolutely *not!*" Hilkiah's voice thundered from behind Eliakim. "You leave those girls alone! Give them a chance to recover from all they've been through. Such a son I raised! Asking such a thing!"

"But, Abba, it's urgent. She could tell us—"

"Absolutely not. It can wait." Hilkiah pushed past him into the room, pleading with Jerusha. "Please, will you forgive my son? He has a head that he never uses."

Jerusha smiled faintly at the kind little merchant, and her emotions seemed to stir to life after lying dead for so long. She remembered the stranger who had helped her escape, and suddenly she wanted to help Eliakim, to repay the debt she felt she owed.

"There's nothing to forgive," Jerusha said. "I'll go with Eliakim. I'd like to help him."

26

King Hezekiah surveyed the somber faces of his councilmen as they assembled to hear his plans for the nation's defense.

"Is everyone here? Can we begin?" he asked Shebna, seated beside him.

"No, Your Majesty—we are waiting for Eliakim. He has the drawings."

Eliakim hurried in with his arms full. "I'm sorry for being late, Your Majesty, but I've brought a guest—someone we all should listen to."

"No. You need to clear all visitors with me first," Shebna said. "It is too late to change our agenda now."

"But I didn't have any advance notice myself. We met for the first time late last night. Please, Your Majesty—I promise it'll be very helpful to our discussion of Judah's defenses."

Hezekiah hesitated, then decided to trust Eliakim's judgment. "All right. Bring him in."

"Well, it's—uh—it's a woman, Your Majesty."

"A woman in council?" Shebna cried. "No. That is unheard of."

Hezekiah held up his hand to stop the whispering among his advisers. "Are you certain this is relevant, Eliakim?"

"Yes. Very relevant." Again he hesitated before making such an unprecedented decision. "Bring her in."

Shebna slouched in his seat, but Hezekiah's advisers sat up in amazement as Eliakim motioned to his guest. The woman who entered was painfully thin, her face so shrunken that her cheekbones protruded. Haunting green eyes dominated her face, and fear dominated her skittish movements. She seemed terrified by the somber atmosphere and staring faces. How could this half-starved young woman possibly help with Judah's defenses?

"You may begin, Eliakim, whenever you're both ready."

"Your Majesty, this is Jerusha, daughter of Jerimoth. She is a refugee from Israel."

An eerie silence crept over the room. Hezekiah knew that the Assyrians had pronounced a death sentence on Israel, but to see living proof of it in this emaciated woman unnerved him.

"The fact that Jerusha is here is a miracle," Eliakim continued. "She was captured by the Assyrians and lived with their army for more than three years."

A murmur of astonishment swept the room. Hezekiah leaned forward. "I would like to hear everything you can tell us about the Assyrians, Jerusha," he said. "Would you share your story with us?"

Jerusha's trembling legs could barely hold her. Hezekiah waited, watching her anxiously. Eliakim took her arm to support her and spoke quietly to her: "Take your time. You've been through so many terrifying events already. Don't be scared now. You're among friends."

She spoke in a voice so soft that Hezekiah strained to hear her. "I lived with my family on my father's land until the Assyrians raided our village. They captured my two cousins—and—and—"

"It's all right—take your time," Eliakim soothed. "Forgive me for making you relive this, but it's so important. Please, Jerusha?"

She took a deep breath. "They killed my cousins, but I was allowed to live as—as their slave. I served as a cook for four army officers, and I traveled with them as they waged war."

Hezekiah could scarcely stay seated. "You actually lived with their army? You watched how they besiege cities?"

"Yes. I will tell you what I can about them."

"That would be a tremendous help to us, Jerusha," Hezekiah said. "But first, I'm curious to know how you escaped."

"I didn't escape. They set me free, just for fun. It was a contest to see who could track me down again."

"That's outrageous!" General Jonadab cried. "What kind of men would do such a thing?"

Hezekiah shook his head in disbelief. "And yet they obviously didn't recapture you. How did you escape from them?"

"I—I walked night and day—across the mountains—and I made it back to my father's land. But they caught up to me and—" Tears filled her hollow eyes and slipped silently down her thin face. "My sister and I hid in a cistern beneath my father's house—the Assyrians killed my parents. Then we wandered everywhere, searching for our relatives, but no one is left. The country has been destroyed—thousands of people—it is a holocaust."

Hezekiah remembered Isaiah's prophecy: *Until their cities are destroyed—without a person left—and the whole country is an utter wasteland.* He fought a surge of fear, the same fear that had destroyed his father.

"So my sister and I walked to Jerusalem," Jerusha continued, "to stay with my father's friend, Master Eliakim. We traveled at night over the mountains, avoiding the roads and Assyrian horse patrols. It has taken us three months to get here. We hid in caves and in tombs, sometimes for days, until it was safe to come out again. The Assyrian armies swarm all over Israel, but we finally escaped and crossed the border into Judah."

The men stared at her in awe and respect. "I commend you for your incredible courage," Hezekiah said quietly. "Now tell me—do you think the Assyrians will be able to conquer Samaria?"

"Yes, I'm certain they will."

General Jonadab stood up. "Wait a minute—Samaria is a great fortress city with strong, thick walls. And it's built on a steep hill, much like Jerusalem. How can they defeat it?"

"The Assyrians use powerful weapons of war and machines that can break down even the strongest walls. Besides, they don't accept defeat. I've never seen them lose. They're willing to wait many years until a city starves to death or dies of thirst."

"And that is Jerusalem's greatest weakness—," Shebna said, "—our water supply. We could never withstand an Assyrian siege."

Jonadab nodded in agreement. "Can you tell us about these war machines?" he said.

"They build powerful battering rams on wheels, fortified so they can attack the walls without being set on fire from above. The men inside them are armored against arrows and spears. The machines keep attacking the wall in the same place until a breach is made and the wall crumbles."

"But if the city is on a hill like Samaria, how do these machines get near the base of the walls?" Shebna asked.

"They send men out ahead of the army to chop down trees and clear a path for the marching troops. The trees are used along with rocks or mud bricks to build ramps up to the walls. They have men who are trained to build these earthworks and handle the machines of war. They also have men who tunnel under the wall."

Hezekiah thought about Jerusalem's ancient, crumbling walls and knew the Assyrians already outmatched him. "What about their other weapons?" he asked grimly.

"Every soldier is well armed and extremely well trained. Discipline is very important to them. Cruelty is honored. All the soldiers wear thick, protective clothing and helmets, besides carrying shields. Their foot soldiers are highly skilled with bows and arrows and slings. They spend all their spare time practicing, and their aim is deadly accurate."

"What about the cavalry?" General Jonadab asked.

"For every 100 foot soldiers there are 10 cavalrymen. They're sent ahead of the army to scout for ambushes or to size up the enemy. These horse patrols are so swift and skilled that they can appear and disappear suddenly before their enemies' eyes like ghosts, terrifying them. Some have spears and swords, some bows and arrows, but they all carry a short dagger for hand-to-hand combat. They can use all these weapons with deadly skill even while riding on horseback at great speed. They guide their horses with their knees and both hands remain free to aim and shoot."

Shebna muttered a curse and shifted in his seat. "What about chariots?"

"For every 10 cavalrymen there is a chariot, heavily armed with strong metal plates. Each chariot holds three men—the driver, the warrior who's armed with bows and spears, and a third man to shield the other two. The chariots are pulled by two horses and are extremely fast. Some even have a third horse tied behind in case one of the others gets injured."

Jerusha shuddered, then summoned the strength to continue. "The chariots usually charge first, and very few armies can survive the first attack. Just the sight of them and the sound of their pounding wheels usually causes the enemy to run. The chariots fan out in pursuit, crushing the enemy beneath their wheels."

"You've painted a very vivid picture of our enemies," Hezekiah said. "Trained, disciplined, professional soldiers too numerous to count. We're not prepared for an assault by such a powerful foe. Do you have any idea what their plans are after they finish with Israel?"

"No, Your Majesty. I have no idea. But when they're ready to march they can move with lightning speed."

"Are they as brutal and bloodthirsty as they're rumored to be?" Jonadab asked.

"They—they—" Her eyes darted wildly about, as if the Assyrians might be hiding in the next room, and her fear quickly became contagious. Hezekiah saw it written across the bloodless faces of his advisers.

"They are not human," she said. "They study their enemies' weaknesses and use warfare of the mind to terrify them before they attack. After the battle, the soldiers make huge pyramids of severed heads, and they get paid for each head. Then they turn to their prisoners of war. The lucky ones are killed quickly. They're made to kneel down as the soldiers smash their skulls with clubs. Others are carried away into slavery like I was. The least fortunate prisoners are the nobles and kings—" She stopped as if suddenly remembering to whom she was talking.

"It's all right," Hezekiah assured her. "You may continue."

She twisted her thin hands nervously. "The Assyrians love to torture their captives. They prefer slow, agonizing deaths for the highest-ranking officers and nobility, torturing them for several days before impaling them on stakes and leaving them to slowly die. But they torture the king most horribly of all. They—they stake him to the ground and—and gradually skin him alive—"

"That's enough!" Shebna shouted. He leaped from his seat, and Jerusha shrank back in fear.

"You don't have to yell at her," Eliakim said. He moved to put his arm around Jerusha, but she shrank away from him too.

"She has made her point," Shebna said. "The rumors of Assyrian atrocities are true. There is no need for her to continue."

Hezekiah felt the tension in the throne room. The Assyrians were a formidable enemy, mobilizing their entire empire into a massive war machine. No one could defeat them. Yet he had rebelled against them. He forced himself to appear calm and controlled.

"After Jerusha's report I think we all realize the critical situation we face. We must strengthen and fortify this city as well as others throughout Judah—" Hezekiah stopped, watching Jerusha with growing concern. She trembled as if shaken by a mighty wind, and her gaunt face had turned pale. Her eyes widened, staring in horror, and she looked as though she might collapse.

"Let's take a break," Hezekiah said. "I think Eliakim had better take Jerusha home."

———◈———

When Jerusha left the meeting with Eliakim, she could scarcely walk. She heard him talking to her, thanking her for coming with him, telling her how important her information was to the council, but a strange whirring sound, like the flapping of a thousand wings, drowned out most of his words.

Eliakim led her through a maze of corridors, then across an inner courtyard, but her legs felt heavy and slow. By the time they reached the outer courtyard of the palace, her knees buckled beneath her like a rag doll's, and she collapsed on the stone pavement in a heap. As her vision narrowed and darkness crept in, Jerusha saw thousands of demonic creatures swirling around her head, swooping and diving at her with sharp, bloodied beaks. She screamed and closed her eyes, shielding her head with her arms.

"No! No! Get away from me!"

Suddenly she was back in the Assyrian camp again, smelling the smoke and the stench of death, hearing the agonized cries of the dying, witnessing the endless torture and brutality, the forests of impaled bodies, the mounds of human heads, the ever-circling vultures. She began to scream, crying out in horror for all the years she hadn't dared to scream.

"Jerusha? Jerusha, what's wrong?"

Dimly, she heard Eliakim calling her, but his voice wasn't strong enough to pull her back. She began spiraling down into a deep, black pit as she relived the nightmare: the first horrible moment of rape, the years of living in the pit of hell, the day Iddina snatched her baby from her arms. She remembered her escape, running blindly, hopelessly, while the Assyrian army pursued her; being roasted alive in the stifling cistern; then holding her mother's lifeless body in her arms.

As Eliakim tried to help her to her feet, Jerusha remembered Iddina's brutality, and she lashed out blindly at him.

"No! Get away from me! Don't touch me!"

"Jerusha, it's all right! You're safe, now—it's all right!"

He tried to soothe her, but she clawed at him, then struck him with her fists as he struggled to subdue her. Eliakim persevered, patiently enduring her wild blows until he held her tightly in his embrace.

"It's all right, Jerusha. I won't hurt you. God of Abraham, please help her!"

Jerusha never heard him. Once again, she lived the nightmare that never ended, and her screams filled the courtyard.

Gradually the vivid scenes began to fade, and her terrible cries died down to a whimper. As if slowly awakening from a long sleep, she became aware of blue skies above her head, of cobblestones warmed by the sun, of open space all around her. Eliakim knelt on the ground with her, clasping her tightly to his chest. His cheek rested tenderly against her hair. Bloody scratches covered his arms where the whirring creatures had sunk their talons, but Eliakim had fought them off.

"I'm sorry, Jerusha—I'm so sorry," he murmured. "I never should have asked you to relive that. Can you ever forgive me?"

He was so gentle with her, his voice so soothing, that she lay in his arms with her face on his chest and wept for a long time. He made her feel safe, like Abba did, and she didn't want to leave his protecting arms. Then she noticed all the people clustered nearby, staring at her.

"Go on now," Eliakim told the gawking crowd. "Go on! Move along and leave us alone."

She finally managed to speak, her voice hoarse from screaming. "I was back there again."

"Shh—it's all right now."

"It was so real—all their creatures—the idols they worship—horrible things—"

"Jerusha, hush." He covered her lips with his fingers. "Don't talk about it anymore. It's over, and I'll never make you relive it again—I swear."

"But—but what if they come here?" Jerusha shivered, and Eliakim tightened his hold.

"Shh—they won't come here. They're a long way from here."

But she knew how swiftly they marched, how quickly they attacked, almost without warning. And they never lost a battle. Jerusha hadn't known any of the Assyrians' other victims, but now she knew Eliakim, and she had seen King Hezekiah and his nobles face-to-face. She shuddered, knowing what they would suffer at the hands of the Assyrians. Unwillingly, she envisioned King Hezekiah staked out and skinned alive. She saw Eliakim impaled on a stake and left to die slowly. She had tried to warn them, but the king's chief counselor had cut her short. He hadn't wanted to hear it.

She drew a deep breath. "We can go home. I'm all right now."

"Are you sure?" He seemed reluctant to let her go.

"It's all right. I—I'll be fine." He finally released her and helped her to her feet. Her legs felt limp and watery.

"Do you feel like walking a little bit? I think it might help if you breathed some fresh air. And you haven't seen much of Jerusalem yet, have you?"

"It was dark when we arrived last night."

"Come on, then." His arm encircled her waist, supporting her as they descended the palace stairs. "By the way, how did you get through the city gates so late at night?"

"Maacah gave the watchman your name, and he let us in."

"I didn't realize I wielded so much power," he said, laughing. "It must have been someone who knew me. I've been inspecting all the city walls and gates, you see."

He led her down the hill from the palace past the guard tower, then followed the road through the water gate. As they walked down to the spring, Eliakim pointed out the vineyards and olive groves in the fertile Kidron Valley and the carefully irrigated plots of the king's gardens near the lower pool. The green patches and leafy vines reminded Jerusha of home, the way Israel used to look. When they reached the spring, Eliakim coaxed a servant girl into lending them a dipper and drew Jerusha a drink.

"Tastes good, doesn't it?" he said.

"Mmm. And it's so cold. Just like the water from Abba's well." She felt tears burning her eyes, and she blinked them back. As Eliakim returned the dipper, Jerusha noticed the deep scratches on his arms again. She unwound the sash of her dress and dipped it into the water.

"Here. Let me wash off the blood."

When Jerusha finished and tied her sash again, Eliakim spun her around and pointed to the city on the hill above them. "Look up, Jerusha. See? Those cliffs form a natural fortress. And once we strengthen our walls, they'll never be able to topple them."

Jerusha nodded vaguely. It was true that she had never seen the Assyrians besiege a fortress as steep as Jerusalem, but the greater the challenge, the more determined they were to master it. They would find a way. Jerusha was certain of it.

"You're safe here," Eliakim said. "They won't recapture you." She wished she could believe him. Neither of them spoke as they walked up the ramp to the city again, but once inside the gates, Eliakim steered Jerusha toward the market square.

"Come on—I'll show you Abba's shop."

The marketplace in Jerusalem was unlike anything Jerusha had seen before, much bigger and busier than the tiny one in Dabbasheth. She slowed almost to a standstill, trying to take in all the varied sights, the mixture of exotic smells, the strident sounds. She saw piles and piles of pottery bowls and oil lamps, baskets of every shape and size, colorful heaps of fruit and vegetables, bolts of fine cloth and embroidered work, mounds of savory spices. Above it all, she heard the sound of haggling and the shouts of vendors as they hawked their goods. But she stared the longest at a glittering display of gold and silver jewelry—earrings, necklaces, bracelets, and rings, decorated with a beautiful bluish-green stone that Jerusha had never seen before.

She picked up a silver chain with an oval pendant stone. "What is this called?" she asked Eliakim.

"Do you like it? That's an Elath stone. It's found only in southern Judah, by the copper mines of Elath."

"It's beautiful." She caressed the cool, smooth rock, and the deep green reminded her of Abba's fields after the spring rains, the blue of the sky back home on a cloudless summer day.

"How much?" Eliakim asked the old shopkeeper.

The jeweler named an exorbitant price, and Eliakim gasped dramatically. "What? It's not worth half that!"

"Thief! Robber! You would take bread from my children?"

They began to dicker, so loudly at times that Jerusha feared they would strike each other. But before long the jeweler was weighing Eliakim's silver pieces on a scale and smiling as Eliakim fastened the beautiful necklace around Jerusha's neck.

"Look at that—it was made for her," the old man said. "It matches her beautiful green eyes."

"Oh, Eliakim, I can't accept such a gift! I—I don't know what to say."

"Don't say anything. Please, accept it with my apologies. I want you to know how sorry I am."

The old shopkeeper sighed. "Ahhh—young lovers."

Eliakim glanced at him nervously. "Come on, Jerusha. I'll show you Abba's shop."

He led her through the crush of people to Hilkiah's shop, nestled between an Arabian incense dealer and a booth of imported pottery. His servant ran out to greet them.

"Where's Abba?" Eliakim asked.

The man grinned. "You just missed him, my lord. But if you wait here, he might have good news for you when he comes back."

"What kind of news?"

"Oh, I shouldn't give it away! You'd better wait for Master Hilkiah. He'll tell you." The man hopped from one foot to the other in excitement.

Eliakim smiled at Jerusha. "Listen—I hate surprises. Why don't you just tell me where my father went?"

"To a very rich man's house. Royalty, I think."

"What for? Is he buying cloth from Abba?"

"Oh, no, no, no, Master Eliakim! Your father isn't selling cloth! He's bargaining for your wife!"

Eliakim gaped speechlessly, then he began to blush. Jerusha saw his skin turn red, even beneath his curly black beard.

"Come on, Jerusha," he said weakly. "Let's go home."

After the long, stressful day, Hezekiah went up to the palace rooftop with Shebna, escaping the stifling confines of his chambers. The ribbon of walls surrounding Jerusalem seemed flimsy to him, an insubstantial barrier against an impossibly superior foe—one that camped a mere three days' march away. Hezekiah's army remained poorly armed and trained, his water supply unavailable to him in a siege, his situation hopeless. He had tried to reign well for the last four years, to reverse the economic ruin and chaos of his father's rule, but would all his efforts be wasted because of his rebellion against Assyria?

"The plans for the new walls looked good, Your Majesty," Shebna said suddenly. "They should improve our city's defenses."

"I'm doing everything I can to strengthen this nation," he said. "I only hope we don't run out of time."

"I understand your urgency. The woman's report this morning was very vivid. The Assyrians have wasted no time laying siege to Samaria. How long does Jonadab think they can hold out?"

Hezekiah shrugged. "I haven't asked. Samaria has a water supply within its walls, which will help prolong the siege."

He rested his arms on the parapet and stared at his city, feeling discouraged and sick at heart. "Shebna, have I been a fool not to send the tribute these past few years?"

Shebna hesitated. "It would be very unwise to tell the king that he was a fool, my lord."

"Don't play games with me, Shebna. I want the truth."

Shebna faced him squarely. "All right. The truth is that I did not agree with your decision in the beginning. Even so, I must admit that the wealth that would have gone to Assyria has helped Judah prosper again. We would still be impoverished if you had sent the tribute."

"I know. And we'll be able to strengthen our defenses with some of that wealth. But what's going to happen because of it?"

All at once he wished Zechariah were alive. His grandfather had been convinced that rebelling was the right decision. But now Hezekiah had no one to encourage him except Shebna. He leaned against the parapet and stared at his friend gravely.

"Now that Samaria has been besieged, what do you think I should do?" Hezekiah saw Shebna's internal struggle.

"Your Majesty, I think this would be a good time to send a gift to Assyria. Call it a peace offering. If you make an alliance with them now, perhaps they will return to Nineveh peacefully after they have conquered Israel."

"But my father made an alliance with the Assyrians, and you know where that led him."

"I will be glad to audit the royal treasuries and tally our nation's resources, then present a taxation proposal. I will even head the delegation to Assyria to request the alliance if you would like me to. That is my advice—send the tribute quickly."

"But I think I'd be deceiving myself if I thought I could send tribute once and that would solve all my problems. It doesn't work that way. We'd be enslaved to them for life."

"Nevertheless, Your Majesty, becoming a vassal is a better choice than being totally destroyed. My advice stands. Pay the tribute. But if you decide not to take that advice, then for your nation's sake I urge you to form defensive alliances with your neighboring states. I suggest you approach Egypt, then maybe the Phoenicians. Judah cannot possibly face Assyria alone."

Hezekiah pulled on his beard as he wrestled with his decision, remembering Zechariah's warning about making alliances with other nations.

"What makes you so sure a foreign king would sign a treaty with us? Assyria is like a hungry lion aroused from a long slumber. And Judah would be easy prey after Israel."

"Then appeasing Assyria is the only answer." Shebna's advice made sense to Hezekiah, but he hesitated, unwilling to reach the same conclusion that Ahaz had. "Maybe it *would* be better for my people if I paid the tribute. Maybe I could spare them from an invasion—bloodshed—"

His voice trailed off uncertainly. The decision perplexed him. It seemed that both choices ended in disaster. He stood balanced on that narrow wall again, the same place he had stood four years ago when he made his decision to rebel. Yet he saw no way down to safety.

"Your Majesty, I would like to start working on a taxation proposal. If you decide to raise the tribute, it will be ready."

"Yes, maybe you should."

Shebna disappeared, leaving Hezekiah alone, discouraged and depressed. As he stood in the growing twilight, a gentle breeze from the north carried the sweet aroma of roasting meat down the hill from the Temple. And as the fragrance of the evening sacrifice reached him, Hezekiah suddenly remembered Yahweh. He had stopped paying tribute because he had put his faith in God. Hezekiah tried to recall that Passover night when his faith had seemed so much stronger. He had worked hard to obey God's Laws since then, purging the idolatry from the land, but had he done enough? Would Yahweh spare his nation because of his faithfulness? He wished he knew the answer.

He returned to his chambers, wandering idly through his rooms, his mind in turmoil. Had he done everything he could for

God? Should he do something more? He rummaged through his scrolls until he found the one he had written with Zechariah, then sat down beside the lampstand, searching for something he may have missed. When he read the words *"He must not take many wives, or his heart will be led astray"* he stopped reading. Four years ago he had forsaken all his concubines for Hephzibah. But except for the baby that had died, Hephzibah had given him no children. Why hadn't Yahweh provided an heir?

"Where am I going wrong? Why is everything falling apart?" God had forsaken him, betraying him to his enemies. Hezekiah sat alone for more than an hour, allowing the winds of self-pity to blow, piling doubt all around him. His faith in Yahweh had been in vain, the promises of God, a lie. He remembered his last afternoon with his grandfather, and Moses' parting words: "Yahweh himself goes before you and will be with you; he will never leave you nor forsake you. Do not be afraid; do not be discouraged." He longed to have more faith in God, and he remembered how Zechariah had snatched the Torah scroll out of his hand, saying, "Either your faith in God is absolute, or it's worthless."

Hezekiah slowly paged through the Torah, longing to discover the source of Zechariah's unshakable faith in God, searching for a promise he could cling to. He stopped when he found these words: "When you go to war against your enemies and see horses and chariots and an army greater than yours, do not be afraid of them, because the Lord your God, who brought you up out of Egypt, will be with you."

Hezekiah bowed his head and prayed for the strength to believe that promise, for the courage to stand firm in his decision not to send tribute, for the power to become a man of faith.

The struggle is always in the will, Zechariah had told him. Hezekiah willed to believe. He silently vowed never to doubt Yahweh's word again. He left the scroll open to the promise he had found and browsed through the stories of his childhood hero, King David, drawing strength from them, until he stumbled upon the words that Nathan the prophet had spoken to David: "Your house and your kingdom will endure forever before me." It was Yahweh's promise, to David and now to Hezekiah. His reign would endure; he would have an heir.

He rolled up the scroll and put it away, then walked to Hephzibah's chambers. She was his oasis in the desert, and he longed for the comfort of her arms. But Hephzibah didn't run to him as she usually did. She never moved from her seat beside the window. He bent to kiss her and saw tears in her eyes.

"Hephzibah, what's wrong?" She didn't answer, and he lifted her chin to make her look at him. "Please tell me."

"My lord," she began tearfully, "I'm so afraid—"

He thought of Jerusha's chilling report that morning and felt his stomach turn. "What are you afraid of, my love? Tell me. You know I'd do anything to make you happy."

"Would you really do anything?" she whispered.

"Tell me, my love."

She inhaled as if summoning courage. "My lord, I'm so afraid you'll have to divorce me because I'm barren. I beg you—please, go to one of your concubines tonight instead of me. Just until she gives you a child—just until you have an heir. The child could become ours. Please, my lord?"

Hezekiah's faith in Yahweh's promises blew away in a gust of doubt: Hephzibah was barren. She would never give him an heir.

For a moment he considered doing what she asked. Then anger exploded inside him—anger at himself for doubting so soon after his vow of faith, anger at the impossible decisions he faced, anger at his own helplessness. He hated his helplessness most of all, remembering how he had stood helpless before Molech.

"No!" he shouted as he pushed Hephzibah away. "No, no, no! Yahweh promised that the house of David would endure forever! Do you think He's going to break His promise now?"

"Can't the promise be kept through a concubine?" she asked, trembling. Her stubbornness infuriated him.

"No, it can't! God promised Abraham an heir, but he listened to his wife and fathered Ishmael! *Isaac* was the son of the promise, *not* the concubine's son! I won't listen to you. Don't you have any faith in Yahweh at all?" She covered her face. "Why don't you stop feeling sorry for yourself and start trusting God?"

He strode from the room, banging the door shut behind him. The irony of his words struck him as he walked back to his own chambers. He was as guilty of doubt and self-pity as Hephzibah was. And he knew that the great anger he felt was not toward his wife but toward himself.

27 ⊷

Eliakim rummaged through his scrolls and drawings, making a mess of his tiny workroom.

"We're all waiting for you," his father called. "Are you eating breakfast or not?"

"Start without me. I'm busy." He gazed at the mess he had made.

"He's busy!" Hilkiah said, loudly enough for him to hear. "He's always busy, but too busy to eat? Well, never mind. We'll eat without him, won't we, girls? No sense in all of us starving."

Eliakim sorted uselessly through the mess for a few more minutes, then finally wandered out to where the others were seated around the low table. He bent to scoop up a handful of olives and cucumbers, then stood beside the table chewing absently, his mind on the dozens of projects he supervised for King Hezekiah.

"What now?" Hilkiah scowled. "You're too busy to sit down?"

"What did you say, Abba?"

Hilkiah bowed with exaggerated politeness, indicating Eliakim's empty cushion. "Would you care to join us?"

Eliakim glanced across the table at Jerusha as he sat down, then quickly looked away. She wore the Elath stone necklace he had given her and the lovely deep-blue dress she had worn the day she accompanied him to the king's advisory meeting. Hilkiah had bought the girls a dozen new dresses, but Eliakim's favorite was still this beautiful blue one. He had admired her courage so much that day, and he also recalled his panic when she collapsed in his arms, struggling for sanity. But Jerusha had tremendous inner strength. Not many people could have survived her ordeal.

"What is it that has you too busy to eat?" Hilkiah asked.

Eliakim gulped down some yogurt, feeling foolishly self-conscious. "The city walls. There are still a dozen places that have to be reinforced, besides the new walls that—" He stopped midsentence as the idea struck him. He could take Jerusha with him to inspect the walls, and she could explain how the Assyrians would attack them. He looked up to ask if she would come with him, then abruptly lost his train of thought. Her hair had grown, and it now reached her chin, curling softly around her lovely face. He had never seen a woman with short hair before. It was unheard of. But it looked extremely attractive on Jerusha.

"Did you swallow an olive pit or something?" Hilkiah asked.

Eliakim looked at his father. "What—?"

"You stopped in the middle of your new wall. I thought maybe you were choking on the food you've been bolting down. Have you bothered to taste it at all?"

Eliakim's face felt hot. Explaining his preoccupation would only make matters worse. "Uh—the food's excellent. And we're laying the foundations for the new walls."

He didn't know what else to say, so he silently pondered the idea of taking Jerusha with him. It made a lot of sense, but he decided to wait until his father left for work. Hilkiah was fiercely protective of his girls.

At last Hilkiah pushed away from the table. Maacah walked him to the door, leaving Eliakim alone with Jerusha. He watched her gather up the bowls and serving dishes, debating how to ask her without breaking his promise not to remind her of her ordeal. He remembered how it felt to hold her frail body as she trembled with terror, and he cleared his throat nervously.

"Uh—Jerusha? I was wondering—"

She stopped stacking dishes and looked at him, fingering her necklace. He wished she was wearing a different dress.

"It, uh—it just occurred to me that you could help me with the walls—if you don't mind, that is."

"The walls—?"

"Yes. I'd like you to come with me and see what we've done and what we've got planned, and maybe—you know—give us a different perspective—how the enemy would see it."

"I don't know anything about walls, Eliakim, but I'll come if you think it would help."

"Yes! I think you'd be a big help! Listen—I have to gather my things together, so you have a few minutes—if you want to go change your clothes or something—"

She looked down at her dress in dismay. "Is there something wrong with this dress?"

"No, no! It's fine! It's just that it's so nice, and we'll be—you know—climbing on walls and—"

He left the sentence dangling and fled to his workroom to gather his project drawings and his wits. He hoped she would change out of that beautiful, distracting dress. He couldn't seem to think straight when she wore it. When Jerusha reappeared she had changed, but that dress proved every bit as distracting as the first. He sighed in resignation and they headed out the door.

For the first part of the morning they visited the older sections of the wall that had been damaged during King Ahaz's reign. Eliakim explained terms like "casemate" wall and "header and stretcher" construction, and Jerusha took an interest in everything, asking questions, offering comments.

Still, she had an eerie coldness about her, a lack of emotion that intrigued and challenged him. Eliakim found himself trying to amuse her, trying to make her laugh and come alive. Her smile, when it finally spread across her face, reminded him of the first tiny wildflowers that bloom after a freezing winter.

Shortly before noon he took her to one of the highest points on the wall, above the steep cliff overlooking the Kidron Valley. He watched her face as she stood with her hands resting on top of the wall, looking across the beautiful valley toward the Mount of Olives. A gentle breeze rustled her skirts, and the sun shone on her hair, edging it with gold.

"It's so beautiful up here!" she said. "Look how far you can see!"

"Yes. Isn't this some view?" He felt strangely short-winded, as if he had run up a steep hill. "Look—you can even see the Judean wilderness, way over there."

As Jerusha gazed at the horizon, Eliakim stared breathlessly at her long, slender neck. He felt an almost unbearable urge to kiss the hollow of her throat, and he gripped the parapet with sweating hands, forcing himself to look away.

"I think I see it—" She pointed to the distant horizon. "Those brownish-gray hills?"

"Uh-huh. That's where the wilderness starts."

When she lowered her hand it accidentally brushed against his, and an alarming, thrilling shock soared up Eliakim's arm and through his body. He had never felt anything like it before.

"It seems odd to be looking down from the top of the walls instead of being in the valley with the Assyrians," Jerusha said. "The city feels so secure up here, but—"

"But what? Tell me. That's why I asked you to come."

"The Assyrians would scarcely worry about these walls. They're just a trivial annoyance standing in front of their goal."

A wave of fear and frustration washed over Eliakim as Jerusha's words reduced months of hard work into rubble. "But they can't get their battering rams up to the base of these walls! Look how steep that cliff is!"

"They wouldn't attack here. They'd choose a weaker place."

Eliakim ran his fingers through his tousled hair. "Like the northwest section. I know—that's why I plan to reinforce that area and build a casemate wall." Jerusha didn't reply.

"Now what are you thinking?" he asked anxiously.

"You're working so hard, Eliakim, and all of your fortifications will certainly slow them down—"

"Slow them down!"

"But the Assyrians don't care how long it takes. Six months or six years—it's nothing to them."

"So I'm wasting my time and the king's money? If they decide to attack Jerusalem, nothing can save us? Is that it?"

"I don't know. It's just that I've never seen them lose."

"So if they decide to attack us—then what? It's hopeless?"

She stared into the distance, her eyes wide. When she spoke, something much deeper than ordinary fear edged her voice. "If I heard that the Assyrians were coming to besiege this city I'd run away—into the desert somewhere." The wind blew her hair into her face, and as she brushed it away her hands shook.

Eliakim felt ashamed of what he had done, and for a horrible moment he feared that she would collapse again. But when she spoke again her voice sounded normal.

"I'm sorry, Eliakim, but you wanted to know."

"I'd better take you home. It's nearly lunchtime."

"Eliakim, wait." Jerusha touched his arm, and Eliakim's heart raced. "I'm really sorry. You've worked so hard on these walls, and I called them useless. They're not—it's just that I'm still so afraid—I'm sorry. Can you forgive me?" Her beautiful green eyes filled with tears, and Eliakim's heart squeezed.

"I asked for your honest opinion, and that's what you gave me. There's nothing to forgive. Come on. Abba will worry if we're late." With his heart thudding uncontrollably, he took Jerusha's arm and helped her down the steep steps from the wall.

◆

Hephzibah sat in her parents' garden beneath her favorite fig tree, but she found no comfort in the familiar surroundings. Once again she had failed to conceive, and so she had come home rather than endure the bitterness of not being held by her husband. Mama would hold her and comfort her. Mama didn't care if she broke Yahweh's law. She tenderly stroked Hephzibah's thick hair.

"I know I should mind my own business," Mama said, "but can't you tell me why you're so sad? Are you still mourning your baby?"

Hephzibah nodded, fighting tears. "It's been almost four years. Why do I still feel so empty?"

Her mother drew her close. "I know—I lost a baby too."

"But you had nine children, Mama. I have none."

"You will, darling. You will." Hephzibah's mother was silent for a moment, then fumbled for words. "I know we've never discussed your private life before—but—I just wondered—do you see your husband very often?"

Hephzibah guessed what her mother was trying to ask, and since she had no one else to talk to about her fears, she opened her heart to her mother.

"My husband has no other wives or concubines except me. I should have conceived by now. I feel like a failure."

"The king has no harem?" her mother asked in astonishment.

"He says it's against Yahweh's law." She heard the bitterness in her voice and recognized a familiar prickle of jealousy at the mention of Hezekiah's God.

"You're the king's only wife?" her mother repeated.

"He says Yahweh's law allows him only one wife. But that's the problem—don't you see? If I don't give him an heir, he'll have to divorce me and marry someone who isn't barren." She hated that word. It reminded her of the lifeless Judean wilderness, and she imagined her womb dry and shriveled like a withered leaf that would crumble at the touch.

"Couldn't a concubine give him a son?"

"No, he got very angry when I asked him that question. I've never seen him so angry. He made it very clear that he would never take a concubine."

"That doesn't make any sense."

"I love him so much, Mama, yet I can't enjoy being with him anymore. Every time he comes to see me I wish he would go away, because I know I'll fail him again. Yet I don't want him to go away! I love him, and I'm so afraid he'll leave me forever! I'm not even making sense, am I?"

Hephzibah cried quietly as her mother held her. "Sometimes I'm filled with hope: maybe this time, maybe this month. But then my time comes, and I've failed again." She tried to wipe away tears that wouldn't stop. "Do you think Yahweh is punishing me?"

"Punishing you? Why would He punish you?"

"After our baby died I was supposed to bring a sin offering to the Temple, but I didn't do it. Why should I? I didn't sin."

"Of course you didn't sin. Where did you hear such a thing?"

"The king said it's Yahweh's law."

"Well, I don't care if your husband *is* the king—it's not right! How can he put one woman under so much pressure to give him an heir? That's why kings have harems. Everyone knows that as soon as a husband takes a concubine, his wife gets pregnant. Wasn't Isaac born after the concubine's son?"

"I guess so." She was glad she had confided in her mother. She felt better after sharing the feelings she had hoarded so long.

"Listen, Hephzibah—I've never had much use for Yahweh and all His rules. He's an angry god, full of wrath and vengeance. Asherah gave your father and me children, not Yahweh. She understands women. And didn't she answer your prayers before? Didn't you pray to Asherah when you wanted to marry the prince?"

"Yes."

Mama pondered something for a moment. "I'll be right back."

She returned a few minutes later with a small bundle, wrapped in an embroidered cloth. At first Hephzibah thought it was a baby and wondered where it had come from. Then her mother unwrapped a golden statue of Asherah and thrust it into Hephzibah's arms.

"Here. I want you to have this. She has blessed our house with seven sons; now let her bless yours."

"The king has forbidden it! He worships no god but Yahweh."

"And has Yahweh given him a son? Of course not! Asherah is the goddess of fertility, not Yahweh. Your marriage is unfruitful because the king has angered her. He's turned his back on Asherah and destroyed all her sacred groves and altars, banished all her priests. Of course she's punishing him. And you're suffering because of it. But if you worship her faithfully and renew your vows, maybe she'll show forgiveness. Take this. Your husband doesn't even have to know about it."

Hephzibah hesitated, not sure if she could deliberately deceive Hezekiah. But what if her mother was right? What if he had offended Asherah? Yahweh seemed cold and forbidding, demanding animals and sacrifices and blood. Asherah embodied life and love. The goddess would give her a child, not rip it away from her. She looked down at the golden figure with the full bosom and pregnant belly. Then Hephzibah wrapped the idol in the embroidered cloth and held it to her breast.

"Thank you, Mama," she whispered.

28 ⊰─○──

Jerusha sat on the stone bench in Hilkiah's tiny garden and stared up at the starry sky, pretending she was home. She had grown accustomed to the confinements of city life, but her heart still longed for rolling green hills and open spaces. She remembered how millions of stars had twinkled in the clear night sky—"sons of Abraham," Abba called them. She missed the sound of the wind in the trees outside her window, the soothing hum of insects, the soft crunching of straw as the oxen chewed their feed in the stall beneath her room. City sounds were so different. They were strident noises, rushed and wearisome.

"It's a beautiful night, isn't it?" Eliakim stood beside her. "Mind if I join you?"

"Of course not." She moved to make room for him on the bench. "Do you like to look at the stars too?"

"Yes, but—I have to confess, that's not why I came out here. I came out to escape."

"What are you escaping from?"

"Another marriage proposal. They're becoming embarrassing." He sighed as he ran his fingers through his rumpled hair.

"Don't you want to get married?"

"Sure, but how am I supposed to choose? The best price? The prettiest maiden? The most impressive papa? It's all ridiculous, and I'm getting sick of it. I'm hardly worth haggling over."

He sighed again and fell into a long silence, not looking at the stars at all, but sitting hunched with his arms on his legs, hands dangling between his knees. Jerusha understood why all the proud fathers fought over someone as handsome and important as Eliakim. As a country farmer's daughter, Jerusha had been content to marry Abram, a poor, hardworking farmer like Abba. But she was no longer a suitable wife for any man.

"Why don't you just pick one, then, and get it over with?" she said at last. She played with the smooth Elath stone necklace he'd given her, envying the woman he chose.

"I probably should. Abba's disgusted with me for giving him such a hard time about it. But choosing a wife is a major decision, and I don't want to make it arbitrarily. After all, I'll be living with my choice for the rest of my life."

"Don't you like any of them?"

His eyes narrowed as he considered. "Want to know the truth? They're all shallow, pampered, overpainted brats."

"Eliakim!"

He laughed scandalously. "Well, it's true. Anyhow, I'm sick of talking about it. Let's talk about something else."

"How's your work on the walls coming?"

"Great! Remember that older section I showed you near the Dung Gate? You should come and see what I'm doing there. It will take an army to move that wall when I'm done with it!" They laughed at the irony of his words. "Anyway, you know what I mean."

"Yes, I know. What about the new northwest wall?"

"Well, I'd planned a casemate wall for that section, but after what you said the other day, I'm still not convinced that it's going to be strong enough." He scratched his beard thoughtfully. "I just don't know what to do there. Any ideas?"

Eliakim was so kind and gentle, so serious, yet so boyishly natural. Jerusha knew she could easily fall in love with him, but she must never allow herself to do such a foolish thing. It was more than the obvious class differences or the fact that she was a penniless orphan and he was a wealthy aristocrat. Eliakim deserved someone pure and unsoiled for his wife, and Jerusha had been with many men. Falling in love with Eliakim was a hopeless folly that could lead only to disappointment in the end.

"I don't know, Eliakim," she finally answered. "I think a casemate wall will probably be strong enough, won't it?" She couldn't bear to remind him that no wall was strong enough to keep the Assyrians out once they determined to get in.

"Why doesn't King Hezekiah appease them with tribute payments? Then he wouldn't have to worry about the walls."

"Because we'd forfeit our freedom. We'd be their slaves."

Jerusha looked away. "You mean, King Hezekiah would rather die than be a slave to the Assyrians?"

"Well, it's a lot more complicated than that, but yes, that's basically what it boils down to."

A deep shame filled Jerusha. She had faced the same dilemma and had made the coward's choice. If she could go back in time, she would let Iddina plunge his dagger into her heart rather than submit to him. She shivered.

"Hey—you're getting cold. Maybe we should go inside."

"No, I'm fine. I want to look at the stars a while longer."

"Are you sure? The proud papa is probably gone by now. Maybe it's safe to go back in." Eliakim's mischievous grin made her smile. She hurried to change the subject, to say something to break the strong pull she felt toward him.

"Can I ask you a question?" she said.

"Sure—anything."

"It's silly, really, but I just wondered how you got that scar on your neck."

"This?" He rubbed the thin line beneath his Adam's apple.

"It looks like someone tried to slit your throat."

"That's exactly what happened," Eliakim said, laughing. "This is General Jonadab's handiwork, the commander-in-chief of King Hezekiah's army. But we're good friends now."

"After he almost killed you?"

"Well, at the time he thought I was a dangerous rebel, plotting to overthrow King Hezekiah."

"You?"

He drew himself up straight and proudly threw back his shoulders. "Yes, me!"

The thought of gentle, scholarly Eliakim plotting a revolution made Jerusha laugh out loud. Against her will, she was drawn to him even more hopelessly than before. She knew she was a fool. When Eliakim finally married his rich wife, she knew her heart would break, but she was powerless to stop herself.

As a silvery moon rose above them, Eliakim laughingly told her the story of the night Micah prophesied to the king.

———◆———

Hezekiah watched as the oxen strained to move a massive building block for the new city walls. A cheer rose from the workmen as the stone fell into place on the bedrock, and Hezekiah relaxed the muscles he had been unconsciously tensing. As he ran his hand over the stone's rough surface, it seemed inconceivable to him that an army could topple such massive rocks. The fact that the Assyrians had toppled countless walls underscored the awful power of his enemies.

"God, help us," he murmured.

Eliakim climbed out of the trench, his face and neck sunburned beneath a layer of dust and sweat. He stood with his hands on his hips, waiting for Hezekiah's reaction.

"Very impressive, Eliakim. Now, let's get out of this sun."

Eliakim followed him to a square patch of shade beneath the foreman's tent where Shebna and Jonadab waited, fanning themselves. They both looked wilted, and sweat poured off Jonadab's bald head in a steady stream.

"Don't you have any water around here?" Jonadab asked Eliakim.

"Just this." Eliakim produced a dusty waterskin, sloshing it to see if there was any left. "It's probably warm—"

"I don't care!" Jonadab grabbed it and tipped the spout to his lips, gulping noisily, then held it out to Shebna.

Suddenly a look of horror crossed his face when he realized that he had quenched his own thirst before offering it to the king. "I—I'm sorry, Your Majesty," he stammered, wiping the spout on his tunic. "I didn't mean to—"

"No, thanks, Jonadab," Hezekiah said. "But you've underscored a point I was about to raise—our critical need for water. The double walls, the weapons in the citadel, the fortifications will all be useless if we die of thirst. The four of us are going down to the Gihon Spring, and we're going to find a way to safeguard our water supply."

Hezekiah led the way out of the tent, climbing over the clutter of rocks and debris from the construction. After filing through the gap where the new gate would stand, they followed the road down to the spring. Goats quietly grazed along the steep hillside beside the aqueduct, while across the valley workmen vigorously shook the first ripe olives from the branches. Life went on unhurried, as if the Assyrian army didn't exist. But the peaceful scene in the Kidron Valley belied the sense of restless urgency Hezekiah felt.

When they reached the spring, Hezekiah squatted beside the water, cupping his hands for a drink, splashing some onto his face and neck. The sun blazed in the hazy sky like the fires of Molech, and Jonadab found a patch of shade where they could sit, on the low wall of a terraced olive grove. As Hezekiah stared at the city above him, the golden stones shimmered in the heat. He traced the line of ancient walls that encircled the old city, then Solomon's walls, added to protect the upper hill and the Temple. The fortifications looked impressive from the valley.

Jonadab looked up at the city too. "It's an ideal city to defend, Your Majesty. It's a natural fortress, built on such a steep mountaintop that my armies could defend it forever if—" He stopped abruptly and looked at Hezekiah.

"I know," Hezekiah said. "If only we had water. But I refuse to give up. The defense of Jerusalem depends on it."

Shebna's blue-black hair glistened with sweat. He wiped the back of his hand across his brow. "We could construct more cisterns inside the walls, haul water up to fill them during peacetime, then use it in times of war," he said.

"That's a possibility," Hezekiah said, "but a temporary water source such as a cistern causes problems with morale. People know that sooner or later they'll run dry, and they start hoarding water or trampling each other to get at it."

"I've considered constructing walls around the spring," Eliakim said, "but it would be impossible to connect them to the city walls. The slopes are too steep."

Hezekiah shaded his eyes and stared up at the city again, trying to see it from the enemy's viewpoint. "I came here with my grandfather when I was a child, and he told me the story of how King David's armies conquered Jerusalem."

"I learned that story too," Eliakim said. "David's men found a secret passageway, didn't they? And it led into the city?"

"I do not think we can put much faith in those stories," Shebna said. "King David's exploits were greatly exaggerated after his death until they reached mythical proportions."

"Then how did they get inside the walls?" Eliakim asked.

"That's a fair question," Jonadab said. "Jerusalem would be hard to conquer by conventional methods of war, especially in King David's time."

Hezekiah scooped up a stone and tossed it from one hand to the other as he spoke. "My grandfather said the Jebusites dug a shaft so they could draw water during a siege. David's men found the entrance here at the spring and crawled up the shaft into the city."

Shebna frowned skeptically. "That mountain is made of solid rock. How could they dig a tunnel through it?"

Hezekiah didn't answer. He had suddenly noticed a slight depression where the spring bordered the slope of the hill. He tossed down his stone and leaped to his feet.

"Do you suppose the tunnel is still here?" Eliakim asked, following Hezekiah as he skirted the water's edge.

"I don't know. But my grandfather trusted the chronicles of David to be accurate."

When Hezekiah got as close as he could along the bank, he shed his sandals and outer robe, tucked the hem of his tunic into his belt, then waded into the icy waters of the spring. By the time he reached the curious depression on the side of the hill, he was soaked to his thighs.

For several minutes he and Eliakim worked to pull out the over-hanging weeds and stones until they saw a small, cavelike entrance leading into the side of the cliff.

"Get a torch!" Hezekiah shouted.

Jonadab hurried up the ramp to the guard tower by the water gate. While they waited, Eliakim and Shebna helped Hezekiah remove more rocks and rubble that had accumulated in front of the entrance to the cave. By the time they had cleared an opening large enough to squeeze through, Jonadab returned. He handed the torch to Eliakim, who ducked through the hole and disappeared into the side of the hill.

"God of Abraham!" he shouted. "You've got to see this!"

Hezekiah squeezed through behind Eliakim and found himself in a narrow slit between two high rock walls. Eliakim stood several feet in front of him, holding the torch, but beyond him the walls disap-peared into inky darkness. The floor beneath Hezekiah's bare feet felt very rough. The walls, which were only a foot apart at the bottom, gradually grew wider apart until they reached the ceiling, just inches above his head.

"Shebna, come see this," Hezekiah called. He waded into the tun-nel to make room for him. In the murky light he saw his friend gaze around, stunned.

Then Shebna leaned against a wall, mumbling, "I cannot believe it!"

"How far back does it go, Eliakim?"

"I don't know, Your Majesty. Let's find out."

Eliakim sloshed forward into the darkness, and Hezekiah waded behind him, barely able to see, feeling his way along the walls. The rock seemed to absorb what little light they had, and Shebna, who was in al-most total darkness, held on to Hezekiah's belt as they groped through the icy, knee-deep water. The crudely cut slit meandered as it wound for several yards into the mountain; then the ceiling gradually lowered until the tunnel ended in another archlike entrance close to the water's surface. Eliakim ducked through first, momentarily plunging Hezekiah and Shebna into total darkness.

"God of Abraham!" Eliakim cried. "Come look at this!" Hezekiah entered a large, cavelike room, nearly round, with walls much smoother than the tunnel's walls. "It's a holding tank!" Eliakim ex-claimed. "For the water!" He raised the torch as high as he could and shone it all around. "Look! There it is! That's where the shaft was!"

Hezekiah spotted a depression in the middle of the smooth ceiling, no wider than a small man's shoulders. Someone had packed it tightly with rocks and rubble. "King David probably didn't want his enemies to find it," Hezekiah said.

Eliakim's eyes were wide. "And I thought it was just a bedtime story! Who would have believed it?"

"It certainly looks man-made," Shebna said as he ran his hand across the walls.

"It probably was a cave originally," Eliakim said, "and the Jebusites enlarged it. The limestone in this area has a lot of natural caves and fissures. The spring itself comes from underground somewhere."

Hezekiah gazed around in amazement, not sure which astounded him more—discovering a way to secure their water supply or learning that the ancient stories were true. This narrow, black tunnel carved in the mountain had encouraged him, inspired him, and renewed his faith.

"Let's go," he said. His legs had begun to ache from the numbing water. He followed Eliakim out, then sat in the sun to warm himself.

Shebna bristled with excitement. "If that truly is a shaft that leads up to the city, then this could be our answer. We could reopen it, and—"

"I don't know," Jonadab said, frowning. "We'd have to get rid of the aqueduct and hide the spring, or the enemy could find the tunnel as easily as we did. I'd hate to risk it."

"Besides, our population is 10 times the size of Jebusite Jerusalem," Eliakim said. "Without the spring or the lower pool, we'd never be able to draw enough water for the entire city from one narrow shaft."

"Maybe we could widen the shaft," Shebna said.

Eliakim thought a moment. "I suppose that's possible, but I'd estimate that the city is more than a hundred cubits above the spring. That's a long way to haul water every day."

"We would need to use it only in times of siege," Shebna argued.

Jonadab shook his head. "No, I don't like it. As long as the spring and the lower pool remain exposed, the enemy could find the shaft. And if we made it wider, we'd make it easier to crawl through too."

"Let's consider this," Hezekiah said. "If the Jebusites could tunnel through solid rock, why couldn't we? We certainly have better tools than they did three or four hundred years ago. Let's forget the shaft and lengthen the existing tunnel. We could channel the water underground to a new pool inside the walls."

Eliakim grinned. "Then we could get rid of the aqueduct and hide the spring underground! They'd never know it was here!"

Jonadab mopped his forehead with his sleeve. "I'd like to see how long the Assyrians could last out here if *they* were the ones without water."

Hezekiah turned to Eliakim. "Do you think we could do it?"

"I can think of a few problems," Eliakim answered. His high fore-head furrowed in thought. "But I won't say it's impossible. I'd like to come back with more torches and look it over carefully. Then I can give you a better answer."

"If it *is* possible," Jonadab said, "then I'd say the king's idea of an underground watercourse is brilliant!"

As they walked up the hill, Hezekiah felt more encouraged than he had in months, and he was eager to begin work immediately. The men gathered in the council chamber with Eliakim's blueprint of the city spread in front of them.

"I'm impressed by the Jebusites' tenacity," Eliakim said. "It must have been difficult to carve through solid rock with primitive tools."

Hezekiah agreed. "I understand the Phoenicians are experienced in mining operations like this. I'll send our trade minister to Tyre to ne-gotiate for the tools we'll need."

Shebna seemed unusually quiet and moody. "What are you thinking?" Hezekiah asked him.

"I think your tunnel is an excellent idea, Your Majesty, but I do not believe we will have enough time to dig it. We should concentrate our efforts on reopening the shaft first. That would provide a backup system."

"But why waste time on a temporary solution?" Eliakim said. "It would take a major operation to unblock the vertical shaft, because there's no trace of the other end up here in the city. And if we dig from the bottom up, all that rubble is going to come down onto our heads."

"Eliakim's right," Hezekiah said. "If we're going to spend time and money digging, then I'd like to dig a new tunnel that would chan-nel the water over here." He pointed inside the southern wall of the city. "Could it be done?"

Eliakim studied the drawing. "Well, I see at least three obstacles, Your Majesty. First, it's a long way to dig—I'd say almost a third of a mile, maybe longer. Tunneling would be slow, and we'd have to trans-port the rubble a long way to the surface."

"What would we do with all the rubble?" Shebna asked. "If it is a secret project, piles of rock in the valley would certainly give it away."

"Second, it would be difficult to get fresh air into such a long tun-nel," Eliakim continued. "And our torches would eat up more air. If we bored air shafts from the surface, it would add years to the project."

Hezekiah frowned. "We can't afford that kind of time."

"The Jebusite shaft has already been dug," Shebna insisted. "We should dig more cisterns and use the shaft when the cisterns run dry."

"And what if the enemy finds it?" Jonadab asked.

Shebna gave him a scathing look. "Only one soldier could climb up at a time, General. Surely your men could fend them off! Besides, they could find a tunnel just as easily."

"No, if we had a tunnel we would bury the spring beneath the surface of the ground," Eliakim said.

Shebna's voice slowly rose in volume. "So then why not bury the spring and use the shaft? It is already dug for you."

Eliakim's voice rose to match his. "Because the spring is a natural fountain. It surges, and the runoff has to be channeled somewhere. That's what the aqueduct and lower pool are for. If we dug a tunnel, we'd make a pool inside the walls to hold the runoff."

Hezekiah grew impatient. "We could probably find a solution if you two would quit bickering. You said there were three obstacles, Eliakim. What's the third?"

"If you look at the underground route, the shortest, most direct path would take us right through here—"

"I see," Hezekiah sighed. "The tombs of King David and Solomon are in the way."

"Unfortunately, yes."

"Even so, I refuse to give up the idea," Hezekiah insisted. "A water supply is crucial in siege warfare, and I know we have the skills to do the physical labor and planning. After all, the Jebusites did it. Keep working on it, Eliakim. Hire any extra help you need. But whatever we decide, let's keep one thing in mind: the Assyrians are camped less than 50 miles away. We may not have much time to find a solution."

29

When the evening meal ended, Hilkiah leaned against the cushions and sighed with contentment. Jerusha and Maacah excused themselves, and Eliakim started to his feet.

"Oh, no, you don't," Hilkiah said, pulling him back. "You're not leaving this table until you give me your answer."

"What was the question?"

"Eliakim, do you listen to anything I say, or do my words simply bounce off your ears?"

"I'm sorry, Abba. I have a lot on my mind. Ask me again."

"All right," he said with exaggerated patience. "As I told you at breakfast, I have two eager fathers who are waiting for your answer. Are you going to marry their daughters or not?"

"Both of them? I have to marry *two* wives, now?" Eliakim grinned.

Hilkiah wasn't amused. "Eliakim—they are from good families. Doesn't either of them appeal to you?"

"What's the big hurry? Why the rush to marry me off?" As usual, the subject irritated Eliakim.

"So you don't want to get married at all?"

"I didn't say that. I just wondered—what's the big hurry? Am I the last eligible bachelor in Jerusalem?"

Hilkiah sighed. "You want me to turn them both down?"

"Would you? And no more proposals for a while, Abba. I need a break from all this nonsense."

"If that's what you want." Eliakim glanced at his father to see if he was angry, but to his surprise Hilkiah was grinning.

"What's so funny?"

"Nothing! This matchmaking is serious business!" Hilkiah's eyes twinkled merrily as he began a long, rambling speech about the intri-

217

cacies of the process and all the hardships Eliakim had put him through.

Eliakim stopped listening, thinking instead about King Hezekiah's water system. He was anxious to go back to his room and work on it, aware that he had to come up with a proposal soon or the king would choose Shebna's plan to reopen the Jebusite shaft. Eliakim couldn't allow that to happen. He'd promised Jerusha that the Assyrians would never get into the city, and Shebna's plan was too risky. Gradually Eliakim became aware that his father was still talking to him.

". . . and it seems like they've always been part of our household, doesn't it?"

"Huh? What did you say, Abba?"

"The girls, Jerusha and Maacah." Hilkiah nodded toward the kitchen area, where they'd gone to supervise the servants.

"Uh, yes, Abba—I can't remember what it was like without them."

"Yes, and it'll certainly be quiet again after they're gone." Hilkiah sighed and sadly shook his head.

Eliakim suddenly woke up. "Gone? Where are they going? Not back to Israel?"

"Don't be absurd. I mean when they get married and move into homes of their own."

"What are you talking about?" Eliakim felt a surge of panic that he couldn't explain.

"Well, I'm their adoptive father, so it's my duty to see that they find husbands. And what wonderful wives they will make, eh? They're such beautiful girls, aren't they?—now that they've put some meat on their bones."

"Yes, lovely. But what's the hurry, Abba? I think you're getting a little carried away with all this matchmaking business. Have they told you that they want to get married?"

"Well, no, but they're of age, and is there a healthy young woman who doesn't want to get married and have a family? Just because *you* want to stay single doesn't mean everyone else does."

Eliakim tugged on his beard, his concern about this conversation rapidly mounting. "I suppose that's true—"

"So I've begun to inquire around about husbands and—"

"You've *what?*"

"—and if I provide a nice dowry, it should be very easy to find suitable husbands for both of them."

"Abba, why are you rushing into this? The girls seem happy here."

"Yes, they do. And Jerusha has taken quite an interest in your building projects, eh?"

"She understands everything, Abba. She's very bright and so easy to talk to, not silly and shallow like other women—" Hilkiah's laughter interrupted him. "What's so funny? What did I say?"

Hilkiah wiped his eyes, then spread his arms wide as he looked toward heaven. "God of Abraham? How is it possible that my son, the brilliant engineer, is so stupid?"

"Stupid? Are you laughing at me because I think Jerusha is intelligent? How do you think she survived? Have you ever talked to her? Well, I've spent a great deal of time with her these past few months, and I'm telling you she's a beautiful, bright, wonderful woman who—"

Eliakim stopped short. Hilkiah had dissolved into laughter again, holding his stomach and shaking his head.

"Abba, why are you laughing at Jerusha this way?"

"I'm not laughing at Jerusha—I'm laughing at you!"

"At me? Why?"

"Because you're in love with her, and you're too thickheaded to realize it!"

Eliakim was speechless. He had never considered the possibility before. Was that why panic had seized him when his father spoke of her leaving? He tried to imagine the long evenings without Jerusha to talk to, and when he thought of her marrying another man, his heart leaped with fear. He stared at his father in amazement.

"Am I?"

"Yes, you crazy fool! Why else would you refuse at least two dozen excellent marriage proposals?"

Eliakim couldn't imagine marrying any other woman. None of them could compare to Jerusha. "I—I don't know what to say. Maybe you're right, Abba."

"Ah! At last!" Hilkiah leaned across the table toward him. "Now, what should my brilliant son the engineer do about it, eh?"

"Should I ask her to marry me?"

"Well, you'd save me the cost of a dowry if you did!"

Eliakim eyed his father suspiciously. "Have you really made inquiries about finding Jerusha a husband, or was that part of your little plot to trap me?"

Hilkiah rose from his seat and patted Eliakim's shoulder. "As the proverb says, *'A wise son brings joy to his father.'*" He whistled as he disappeared through the door.

Eliakim sat alone at the table for several minutes, thinking about what Hilkiah had said. The entire conversation seemed absurd. He had work to finish. But when Eliakim returned to his room, he found it impossible to concentrate as his mind wandered back to Jerusha. He picked up a clay tablet and dipped his finger into the bowl of water to wipe it clean, but his hand shook, and drops of water splattered all over his parchment scrolls. He chided himself for acting so foolishly and dried his sweating palms on the front of his tunic. He was a grown man, not a lovesick youth. He had never acted this way before. But he had never met a woman as captivating as Jerusha. He picked up the tablet again. What if his father was right? What if Jerusha decided to marry someone else? Jerusha, in another man's arms? Unthinkable!

He recalled the strange thrill he felt when he worked beside her, the sound of her voice, her sweet scent. He remembered the foolish, giddy feeling he'd had when her hand brushed against his and the nearly uncontrollable urge he had felt to kiss the lovely hollow of her throat. He felt a constant longing to be near her, and when he realized that she was probably sitting out in the garden, his heart began to race. His father was right. He was in love with her. And suddenly it mattered very much to Eliakim to know if she loved him too.

He sprang to his feet and looked at himself in the mirror. She could never love him. He was too thin, his forehead was too high, his hair never stayed in place. And Jerusha was so beautiful. He tried to smooth down his tousled hair, but it stayed hopelessly rumpled. Then Eliakim raked his fingers through his beard, straightened his shoulders, and made his way breathlessly to the garden, hoping she was alone. She sat on the stone bench, gazing up at the first few stars that twinkled in the sky.

"Hi. May I join you?" His voice felt out of control.

"Of course."

Eliakim sat beside her, convinced that his nervousness was obvious. He was afraid to look at her, afraid his heart would burst if her beautiful green eyes met his gaze. He cleared a lump from his throat.

"You look so serious tonight," he said. "What are you thinking about?"

She brushed her hair from her eyes. "I was listening to your father's laughter—" Eliakim felt a stab of fear. Had she overheard them? "—and thinking about my own father. I really miss him."

Eliakim played with the hem of his tunic. "Your father was a good man, Jerusha, and a good friend. I miss him too. He once told me that—that he wished I was his son."

They sat in silence, and Eliakim was distressed to find himself speechless. He wanted to tell Jerusha in a beautiful, memorable way exactly how he felt about her, but his mind spun.

"Jerusha—," he began and cleared his throat again. "I've decided who I want to marry."

She whirled around to face him, surprised. "You have?"

"Yes. I wish I was more eloquent, but I'm not, so I'll just say it. I . . . I love you. I want to marry you." He reached to take her hand.

"No!" she cried and leaped from the bench, jerking her hand away as if his touch had scalded her. She shrank back from him, then covered her face and wept.

Eliakim stared down at his empty hands, stunned. He felt as if he'd been punched in the stomach and couldn't catch his breath.

"Oh, Eliakim, I'm so sorry," she sobbed, "but I can't marry you. I—I can never marry anyone."

Eliakim saw the anguish in her beautiful face, and he longed to hold her and comfort her. "Jerusha—please tell me—why not?"

She struggled to force out the words as if pulling arrows from her flesh. "Because I'm not a suitable wife for you. I—I've slept with many men."

Eliakim swallowed a lump of grief that had risen in his throat to choke him. "Did the Assyrians rape you?"

"Yes."

"Jerusha, no one can blame you for that—," he began, but it was as if she didn't hear him. With tears streaming endlessly down her face, Jerusha told him the truth.

"It was more than rape, Eliakim. That was only the beginning. I wasn't their cook—I was their mistress. I had a child. I don't even know—which one—was her father."

"Oh, God of Abraham," Eliakim groaned, and a fist rammed into his stomach again at her words.

"She was such a beautiful baby, so tiny and perfect—with huge, dark eyes like they have, and soft, curly hair—so shiny and black—"

"Jerusha—," he whispered. He wanted her to stop. He could see that the memory caused her pain, and he felt her suffering as if it was his own.

"But they took my baby away from me the day after she was born and—and I never saw her again. They have rituals, for their gods—they take newborn babies and—"

"Jerusha, don't!" he said harshly, then his voice softened. "Please—"

"I've never told anyone about her before, not even Maacah."

221

He wanted to hold her in his arms as he had that first day, but the memory of how she had recoiled from his touch was still sharp and painful. "Jerusha, it doesn't matter to me. You were raped—you had no choice."

"No, Eliakim. That isn't true. You don't know what I really am. You don't know what they've done to me."

"It doesn't matter—" Eliakim loved her, and he couldn't bear to hear what the Assyrians had done to her. But Jerusha told him anyway, and her words tore through his heart like hot irons.

"I let them make me into a harlot. I became a prostitute. I let them all do whatever they wanted to me, because I was a coward. That's why I lived when my cousins and all the others died."

Eliakim covered his face. "Oh, God, no—no—"

"I didn't want to die, so I let them own me and use me like an object, for their own pleasure. But I did die, Eliakim. I died inside."

"Please, Jerusha—stop!" He didn't want to believe what she was telling him.

"You couldn't possibly want me for your wife and the mother of your children. You don't know how filthy I feel inside. And I could never be pure and clean again. I would pollute you. You deserve someone better than me. I'm filth—I'm garbage—"

"But you had no choice—" It was what he wanted to believe.

"Oh, yes, I had a choice," she said bitterly. "And I chose to be their prostitute."

Eliakim felt sick to his stomach. "Dear God—," he moaned. "It's not true—"

"I'm sorry, but it *is* true. I never meant to hurt you, Eliakim. But I knew you could never say you loved me if you knew the truth about me. You would hate me, as much as I hate myself."

Eliakim felt numb with grief and rage. The Assyrians had used and destroyed this beautiful girl whom he loved so deeply. Anger and hatred rose up inside him, until they seemed to strangle all the joy and love he had ever known. He wanted to mutilate the Assyrians, by the thousands and tens of thousands, for what they had done to Jerusha—and to him, for it was as if they had violated him as well. He would get even. Somehow he would make them pay.

"Eliakim, please—marry one of your father's brides, a virgin, someone who could give you a happy home. You're a member of the king's royal council. You can't marry a harlot."

Eliakim looked at her. The thought of Jerusha willingly sleeping with dozens of men was more than he could bear. He rose from the bench and walked silently into the house.

———◆———

When he was gone, Jerusha stood alone in the courtyard. Above her head the dazzling stars floated and swam as she gazed at them through silently falling tears. The moon on the horizon shone nearly as brightly as the sun, bathing the empty bench where Eliakim had sat in pale yellow light.

Gentle Eliakim, with his dark, tousled hair and warm brown eyes—Jerusha loved him. In spite of all her resolve, all her efforts not to, Jerusha loved him, so much that she had told him what she had hidden from her own family—the truth about herself. Jerusha had suffered the loss of her child, her parents, her freedom, her dreams. She had felt the deep wounds of death and sorrow and grief. She had known anguish and despair and pain. But on this achingly beautiful starlit night, none of those feelings seemed as painful to her as love. Eliakim loved her. But she could never belong to him. And she would have to live the rest of her life without him.

———◆———

Eliakim slumped at his worktable, staring blindly at the drawings in front of him while Jerusha's words echoed painfully through his heart: *Many men . . . I chose to be a prostitute.* The hatred that he felt toward the Assyrians was such a new feeling to him, yet so strong, it paralyzed him. In his imagination he held a sword, slaughtering thousands of them, avenging Jerusha's shame. They would never get past his walls. They would never get their cursed hands on Jerusha again.

Eliakim wasn't a warrior. He couldn't fight the Assyrians with a sword. His only weapon was his agile mind and his ability to plan and build. As the drawings in front of him slid into focus, Eliakim suddenly realized how he would fight the Assyrians.

The water tunnel—it had probably taken the Jebusites years to expand a natural cave into a usable water system, yet the tunnel King Hezekiah had proposed would be four times as long and nearly impossible to dig. How could he work fast enough to complete it before the Assyrians marched south to Jerusalem? But if he told the king it couldn't be done, the Jebusite shaft would be reopened, and now Eliakim knew that he would never risk even one Assyrian soldier crawling up that shaft into his city.

Fighting his anguish and grief, Eliakim lit three more oil lamps and bent over his drawings with renewed determination. He would find a way to do the impossible, a way to bring water into his city, a way to defeat the cursed Assyrians. He would get revenge in his own way.

When the morning sun began to light up the eastern sky, Eliakim was nearly finished. He heard sounds of activity in the kitchen as the household began to stir, and he sketched one last drawing. He was ready to present his plans to the king.

"Eliakim—are you almost ready to go?" Hilkiah called from the hallway outside his room. Eliakim knew he couldn't go with his father to worship God. He couldn't praise or give thanks. He had nothing to pray for except revenge.

"Uh—I'll have to skip the sacrifice this morning," he called back. "Go ahead without me." He should have known that a moment later Hilkiah would hurry into his room.

"Why not? What's the matter? Are you sick?"

"No, it's just that—"

"You look terrible!" Hilkiah gasped.

As Eliakim rose to his feet, he caught a quick glimpse of himself in the mirror. He looked pale and tired, and his bloodshot eyes had dark circles beneath them. He could have feigned illness quite easily, but he'd never lied to his father.

"I've been up all night working on these plans for the king," he said as he pushed his hair off his forehead. "I need to get washed up before the meeting at the palace. Go without me."

Hilkiah studied him carefully, looked down at the cluttered worktable, then back at him. "You proposed to her, didn't you?" he said softly. Eliakim could only nod. "And she must have said no? I'm so sorry, Son. I truly am."

Was his grief that obvious? Could his father and everyone else in Jerusalem look straight into his heart and see that it was shattered? The only way he could get through this day and the days and months to follow was to do what he had done all night—make the tunnel his reason for living, his obsession. The blast of the shofar broke the silence.

"You're going to be late, Abba," he said hoarsely. "Go without me." Hilkiah turned without a word and left.

Eliakim slowly gathered into a pile the drawings he'd worked on all night. They were more than a design for a water tunnel. They were his plans for revenge. He slammed his fist on the table with all his strength.

"I hate them! May God curse them all!"

Eliakim ducked out of the house through the servants' door, afraid that he would run into Jerusha in the hallway or on the stairs. If it hurt this much to think about her, how could he bear to face her? His stomach rumbled as he trudged up the hill to the palace, but the thought of food made him sick.

The court chamberlain gave him an odd look when he arrived at the throne room. "You're much too early to meet with the king, my lord. He always goes to the morning sacrifice, and then—"

"I'll wait." Eliakim found a bench outside the throne room and collapsed onto it. He was tired. The deep ache inside would probably never go away. He twisted one of the parchment scrolls in his hands, rolling it up tightly, then unrolling it again as he waited. When he remembered that he would have to face Shebna, he cringed. Shebna hated him. He would probably argue against any plan of Eliakim's. But these plans would succeed. They had to.

At last a scribe emerged from behind the closed door and Eliakim followed him inside, their footsteps echoing hollowly in the high-ceilinged room. He remembered the day he had brought Jerusha here and felt the balled fist slam into his gut again.

"Your Majesty, with your permission I would like to begin construction immediately on what I've called the Siloam tunnel. As you've requested, the water will flow underground from the Gihon Spring to a new retaining pool within the city's walls." He produced a diagram showing the location of the Pool of Siloam.

The king appeared surprised but pleased. "Then you've found solutions to all the obstacles we discussed, Eliakim?"

"Yes, Your Majesty, I have. And I also believe we can complete the tunnel in less than a year's time."

"Oh, really?" Shebna said. "That sounds too good to be true."

"Yes, it does," Hezekiah said. "How are you going to accomplish all this?"

Eliakim tried to sound confident. "The first problem is the Tombs of the Kings. Since it would be a sacrilege to exhume them, we will simply tunnel around them."

"But that will take even longer," Shebna said.

"True, but I have two other ideas that will make up for the time we'll waste. They will also solve the second problem, which is a fresh air supply."

King Hezekiah sat forward on his throne, peering anxiously at Eliakim's drawings. "Let's hear them."

Eliakim was so tired the room swam, and he felt as if his speech was slow and ponderous. "The old Jebusite tunnel seems to meander aimlessly, as you may recall, and I wondered why. But when I looked more closely, I discovered that the Jebusites followed a natural fissure in the limestone and a vein of softer, more porous rock. The holding tank and shaft were part of a cave system, which was probably already there."

"Perhaps they were in a hurry too," Hezekiah said.

"If we followed natural fissures and used caves too, it would make the tunneling proceed much faster. Now as Shebna pointed out, there's also the problem of the accumulated rubble from the tunnel giving away our secret. To solve it, I have redesigned the northwest wall." That was the wall Jerusha had said was the easiest to attack.

Suddenly a vision of Jerusha filled Eliakim's tired mind. She was standing on the wall beside him, looking down at the city, her hair blowing gently in the wind. Lovely Jerusha—a prostitute. Eliakim cleared his throat.

"As you know, that wall is very vulnerable to Assyrian battering rams. So instead of a casemate wall, hollow in the middle, we will fill in the space, some 20 feet thick, with the rubble from the tunnel. When enemy battering rams attack it, the rubble will avalanche down on them."

"Brilliant!" Hezekiah exclaimed, and even Shebna showed grudging respect.

But Eliakim knew his final proposal was the one most likely to meet with opposition. He drew a deep breath. "Finally, to solve the problem of fresh air in such a lengthy tunnel and to greatly accelerate the digging schedule, I propose to begin digging at both ends of the tunnel simultaneously and work toward the middle." Silence met him as Shebna and Hezekiah stared in disbelief.

"There would be fewer problems with fresh air in two short tunnels than in one long one," he hastily explained. "And two work crews, digging day and night, could accomplish twice as much as one."

Hezekiah stroked his beard thoughtfully. "I understand that, Eliakim, but how would you get them to meet in the middle?"

"Especially if you are following natural fissures in the rock instead of tunneling in a straight line?" Shebna added.

Eliakim produced another diagram. "Look—the tunnel that will start at the new Pool of Siloam will be running approximately west to east as it detours around the graves. And the tunnel that begins at the Gihon Spring will curve like this and end up running approximately north to south. Eventually they will cross paths in the middle."

Shebna frowned skeptically. "Not necessarily. If you follow the natural fissures in the rock like the Jebusites did, the tunnel would twist and turn in all directions. How on earth would you ever make two meandering tunnels meet in the middle? You would have no way of knowing where they were, underground."

"No, my lord—I am sure it would work," Eliakim said defiantly. He knew he could never explain to them the power of hatred that would drive him until he succeeded. "We'll dig the shaft just wide enough and high enough for the workmen to squeeze through, at first. Then once the two tunnels join, we can enlarge them and adjust the angle of descent so the water will flow. I will make careful measurements of all the distances and plot all the twists and turns on a map. We'll be able to hear the sound of the picks from the other side once we're close. I know it will work, Your Majesty. I know it."

Hezekiah took the scroll from him and studied it. Eliakim waited tensely, suddenly aware of how badly he needed to sleep. The only sound he heard was the chirping of birds in the trees outside the palace window, and it annoyed Eliakim, as if they had no right to be so happy. Then a sparrow picked up the refrain that had been sounding in his ears all night and sang it to him over and over again: *many men . . . many men . . . many men.*

At last the king spoke. "Digging one tunnel through solid rock would be a challenging project for anyone to tackle. But digging *two* zigzagging tunnels that have to eventually meet in the middle has to be nearly impossible. Can't we find another way to—"

"No!" Eliakim felt sick with rage and disappointment. He knew better than to argue with the king, but he no longer cared what happened to him.

"No, Your Majesty! If we do it any other way it will take too long! We don't have time! If the Assyrians attack us next—" He stopped short, startled to find he was shouting at the king. He lowered his voice. "I know I can do it, Your Majesty—I know I can. Please give me a chance."

The king looked at Shebna for a moment, then back at Eliakim. "We all understand the seriousness of the Assyrian threat and the critical need for water during a siege—" Hezekiah paused, and Eliakim waited in agony for him to finish. Sweat ran down Eliakim's face and the back of his neck, even though the air in the throne room was cool.

"—If you're sure this is the only way, Eliakim—very well. You may dig your tunnels."

———◈———

"*I am my beloved's, and he is mine*—" Hephzibah sang. Her sweet voice had the power both to soothe and to stir Hezekiah, and he leaned back against the cushions. The love he felt for her overwhelmed him. Hezekiah had deeply regretted losing his temper with Hephzibah and had worked hard to reassure her of his love.

"I don't care about an heir," he had told her. "I belong to you." The thought of sharing himself with anyone else repulsed him, just as he would never want to share Hephzibah with another man.

"Place me like a seal over your heart, like a seal on your arm; for love is as strong as death, its jealousy unyielding as the grave. It burns like a blazing fire, like a mighty flame."

He watched her delicate hands as they plucked the harp strings and thought of what Zechariah had once told him—God dwelt in the midst of married love. Hezekiah silently thanked God for making his love for Hephzibah possible. If he hadn't obeyed the commands to the king, he might have had many concubines, but he would never have known love. For the first time, Hezekiah saw God's laws not as negative commands but as His loving provision for His people.

"Many waters cannot quench love; rivers cannot wash it away. If one were to give all the wealth of his house for love, it would be utterly scorned."

As Hephzibah sang the beautiful words, a deep contentment filled Hezekiah. He knew love and joy and the rich blessings of God as his nation continued to prosper. Only the threat of Assyria cast a shadow over his kingdom.

Hephzibah finished her song and laid down her harp. "What is it, my lord? You looked so content lying there—then suddenly you looked worried." She nestled close to him, melting into his arms as if she were part of him.

"It's nothing, my love, nothing," he murmured. Her arms twined tightly around his neck, and her skin felt cool and smooth.

"I love you, my lord."

Hezekiah sighed. Something about his beloved wife calling him "my lord" saddened him, and he struggled to define it. "Sometimes it's lonely being the king, Hephzibah. Everyone must keep their distance from me, and it's almost as if there's a fence all around me like—like the barrier around the royal dais at the Temple. No one dares to cross it. No one dares to be honest with me. No one dares to anger me. They tell me only what they think I want to hear. It's all necessary, I suppose—but it's lonely sometimes. Even those closest to me, like you and Shebna and Jonadab—you all call me 'Your Majesty' or 'my lord,' and the invisible barrier can never be crossed."

He stopped and shook his head, not sure what he was trying to say. "Sometimes I wonder about God. I wonder if He truly delights in all our religious forms and rituals or if they are barriers that keep us at arm's length from Him. I wonder if He wouldn't rather have our simple love, like a father with his children, instead of as a king and his subjects. Am I making any sense?"

Hephzibah took his face in her hands, gently smoothing his thick beard. She kissed him softly, then looked into his eyes. "Yes. I understand. And I love you with all my heart, Hezekiah."

Later that night, after Hezekiah left, Hephzibah knelt by the carved wooden chest beside her bed. She removed the small bundle wrapped in an embroidered cloth and took out two incense burners and a golden lampstand. She carefully spread the cloth on top of the chest and set the golden statue of Asherah in the middle of it. Then, murmuring the proper prayers, she laid out her offerings of grain and oil and incense before the smiling goddess. She gazed at Asherah's swollen belly, longing more than anything else in the world to give Hezekiah a son, an heir to rule after him in the land he loved so deeply.

"Please, my lady. I love him so much! Please forgive his unbelief and grant him a son."

Part

3

Hezekiah did . . . what was good and right
and faithful before the Lord his God. In
everything that he undertook in the
service of God's temple and in obedience
to the law and the commands, he sought
his God and worked wholeheartedly.

—2 Chron. 31:20-21

King Hezekiah ducked inside the foreman's tent beside the Gihon Spring. "I've come for that tour you promised me, Eliakim."

Eliakim sat hunched on a low stool behind a makeshift table that was piled with scrolls, clay tablets, and chunks of rock. He looked up in surprise, then scrambled to his feet.

"Certainly, Your Majesty. We've accomplished quite a lot already." Eliakim's words lacked enthusiasm, and he looked thin and haggard. His shoulders sagged as if still bent over the table.

"Are you ill, Eliakim? Do you need some time off?"

"No, I'm fine." But his boyish grin was missing, and dark circles rimmed his eyes.

"All right, then. Lead the way." Hezekiah stood aside.

Shebna waited outside the tent, kicking a huge mound of rock with his foot. "I thought you had a plan to get rid of all this rubble, Eliakim."

"I do. We're filling in the new extensions on the northwest wall, making a solid wall 20 feet thick."

"Then why are all these piles still here?"

"Well, we can't haul it away instantly. It's a long, slow process, requiring a lot of manpower. In the meantime, it accumulates down here."

A work crew emerged from the tunnel with another load of rubble and added it to the pile as if to underscore Eliakim's point. Shebna shook his head in disgust. Hezekiah had no idea what caused the friction between Shebna and Eliakim, but it wearied him. Eliakim was the only man on his council whose intellect matched Shebna's, and they could accomplish a great deal if they put their minds together. Instead, they never failed to antagonize one other.

"Is it piling up by the other tunnel too?" Shebna asked.

"Yes, but I can't help it. It'll all be used as fill eventually. I don't see the problem."

"It is ruining any secrecy we may have hoped for," Shebna said. "If we were mining the rock for fill, we would not be digging it out faster than we are using it."

"I'm supposed to dig this tunnel as quickly as possible and—"

"Hire more workmen to haul it away," Hezekiah interrupted, "but don't slow down the digging. Now, we came to see the tunnel."

They skirted piles of tools and more rubble as they walked to the edge of the spring; then they stopped again as Eliakim explained the work to them. His obsession with the project was clear, despite his fatigue and depression.

"We start with a natural fissure and dig a tunnel wide enough and high enough for one man to crawl through. Then a second crew enlarges the tunnel. My men work day and night—there's no difference down there. Each crew rotates jobs; digging for a while, then hauling out rubble, then resting. It's going very smoothly."

"Are we going to stand out here all day, or are you going to let us go inside?" Shebna said.

"I have to get the work crew out first. I just told you—it's wide enough for only one man."

Hezekiah flashed Shebna a warning look as Eliakim went inside to order the workmen to take a short break. Only the worker at the tunnel's end was allowed to continue. When it was clear, Eliakim led the way inside. He had enlarged the entrance and channeled the water down into the valley. Inside, he had cut grooves in the walls, several cubits apart, to hold oil lamps.

"It's a lot brighter in here that the last time we visited," Hezekiah said. "Where did you get these lamps?"

"I designed them. We can carry them like this or fit them in the grooves." He gave them each a lamp to carry.

"Are they not burning your air supply?" Shebna frowned.

"Yes, but that's better than stumbling around in the dark and bumping into walls. Would you like me to extinguish them and show you how dark it is?"

"No, that's not necessary," Hezekiah said. "I remember how dark it was."

They wound through the narrow slit in the rock until they reached the old Jebusite holding pool. The water barely reached their knees. The entrance to the new tunnel stood off to Hezekiah's left and a small dam kept the spring water out.

"Why do you not dam it up on the outside?" Shebna asked. "You could keep all of this dry."

"When the tunnel is farther along we'll let some of the water trickle through the natural fissures and watch for seepage in the other tunnel."

"I still do not understand how you think they will meet."

"It's my job. I know what I'm doing."

Hezekiah grew tired of listening to them. "This arguing is unnecessary," he said sharply. "

With Eliakim leading the way, the three men started down the new tunnel. Hezekiah had to crouch down, ducking his head to keep from smashing it on the ceiling. His broad shoulders scraped both sides, and he twisted sideways, fearing he would become stuck. It was such a tight fit he wondered if he could turn around again, or if he would have to back out. Even with the oil lamp it felt dark and oppressive. Unlike the ragged Jebusite tunnel, the walls and ceiling of the new tunnel were neatly squared off. Hezekiah ran his hand along the wall, feeling the slanting pick marks.

"We've only had one or two false starts," Eliakim explained as they came to an alcove along one side. "We struck a vein of harder rock after a cubit or so and had to change direction."

They walked several more yards, winding first to the right, then meandering to the left, until Hezekiah lost all sense of direction. He could hear the clanging of a pick against stone in the distance.

Suddenly Eliakim stopped and the opening lowered to knee height. The rhythmic ring of hammer and chisel was close. "This is as far as we can go, unless you'd like to crawl."

"No, thanks," Hezekiah said. "This is cramped enough." He could almost feel the weight of the mountain above his head and his own frailty beneath the tons of solid rock.

"How can the workmen stand it in here?" Shebna grumbled.

"We're all used to it, I guess."

"Well, it is too confining for me," Shebna said. "I am getting out." They managed to turn around, and Shebna, who had been last, led the way.

"I'm very impressed," Hezekiah told his engineer when they were outside in the warm air again. "You've made incredible progress in the last four months."

Eliakim managed a tired smile. "Thank you, Your Majesty. We're not quite halfway to where the two tunnels will meet."

"If they meet," Shebna mumbled. "Have you dug this much of the other tunnel too?"

"No, that side's been going a lot slower. The Jebusites gave us a head start on this end—remember? We had to clear the land, then dig a shaft down to the starting level, then find a cave system with a vein of the softer limestone. We're also digging the new Pool of Siloam to hold the water once the tunnel is functioning."

Eliakim turned to Shebna. "Is there anything else you'd like to see, my lord?" Shebna shook his head.

Hezekiah knew the brooding Egyptian well enough to know that he was deliberately holding back whatever opinions he held. "Good job, Eliakim," the king said. "Thank you for the tour."

"Any time, Your Majesty."

The sun blazed down on them as Hezekiah and Shebna followed the shadeless path up the ramp to the city. Hezekiah almost envied the workers in the cool tunnel. When they reached the water gate, Hezekiah finally turned to the scowling Egyptian.

"All right, Shebna. Let's hear what you're thinking."

Shebna shook his head. "He will never do it, Your Majesty. You saw how that tunnel meanders. He will be groping like a blind man down there, trying to find the other end."

Hezekiah stopped walking and paused to catch his breath. "What is it between you two? What do you have against Eliakim?"

"It is nothing personal. Merely a difference of opinion."

"I've known you a long time, Shebna, and I think it's deeper than that. Are you still holding a grudge because of that refugee business when Eliakim came to me at the Temple?"

Shebna started walking again, and Hezekiah kept pace beside him. "Maybe you should ask him why he has never respected me."

"I wish you would work together instead of fighting all the time. Can't you forget your differences long enough to help him? We need this tunnel."

Shebna stopped abruptly. "There is nothing I can do to help him. I have studied his plans, and he will never get those two tunnels to meet. He is attempting the impossible."

Hezekiah remembered how crazily the tunnel had meandered, and he wondered if Shebna was right, if finding the other tunnel would mean groping in the darkness like a blind man. *My God turns my darkness into light,* he recited to himself, and he hoped that Eliakim was praying.

❖

"May I bring you anything else, Your Majesty?" Hezekiah's servant asked as he helped him remove his royal robes.

"No. I'm waiting for Shebna to bring me some documents. Then I will be going to see my wife."

Hezekiah sank down onto the window seat and stretched his long legs. The day had been hot, and all the shutters in his private chambers stood open to allow in the evening breezes. They carried with them the fragrance of the sacrifice from the Temple, and Hezekiah closed his eyes, trying to recall the words of the evening prayers: *"Find rest, O my soul, in God alone; my hope comes from him. He alone is my rock and my salvation; he is my fortress, I will not be shaken."*

The words of David's psalms comforted him, and he made an effort every night to read and memorize some of them. He picked up his Torah scroll and unrolled it.

"Lord Shebna is here, Your Majesty," his servant announced.

"Good. Send him in."

"I am sorry for interrupting your privacy," Shebna said when he saw Hezekiah stretched out comfortably with the Torah scroll.

"No, I've been expecting you." He laid the scroll aside.

"I've completed the itinerary, but it could have waited."

"I want Eliakim and Jonadab to get an early start in the morning. Let me see it." Hezekiah studied the list of cities the two men were scheduled to visit, scattered along all the possible invasion routes. The men had orders to inspect the fortifications and offer advice on reinforcing them. As usual, Shebna had taken care of every detail, and the document was ready for Hezekiah's seal.

"You think it will take them about two months, then?"

"Two months at the very least, Your Majesty."

"It looks excellent, Shebna." Hezekiah pressed his ring into the small lump of clay, then handed it back to him. Shebna looked tired. "You work too hard, my friend. You should learn to relax. Would you like to take some time off?"

Shebna blinked in surprise. "No, of course not."

Hezekiah remembered how Eliakim had given him the same answer, and he realized again how much alike the two men were. The tunnel foreman had told him that Eliakim rarely went home, staying in the tunnels almost day and night. Maybe traveling would be good for Eliakim.

"Would you like to go along on this trip too, Shebna?"

Shebna stared, then quickly shook his head. "Travel is not for me. I prefer my own bed at night. And I will need to observe the progress on the walls and the tunnel while Eliakim is away."

"I realize that's asking a lot of you, Shebna, but Eliakim has assured me that his project foremen are capable men. All the preliminary work is finished."

"Of course, my lord. I am happy to do it."

Hezekiah smiled slightly. "I know you don't think much of Eliakim's tunnel—"

"It is your tunnel, my lord, and it must be completed."

"I'm glad you see it that way, my friend."

As he stood up to stretch, one of his servants hurried into the room. "Your Majesty, General Jonadab wishes to see you right away."

Shebna turned on him. "Unless we are being invaded, it can wait! The king is tired, and Jonadab has no right to intrude in his private quarters."

"But the general said it was urgent—"

"Send him in," Hezekiah said. "I don't think Jonadab would come at this late hour unless it was important. Maybe it concerns tomorrow's trip." He sank down onto the window seat to wait.

When Jonadab entered he seemed deeply shaken. He was a battle-hardened soldier, but as he groped for words Hezekiah saw how upset he was. "I'm very sorry to disturb you, Your Majesty, but something terrible happened tonight, and—"

"Sit down, Jonadab, take your time."

"Your Majesty, one of my watchmen at the valley gate saw a man and woman leave the city after sunset, carrying a bundle. They headed down toward the Hinnom Valley, and a few minutes later he saw what looked like a bonfire over by the cliffs—"

An icy chill passed through Hezekiah. "Oh, no—"

The general drew a shaky breath. "I'm sorry—but we were too late. By the time we arrived, the baby was dead. This is all that was left."

He handed Hezekiah a small funeral urn. Tiny, charred bones lay on the bottom. Hezekiah's stomach turned as he read the inscription. The baby had been sacrificed to the goddess Asherah to fulfill a vow.

"Where is the couple now?"

"Outside your throne room."

"Let's go."

When Hezekiah was seated on his throne, Jonadab's soldiers brought in the prisoners. The handsome couple was dressed as if attending a lavish social function. The woman was adorned with expensive jewelry. But panic showed on their chalky faces as they cowered before the king, staring at the floor. The woman's shoulders quaked with silent sobs.

"Why did you do it?" Hezekiah asked, but they made no reply. "I asked why you sacrificed your child!" he shouted. "Answer me!"

The husband finally looked up. His voice had the defiant tone of a man who knows he stands condemned and has nothing more to lose. "We made a sacred vow to the goddess a year ago. She answered our prayers and granted me what I asked for, so we've kept our part of the vow in return."

"You vowed to kill your own child?"

"He's our son. Aren't we free to do whatever we want with him?"

Hezekiah gripped the urn until his knuckles turned white, controlling his anger with great effort. He didn't need to consult the Levites. He knew what the Torah said. When he finally passed the tiny remains back to Jonadab, his hands shook.

"Give this little one a proper burial, then take his parents out of the city and stone them to death."

"*No!*" the woman screamed, dropping to her knees. "Have mercy on us, *please!*"

"The same mercy you showed your own son?" Hezekiah cried. "You burned him alive, and you're asking for mercy?"

"We have other children at home," she pleaded as the soldiers hauled her to her feet.

"Stone them both."

Her cries gradually faded as the soldiers hustled her away. Jonadab remained behind, clutching the urn. The room fell silent as Hezekiah struggled to compose himself.

Finally Shebna spoke for the first time since the incident began. "You should have waited until morning for this, Jonadab. Besides, the law is very clear in this case. A lower court could have judged them without disturbing the king."

"No, he did the right thing," Hezekiah said quietly. "I asked him to report any incidence of idolatry directly to me."

"But why upset yourself with matters that can easily be judged by—"

"Because I started these religious reforms, and it's important to me that they succeed. It's important to our nation too. Don't you understand that yet?" But Hezekiah knew that he didn't. He sighed wearily and walked out to the hallway with them. "Go home and go to bed, General. It's been a long night for all of us."

But as Jonadab turned to leave, Hezekiah stopped him. "Wait. Make sure that their other children are cared for, first."

"Yes, Your Majesty." The incident left Hezekiah badly shaken. An hour later he was still trembling, and he debated whether or not he should go to see Hephzibah. He needed her to help him erase the events from his mind, but he didn't want to burden her with what had been a revolting duty. At last he decided to go but to remain silent about what he had been forced to do.

"What happened, my love?" she cried the moment she saw him. "What's wrong?"

Hezekiah drew her into his arms, clinging to her. "You don't want to know."

"Please tell me. Maybe it will help if you talk about it."

He finally released her, and she led him over to a pile of cushions in front of the empty charcoal brazier. He sank down and stared at the smudges of soot on the bronze, feeling sick, while Hephzibah gently rubbed his shoulders.

"I just ordered a couple to be executed," he said at last.

"Why?"

"They sacrificed their son to Asherah." For a moment Hephzibah's hands froze on his shoulders. "I remembered how we grieved when our son died. We both wanted a son, and I—I just can't—I don't know how anyone could do that, Hephzibah. Sacrificing their own child to a—to a lifeless slab of stone."

Hezekiah hadn't thought of his brothers in many years, and their faces had faded with the passing of time. But he remembered all too well the heat of the flames, the terror, and the stench of their burning. He pulled Hephzibah into his arms again and opened his heart to her, hoping to find relief from his painful memories.

"When I was a child my father ordered the priests to sacrifice me to Molech."

"Hezekiah, no!"

"First he sacrificed my brother Eliab, and I had to watch him die. But that wasn't enough. He ordered them to sacrifice me too." Hephzibah clung to him fiercely, and he remembered clinging to his mother the same way, desperate for her protection. "Someone made a mistake—and they sacrificed my brother Amariah instead of me. He died in my place, Hephzibah. But I was the oldest son. I was supposed to die—like the little boy who died tonight."

Hezekiah stared at the cold, black charcoal and heard the sound of the drums pounding in his ears. "My own father—ordered his children put to death because he was in trouble. How could anyone do that, Hephzibah—to his own children?"

He felt her warm tears on his chest, but she didn't answer. "And then tonight. I thought I'd purged such abominations from my land. I thought I'd smashed all the idols. I thought—I thought my people knew better than to worship lifeless stones."

Grief overwhelmed him, and he covered his eyes. "If you could have seen those tiny bones—he was so small—so small and helpless—" His voice faded away as his heart raged at the monstrous injustice. "We want a child so badly," he said at last. "We've been praying for one, trusting God for one, and I had to condemn two people to death for murdering their own son."

31

Eliakim winced and shifted in the saddle, trying to find a comfortable position—after riding horseback for three days, there wasn't one. "Are we still behind schedule?" he asked Jonadab.

The general smiled slightly. "Why? Do you want to walk awhile?"

Eliakim nodded sheepishly. They dismounted, and Eliakim groaned with relief. "I'm sorry, General, but I'm a city boy. Horses are a new experience for me."

Jonadab laughed. "That's OK. I think Shebna wants to kill us both with his crazy schedule. He didn't even give us time to enjoy the scenery."

The road followed the banks of the winding Sorek River with the beautiful rolling green hills of the Shephelah surrounding them on every side. It felt good to walk again.

Eliakim drew a deep breath, inhaling the sweet scent of the Sorek vineyards. "This certainly is beautiful country," he sighed.

"I led the military campaign when we won this territory back from the Philistines—one of the wisest decisions King Hezekiah ever made. It's as fertile as Eden. My wife's from around here. I miss her already. But you wouldn't know about that. When are you going to get married and find out what you're missing?"

Eliakim hadn't thought about Jerusha for several days, and his depression had begun to lift for the first time in months. But Jonadab's gentle teasing reminded him, and Eliakim felt the familiar twisting pain in his gut. *Many men.*

"Sorry—guess it's none of my business," Jonadab mumbled.

Eliakim sighed and ran his fingers through his hair. "No, it's all right. I, uh—might be getting married when I get back home."

"You don't sound too thrilled. Is she ugly?"

Eliakim thought of beautiful Jerusha and smiled weakly. "I don't really know. My father has several prospects for me. I'm not sure which one we'll choose."

Jonadab studied him as they walked. "But you're in love with someone else—is that it? And your father is against it—or maybe hers?"

"Yes, something like that."

"Tell you what: I'll give you a little sword practice, and when you get home you can ride your horse up to her house and carry her away." Jonadab slapped Eliakim on the back good-naturedly. "What do you say?"

"When I get home I'm never getting on a horse again."

Jonadab laughed, but when he looked at Eliakim's grim face his smile changed to a frown. "Is it really that hopeless—with your girl-friend, I mean?"

Eliakim looked down at the road. "Yeah, it's hopeless."

"That's too bad. I'm sorry."

They walked along in silence for a few minutes, with the heavy plodding of the horses and the sweet chirping of birds sounding in their ears.

"Listen, Eliakim, if it's any consolation, I never met my wife until the day we got married. My father chose her for me. But I love her with all my heart now. We've had five children together and three grandchildren so far. Maybe you should give one of your father's brides a chance."

"Thanks. Maybe I will." But as they walked along he wondered if he could learn to love anyone the way he had loved Jerusha.

They approached the outskirts of Lachish shortly before sunset, riding once again, but several hours behind schedule.

"I'm dreading this visit," Jonadab said.

"Why is that?"

"The governor of Lachish is the king's brother, Prince Gedaliah. Ever meet him?" Eliakim shook his head. "I tutored him for his military training, just like I tutored the king. But Gedaliah is very different from King Hezekiah, as you will soon see and—well, maybe I should let you decide for yourself."

"You'd better tell me now, since we'll be working closely with him."

Jonadab scratched his beard. "I never liked Gedaliah. Never trusted him. It's hard to explain why exactly. King Hezekiah has a certain—royalty about him. He gives an order, and you feel like obeying it. His brother gives orders too, but they rub me the wrong way. Like petting a dog from the tail to the head—you know what I mean?"

"I think so."

"I've always known the king to be fair, even when the decisions were tough. But Gedaliah? He's always in it for himself. Selfish little runt, a lot like his father. I'd be willing to bet that he's lined his own pockets pretty nicely since he was appointed governor of Lachish."

"Does the king know what he's like?"

Jonadab shrugged. "That's hard to say. Anyway, it was your friend Shebna who recommended him for the position of governor."

"My friend?"

Jonadab slapped his back. "Someday you'll have to fill me in on why you two hate each other so much."

"It's not *that* bad."

"Come on, you and Shebna can't be in the same room together without going straight for each other's throats."

"I don't really know how it started with Shebna. I never liked him, and he never liked me. He's sure getting his revenge on this trip, though." Eliakim shifted in the saddle uncomfortably. "But don't ever tell him that."

"Your secret is safe with me."

"I don't know. It's Shebna's beliefs, I guess—or lack of beliefs. I have no use for people who don't believe in God. You can blame my father for instilling me with that prejudice."

"Then you won't like Gedaliah either."

"He's an unbeliever?"

"Worse. He'll worship anything to further his own selfish ambitions."

"You're right. That's much worse."

By the time they rode through the triple gates of Lachish, Eliakim was convinced he would have to eat dinner standing up. They were welcomed by Governor Gedaliah, who conducted them on a tour of the impressive fortifications.

"Lachish seems well prepared for an Assyrian siege," Eliakim said when they returned to the sumptuous governor's palace.

"I've made sure of that," Gedaliah said. "It's an important city, safeguarding the entire valley. The Assyrians could never conquer it."

"It would be a dangerous mistake to underestimate them," Jonadab warned.

"They'll *never* defeat Lachish. But enough business. Time to relax. How long do you plan on visiting? I'd like to make your stay comfortable."

"We're scheduled to stay two days," Jonadab said.

"Stay as long as you like. I've assigned some slave girls to make sure all your needs are met. Let me know if you want anything else."

"There is one thing," Eliakim said. "I understand this area manufactures pottery. I'm trying to locate a friend, a potter by the name of Saul of Dabbasheth. He's a refugee from Israel."

Gedaliah turned to one of his aides and snapped his fingers. "You! Take care of it."

Outside the palace windows, Eliakim heard the blast of a shofar, identical to the call for the evening sacrifice at the Temple in Jerusalem. "Ah, it's time for the evening sacrifice—would you like to accompany me?" Gedaliah asked.

Eliakim stared. "How can you conduct a sacrifice here? The king has centralized all worship in Jerusalem."

"Some of our customs date back many centuries to a time when Lachish was under Egyptian influence. My brother is naive to think he can change centuries of worship with a single edict."

"That might explain why the local people worship other gods," Eliakim said. "But why do you?"

"I'm their governor. It's a token gesture to their customs."

"Has it occurred to you that you represent King Hezekiah? Perhaps you should make a token gesture to *his* wishes. And he would never want you to condone idolatry by participating in it."

The prince's icy gaze told Eliakim that he had made an enemy. Jonadab's opinion of Gedaliah had been confirmed. "Since you obviously don't care to join me in worship, you'll have to excuse me," Gedaliah said. "The servants will show you to your rooms."

When the prince was gone, Eliakim turned to Jonadab. "Are you sure he's the king's brother?"

—◆—

Jerusha sat at the dinner table beside Maacah and listened as Hilkiah recited the blessing over their food. She wouldn't bow her head for the nightly ritual, nor would she pray. She didn't believe in God. They were about to begin eating when they heard the front door open. A moment later Eliakim strode into the room.

"Son!" Hilkiah cried, and he leaped up to embrace him, kissing Eliakim on both cheeks. "Welcome home! Look at you! Oh, how I've missed you!"

"Me, too, Abba."

Eliakim returned the embrace warmly. He nodded politely in Jerusha's direction but didn't look at her. Eliakim appeared older, more mature, and Jerusha saw a network of fine wrinkles around his tired eyes. But traveling had obviously agreed with him. His slim body had filled out, and with his skin deeply tanned from the sun, he looked even more handsome than before.

"You look tired, Son. Did you just get in?"

"No, a little while ago. I stopped to check on the tunnels."

"Well, here—sit down, sit down. We've just said the blessing, and we're about to eat."

"I'm really not hungry." Eliakim seemed ill at ease, but his father bustled him over to the table and made him sit in his usual place across the table from Jerusha.

"Sit down and talk to us. Tell us where you've been, what you've been doing. We haven't seen you in months! Oh, you look marvelous, Son! Marvelous! And everyone I meet tells me what an important man my son is now!"

Eliakim remained strangely subdued. He looked down at the table or up at his father, but he avoided looking at Jerusha as if unable to stand the sight of her.

"So where have you been all this time?" Hilkiah asked.

"I've been everywhere, Abba, from Beth Horon to Elath."

"All the way to Elath? Tell me. What's it like?"

"Beautiful. But very hot. Almost unbearable."

Jerusha put her hand to her throat and felt the outline of the Elath stone necklace Eliakim had given her, beneath the fabric of her dress.

"I understand it's a major seaport now," Hilkiah said, "with ships coming and going from all over."

"It is. We watched some of them unloading, but we could stay only a few days."

Hilkiah passed him a basket of bread. "Here—eat something. You're not eating."

"I haven't washed, Abba."

"Well, where are those servants? Somebody bring him some water!"

Jerusha hadn't seen Hilkiah so flushed and excited in months, and she suddenly realized how lonely he must have been without his son. The two of them had shared a close relationship before she got in the way. The servants brought a basin and pitcher of water, and as Jerusha watched Eliakim perform the ritual, pouring water over his work-hardened hands, she remembered the night those strong hands had reached out to take hers.

"How many days did it take you to travel back from Elath?"

"We made so many stops I lost track, Abba. We came back through Arad and Beersheba, then up through the Negev."

There was no enthusiasm in his voice, and Jerusha saw that in spite of his exciting travels, his depression hadn't lifted. Even Hilkiah seemed unable to draw his son into the warm, animated conversation they had once shared.

"What about Uncle Saul?" Maacah asked. "Did you have any luck finding him?"

"No, I inquired everywhere I went, but there are so many displaced persons, it was hopeless."

"Well, he's a potter," Hilkiah said. "Did you try looking for him in the main pottery districts?"

"Yes, but I don't see how he could possibly work as a potter anymore—"

"What do you mean?" Jerusha said. Eliakim didn't answer, and suddenly Jerusha remembered the brutal slash of the soldier's sword and her uncle's bloody, amputated hand.

"They cut his hand off!" she cried out. An awkward silence filled the room.

Finally Hilkiah cleared his throat. "I was hoping you'd be able to locate him, Son, and urge him to come live with us. He doesn't even know he has two nieces."

"I tried, Abba."

For the remainder of the meal the conversation felt strained, and Jerusha knew she was the cause. Eliakim had avoided coming home because of her, and she felt guilty for interfering in the life of this once-happy family. If only they could find Uncle Saul. If only they had someplace else to go. She stole a final, fleeting look at Eliakim as he excused himself from the table, but as far as she could tell, Eliakim had never once looked at her.

——◈——

When the meal finally ended, Eliakim fled to his room. He had longed to go home so many times during his travels, but now that he was here he felt like an outsider. It was so hard to see Jerusha again, so difficult to be in the same room with her. He had hoped that his feelings would fade with time, but when he saw her at the table, his longing for her seemed greater than ever. Eliakim had two days off before continuing his travels, but he knew he couldn't spend them at home.

He folded one of his tunics carelessly and stuffed it into a leather satchel with his scrolls, then paused to consider what else he needed to pack. Someone knocked on his door, and he suddenly felt sick inside.

"Who is it?"

"May I come in, or do I need an appointment to see you?" Hilkiah asked.

Eliakim opened the door, relieved to see that his father was alone. "Of course not, Abba. Come in."

"If we'd known you were coming home tonight we would have had a welcoming party for you, and—" His smile faded. "What are you doing?"

"Packing a few things."

"You're not planning to leave again?"

"Yes, I—"

"When?"

"Tonight."

"But you just got home!" "You've been gone for months, and now you're leaving us again? Where do you have to go this time?"

"Back to Timnah and then—"

"How long will you be gone?"

"I don't know—until I'm finished," he said irritably.

"And then you'll probably work all day and half the night at the tunnel again?"

Eliakim wadded up his prayer shawl and stuffed it into the bag. "Probably."

"Son, you need to slow down. I know why you're driving yourself, but—"

"I'm not driving myself, Abba. This is my job."

"It's your job to work day and night for six months and never come home?"

"Yes! The king has building projects all over the country, and it's my job to oversee them. We're fortifying dozens of cities. Lachish is a major fortress now, and we've started an underground water system there too. I also have to stop at Timnah for a few days and check on their new fortifications and—"

"I'm tired just listening to you. I'm worried about you."

"Well, don't be. I appreciate your concern, but I enjoy my work. It's very fulfilling." It was only partially true. Although he enjoyed the challenges of his job, Eliakim felt an emptiness inside that his work couldn't fill.

"And working so hard helps you avoid coming home to face Jerusha," Hilkiah said quietly.

Eliakim sighed and sank down on his bed. "That's probably part of it." He played with a loose thread on the coverlet. "I guess I still haven't gotten over all that yet."

Hilkiah's face reflected his love and concern. Eliakim missed being with his father, laughing with him, sharing his work with him, going to the Temple together. By avoiding Jerusha he had cut himself off from his father as well.

"Maybe I'll take some time off when I get back," he said. "We haven't talked in a long time, and I have so much to tell you about the tunnel."

"How is it coming along?"

"Great. You should stop down and see it." As always, Eliakim grew excited when he talked about his tunnel. It would be an engineering masterpiece when it was finished. "I'd say we're about three-quarters finished, so we'll have our water system in less than a year, just as I promised the king. When I get back in a few weeks, I'm going to start a signaling system so we can listen for sounds from the other side. It's going to work, Abba. I'm going to prove Shebna wrong. The two tunnels are going to meet."

"Then what will happen to the old aqueduct?"

"Once our water is flowing underground to the new Pool of Siloam, we'll get rid of the old aqueduct and bury the Gihon Spring underground. You'll never know it was there. Everything will be so well hidden the Assyrians will never find it."

"Does King Hezekiah think we might be invaded next?"

"No one knows. But we're working to fortify more than 40 cities throughout Judah, so we'll be ready for them."

"God of Abraham, I just pray it'll never come to that."

"Me too, Abba." He gazed affectionately at his father for a moment, then pushed the loose ends of his prayer shawl into the bag. "And now I'm sorry, Abba, but I have to go."

"All right, Son. I understand." He pointed to Eliakim's overstuffed bag and smiled. "But I suggest you let the servants fold those things up properly for you, or you're going to arrive looking even more rumpled than you usually do."

❖

The inside of the windowless storehouse felt cool and damp, offering Hezekiah blessed relief from the hot sun. By the dim light of a torch, he followed Eliakim to a tall pile of earthenware jars, stacked on their sides like cordwood. Each handle was inscribed with Hezekiah's seal, "Belonging to the king," and the name of the distribution city.

Eliakim rested his hand on one of the jars. "We're building storehouses like this all across the nation for army supplies. We'll be well prepared for an Assyrian siege."

"Tell me about Lachish," Hezekiah said. "I understand you and Jonadab just spent several days there." He had heard unsettling rumors about the way his brother governed the city, and he trusted Eliakim to tell him the truth.

"Lachish is a very impressive fortress, Your Majesty—one of the strongest cities in Judah."

"How is my brother Gedaliah?"

Eliakim brushed invisible dust off the storage jars. "He's fine. He lives well. It's a very prosperous city."

"He's doing a good job as administrator, then?"

Eliakim wiped his hands on his tunic. "That's really not for me to judge. I'm only an engineer."

"I'm asking for your honest assessment, Eliakim. Forget that he's my brother—I need to know."

"The city appears to be running smoothly, and their standard of living is very high, if that's any indication of his leadership ability." Eliakim glanced briefly at Shebna. "But personally, I don't agree with all the decisions he's made. And I don't think you would either."

"Which decisions?"

"He allows the people to worship at a temple to the sun god."

"It is not such a simple matter, Your Majesty," Shebna interrupted. "The elders of Lachish are very powerful men, and Gedaliah has had to deal carefully with them. Most of them never agreed with your religious reforms and would rebel against your brother if he pushed too hard."

Eliakim frowned. "I got the impression that he wasn't merely appeasing them, Your Majesty. I seriously question if Gedaliah himself supports your religious reforms."

"Are you saying my brother is an idolater?"

"He worships at the temple to the sun god—twice a day."

"Maybe he is pressured!" Shebna shouted. "You would do the same thing in his place."

"No, I would resign before I'd worship idols."

Shebna folded his arms across his chest. "Listen, Your Majesty—I am sure Lachish is not the only city that still has a foreign temple."

"It's the only one Jonadab and I found," Eliakim said. "The people have destroyed all the others. In Beersheba they not only tore the temple down—they brought me the pagan altar for building material. I used it to reinforce the city wall."

Hezekiah smiled slightly. "That's putting it to good use." He decided to steer the conversation to another topic. "Jonadab has requested some leave time before he takes over our military training program. Would you like some time off as well, Eliakim?"

"No, I'll be needed down at the tunnels. We're very close to the middle."

"Keep me informed, Eliakim. Let me know as soon as you hear the signals from the other side."

As they walked back into the sunlight, Hezekiah felt a surge of confidence. He had excellent men working for him, and he had spared no expense. When his plans were complete, every citizen in Judah would be within traveling distance of a well-fortified, well-supplied city. At the first sign of an Assyrian attack, they could take refuge behind fortressed walls and wait out the siege. Now all Hezekiah could do was pray that his plans and fortifications would never be needed.

32

Eliakim crouched in the coffinlike tunnel with his measuring cord and clay tablets, checking his calculations for the third time. In the distance chisels clashed against stone, and one of the laborers hummed tunelessly as he worked. Eliakim bent close to the lamp to read his figures, and the oily smoke stung his eyes. These calculations couldn't be right! But where had he made a mistake? He wiped his stinging eyes and added the numbers again.

"We're hitting harder rock where you told us to dig, sir."

Eliakim looked up; his burly foreman filled the tunnel in front of him. The chiseling and the singing had stopped. "Not again."

"Afraid so, sir. The fissure in the limestone takes another twist to the left."

"Show me."

Eliakim pushed his measuring cord and tablets aside as the foreman ordered the workmen to take a short break. Then Eliakim led the way, crawling on his hands and knees toward the wall of rock at the end of the tunnel. Only one small lamp burned, mounted on the wall a few feet behind them. Their crouching shadows danced eerily on the wall. In the inky gloom, Eliakim couldn't see any fissures in the rock. He picked up a hammer and tapped the wall, listening for changes in pitch. Maybe the foreman was wrong; maybe the vein of limestone they followed would continue in a straight path. But after several minutes of testing, Eliakim knew the tunnel would have to make yet another sharp turn to the left.

He threw the hammer to the floor and crouched in the semidarkness, resting his forehead on his clenched fist. Silence filled the tunnel. Even the mumbling of the workers had stopped, and all he heard was the foreman's chesty breathing. The air felt damp, his skin clammy.

"What do you want us to do now, my lord?"

Eliakim tried to recall his latest measurements and to calculate in his head, but exhaustion slowed his efforts, frustrating him. "I don't know—follow the softer rock, I guess." He turned around to crawl out and cracked his head painfully on the low ceiling.

"Wait a minute, my lord. If we follow the vein, won't we be veering away from the other tunnel again?"

Eliakim didn't know where the other tunnel was. That was the problem. According to his calculations, the two tunnels were perfectly aligned and within a few cubits of breaking through. But in reality the tunnels didn't seem to match his calculations. He rubbed the rising welt on his head and inched back to the end of the tunnel. He pressed his ear to the wall like an anxious physician on a dying patient's chest, listening in several places for sounds from the other side. If they were as close as he thought they were, he should be able to hear the ringing vibrations from the other tunnel, conducted through the stone. He heard nothing.

"Are you sure they're digging over there?" he asked.

"I can check—"

"Never mind. Let's try the signals again. We'll listen here, and then over here, where the softer vein lies."

"First thing tomorrow morning, you mean?"

"No! Right now! How else can we dig?"

"But it's the middle of the night—"

"I don't care!"

"But they have to blow the shofar to let us know when they're ready to signal, and we can't go blasting shofars now. We'll wake up the entire city. They'll think the Assyrians are coming."

The Assyrians. They were the reason he had gotten into this mess. Eliakim slumped against the cold stone wall in defeat. "I can't even remember if it's day or night anymore."

The foreman nervously toyed with his hammer. "Sir? You can tell me to mind my own business, but I think you should go home and get some rest. Maybe things will look different in the morning."

"Torches!" Eliakim suddenly shouted. "We can signal with torches instead of shofars!"

He squeezed past the stunned foreman and scrambled down the tunnel on his hands and knees to issue the orders. "Send a runner over to the other side and tell them to try the signals twice. Tell them to light a torch when they're ready to start and extinguish it when they're done. We'll do the same. Got that?"

Eliakim brushed the loose dirt off his knees and crawled back to his foreman. "You listen there, and I'll listen here, then we'll switch."

The foreman's slippery sweat soaked Eliakim's tunic as they maneuvered into position, side by side, in a space large enough for only one man. The ceiling was just inches above Eliakim's head, and the man's salty odor nauseated him. At last, word traveled down the tunnel that the signaling had begun. Eliakim pressed his ear against the cold wall, now damp with his own condensed breath, and listened. Nothing. He watched the foreman's face, just inches from his, but it remained fixed in a scowl. When word reached them that the signaling was over, the foreman shook his head.

"All right. Switch places."

In his haste, Eliakim smacked his head on the ceiling again and grunted in pain. As he listened for the second set of signals, he knew that if he closed his eyes he would fall asleep on the hard stone floor. He was sticky with sweat, his own and the foreman's, and coated with a layer of dirt. When the signaling ended he would go home, get washed, and go to bed. It was hopeless. The signaling had ended. He heard nothing. The foreman held out the hammer.

"Do you want to pound the signal, sir, or should I?"

"You do it. I'm going out for some air." He crawled down the tunnel to where he had left his drawings, then slumped against the wall and promptly fell asleep.

When he opened his eyes, the foreman was crouching beside him. "We can't dig until you tell us where, sir. The other side didn't hear our signals either." Eliakim looked down at his measurements, but they dissolved into an unreadable blur. "Follow the vein of softer rock."

"But, that means—"

"Then do whatever you want! It doesn't matter anymore. I'm going home to get some sleep."

———◆———

Hilkiah lay in bed, staring into the darkness, listening. Eliakim had promised to come home for supper, but it was already after midnight, and he hadn't arrived. Hilkiah tried not to imagine a cave-in at the tunnel or some other disaster. Months had passed since he'd talked to Eliakim about slowing down, but if anything, he'd been working even harder. He was digging the tunnel to bury his broken heart.

Hilkiah couldn't remember when Eliakim had last gone to the Temple with him—or laughed or smiled. His depression was as deep and black as the tunnel shaft. Wealthy fathers continued to line up at Hilkiah's door, offering to match their daughters with Eliakim.

Maybe his heart would heal faster if he arranged a match for him. But Eliakim had been so short-tempered lately that Hilkiah was afraid to suggest it.

At last Hilkiah heard the front door creak open, then slam shut. He leaped out of bed, grabbing his robe and an oil lamp on the way out. He saw by Eliakim's face that the news wasn't good.

"Abba, why are you still up?"

"I was worried about you. You said you'd be home for dinner."

"Yes—well, I'm sorry. I guess I forgot. I lose track of day and night when I'm inside the tunnel."

"We waited to eat—we were all worried about you."

Eliakim peeled off his dusty outer robe and let it drop to the floor. "Don't you have anything better to do than worry about me? You've got the girls now. Worry about them."

Eliakim smelled like stale sweat. He looked exhausted, but he stumbled around the front hall as if filled with nervous energy, his bloodshot eyes darting restlessly. "Look—if I'm causing you so much worry and distress, maybe I should move out for good. Then it won't matter when I come or go, and you can stop losing sleep over me."

"You hardly live here now as it is."

"We've been through all this before," he said wearily. "It's my job—you know that."

"And it's my job as your father to worry about you."

Eliakim rubbed his eyes, and Hilkiah saw that his hands were shaking. "I'm sorry, Abba. Maybe once the tunnel is finished we can all relax again."

"Any sound from the other side yet?" Hilkiah hated to ask.

"No. Nothing."

"How about water seepage?"

"We've *got* to be close! That's why I'm so late. I measured it all over again, and we've *got* to be within hearing range by now! I don't understand it!"

"I never did understand how you could get two narrow, winding tunnels to meet."

"You sound like Shebna. He's convinced I can't do it, but I know they're close. I *know* they are!" Eliakim's hands balled into fists.

"Then why are you so upset? I should think you'd be happy."

Eliakim stopped pacing, and his whole body sagged. "King Hezekiah received a report today. They've spotted Assyrians in Judean territory."

"God of Abraham! Are they invading us?"

"Not yet, but it doesn't look good."

"They're scouting Judean territory." The voice came from behind Hilkiah, and he jumped in surprise. Jerusha stood in the shadows, hugging her robe tightly around herself. She looked beautiful in the pale lamplight. No wonder his son was smitten.

"The siege must be nearing an end," she said. "That's why they're sending out their scouts."

"Oh, Jerusha. Are you sure?" Hilkiah asked.

"Yes, I'm positive. They scout their next target when the siege is about to break through."

Hilkiah wrung his hands. "God of Abraham! It's time for our nation to cry out to Yahweh. The Torah says that sometimes the Holy One sends a crisis to wake us up. Sometimes that's the only time men will call on Him, and the Torah also says—" Hilkiah stopped when he saw his son's face. All the color had drained from it, and he looked as though he might collapse. "Son, what's wrong? Are you all right?"

"I have to go back to the tunnel."

"Go back? It's the middle of the night. You can't—"

"I told them to follow the softer rock, but they have to go straight!" Eliakim picked up his outer robe and struggled to put it on. His motions were jerky and out of control. Before Hilkiah could stop him, Eliakim disappeared through the door.

"God of Abraham, when does he eat? When does he sleep? What can I do with such a son?" He turned to Jerusha. "What's wrong?"

"Why did I ever think I'd escape from them?" she wept. "Iddina's stalking me—and there's no place left to hide!"

33

King Hezekiah sat on his throne, holding court as usual, but deep inside, faith and doubt battled like two armies locked in mortal combat. Assyrians had been spotted in Judah, and Hezekiah knew he faced one of the greatest crises of his reign. Outside his throne room the air was still. No branches stirred, no birds sang, as if nature tensed with the strain of waiting. The steady pounding of hammers sounded in the streets as workmen labored to complete the walls around the palace complex and military fortress. The sound seemed to echo the Assyrian battering rams as they hammered against the walls of Samaria in the north. When the scribe announced that Jonadab had arrived, Hezekiah knew why.

"Your Majesty, the siege of Samaria is over. The city fell to the Assyrians three days ago."

In the hush that filled the throne room, an overwhelming sadness filled Hezekiah. Israel was defeated. All the territory that had once belonged to the 10 northern tribes was conquered. How could all those descendants of Abraham, once as numerous as the stars of heaven, be lost?

"It was inevitable," Hezekiah said. "No one has ever defeated the Assyrians."

"Samaria held out bravely for three years," Jonadab said, "but the remaining inhabitants neared starvation at the end. They'd resorted to cannibalism."

"How does news like that find its way here?" Shebna grumbled.

"The Assyrians will make sure every man in Judah hears about it," Jonadab said. "It's part of their plan to demoralize their enemies so they'll give up. They're masters at it. They'll keep some of the victims from Samaria alive until they reach the next city—then they'll impale the poor souls around the walls and leave them there to die. Do you have any idea how terrifying that is to the people watching from inside the walls?"

"Yes, and if they attack Judah next, those Israeli prisoners will remind us that Israel was always larger and stronger than our nation." Hezekiah passed his hand over his face. "What else, Jonadab?"

"The Assyrians will deport the survivors as slaves. By the time they finish, not one Hebrew will remain in Israel. It will be as if they disappeared from the face of the earth."

Hezekiah felt a chill. That was what Isaiah had prophesied during the first year of his reign. He wondered if this, the seventh year of his reign, would be his last.

"Has anyone learned what Assyria's next move will be?"

"No, Your Majesty. No one seems to know."

Hezekiah drew a deep breath and grimly faced the two men. "Use the signal fires to keep me informed on the Assyrians' movements. I want to know as soon as they march. As I see it, we have two choices—submit and become a vassal nation to Assyria again, or call upon any allies we can find and fight back."

Shebna gnawed his fingers. "Whatever you decide to do, you had better do it quickly. Once the Assyrians cross our borders it will be too late for tribute."

"We shouldn't wait to start mobilizing our allies or our troops either," Jonadab said.

"Are we prepared for a fight, General?"

"Not as ready as I'd like to be. We need more time to finish our fortifications and train our forces. But this is our land, Your Majesty. The men of Judah will fight with all their hearts to save it."

Shebna stared at the floor and shook his head. "Their love for the land will never be enough. We are a nation of farmers and craftsmen; the Assyrians are professional soldiers. Without allies we are doomed, outnumbered a hundred to one."

"Is slavery preferable to annihilation?" Hezekiah wondered aloud. "Would the men of Judah prefer to live, laboring in their fields for foreign masters for the rest of their lives?"

"Given the choice, I think they would," Shebna said.

"No! Only the cowards would choose to surrender," Jonadab said. "We were outnumbered when we faced the Philistines too. We should fight for what is rightfully ours."

Hezekiah looked at the two men for a long moment. "The decision isn't mine to make," he said at last. "It's God's. I'm not going to choose either alternative until I know what God's will is. Find Rabbi

Isaiah. Ask him to seek the word of the Lord for me. Tell him I'll do whatever Yahweh says."

Shebna slumped in his seat and stared at the floor. Jonadab went rigid. "Shouldn't I mobilize my troops, just in case—?"

"Not until I talk to Isaiah, but in the meantime we can pray. Tell the priests and Levites to organize a special sacrifice at the Temple. Then send for Eliakim. If we ever needed a secure water supply, the time is now."

<hr>

When the blast of the shofar announced the service at the Temple, Eliakim was crouched deep inside the south tunnel, listening in vain for a sound from the other side. When he heard the news, he dismissed all the workmen, then hurried home to change his clothes.

Maacah met him at the door. "What's going on, Eliakim? Why are the shofars blowing?"

"It's a special assembly at the Temple."

"Why would they call one now, in the middle of the day?"

Samaria had fallen. There could be no other reason. Jerusha and Maacah would find out eventually, but Eliakim didn't want to be the one to tell them. He pushed past Maacah.

"I don't know. I've been in the tunnel all morning. Excuse me—I have to get ready."

Eliakim bathed in the mikveh, then changed into clean clothes. But as he hurried across the courtyard he heard Jerusha's voice through the open bedroom window.

"I'm packing some food and water and getting out! I'm not staying in Jerusalem. I'm not!"

"We can't leave—not after all Uncle Hilkiah has done for us!" Maacah said. "Besides, where would we go?"

"We'll find Uncle Saul and live with him."

"But if Eliakim couldn't find him, how will we?"

"I don't know! I don't care! We've got to get out of here!"

"We're safer behind the city walls—"

"No, we're not! The Assyrians could easily topple these walls. I've watched them do it!"

Eliakim felt a knife twist in his stomach. He groaned and leaned against the wall of the house.

"Maacah, I've seen them attack walls much thicker than Jerusalem's. And I've witnessed the horrible things they do once those walls were breached. I pitied the people who were trapped inside, and I won't become one of them! I won't!"

Eliakim felt a hand on his shoulder. "Are you ready to go, Son?" Eliakim nodded. He didn't want to hear any more.

Eliakim and Hilkiah joined the crowd that stood before the sanctuary, anxiously waiting to hear the king's announcement. Finally Hezekiah mounted the royal dais, and the murmuring fell silent.

"Three days ago Samaria fell to the Assyrians." His strong voice carried no tremor of fear, and he stood with his shoulders straight, his head held high. "We need to remember our brethren and to pray for them. And we need to pray for ourselves as well."

As Eliakim bowed down in the courtyard, one overwhelming thought filled his mind: his tunnel wasn't finished. Eight months had passed since he had first begun to dig, and according to his calculations it was almost complete. But *almost* wasn't good enough. His long months of digging had been wasted. The Assyrians were going to win again.

The priests pleaded with God for help, but Eliakim was too panicked to pray. His mind raced in every direction at once, trying to figure out how he could make the tunnels meet.

When the priests slew the sacrifices, Eliakim rose with the other men as they crowded around the altar. But he didn't hear any of their words as he frantically struggled to recall the latest measurements of the tunnels and to calculate how many more cubits they had to dig. Once again, he asked the question that had haunted him day and night: why hadn't they heard the signals?

As the fire ascended heavenward, the Levites began their song of praise to Yahweh: *But I will sing of your strength, in the morning I will sing of your love; for you are my fortress, my refuge in times of trouble.*

Before Eliakim realized it, the service had ended. How could the lengthy sacrifice have passed so quickly without his hearing a word of it? As the men filed through the Temple gates to go home, panic gripped him. King Hezekiah was going to ask for a report on the tunnel. Time had run out, and Eliakim had failed.

Forgetting his father, Eliakim elbowed through the slow-moving crowd. Once outside the Temple gates, he ran through the streets to the foreman's tent at the south tunnel. He was the first one to return, and when he realized that the work had stopped for the sacrifice, he grabbed a hammer and chisel and scrambled down the shaft to dig. Then he remembered that he had calculations to make before King Hezekiah sent for him, and he threw down the tools and raced back to the tent. Sweat dripped from his forehead and ran down his neck as he bent over his scrolls in the suffocating tent.

At last he heard the laborers return and the clanging of their tools as they went back to work. Minutes passed; then Eliakim finally heard footsteps approaching. He mopped the sweat from his brow and looked up.

"A messenger has arrived from the palace, my lord. King Hezekiah wants to see you at once."

—◈—

"What do you mean, you can't find him?" Hezekiah stared at the messenger as if he had misunderstood.

"Rabbi Isaiah's house is empty, Your Majesty. His neighbors say he left about a week and a half ago."

"And *no one* knows where he went?" Shebna asked.

"No one, sir. But we'll continue searching for him."

Hezekiah groaned. He couldn't afford to wait for the prophet; he had to make a decision. He yearned to take action in this crisis, to issue commands instead of sitting around waiting for Isaiah. But he needed to hear from God first. He wondered if the prophet had fled because Judah was about to be invaded, and all of a sudden God seemed very far away. He clenched his fists.

"You have to find Isaiah!" While Hezekiah debated what to do next, his engineer arrived.

Eliakim entered with his head bowed and his shoulders sagging. The proud confidence he had displayed when he first unveiled his plans for the tunnel had vanished. Hezekiah knew without asking that the tunnel wasn't finished, and his anxiety deepened.

"I assume you've heard the news about Samaria, Eliakim. I'd like a report on the tunnel."

Eliakim cleared his throat. "According to my calculations, the two tunnels are within a few cubits of breaking through."

Shebna leaned forward. "Have the workmen heard the signals from the other side?"

"Uh—no—we still haven't heard them but—"

"Then this breakthrough you are talking about is only a theory."

"There's every indication that—"

Shebna's voice rose to a shout. "Can you guarantee that we will have a water system within the next few days or not?"

"No. I can't."

Shebna slapped his thighs. "That is great! Not only will the Assyrians be able to use our water supply—maybe they can finish digging the tunnel for us. You have given them a convenient door into the city so they will not *need* their battering rams!"

"Let him finish, Shebna," Hezekiah said. "How much longer do you think it will take?"

Eliakim sighed and ran his fingers through his curly hair. "Your Majesty, we must be very close. I've been expecting a breakthrough for over a week. Just a few more days and—"

"—and the Assyrians will be camped out there helping you dig!" Shebna finished. "Besides, how do you know that the two tunnels are even in alignment? How do you know that they will *ever* meet? Maybe they have passed by each other already!" Shebna gestured with his hands, sailing them by each other without touching. Eliakim stared at the floor.

"That's enough, Shebna," Hezekiah said.

"I am sorry, my lord." He sat back and crossed his legs.

"Eliakim, assuming that you break through in the next day or two, how long until the tunnel is ready to use?"

"The new Pool of Siloam is ready. We could probably start diverting the water from the old aqueduct right away."

"The problem is—we can't conceal the spring until the tunnel is finished, right?"

"Yes, Your Majesty."

"And if it isn't finished in the next two days," Hezekiah continued, "there won't be enough time to conceal it properly. Shebna's right. The Assyrians will be here to help us dig." Eliakim closed his eyes in defeat.

"Now, we can spend the next two days digging and hope for a breakthrough," Hezekiah said, "or we can spend that time erasing all traces of the half-finished project. Shebna, what do you say?"

"I am not a man who likes to gamble, Your Majesty. Forget the tunnel and prepare for a siege."

"Eliakim, what do you think?"

"The two tunnels should have met by now," he mumbled. "I don't know why they haven't. I—I can't offer any advice."

Hezekiah felt torn. They would desperately need water if the Assyrians laid siege to the city, but did he dare take a chance that the enemy would find the unfinished tunnel? How he wished Isaiah was here to tell him what Yahweh had to say! But Isaiah wasn't here. And Hezekiah had to make a decision.

"Go back and keep digging," Hezekiah said at last. "I'll let you know if I change my mind."

◄◈►

Shebna stormed back to his chambers, angry and frustrated. King Hezekiah was making a terrible mistake. It would take the workmen days to hide every trace of the unfinished tunnels, but instead of ordering them to begin immediately, Hezekiah allowed them to continue their useless digging. What a tragic waste of valuable time! The tunnels would never meet. The king should have listened to his advice and reopened the water shaft. At least that project would have been finished by now. It seemed to Shebna that the king was faltering in this crisis, unable or unwilling to make a decision. He was deeply disappointed in Hezekiah, and for the first time ever, Shebna wanted to distance himself from the king and be alone. But when he opened the door to his private chambers, Prince Gedaliah and the elders of Lachish were waiting for him.

"Give us an audience with the king," Gedaliah said abruptly.

Shebna folded his arms across his chest. "What for?"

"Surely you've heard the news, Shebna. Samaria has fallen, and we're probably going to be next." He slapped a document into Shebna's hands. "This petition asks the king to send tribute before we're wiped out like our brothers to the north."

"How did you get to Jerusalem so fast?"

"The news is all over Judah that Assyrian patrols were seen in our territory. We didn't wait for the ax to fall. We decided to come with our petition right away. We just happened to arrive in time to hear the news. Now—do we get our audience or not?"

"It would be a waste of time. Your petition will not matter one way or the other," Shebna handed it back to Gedaliah.

"Haven't you had enough of him yet?" Gedaliah shouted. "Can't you see that my brother isn't fit to rule?"

The elders' angry faces told Shebna that they agreed with the prince. And after Hezekiah's wavering indecision this morning, Shebna wondered if perhaps they were right. But if Gedaliah wanted to plot a rebellion, Shebna didn't want any witnesses to his part in the conspiracy.

"I will see that the king gets your petition. Now, if you have anything more to discuss with me, Gedaliah, you will have to do it privately."

"Oh, stop playing your stupid games. We all know you're as disgusted with Hezekiah as we are."

"You are mistaken."

"Oh really? Then why have you been working until midnight every night on tax proposals and petitions for alliances?"

The knowledge that he was being watched made Shebna shudder. "I drew up those documents in case the king decides to use them. I have no intention of implementing them myself."

Gedaliah turned to the city elders. "You'd better leave and let me talk to him in private. He can be pretty stubborn." The men muttered their discontent as they filed from the room. "Now then," Gedaliah said when they were alone. "Can we cut out all the loyalty garbage and talk seriously?"

"That depends. What exactly do you want from me?"

"I thought you were smart, Shebna. But if you want me to spell it out for you, I will." His voice rose to a shout, and Shebna backed away from him. "We're about to be invaded by the most powerful nation on earth—all because Hezekiah became a religious fanatic and stopped sending tribute! There's only one thing left for any king to do—either send the tribute with his humble apologies or find some very strong allies, fast!"

"That is what I have been advising—no, begging—him to do."

"But he isn't listening, is he? Even his military advisers are telling him to marshall the troops, but is he listening? I'm telling you—he's incompetent!"

"If you make that accusation again, I swear I will—"

"Then what is he waiting for? Does he *want* to be wiped out?"

Shebna hesitated, reluctant to disclose the reason for Hezekiah's inaction. Shebna knew that the king was a very competent ruler, even if he didn't always agree with his decisions. He could no longer bear to hear the prince's criticism.

"King Hezekiah consults his god in every decision he makes. He is waiting for Isaiah to tell him what Yahweh wants him to do."

Even as he spoke the words, Shebna realized the foolishness of what Hezekiah was doing. There was no god to answer him or to come to his rescue. The king had no right to risk his nation's future on the basis of a myth.

Gedaliah spat out a string of angry curses. "Just who is running this nation—Hezekiah or Isaiah? And if you're supposed to be his chief adviser, why is he ignoring your advice and going to someone else?"

This time Gedaliah's words hit their mark. Hezekiah had ignored Shebna's advice for weeks, and no amount of pleading had changed his mind. Even this morning the king had asked for Shebna's advice on the tunnel, then promptly disregarded it. But Hezekiah wouldn't ignore Isaiah's advice. Shebna's anger and frustration finally reached their limit.

"What do you propose, Gedaliah?"

"It isn't just my proposal. All the city elders agree—some of the army commanders too. If King Hezekiah won't listen to reason, then we need a different king."

Shebna turned his back on Gedaliah and stared through the open window at Ahaz's clock tower. Disappointment and resentment consumed him, and for the first time in his life he couldn't seem to think clearly.

"Will there be an assassination?" he finally asked.

"I could never kill my own brother." Gedaliah's voice was as smooth as olive oil.

Shebna knew he was lying. "Who do these elders have in mind as their new king?" he asked bitterly.

"My first action as King of Judah would be to do exactly what you've advised, Shebna—send tribute to Assyria in order to avert this disaster that's hanging over us. Unlike my brother, I would take your advice very seriously. I'm asking you to serve as my palace administrator."

Shebna didn't answer. He hated Gedaliah. The prince was a power-hungry traitor, but he was also right. The nation faced certain annihilation if Hezekiah refused to act. Shebna's friendship and loyalty to Hezekiah spanned more than 20 years. He greatly admired the king for his integrity and courage, qualities that Gedaliah certainly lacked. But the frustration of having his advice ignored for the past several months had strained their relationship. The fact that Hezekiah turned to Isaiah in a crisis instead of him angered him the most.

Shebna understood the consequences of supporting Gedaliah if the takeover failed. But he also understood the consequences of remaining loyal to Hezekiah if the plot succeeded. It was simply a matter of betting on which brother would win—or deciding which brother he was willing to die for. He felt trapped.

"Are you with us or not?" Gedaliah asked.

"When is this going to take place?"

"I'm not stupid enough to tell you everything until I know where you stand."

"I need time to decide." The only way for Shebna to escape this trap was to find Isaiah and hope that the prophet's advice would finally cause Hezekiah to take action.

"You're stalling!" Gedaliah cursed.

"No! You are asking me to put my life in jeopardy. I will give you my decision tomorrow. Not before."

"We can't wait that long."

"If you want my support, you will have to. Now get out!"

34

Eliakim left the palace and walked down the hill in a daze of guilt and failure. He had seen the anxiety and disappointment on King Hezekiah's face, and he knew he was to blame. He had been so sure he could do the impossible. Now he had failed. *Keep digging*, King Hezekiah had said. But what was the use? Eliakim knew his two tunnels were never going to meet.

As he walked through the water gate and down the steep ramp to the spring, the beautiful Kidron Valley lay before him. But instead of the green patchwork of gardens and olive groves, Eliakim saw thousands of Assyrian troops trampling the earth beneath their chariots, staining the brook red with blood. With a gnawing ache in the pit of his stomach, he made his way to the tunnel entrance and found his foreman.

"I need to measure the tunnel again," Eliakim told him. "We must have strayed off course somehow, and we need to get back on track."

Eliakim tried to sound confident, but anything he tried would be a stab in the dark. It seemed useless to continue digging, but he didn't know what else to do except obey the king's orders.

"Have all the men take a break. Send them out here so they'll be out of my way. I need space to measure properly."

"Even the laborer at the end, my lord?"

"Yes. And bring all the torches out to conserve air; it's getting stuffy in there. I'll need only one lamp."

The foreman shrugged. "Whatever you say. You're the boss."

Eliakim waited, wishing in vain that he was *not* the boss. When the workmen had cleared out, Eliakim slowly crawled through the tunnel, remeasuring carefully, comparing the results with the figures in his diagrams. The twisting path of the fissure probably caused all his problems in this tunnel. And the huge curve he had dug to avoid the kings' graves had thrown him off course in the other one. He wished for the hundredth time that he had dug the tunnel straight instead of following the fault line.

But as Eliakim crouched in the cramped, suffocating darkness he knew that he wouldn't find a mistake in his calculations. His mistake had been pride, reckless overconfidence fueled by hatred. Arrogance had convinced him that he could tunnel from opposite ends and meet in the middle. Revenge had induced him to attempt this impossible feat. He had been a conceited fool.

With rising despair, Eliakim inched through the dark, stuffy tunnel, measuring carefully, pulling his lamp and his drawings along with him. When the ceiling lowered, he ducked his head and crawled on his hands and knees for the last few cubits until the tunnel ended abruptly in a wall of rock. He crouched in a space barely three feet high and as wide as his shoulders, surrounded on three sides by solid rock. Unyielding, impenetrable, immovable rock. He hadn't dug a tunnel after all, but a tomb—twin grave pits in which to bury the people of Jerusalem. He had failed.

"NO!" The gloomy walls absorbed the sound of his voice as they closed in around him. "NO! NO!" He pounded his fists against the silent, jagged wall until they were bruised and raw.

"Where are you, you cursed tunnel?" he cried as he clawed at the stone, trying to dig it away with his hands. "Do you want them to win? Those heathens are going to win again! Where are you?" Jagged rock tore at Eliakim's skin until his hands bled, but he never noticed the pain as he beat against the wall again and again. At last he slumped to the ground, exhausted, defeated. His chest heaved from exertion, and he tasted the bitterness of failure. He lay inside his grave, staring up at the ceiling.

Then slowly, the black, uncaring walls began to close in on Eliakim. The place where he lay gradually grew smaller and smaller. In a few minutes the walls would crush him to death. He couldn't catch his breath. His heart pounded savagely as his panic soared and his lungs strained for air. He had to get out! The walls were closing in and the tunnel was out of air! He grabbed his oil lamp and pinched out the flame. The moment he did, Eliakim realized his mistake. He cried out as he plunged into total, impenetrable darkness.

"Help me!" The walls absorbed the sound of his screams. He tried to scramble to his feet, but cold, hard rock smashed into him on every side. He groped in the dark like a blind man, striking his head against the ceiling, feeling along the walls for the way out. He couldn't find it. He'd been buried alive.

"Oh, God—help me!"

Eliakim found the opening and clawed his way forward on his face. Dirt filled his mouth and throat as his lungs screamed for air. Then the tunnel widened, and he could stand. He pulled himself to his feet, but his trembling legs barely supported him. He gasped for each breath of air. The ceiling was pressing down on him, the walls still closing in. At any moment he would be crushed to death beneath millions of tons of rock.

Eliakim began stumbling forward through the blackness, his arms outstretched. But the sharp twists and right angle turns of the tunnel continually blocked his escape as he smashed into barriers of stone.

"Somebody help me!" On and on in maddening blindness, searching for a way out, finding none. It wasn't a tunnel, but an endless maze, a hopeless labyrinth. He couldn't breathe. He was going to die. He had dug his own tomb.

"Oh, God!" he screamed. *"NO!"*

Suddenly Eliakim tripped and fell headfirst. Cold, black water slapped his face, then surrounded and engulfed him. The icy shock brought him to his senses. He struggled to his knees, coughing and choking for air. He knew where he was now—he had tripped over the dam that held back the spring water and had fallen headlong into the old Jebusite holding pool. He pulled himself out of the water, leaned against the wall, and vomited. When his stomach finished heaving, Eliakim knelt beside the water for a long time, gulping air, waiting for his panic to subside. He made a shaky attempt to wash off the vomit and blood, then slowly rose to his feet and groped down the narrow slit of rock. At last he saw the opening, and he waded into the sunlight.

As he emerged dripping wet from the tunnel, the foreman and work crew standing nearby suddenly fell silent. Eliakim saw them staring at him and realized that he hadn't marked where they should dig. He didn't even have his drawing with the measurements. He turned around and staggered back toward the tunnel, but when he recalled the suffocating panic that had engulfed him, he knew he couldn't crawl back inside. Eliakim turned back to the waiting men. Bile burned his throat, and his bloodied hands throbbed painfully. The men were watching him curiously, staring at him. He cleared his throat, not certain if he could speak, and thrust his hands behind his back to hide the blood that still oozed from his raw flesh.

"There's—uh—no need to change direction. Just—uh—just keep going straight until—uh—until we try the signals again."

The foreman took a tentative step toward him. "Are you all right, my lord?"

"Yes," Eliakim replied too quickly. "I—uh—I fell." He edged away from him.

"But sir, you're—"

"Listen—I'll be down at the other tunnel if you need me." He continued to back away. No one moved. Why were they staring?

"Quit standing around!" Eliakim shouted. "Get back to work!"

He fled down the valley, through the lower gate, and into the new section of the city where the empty Pool of Siloam marked the entrance to the other tunnel. He stayed inside the foreman's tent all day and into the evening, eating nothing, barely speaking, totally incapacitated by failure and guilt. It took a long time for his limbs to stop shaking, and he refused to crawl inside either tunnel to listen for the signals.

"Your ears are just as good as mine!" he growled when the foreman questioned him about it. He waited to return home until after the supper hour to avoid Jerusha. How could he tell her that the Assyrians were going to win? She was going to become their slave again. They all were.

When he finally trudged through the door, his father bustled around him, worrying over him, insisting that the servants fix him something to eat. Eliakim's stomach turned queasy at the thought.

"I don't want any food," he mumbled.

"What's all over your tunic? What did you do to your hands? Is that blood?" Hilkiah wanted to know.

"Yeah, I—uh—I slipped—fell on some loose rocks—" He no longer cared if he lied.

"Well sit down. Let the servants put balm on your hands." Hilkiah tried to coax Eliakim to a couch, but he pushed him away.

"Leave me alone. I don't need anything."

"Son—?"

He couldn't stand his father hovering over him. "Just leave me alone!" A servant entered with a tray of food and held it out to Eliakim. "I said I don't want it!" he shouted, and knocked it out of the servant's hands, sending the plates crashing to the floor, spilling food everywhere. Then Eliakim turned and fled to his room, slamming the door behind him.

◆

To Hezekiah the long, dreary day filled with distressing news seemed as if it would never end. Samaria had fallen. The tunnel remained unfinished. No one knew for certain where the Assyrians would attack next. And the prophet Isaiah still hadn't been found.

Hezekiah's troubles piled one upon another, threatening to topple over and crush him beneath their weight. He had gone to the top of the wall at sunset and stood with the watchmen, waiting for the signal fire. When the message finally came it told him nothing new. The Assyrians still camped at Samaria. They hadn't begun to march.

Tonight Hezekiah needed his wife more than ever before. She ran to his arms, but he lacked the strength to return her kisses.

"My lord, I've never seen you this discouraged. Is there anything I can do?" He didn't answer. He didn't know the answer. "Shall I sing for you?"

"Only if you know a funeral dirge." Her lovely smile vanished.

"I'm sorry," he said, pulling her close. "But I can't help mourning for Israel. They were our brothers, and now they're gone."

Her hair brushed against his face with a lovely floral fragrance. He tried to determine what the scent was, but it eluded him.

"Have you ever been up north, to Israel?" he asked.

"No, Hezekiah. What's it like?"

"I've been there only once, a long time ago, when my father was still king. It was a beautiful land back then, much richer than ours and not nearly as rocky. They have a lake, shaped like your little harp, and it glitters in the sun as if filled with a thousand diamonds. The water is sweet and full of fish."

"Come. Sit down and tell me more, my love." She led him over to a couch near the window and sat down beside him with her head on his chest.

"Farther north there's an old man of a mountain with snowy white hair, called Mount Hermon, and the air is fragrant with the scent of cedar. The Jordan River is born on that mountain, and as it winds south toward our land it passes through farmland that's fertile and rich and green."

"You make it sound so beautiful," she murmured.

"Mmm—it was." Thinking of Israel in the past tense seemed strange to Hezekiah and profoundly sad. "Have you ever been down to the Jordan River, Hephzibah?"

"No, I've never traveled far from Jerusalem."

"Then you have no idea what a beautiful land you live in."

"Tell me about it."

"All right, but first I promise you that someday—in better times—we'll travel to all these places and see them together."

She held his hand to her cheek and kissed his fingers. "I would love that."

"First, we'll go down to Jericho. And I do mean down, because it rests in the deepest valley I've ever seen. It's an oasis, a glimmering green emerald in the dry, barren desert. We'll sit on top of the city walls, and I'll read you the story of how Yahweh worked a miracle to help Joshua conquer Jericho.

"Then we'll go down even farther to the Dead Sea. It's as blue as the sky on a cloudless day, but its waters are bitter and dead. There's no life in it at all."

"Why not?"

"It was poisoned by God's judgment on Sodom and Gomorrah. Surrounding the Dead Sea, the Judean wilderness looks barren and lifeless, but it has a beauty I can scarcely describe."

"How could something dead and barren seem beautiful?"

"I don't know," he shrugged, "but I think it's very beautiful. Maybe because it's part of God's creation or maybe because it belongs to me—I don't know. But I'll show it to you, and you can tell me what you think.

"Then we'll go through the Arabah and down to Elath on the Red Sea. Ships from all over the world sail there, bringing apes and ivories and exotic spices from faraway places. We'll sit for a while beside the warm, clear water and watch the ships come and go."

When Hezekiah closed his eyes he could almost hear the sound of the waves lapping gently against the shore. "Then we'll go north again and visit the Negev, and I'll show you the rolling prairies and how the grain ripples in the breeze like a golden sea."

He paused, and when he looked into Hephzibah's shining eyes, her long, dark lashes were moist. "You really love your nation, don't you, Hezekiah," she said.

"With all my heart." He swallowed back the sadness he suddenly felt and stroked her soft cheek. "Last of all, before we return to the rock-strewn Judean hills, we'll go through the Shephelah, where there are sycamore groves and almond orchards, pomegranates and olives and grapes. We'll stand in the Valley of Elah together and look out over the plain where a small boy named David once challenged the giant that paralyzed armies and kings.

"'You come against me with sword and spear . . . '" he quoted softly. "'But I come against you in the name of the Lord Almighty. . . . and the whole world will know that there is a God in Israel.'"

Shebna would say it was only a myth, the exaggerated exploits of a departed king. Hezekiah fell silent for a long time; then his arms tightened around Hephzibah.

"You are so precious to me. I love you. I want you to know that— no matter what happens."

He wanted to tell Hephzibah that he was sorry, that if his nation came to an end like Israel the fault was his alone. But instead, he held her close and wondered what would happen to both of them.

After Hezekiah left, Hephzibah sat for a long time, weeping for all she might lose. She loved Hezekiah deeply, and she feared for his life more than she feared the horrors of siege warfare. If the nation fell to the Assyrians, his punishment would be the most severe. She was powerless to help him, and she thought she understood a little of the helplessness he felt. She would do anything, sacrifice everything, if it would allow him to continue as king of the nation he loved.

She knelt in front of the small carved chest beside her bed and reverently laid the lamps and incense burners before the smiling statue of Asherah. Then Hephzibah bowed with her forehead pressed to the floor.

"Oh, Lady Asherah, please forgive my husband's unbelief. Please, save him from invasion and make his kingdom secure. Please—please—may he live to reign a long time—"

Suddenly Hephzibah stopped. She had nothing to offer the goddess in return. She needed a sacrifice to guarantee that Asherah would answer her prayer. Only one sacrifice would be suitable, the highest gift of love and devotion.

Hephzibah ran to the adjoining room, where her maid slept. "Get up, Merab. I need your help."

She gazed at her sleepily. "Now? In the middle of the night?"

"I need an unused urn. Find me one quickly."

Merab pulled on her outer robe and smoothed down her hair before hurrying off. She returned with one of the king's storage jars, bearing his royal seal. "This is all I could find, my lady."

"It's perfect."

Hephzibah removed a lump of charred wood from the grate. Clutching the urn, she knelt before Asherah again. Her hands trembled at the enormity of what she was about to do, the great risk she was taking.

"Oh, Lady Asherah, if only you would allow my husband to rule over his land—I pledge to you—I solemnly vow—that I will sacrifice the first child you give me—the firstborn of my womb."

She opened her eyes and, with trembling hands, drew the symbols in black on the urn that would hold her baby's remains: the symbol for Asherah, the symbol for sacred vow, the symbol for firstborn, the symbol for death. Then Hephzibah covered her face with sooty hands and wept.

35

Hilkiah's distress deepened as he watched his son disappear into his room. Eliakim hovered on the verge of collapse, and Hilkiah guessed that his hands, which trembled uncontrollably, were not bruised and bloody from a fall. The anxiety his tunnels produced, coupled with his grief over Jerusha, had finally brought Eliakim to the breaking point.

As the household settled down for the night, Hilkiah knew he would never be able to sleep. Instead of going to his room, he walked through the darkened house and outside to the courtyard. It was a perfect night, quiet and clear, with a gentle breeze that cooled the air. But Hilkiah didn't notice the beautiful night or the millions of stars that sparkled in the cloudless sky. He sank down on the stone bench and buried his face in his hands.

"God of Abraham, what am I going to do? You see how my son suffers. You know how I suffer with him and how much it hurts me to see him like this. But how do I help him? If I could spare him this pain or take his pain on myself somehow, I would gladly do it. How I wish I suffered instead of my beloved son!"

Hilkiah wiped his tears with the back of his hand, then looked up into the sky for the first time, gazing at the rippling white curtain of stars. Suddenly God drew near to Hilkiah. The breeze was His breath, the silence His voice, the stars the light of His wisdom. And as the Spirit of God soothed Hilkiah's grieving heart, He provided understanding as well.

"God of Abraham!" he whispered. "My son hasn't called on You, has he? He hasn't sought Your wisdom and help." The stars twinkled in silent reply. "Yes, yes—that's it," he groaned. "He wanted to do everything himself so he would get all the glory. But now he needs Your help, Lord, and he's too proud to ask."

Once again Hilkiah covered his face. "I'm sorry, Lord. It's my fault too. I tried to raise him to have faith in You. I don't know where I went wrong."

His shoulders shook as he wept for Eliakim's pain and now for his own, at having failed God. He longed to go to his son, to beg him to turn to God and pray, but he knew he couldn't. Eliakim was a grown man, and no matter how great Hilkiah's faith in God, no matter how much he loved his son, Eliakim had to stand face-to-face with God by himself.

"Show me what to do, Lord!" Hilkiah was so deep in prayer he never noticed that Jerusha had joined him in the courtyard until he felt her comforting hand on his shoulder. He looked up.

"What's wrong?" she asked. "Can I do anything to help you?"

"No, my child, no. I'm not weeping for myself, but for my son. You've seen how he is—how he looks—he's a broken man."

He wiped his eyes again and sighed deeply as Jerusha stood by his side. "It's his tunnel. He's run out of time, and his tunnel isn't finished. He needs a miracle. He needs to pray."

Hilkiah closed his eyes, remembering the night he had argued with Eliakim over Jerimoth, remembering the bitterness in his son's voice: *Why did Mama die? Why didn't God answer our prayers?*

"But Eliakim won't pray," Hilkiah said. "He doesn't believe God answers prayer." He looked up at Jerusha, and suddenly he knew that she was God's answer. She was the only one who could help Eliakim.

"Jerusha," he whispered, "he won't listen to me—but he would listen to you."

"But I don't believe in prayer either. There is no God. He never answered any of my prayers."

"My sweet child—I think He has answered them, but you refuse to recognize it."

She looked startled, as if she had been slapped.

"Forgive me, Jerusha. I know that your ordeal must have been unbearable, but look around you! Are you still a slave? The Holy One has raised you from the dead! You're back from the grave in answer to your dear father's prayers. You have life again, and love, but you refuse to see it. In your mind and in your heart you're still their slave. You're hanging on to all your hatred instead of letting it go, and that hatred is keeping you captive. But even worse, you're robbing God of the glory that is due Him."

"God could have saved me from being captured in the first place!" she cried. "But He didn't! Why did He allow me to suffer like that? It was so horrible—!"

"Oh, my child. I can't even imagine how you've suffered. The world is an evil place because of man's choices, not God's. Yet I know that just as your father suffered and wept over you, and just as I weep and share in Eliakim's pain, our Heavenly Father felt all your sorrow and suffered your pain along with you."

"Then why did He allow it to happen?"

Hilkiah drew a deep breath and slowly let it out. "I asked 'Why?' when Eliakim's mother and our two little sons died. And what was God's answer? 'Look up!' There *is* a God of the heavens and the earth, my child. He orders all the stars in their courses and the moon as it waxes and wanes. He sends the rain and the sunshine and causes the earth to bloom. So if there is an order and a purpose in all He's made, then surely we can trust Him to order our lives too—without needing to know why."

"But I can't forget what they've done to me—or what I chose to become."

"What they've done to you can never be changed. But now you face another choice, Jerusha. How will you live the rest of your life? You can let the past make you bitter and unforgiving and unloving. Or you can turn the pain into something beautiful by choosing to do so."

"I don't see how."

"My dear child, tonight you saw me weeping, and you had compassion on me. Why? Because you've wept many hours yourself. You know what it's like to suffer. Because of what you've been through, you can reach out to others—but first you have to stop thinking of yourself. Did your father and mother die to save you so that you could be crippled with self-pity the rest of your life?" She didn't answer.

"Jerusha, Eliakim needs you—as a friend. I'm not asking you to be anything more. He doesn't trust God to answer his prayers, but he knows—*he knows* you're alive because of your father's prayers. If you want to help me, I beg you—go to him. You're a living testimony, Jerusha. He needs to be reminded of your father's great faith in God and that God does indeed answer prayer. Please, Jerusha?"

Jerusha stared at the ground. She wouldn't look at Hilkiah.

"I—I can't—," she cried. Then she fled into the house.

◆

Jerusha lay on her bed for a long time, clutching her baby's blanket and listening to Maacah's steady breathing as she slept. She had seen how Eliakim suffered, how haggard and defeated he looked, and it broke her heart. She loved him. But he had avoided her ever since the night he proposed, and she was certain that he hated her. How could she go to him now?

You're a living testimony that God answers prayer. Abba had believed in God and had prayed for her throughout her long ordeal.

"Oh, Abba!" she sobbed, remembering his smile, his strong, tanned arms, his warm green eyes. "My happy little bird," he used to call her. But that was before they took her song away. Before she'd been forced to witness the brutal deaths of thousands of people. She shuddered, remembering the endless days of hard labor, the long nights of suffering. *Turn it into something beautiful.* But how?

As Jerusha buried her face in the blanket, she suddenly remembered how her beautiful, perfect baby had been created through rape and pain. Could Hilkiah be right? Was it possible to find beauty from suffering? She raised her head and gazed around the room as if seeing it for the first time. Hilkiah was wealthier than Abba had dreamed of being. His luxurious home lacked nothing, and he had opened it freely to her, never asking for anything in return until tonight.

She thought about Hilkiah's stern words. Was she really as blind and ungrateful and filled with self-pity as he said? Was there really a God after all—a God who could forgive what she had done, a God who may have allowed her to suffer so that He could use her as His instrument of compassion?

Suddenly she remembered her father's final prayer as he blessed her and kissed her good-bye, then sacrificed his life so that she could live: *You saved Jerusha for a reason . . . May she find that reason and be a living testimony to Your goodness and grace.*

Jerusha went to the window and looked up into the star-filled sky. "God?—If You're really there, God—please help me. I—I don't know what to say to him!"

◆

As he sat in his room late that night, Eliakim's tortured mind barely functioned. With his drawings spread in front of him, he worked through his calculations one more time. And once again, he reached the same conclusion: the two tunnels were perfectly aligned. They should have broken through. He pounded his fist on the table, reopening the wounds on his raw, bruised hands. It was past midnight, and the dim light of the oil lamp strained his eyes. There was nothing more he could do.

Eliakim snuffed out the lamp and climbed the staircase to the darkened rooftop. The night was bright with stars, and he gazed down at the buildings and houses below him. His father's house sat high on the city mound, just below the king's palace. From his roof the vertical drop was at least 30 feet. Eliakim knew his tunnel would never be finished on time. There was no remedy for his failure. He didn't want to watch as thousands of soldiers surrounded Jerusalem, a city left without water because of him. He couldn't bear to hear them beating against his walls until they finally broke through, until they defeated him once again. They'd destroyed Jerusha, and soon they would destroy his nation. There was nothing left to live for.

He pried at the stones of the parapet that guarded the edge of the flat rooftop. For Hilkiah's sake, he would make it look like an accident, as though the wall had collapsed and he had fallen. But Eliakim couldn't get a firm grip with his sore hands. He kicked at the unyielding stones, then hurled his body against them, but the stones didn't budge. Like the wall at the end of his tunnel, the cold gray stone seemed to mock his efforts. He would have to climb over and jump.

"Eliakim, *don't!*"

He spun around. Jerusha looked so beautiful in the soft moonlight, with her long hair blowing in the breeze, that she might have been a mirage. Eliakim felt the familiar, painful longing for her beneath his despair.

"Don't do it, Eliakim—*please*—"

"What?" She couldn't have guessed what was on his mind.

"You were going to jump."

"No—I wasn't—I—" He moaned and leaned against the wall. Why bother lying anymore?

"Is it because of your tunnel?"

"My wonderful tunnel! The two shafts should have met days ago, but it's useless. All I can do is grope around down there—digging and digging—night and day—" He stopped, not trusting his voice.

"Then it's only a matter of time, isn't it? They have to meet up sooner or later."

"But we've run out of time—don't you understand? There *is* no more time! How long will it take the Assyrians to march here from Samaria? Tell me, Jerusha! You know the answer! Our time is up!" He turned away from her to look down once again at the 30-foot drop that could end all his anguish in a moment.

"Surely the king doesn't blame *you*, does he?"

"I told him I could do it. I promised him I could make it work. I was so sure." He whirled around to face her again. "This was the only way I could fight them—don't you see? I'm not a soldier. I can't fight with swords and weapons. This was my way of getting revenge. But they're going to defeat me anyway. You know it as well as I do. They're going to tear down my walls, and they're going to win. I don't want to live to see it."

She stared at him silently for a moment. "Why do you hate them so much, Eliakim?"

He waited for a long time to answer. When he spoke, his voice was hoarse. "Because of what they did to you. They crushed your heart and destroyed all your love—then they took away your hope. Nobody has the right to do that to another person. Without love there's nothing to live for except hatred."

Jerusha gave a startled cry. "Oh, Eliakim! I've done the same thing to you! I've destroyed your love and turned it into hatred! I'm no better than they are!" She began to cry.

"No, Jerusha, it's not your fault. You aren't to blame for what they did to you." He yearned to go to her, to take her in his arms and hold her close. He wanted to feel her hair against his cheek, to comfort her the way he had in the palace courtyard. But he couldn't. He wished he had jumped to his death before she came up onto the roof, instead of hesitating. Now she would blame herself for his death. But he knew it was his pride that was to blame. He should have reopened the Jebusite shaft.

"It's not your fault," he said again. "I made the decision to dig the tunnel from both ends. I made all the plans and calculations. I wanted all the glory, to be the man who saved his city. But the failure is mine instead—mine alone. I can accept the blame, but I can't live with the failure—not when I have to watch all the people I love die because of me."

"Eliakim, please—"

"Jerusha, go back to your room. I need to be alone. You're not responsible. Please believe that."

Neither of them moved. Jerusha looked at him for a long time, with tears streaming down her face. When she finally spoke again, her voice was barely a whisper.

"Eliakim, I know what it's like when all your hope is gone. I felt that way once. And I wanted to do the same as you—I wanted to die." She looked so beautiful to him, and his love for her was so great, that he had to look away from the anguish he saw on her face and heard in her words. "I started to search for a way to end my life too," she said, "but the day I decided to die was the day they set me free to track me down again. They gave me hope—a reason to want to live—but it was a mockery. How did I dare believe that I could escape from them?"

Eliakim felt ashamed. "You've been through more than I could even imagine—"

"No. Let me finish. I've realized something tonight. I'm not a slave anymore. I'm free. And I live here in this beautiful home with a family who loves me. Why did I go free when so many thousands of others died or remained slaves? How did I ever make it home again? Escaping from the Assyrians is impossible, Eliakim. So how is it possible that I'm here?"

"Your strength—and courage—," he said feebly.

"No! I know that isn't true. I was a coward. I would have killed myself in another day. That's not courage. I'm here because my father prayed, and God answered his prayers. There is no other explanation. Do you believe that, Eliakim?"

Eliakim remembered arguing with his father over the impossibility of her return. He knew the reason she escaped was because of a miracle of God. He could never deny it.

"What are you trying to say, Jerusha? What does that have to do with—?" He stopped, unable to speak about his tunnel again.

"Have you prayed?" she asked. "Have you asked God for help?"

"No."

It was the simple, honest truth. There was nothing more he could say. He closed his eyes, ashamed. Yahweh was a living God to Hilkiah and Jerimoth, a God they could turn to for help. But in spite of the fact that Eliakim attended the sacrifices and festivals year after year and had never bowed his knee to a false idol, Yahweh remained a distant, unknown God to him. And it had never occurred to him to call on Yahweh for help. He had shut God out of his life, living his own way, on his own strength. And that was arrogant pride. He looked up at Jerusha again.

"No. I haven't prayed."

"I never would have dared to believe God for all this," she said, gesturing. "But I'm here. Ever since they took me captive, I've been bitter against God for allowing it to happen. And my bitterness made me blind to all He's given back to me."

Eliakim remembered the deep bitterness he had felt when his mother died in spite of his fervent prayers. He had felt betrayed, and he had never asked God for anything else, carefully disguising his bitterness and unbelief behind a mask of religious ritual.

"Eliakim, I haven't prayed since they took my baby from me. But I want to pray now—with you—if you'll let me . . ."

She stretched out her hand to him, but Eliakim couldn't take it. Instead, he covered his face in shame.

"*O God!*" he cried out.

Then, overwhelmed by his sin and his pride and his unbelief, he fell to the floor on his face. For the first time since he was a little child, Eliakim wept.

36

Hezekiah awoke while the sky was still dark. His sleep had been restless, and he felt as if he hadn't slept at all. Worry pushed down on him like the weighted beam of an olive press until his head ached from the strain. He would have to make a decision today, whether they found Isaiah or not. Sending tribute to Assyria seemed to be the only solution. He couldn't delay any longer.

Hezekiah rose and began to dress by lamplight when he heard a knock on his door. It had to be bad news at this early hour. His servants were still asleep, so Hezekiah opened it himself. Immense relief flooded over him when he saw Isaiah.

"Rabbi, come in! I've been trying to find you since—"

"Yes, I've heard. I'm sorry you had to wait so long for me, Your Majesty. And I'm glad that your palace administrator was finally able to get in touch with me. Shebna tracked me down late last night and sent the urgent message that you needed to see me."

"Yes, Rabbi, I do. Has Yahweh revealed to you what's going to happen to our nation—to our people?"

The prophet's expression changed, as if he had glimpsed something both wonderful and terrible, awesome and dreadful. "Yes," Isaiah said. "But who has believed our message and to whom has the arm of the Lord been revealed? God has shown me things I'm not sure I fully understand yet. I've seen the promised seed of Abraham, the righteous Servant of Yahweh in whom He has put His Spirit, a Light for the Gentiles and a stumblingblock to our people—the Messiah, who will reign on the throne forever."

"Will God send the Messiah now—to deliver us from Assyria?"

The question seemed to trouble Isaiah. "You don't understand. He will be your offspring, but you and I won't see Him. And when He does come, many will hear Him but not understand."

"Rabbi, what about our present crisis? Have you heard that Samaria fell to the Assyrians, that their soldiers have been seen in Judean territory?"

"No, I didn't know that." Isaiah did not seem to care. An aura of other-worldliness surrounded him, as if his vision of the future made him unconcerned with the present. Hezekiah was desperate to make him see the urgency of their current situation.

"I've been waiting to talk to you about what I should do. I've armed and fortified our nation, and we're ready to fight the Assyrians if that's God's will. Or maybe rebelling was a mistake. Should I appease them with tribute or seek alliances? I have to make a decision today, but I want it to be what Yahweh wants."

He waited anxiously for Isaiah to answer, but the prophet remained silent for several long minutes. When he finally spoke, he seemed deeply burdened and sorrowful. "Your Majesty, you've earned my deepest respect for seeking the will of the Lord, unlike your forefathers. May God grant you the grace to hear it and understand it."

Another change took place in Isaiah, and suddenly Hezekiah was afraid to hear what Yahweh had to say. Was it the fulfillment of Isaiah's earlier vision—the end of his nation? He had to know.

"Tell me, Rabbi."

Isaiah's clear blue eyes held Hezekiah's. "You looked . . . to the weapons . . . , you saw that the City of David had many breaches in its defenses; . . . you counted the buildings . . . and tore down houses to strengthen the wall. You built a reservoir between the two walls for the water of the Old Pool, but you did not look to the One who made it . . . the One who planned it long ago."

Yahweh's rebuke felt like a sword thrust. "But, Rabbi—does Yahweh expect us to remain defenseless when our nation is threatened? Why was it so wrong to stockpile weapons and strengthen our defenses—or to try to safeguard our water supply?"

"Did you seek God's word before you did all these things?"

"No, but I saw the condition my nation was in, and I knew these measures had to be taken. It was common sense."

"So you went ahead with your building projects and your plans, and now you're asking Yahweh to bless them? Now, when you're in trouble? You're not asking for God's will, King Hezekiah. You're asking Him to choose one of the plans you've already initiated."

"No—but—" Hezekiah groaned. "I see what you mean."

He had tried to trust God and control his own life at the same time, trying to reconcile the two sides of himself: his self-reliance and his faith in God. And he suddenly remembered that his grandfather had warned him that he could never do both.

"Yahweh made this present crisis, Your Majesty. He planned it long ago for His own purposes. Your reforms eliminated idolatry from the land, but that's only half of it. Worship of Yahweh without heartfelt commitment only leads to empty ritual. The Lord says, 'These people come near to me with their mouth and honor me with their lips, but their hearts are far from me. Their worship of me is made up only of rules taught by men.'"

"So by trying to take the defense of Judah into my own hands I'm working against Yahweh?"

"Yes—against His plan to chasten His people."

Hezekiah sighed. "So what should I do now?"

"Do you have enough faith to trust Yahweh completely and not rely on your own strength?"

Hezekiah had to be honest with himself and with God. "No. Probably not. But I don't have much choice, do I? The Assyrian weapons are superior to ours, and even our new walls may not stand up to their battering rams. Our tunnel isn't finished either. So my own strength is pitiful, in spite of my efforts."

"The Lord is your strength, King Hezekiah. And Yahweh's word to you is to wait."

Hezekiah stared at him in disbelief. "Wait? And do nothing?"

"They that wait upon the Lord shall renew their strength; they shall mount up with wings as eagles; they shall run, and not be weary; and they shall walk, and not faint."

"Then I'm not to take *any* action in this crisis?"

"This is what Yahweh says to me: 'As a lion growls, a great lion over his prey—and though a whole band of shepherds is called together against him, he is not frightened by their shouts or disturbed by their clamor—so the Lord Almighty will come down to do battle on Mount Zion and on its heights. Like birds hovering overhead, the Lord Almighty will shield Jerusalem; he will shield it and deliver it, he will "pass over" it and will rescue it. . . . Assyria will fall by a sword that is not of man; a sword, not of mortals, will devour them.'"

Yahweh's word should have reassured Hezekiah, but it didn't. He paced anxiously in front of the prophet, wondering if he could obey God's word, wondering if he could sit passively through a crisis of this magnitude without taking action. He had no proof that Isaiah's words were true, no evidence he could see that told him he could trust God.

But when we believe only in things we can see with our eyes and touch with our hands, it is idolatry. Faith in God meant believing the unseen.

"God, give me the faith to believe!" he murmured. In the distance, the shofar summoned Hezekiah to the morning sacrifice.

"Will you worship with me at the Temple, Rabbi?"

"Yes, of course, Your Majesty."

Now that he knew God's answer, Hezekiah would heed the word of the Lord. He would not send tribute, he would not marshall his troops, he would not seek allies. He would wait and do nothing. But it would be the hardest thing he ever did in his life.

—◈—

The sun glowed behind the clouds like the golden embers on the altar as Eliakim stumbled up the hill to the Temple with his father. When the shofar had sounded, it seemed to Eliakim as if God himself had summoned him to appear before Him. Shoulder to shoulder with the other men, Eliakim filed through the narrow Temple gates, through the Court of the Gentiles and the Court of the Women into the inner courtyard.

He approached the basin to wash himself, and never before had he felt so filthy. His sins burned a hole in his heart like the heat from a thousand suns—bitterness, unbelief, and—worst of all—pride. He had taken God off His rightful throne and replaced Him with the works of his own hands, making his own decisions, choosing his own paths. Eliakim allowed the water to wash over his hands for a long time, but they still felt unclean. Hilkiah gently pulled his son's hands from the water and coaxed him to move, but Eliakim felt unworthy to approach God's altar.

As the priests slew the sacrifices, the praises of the Levites crescendoed in the still morning air: *Praise the Lord, O my soul. All my inmost being, praise his holy name.*

The music had never sounded so magnificent, and it answered a cry from deep within Eliakim's soul. Yahweh reigned—majestic, awesome, worthy of praise! Eliakim wanted to fall on his face before God.

Praise the Lord, O my soul, and forget not all his benefits—who forgives all your sins . . . and redeems your life from the pit.

Yahweh. The God of Abraham. The Holy One of Israel. His father had used those phrases all of Eliakim's life, but never before had he fully comprehended their truth. Who was worthy to approach Yahweh? How could a sinner like him even dare to stand in Yahweh's holy Temple, before His holy presence?

The priests in their pure white robes came forward, gently swaying in rhythm with the music. Eliakim smelled the sweet perfume of incense and heard the faint tinkle of bells on the hem of the high priest's garment. He carried a golden bowl, filled with the blood of the sacrifice, the atoning blood. Through it Eliakim could be forgiven, all his sins paid for. He didn't wait for the other men, but threw himself before God, pleading for mercy and forgiveness as the Levite choir sang:

The Lord is compassionate and gracious, slow to anger, abounding in love. . . . He does not treat us as our sins deserve or repay us according to our iniquities.

All glory and honor belonged to God, not man. Yet Eliakim had sought glory for his own works. Vengeance was God's to pay, yet he had sought revenge against the Assyrians. He deserved to die for his sin, and he waited, prostrate, for God's judgment to fall on him. He welcomed it, longed for it. But as the magnificent words of the psalm touched his soul, Eliakim's heart overflowed with love and praise for God:

For as high as the heavens are above the earth, so great is his love for those who fear him; as far as the east is from the west, so far has he removed our transgressions from us.

In all the years he had come to the Temple, Eliakim couldn't remember a service like this one. But had he ever come with his heart surrendered to God before? He had believed that the services satisfied *his* needs, and when Zechariah had disrupted his first sacrifice long ago, Eliakim had been outraged because he felt cheated, not because God had been cheated. He wanted to stay prostrate with shame, but his father gently nudged him to his feet.

As a father has compassion on his children, so the Lord has compassion on those who fear him; for he knows how we are formed, he remembers that we are dust. . . . From everlasting to everlasting the Lord's love is with those who fear him.

The priest laid the offering on the altar, and as the pillar of flame soared into the air, Yahweh suddenly revealed himself to Eliakim. He staggered backward, overwhelmed, as he felt the tender, all-powerful presence of God. Like a blind man recovering his sight, Eliakim recognized that Yahweh, Creator of all the universe, was a Father—a gentle, loving Father. Like Hilkiah, Yahweh would lovingly welcome Eliakim back into His arms, forgiving him, even though he had grievously wounded Him. Like Jerimoth, Yahweh had patiently waited for His child all these years, longing for him to return. Yahweh—a Father who would lay down His own life for His children, even as Jerimoth had. God's presence had been with Eliakim all his life, just as surely as Hilkiah had been with him, but he had been blind to Him.

"Abba!" Eliakim cried as the tears flowed down his face. "Abba! Father God!" The praise cry resounded, as if coming from heaven itself, and Eliakim lifted his hands high in surrender to God.

Praise the Lord, you his angels . . . Praise the Lord, all his heavenly hosts . . . Praise the Lord, all his works everywhere in his dominion. Praise the Lord, O my soul.

—◈—

When the morning sacrifice ended, Hezekiah waited in his private chambers for his advisers to assemble in the throne room. His long purple robe felt hot and very heavy on his shoulders as it dragged across the floor behind him. At last Shebna came to summon him. He looked as if he hadn't slept.

"They are ready for you in the throne room, Your Majesty."

"Shebna, wait. I want to thank you for finding Rabbi Isaiah last night." Shebna nodded slightly. "Listen—I know I don't always take the time to tell you how grateful I am for all that you do, but I'm very grateful. You've been more than my right-hand man—you've been a true friend to me."

Shebna looked away as if unable to meet Hezekiah's gaze. "I trust Rabbi Isaiah has told you what you wanted to know?"

"Yes, and I want you to hear it first before I tell the others. I'm not going to send tribute or mobilize our troops and allies."

"What are you saying?"

"Isaiah told me to wait and to trust in God."

"*No!*" Shebna lunged at Hezekiah, losing control for the first time in all their years together. He clung to the front of Hezekiah's robes, shaking him, pleading desperately with him. "Do not be a fool, Hezekiah! Please! Send the tribute—I beg you! They will kill you! As a friend I am telling you that your very life is at stake! Please!"

Shebna's sudden outburst shook Hezekiah deeply. *They will kill you!* He remembered Jerusha's vivid description of what the Assyrians would do to a conquered king, and he felt his knees go weak. But in the next moment he grew angry at Shebna for his lack of faith in God's word and pried his hands off his robes.

"No, I won't become an Assyrian vassal again. Our nation is in Yahweh's hands. Now pull yourself together. I expect you to stand behind my decision. I need your support."

Shebna covered his face. "They will kill you," he moaned.

"Shebna, stop it! It's time to go."

More than anything else, Hezekiah wanted to get this meeting over with. He walked briskly down the hall to the throne room with Shebna trailing miserably behind him and sat down on his throne feeling tense and overwrought. He studied the anxious faces of his advisers for a moment. Like Shebna, most of them would probably never understand his decision. He wasn't certain he could explain it to them, but he had to try.

"Rabbi Isaiah has returned to Jerusalem," he began with more confidence than he felt. "I met with him earlier this morning, and as a result I've decided not to send tribute to Assyria."

"I'll mobilize our forces, Your Majesty," General Jonadab cried, leaping to his feet.

Hezekiah shook his head. "Our weapons will stay in the armory. We don't need them." A few of his army commanders muttered their objections, but Hezekiah ignored them. "Nor will we seek an alliance with a foreign power, because—"

"That's insane!" Gedaliah leaped to his feet, cutting off Hezekiah's words. "Why do you even listen to a religious radical like Isaiah? You're going to destroy us all. We'll be annihilated like Israel!"

His brother's outburst unnerved Hezekiah. Then elders from various Judean cities stood to their feet and clustered around Gedaliah, shouting at the king and voicing their support for Gedaliah. Hezekiah wasn't prepared for such a violent show of opposition, and it staggered him.

"Don't just sit there, Shebna—tell him!" Gedaliah cried above the noise.

"Tell me what?" Hezekiah turned to Shebna, certain he could count on his friend's support, even if he disagreed with the decision. But Shebna's face was ashen, and his hand trembled as he wiped the sweat from his brow.

"Tell me *what?*" Hezekiah repeated.

For a long moment Shebna was silent, but when he finally spoke, his answer startled Hezekiah. "Your Majesty, your brother is right. You must take some course of action. To sit and wait for the Assyrians is suicidal."

Hezekiah felt his anger rising dangerously. "This *is* my course of action! God promised to deliver us from the Assyrians, and I've chosen to wait and trust in that promise!"

"Let my troops march to defend our borders," Jonadab begged. "Remember how Yahweh helped us defeat the Philistines? They were stronger than us too."

"No troops, Jonadab. Yahweh can deliver us without the sword of man. The Torah says—"

"Those are fairy tales!" Gedaliah shouted, his face flushed with rage. "You're governing a real nation, with real people!"

Shebna clutched Hezekiah's sleeve, pleading with him. "Surely you are not putting your trust in the mythical accounts of your ancestors."

"Those are bedtime stories for children!" Gedaliah shouted. "But this is not a child's game, Hezekiah!"

The throne room erupted into chaos as nearly all of Hezekiah's advisers shouted their objections at once. Their reaction shocked him. Everyone was joining the mutiny, even his close friends Shebna and Jonadab. Anger choked off Hezekiah's reply, and Shebna continued to plead with him in a low voice.

"The opposition to your decision is overwhelming. Please, before they kill you—I beg you to reconsider!"

Suddenly Hezekiah realized what Shebna's words had meant. *They were going to kill him.* Not the Assyrians, but his own officials. If he didn't give in to them, he risked a revolution. But if he changed his mind now, he would forfeit his sovereignty forever—and God's sovereignty as well.

"*No!* I will *not* reconsider!" The hall gradually grew quiet as everyone stared at him.

"Listen to me! When my father faced an invasion 20 years ago, Isaiah told him to wait and to trust God for deliverance, but he refused to listen. Instead of waiting for the crisis to pass, he sent tribute to Assyria and turned us all into slaves. Once again, God has told us to wait. I have sworn a covenant to the Lord, and I'm going to obey Him, no matter how dangerous it seems." The discontented murmuring started up again as the angry men rallied around Gedaliah.

Shebna slowly shook his head. "There is no God to save us," Hezekiah heard him murmur. And his words made Hezekiah angrier than anything else.

"Silence!" he shouted. Instantly the hall grew still. "Shebna, if you and these others say there is no God, then I ask you—what's the point of life? Why govern the nation at all or live our lives by any rules and laws? Why not live in anarchy? Why should we make rational decisions if life is chaotic and irrational, if there's no order to the universe?"

No one moved. No one spoke. "But if there *is* a God and He isn't strong enough to deliver us, then who can? Our meager military forces, Jonadab? Some neighboring nation? How can the arm of man possibly succeed if God himself fails us?"

He slowly rose from his throne and stood to face them. "But if there *is* a God who keeps the heavens and the earth in order and rules sovereignly over all His creation, if He truly *has* intervened in our nation's past to deliver us from slavery and place us in this land, then how can we do anything but trust and serve Him? How can we ever presume to know more than God? All our plans, all our schemes are worthless—foolishness—beside His wisdom and planning."

He stared for a moment at their silent, sullen faces. "Yahweh gave me His Word to be still and to wait for His deliverance. I have chosen to obey that word. And I will *not* reconsider! Gedaliah—Shebna—any of the rest of you who can't support that decision—get out! I don't need you!"

He pointed toward the door, staring down at them boldly, and a tense silence filled the hall. Anger and discontent showed on many faces, and he wondered if there would be an open rebellion, if any of them still supported him, if even Jonadab and Shebna would turn against him. Then he remembered that God had chosen him to rule, and a strange peace filled his heart. His life rested in God's hands. It was enough to know.

"I have nothing more to say. This meeting is over." And King Hezekiah strode from the room.

——◆——

Shebna didn't move from his seat as Hezekiah left, but sat in stunned shock. The king he greatly admired and worked hard to please had just made a fatal mistake. His impassioned speech had convinced no one. It had only sealed his death warrant. Deep sorrow consumed Shebna, and he slumped forward in his seat with his face in his hands, oblivious to the grumbling and arguing of the advisers as they filed out.

"Are you with us, Shebna?" He looked up. Gedaliah quivered with anger. "Yes or no? We need your answer now."

Shebna closed his eyes, as if he could hide from the ugly reality of what he was doing, and nodded. "When?" he whispered.

"Tonight. When he's asleep."

"Cowards! You would rather murder a man in his bed than fight him face-to-face."

"You'll leave in the morning with the delegation to deliver our tribute to Assyria," Gedaliah said. Shebna didn't answer.

Gedaliah's eyes traveled to the row of guards standing nearby. "By the way, don't try to double-cross us. You're being watched."

37

The morning sacrifice left Eliakim exhausted and broken. He wondered how he would make it through the day. He sat in the foreman's tent near the empty Pool of Siloam and stared into space. He no longer consulted his drawings and calculations. They couldn't tell him anything new. All he could do was wait—wait and hope that God would forgive him and answer his prayers.

Outside the tent door he heard one of the workmen grumbling about digging all the way to Sheol. Then his foreman appeared at the door of the tent.

"We're ready for the signals, my lord."

"Thanks. I'll be there in a minute." He looked down at the diagrams on the table in front of him and closed his eyes. The warmth of God's presence filled his soul.

"Lord God—Father—guide us through the darkness," he prayed. "Not for my sake, but for Your glory."

Eliakim rose to go, then froze. When he thought about crawling inside the suffocating tunnel again, he began to tremble. He couldn't do it. He would have to tell his foreman to listen for the signals. He could never go back inside. He emerged from the tent to tell the foreman and was startled to see King Hezekiah standing outside.

"Your Majesty!"

"I decided to come see what you've accomplished, Eliakim. Then we can decide together how to proceed." His voice was kind, not accusing, but he looked as though the burden of his reign weighed heavily on him. "Is this a good time to show me?"

Yesterday the King's unexpected arrival would have thrown Eliakim into a panic, but today he felt strangely numb.

"Certainly, Your Majesty, but the work has stopped so we can try the signals again."

"Then I'd like to go inside and listen with you."

Eliakim's heart galloped with fear. He couldn't go inside. But how could he explain that to the king? "You're welcome to listen, Your Majesty, but it's very cramped down at the end. Maybe we should wait and let the foreman go—"

"I don't mind tight spaces." Hezekiah removed his outer robe and handed it to his servant. Lead the way, Eliakim."

"You'll need a lamp."

Eliakim's hand shook as he handed the king a lamp. Then, lighting another for himself and grabbing a hammer to signal with, Eliakim plunged into the darkness. His heart pounded uncontrollably as soon as he entered the shaft. After a few yards, Eliakim knew he couldn't go on. He had to get out. He turned around but Hezekiah followed right behind him. The shaft was too narrow, the king too tall and broad-shouldered to squeeze past. Unless Eliakim knocked him down and trampled over him, he couldn't get out.

"What's wrong, Eliakim?"

"Uh—nothing."

Eliakim turned around and continued walking, embarrassed to confess his fear. Waves of terror overwhelmed him as he forced himself to creep deeper and deeper into the winding labyrinth. He felt the weight of the mountain above his head, pressing down on him, closing in on him. He was gasping for air and perspiring so heavily that the oil lamp threatened to slip from his sweating palms. Still, he plunged on, with the king following closely.

When the ceiling lowered for the final few yards, Eliakim hesitated again. They would have to drop to their hands and knees and crawl. He couldn't do it. He couldn't go into the coffinlike shaft, but he couldn't get out either. He felt trapped. He gritted his teeth to keep from crying out and told himself over and over that the rock walls were not closing in on him. Then he crawled the last few yards. By the time he reached the wall at the end of the tunnel, Eliakim was dizzy and nauseated.

"I see what you mean about cramped quarters." Hezekiah's deep voice boomed like thunder. Eliakim breathed in rapid gasps, but if the king noticed, he didn't say anything.

"What happens next?" he asked.

Eliakim struggled through waves of terror to remember. "Uh—the shofar will sound—and—uh—the other tunnel—they'll signal 10 times—and—we'll listen."

As he set his oil lamp onto the floor, his hands trembled so badly that he nearly dropped it. He wanted desperately to run out, but he forced himself to stay. Finally they heard the sound of the shofar. Eliakim squeezed to one side as far as he could and pressed his ear against the wall to listen. He wanted to get it over with, to get out. Hezekiah crowded beside him, and they lay side by side, holding their breath, listening. But all Eliakim heard was the sound of his own heart, hammering in his ears. Nothing else. The silent wall of stone refused to reveal the other tunnel's secret.

The seconds ticked by as every muscle and fiber in his body tensed with the strain of listening. The signal must be over by now. He had heard nothing. Then in the distance the shofar announced that the signaling had ended.

Hezekiah crouched beside him. "Could you hear anything, Eliakim?"

"No, Your Majesty."

The king sighed. "Me either. Now what?"

"They'll sound the shofar again; it'll be our turn to signal."

Eliakim gripped the hammer with two hands to control it, then pounded the rhythm on the wall in front of him with jerky motions. He repeated the signal nine times, then crawled out to the higher part of the tunnel to wait. His arms ached from the exertion, his ears rang, and sweat poured from his brow. Eliakim breathed almost normally again, and except for his trembling and the lingering nausea, the anxiety attack had nearly subsided. Before long they heard footsteps coming toward them.

"Your Majesty—my lord," the foreman said, "I'm sorry, but the men on the other side couldn't hear your signal."

"And we didn't hear theirs either," Eliakim said.

Bitter disappointment overwhelmed him. He had been so sure God would answer his prayers. He didn't know what to do. Should the men keep digging anyway? Should he measure again? What did it matter? The Assyrians were probably marching toward them. Eliakim's hopelessness edged toward despair. He wanted to get out of this claustrophobic tunnel before it closed in on him again. He picked up his lamp.

"Would you like to go down to the other tunnel now, Your Majesty?"

In the flickering lamplight, Eliakim saw Hezekiah's expression change. The king froze, then stared intently at him.

"Say that again, Eliakim!"

"Uh—do you want to go down to—?"

"*Down!*" Hezekiah cried. "You said *down* to the other tunnel!"

Eliakim had no idea what the king was talking about. "Uh—yes, Your Majesty—I—"

Hezekiah grabbed him by the shoulders, and his fingers dug painfully into Eliakim's arms. "Eliakim, listen! Is it possible that this tunnel is higher in elevation than the other one—that the reason they haven't met is because the other one is underneath us somewhere? Down there?" He pointed.

"God of Abraham! Yes—of course! That's it!"

It was so simple but Eliakim had been too distraught to think of it. Yet traveling between the two tunnels every day, he had intuitively felt that the valley tunnel was lower.

"That has to be the answer, Your Majesty!" Eliakim turned to his foreman. "Tell them to repeat the signaling process again. But this time, tell them to hammer on the ceiling! Hurry!"

He dropped to his hands and knees, and with the king following behind, Eliakim crawled to the end of the tunnel again. He set his lamp onto the floor and crouched beside Hezekiah to wait. He imagined the messenger running through the streets to the lower gate, then down the Kidron Valley to the spring. The men would go back inside the other tunnel. They would probably think that Eliakim was crazy. But they would pound on the ceiling this time.

The shofar sounded, and the two men pressed their ears to the floor of the tunnel. *God of Abraham—please—* Then dimly, faintly, Eliakim heard a sound. He held his breath. Almost imperceptibly at first, he heard a distant ringing. Clang-clang. Then again, clang-clang. He moved his ear to another spot and heard the rhythmical tapping more clearly now. Eight times, 9 times, 10 times. Then silence. He raised his head from the floor and looked at the king, almost afraid that he had imagined it.

"Did you hear it?"

"Yes, Eliakim! Praise God!"

Hezekiah grabbed him in a bear hug and slapped his back. Then the king hurried down the tunnel ahead of him, shouting the good news. Outside, the shofar began to blow, and a cheer went up from the workers that could probably be heard throughout the city. But Eliakim sat slumped inside the tunnel, weeping and praising God.

❖

Jerusha sat on Hilkiah's roof that same morning and watched the sun rise as if seeing it for the first time. Eliakim's humility and brokenness the night before had deeply moved her, and she knew she also had much to confess before God. After Hilkiah and Eliakim left, Jerusha knew what she had to do. She descended the outside stairs from the rooftop and walked slowly through the streets, up the hill to the Temple. She had never been there, and she felt like a stranger as she wandered past the people milling around in the Court of the Gentiles. A Levite stood in a corner, teaching his students. Men passed through the gates with their offerings, and she envisioned her father coming with a lamb from his flock to pray for her.

She slipped through one of the gates that led into the Women's Court. It was deserted, and she crossed to the low wall that separated it from the inner courtyard. Beyond that wall the morning sacrifice lay on the huge altar, its aroma slowly drifting toward heaven. The smell of the roasting meat reminded Jerusha of weddings and festivals when her family and their neighbors roasted a whole calf or lamb.

As Jerusha gazed at the lamb lying on the altar, it seemed too small to cover her sins. She sank to her knees and closed her eyes, silently confessing her guilt, her hatred and bitterness, her harlotry and unbelief. One by one she offered them up to God, and, like the day Maacah chopped off her hair, she felt lighter, freer as the weight of her sins fell away.

"Do you wish to make an offering?"

Jerusha opened her eyes and looked up. A tall, white-robed priest stood on the other side of the wall. She hastily swiped at her tears.

"What did you say?"

"I asked if you'd like to make an offering." His face, creased with fine wrinkles, looked kind.

"Yes—yes, I've sinned. How—what should I do?"

"You'll need to bring a goat or a lamb for the sin offering."

"But—I don't have anything. I—I have no money."

"The poor may bring a dove or a pigeon."

She shook her head. "I can't—I don't even have—"

"If you're very poor, you may bring a tenth of an ephah of fine flour."

Jerusha knew that Hilkiah would give her money for an offering, yet she didn't want to ask him. An offering that didn't cost her anything wasn't a true sacrifice at all. God had given everything to Jerusha. What could she possibly sacrifice to Him in return?

The priest smiled. "I'll come back later, when you decide."

As Jerusha watched him walk away, her eyes filled with tears. "I'm sorry, God. But this is the only thing I really own." She reached into the fold of her dress and pulled out the torn fragment of blanket that had once swaddled her baby. It was her only link to her daughter—and to her past. Tears rolled down Jerusha's face as she held it out to God.

"It's all I have, Lord. But I'll offer it to You. Please accept my sacrifice. Please forgive me and make me whole again." She held the blanket to her face and wiped her tears with it, smelling its woolly fragrance for the last time. Then Jerusha folded it up and tenderly stuffed it between the stones of the Temple wall.

When she returned home, Jerusha sat in the garden courtyard for a long time, listening to the sound of the birds, feeling the gentle breeze caress her face, savoring the sticky fragrance of Hilkiah's fig tree. She remembered the feeling of being reborn after the Assyrians had set her free, but this was a thousand times better. This time she was *really* free. God had forgiven her, and now she could begin to forgive herself.

Suddenly Jerusha heard a door slam. She jumped up, and a moment later Eliakim burst into the courtyard. His clothes were dusty, his face streaked and smudged with dirt, but his smile was radiant. He swept her off her feet and into his arms.

"Jerusha! God answered our prayers! They're going to meet! The two tunnels are going to meet!"

Jerusha began to laugh and cry at the same time. "Oh, thank God!"

"We finally heard the signals through the rock! It will take only another day or so. One tunnel is higher than the other, but they're going to meet!" He danced in circles with her, clutching her so tightly she could scarcely breathe. "God answered our prayers, Jerusha!"

"I'm so happy for you, Eliakim! I'm so happy!"

Suddenly Eliakim stiffened and practically dropped Jerusha to the ground, shrinking away from her in horror. "Oh, Jerusha, I'm sorry—I didn't realize what I was—I'm sorry!"

She looked at his tired, dirt-streaked face and saw the fear and guilt in his eyes. He was trembling. "Jerusha, you were wrong," he said quietly. "It's not you who's unworthy—it's me. I'm a sinner. I put pride and ambition and revenge before the God of the universe. I'm not worthy of you."

She took his rough, bruised hand in hers and held it to her cheek, letting her tears flow over it. Eliakim gazed at her tenderly, and his eyes filled with tears.

"You're not a harlot, Jerusha. You chose to live. There's not a person in the world who wouldn't have done the same thing, including your cousins. But they never had a chance. If you had died, Jerusha—" He stopped and swallowed hard as a tear slipped down his face. "—if you had died, I never would have seen the power of God. But you're God's gift to me, to show me that He has the power to answer prayer. That's why you lived. It was God's choice, Jerusha. Not yours."

His warm, brown eyes searched hers for a moment; then he took her face in his hands and kissed her. The touch of his lips on hers was the most beautiful feeling she had ever known. How she loved Eliakim, this gentle man who had tunneled through a mountain of solid rock for her! Finally Eliakim drew back.

"I love you, Jerusha. I can't imagine living the rest of my life without you. Please marry me."

His arms encircled her, pulling her close. As she rested her cheek against his dusty chest, Jerusha couldn't imagine living without Eliakim either.

"I love you too," she whispered. "Yes—I want to marry you, Eliakim."

38

The day seemed endless to Hezekiah as he tried to govern his nation as if a crisis didn't exist. Shebna's seat beside his throne stood empty, and the dozens of noblemen who usually hovered around the throne room had disappeared, leaving the palace courtyards strangely silent. Hezekiah had never felt so utterly alone and abandoned. When the evening sacrifice ended, he ordered his supper served in his private chambers.

Then he sat alone, toying with his food, wishing Isaiah had told him how long he would have to wait. When a servant announced that Shebna wanted to see him, Hezekiah felt a range of emotions from relief to rage.

"Send him in."

Shebna approached Hezekiah haltingly, unable to meet his gaze, then bowed low. "I have come to resign," he said quietly. "As you know, I do not support your decision or your faith in Yahweh. I am sorry."

Hezekiah bit his lip, fighting back his anger at Shebna for not supporting him at the meeting, for deserting him now. His closest friend had betrayed him, and he wanted to lash out at him.

"Why, Shebna? Why are you abandoning me now, when I need you the most?"

Shebna didn't look up. His voice was a low mumble. "Because I think you are wrong. I think you are making a disastrous mistake. And my position should be filled by someone who supports your decision."

"Who?" Hezekiah asked bitterly. "Is there anyone left who does support me?"

"Rabbi Isaiah does."

"Well, he's the only one, then. And he doesn't want the job. I asked him seven years ago, remember?" He pushed his plate aside.

Shebna cleared his throat, then spoke haltingly, as if forcing out the words against his will. "Eliakim shares your faith. Now that his tunnel is a success, I am sure he would be pleased to have my job."

Hezekiah had seen the enormous stress the tunnel had placed on Eliakim and the heavy toll it had taken on his health. Eliakim deserved a long rest before he would be ready for the pressures of Shebna's job. Hezekiah couldn't deny the resentment he felt toward Shebna, but he needed him. There was no one else.

"I can't stop you from resigning if that's what you want to do, but I won't accept your resignation tonight. I'll give you three days to reconsider it. Maybe by that time—" He paused, admitting only to himself the tremendous fear he felt. "Maybe by that time, this crisis will have passed."

Shebna didn't answer. He continued to stare miserably at the floor. In spite of his anger, Hezekiah wanted to do something to heal the breach between them. There was no one he trusted as much as Shebna except Hephzibah. Hezekiah pushed the table aside and stood up. Through the open window the first few stars had begun to shine in the sky.

"I'm going up to the north wall to watch for the signal fires. Come with me, Shebna."

When Shebna looked up, Hezekiah saw sorrow in his eyes. "Very well, Your Majesty."

Neither of them spoke as they left the palace and walked up the hill to the Temple mount. Below them, the city seemed unusually quiet and still. Instead of entering the Temple enclosure, they climbed the steep steps to the top of the city wall and followed it along the eastern side of the Temple grounds. The sheer drop to the Kidron Valley was dizzying. They turned at the northeast corner of the wall and continued until they came to the watchtower that Eliakim had constructed. From the top of it, they would have an unobstructed view of the signal fire on the next watchtower to the north. Three young Judean soldiers, posted at the watch, halted their lively banter and bowed nervously as the king and Shebna approached.

"Has there been a signal yet?" Hezekiah asked.

"No, Your Majesty. It's still too light."

"Good. We'll wait for it."

Although the stars hung brightly above the Mount of Olives to the east, Hezekiah could still see the faint glow of the sun behind the mountains to the west.

"The message we received last night said that the Assyrians still hadn't broken camp," he told Shebna. "But I expect that the first few divisions will begin marching any day now."

Hezekiah leaned against the wall, resting his arms on the top of the parapet, and gazed out at the dark silhouette of the mountains to the north. A hushed expectancy fell over the waiting men, a feeling of suspense familiar to Hezekiah. He remembered standing on the platform before Molech, waiting, with Isaiah's promise of salvation his only hope. He had waited, interminably, for the hand to grab him and hurl him to his death. But the hand of Yahweh had rescued him instead.

Now he stood facing an enemy once more, and again Isaiah's promise from God was the only hope he had. Rigid with suspense, he listened to the night sounds in the valley below him as the sunlight gradually faded into darkness.

Suddenly, one of the soldiers leaped to attention. "There it is, Your Majesty!" He pointed to a blinking light on the horizon. Hezekiah's heart felt like a cold stone in his chest. He didn't know how to read the signals. He could only wait tensely for the soldiers to decipher them.

"The Assyrians have broken camp—they have begun to march—"

"Which direction?" Hezekiah whispered.

He waited, an eternity, but the distant mountaintop remained dark. Then the tantalizing light flickered once again.

"Northeast!" the soldier cried. "They're marching northeast! Back to Nineveh!"

A cheer went up from the soldiers beside him but Hezekiah closed his eyes and leaned against the wall, numb with relief. *When you pass through the fire, you won't be burned. The flames will not hurt you. For Yahweh is your God. The Holy One of Israel is your Savior.*

The soldiers were rejoicing, embracing one another and clapping each other on the back. Shebna looked unnaturally pale, as if he might faint.

Hezekiah's eyes bored into him. "Another coincidence, Shebna?"

"Perhaps not," he whispered.

———◆———

Shebna found Gedaliah and the elders of Lachish in the palace, planning the government they would soon form. As he burst into the room, the door slammed backward against the wall, nearly rocking it from its stone sockets. The startled men stared at him fearfully. But before he could speak, the shofars began to blast from the Temple walls.

"That is the sound of your defeat, Gedaliah. There will be no Assyrian invasion, just as your brother's God has promised."

Gedaliah stared at him, too stunned to speak, while in the background the triumphant cry of the shofars sounded on and on.

"Your horses are being saddled. Take your men and get out. Go back to Lachish now! Tonight! Or I swear by Hezekiah's God I will kill you myself!"

———◆———

Hezekiah stayed on the wall alone after the others had left, gazing out from the watchtower toward the darkened hills. Only 40 miles to the north the land of Israel lay destroyed, and except for the grace of God, the land of Judah would have met the same fate.

As the Temple shofars blew, announcing the joyful news, Hezekiah watched the city come to life as the people flooded from their homes into the streets to celebrate. In a few minutes he would go down as their king and lead them in worship. But first he knelt beneath the starry sky and bowed with his forehead to the ground before his Heavenly King.

"We have heard with our ears, O God; our fathers have told us what You did in their days, in days long ago. With your hand you drove out the nations and planted our fathers; you crushed the peoples and made our fathers flourish. It was not by their sword that they won the land, nor did their arm bring them victory; it was your right hand, your arm, and the light of your face, for you loved them.

"You are my King and my God, who decrees victories for Jacob. Through you we push back our enemies; through your name we trample our foes. I do not trust in my bow, my sword does not bring me victory; but you give us victory over our enemies, you put our adversaries to shame. In God we make our boast all day long, and we will praise your name forever.

"Hear O Israel, Yahweh is our God. Yahweh alone."

Epilogue

Jerusha sat in the flower-decked chair in Hilkiah's garden with a carpet of flower petals beneath her feet. She heard the joyful music of the groom's procession and recognized the song; the one she'd sung on the morning of her cousin's wedding so long ago. Maacah stood beside her and as the sound of the music drew closer, she bent to hug Jerusha tightly.

"You're so beautiful! I wish Mama and Abba could see you. They'd be so proud and so happy that you're marrying Eliakim."

Suddenly the music stopped. Eliakim stood in the doorway of the courtyard. His curly black hair was tousled, as usual, but he looked like a prince in his wedding robes. When he saw Jerusha, a boyish smile lit up his handsome face, and she wanted to run into his arms. Beside him, General Jonadab wore the uniform of the King's Royal Army. Dozens of Hilkiah's relatives and guests crowded into the courtyard behind them.

Eliakim's eyes never left hers as he took her hand and squeezed it gently. She rose to her feet to stand beside him. Jerusha silently thanked God for all He had done for her, for the miracle of her restored life, for forgiveness. Then, for the greatest miracle of all, Eliakim's love.

She saw tears of joy in Hilkiah's eyes as he took Jerimoth's place, as father of the bride. How Jerusha loved the dear little merchant! Hilkiah laid his hand on her head as Abba once had, and she remembered her father's words, *Someday God will turn these tears into joy.*

Hilkiah's hand rested on her head for the blessing, but as he spoke the words, Jerusha heard Abba's voice: "May Yahweh bless you and keep you. May Yahweh cause His face to shine upon you And be gracious unto you. May He make you as Sara and Rebecca. May He favor you and grant you His peace. Amen."

"Behold the tunnel. Now this is the story of the tunnel; while the workmen were still lifting up the pick, each towards his neighbor and while there was yet three cubits to excavate, a voice was heard of a man calling his fellow, since there was a split in the rock on the right hand and on the left. And on the day of the excavation the workmen struck, each towards his neighbor, pick against pick, and the water flowed from the spring to the pool for twelve hundred cubits, and a hundred cubits was the height of the rock above the heads of the workmen."

Oldest Hebrew inscription ever discovered, carved in The Siloam Tunnel, Jerusalem, 8th century B.C.

Scripture Credits

Scripture quotation from the King James Version is found on page 281 (ninth paragraph).

Scripture quotations from *The Living Bible* (TLB) are found on the following pages (see page 4 for copyright information): 75, 76.

Paraphrased verses by the author are found on the following pages: 14, 23, 33, 34, 35, 54, 55 (first paragraph), 72, 73, 95, 97, 103, 104, 121, 160 (first, third, and fifth paragraphs), 182 (first paragraph), 200, 227 (first paragraph after break), 228, 280, 297, 299.

All other Scripture quotations are from the *New International Version®* (NIV®). See page 4 for copyright information.

Preview of Book 3

**If you loved *The Lord Is My Strength* and
The Lord Is My Song, you won't want to miss . . .**

The Lord Is My Salvation
Book 3

The Lord Is My Salvation tells of King Hezekiah's later reign and the climax of events surrounding the Assyrian invasion. God has brought him great wealth and power; but after many years, Hezekiah still has no heir. His wife, in desperation, makes a vow to Asherah, the fertility goddess, betraying all that Hezekiah believes in and works for.

As his international stature increases, Hezekiah is tempted by Egypt and Babylon to join a military alliance against Assyria—an alliance that the prophet Isaiah warns him not to join. As the Assyrians match westward with a lust for vengeance and conquest, Hezekiah will discover whether or not his faith in God will sustain him against an overwhelming enemy.